# Dunya 2

*Rasheed's Redemption*

By

Dean Hamid

# Dunya! 2 Rasheed's Redemption

**Part Two, Volume 2**

Dean Hamid

Published by Dean Hamid, 2022.

# Dunya 2: Rasheed's Redemption
# Dean Hamid

F ast forward to 1995. Rasheed. Waseema. Shaheeda. Latif. A different time. A different world. A different... Brooklyn.

Rasheed is trying to make a life for himself. But he still struggles from the demons that haunt his past. Not only his, but his family's as well.

Waseema and Shaheeda make a life for themselves as well, but unsolved conflicts threaten their already fragile relationship.

Latif inherits the family jewels, as well as the headaches that come along with it. Stressed, he makes compromising decisions that threaten the family's financial organization.

They're all one explosive catalytic time bomb from the chaos and high stakes drama that will tear at their family structure. But at the same time, will it bring them closer together?

Dunya 2 picks up quickly where Dunya: The Do or Die left off. Intrigued. Wanting more. Get caught up with Rasheed's Redemption

1

# CHAPTER ONE

The quiet out-of-the way street showed no unusual signs, distractions, or nuances that would have made it seem the least bit bizarre. It was that one city light that glowed brightly midway up the street that gave the whole block a sinister, evil-yet innocent type of countenance, like it was holding back something... a mystery.

This was not typical Harlem, but just a few blocks over would have put you straight into the mix; the hustle and bustle that was typical of the nineties; *'Uptown'*. This hood here was way out in the sticks on the far end of town, closer towards Riverside Park. A quiet Irish working class neighborhood where everyone still minded their own business. That's why it was the ideal location, that's why she picked here for it to go down.

"Shoot him!"

"I-I can't..." Waseema snatched the gun out of Shaheeda's hand and pointed it at the man in the dark suit's head. His hands and feet were tightly bound with duct-tape and his mouth gagged with a bandana wrapped around his head. His eyes were wide open as he gazed up at Shaheeda; a steely-eyed look that, for the most part, right now saved his life. "No... you do it, Ma."

Waseema shook her head in disgust as she snatched the gun away from her and looked down at him. "I knew you couldn't do it... but that's okay." She looked over at Shaheeda and said, "He's a dead man anyway."

Waseema was ice-cold, but her demeanor never showed it, she was pissed-off at best. The man she now stood over trained his eyes on her. "That won't work on me," she said as she stepped closer to him. She pointed the gun to his head and said, "I'll give you one opportunity though...one chance." She snatched the gag from around his mouth. "Why did you do it!"

He spit out cotton lint balls that had built up in his mouth from the bandana and twisted his stiffened jaw around then said, "You don't want to do this, Waseema. I mean, if you wanted to prove a point. I got it."

"Fuck the point! You're a piece of shit! Tell me!" she shouted as she pushed the gun into the back of his neck.

"Whoa...hold on now. Remember, it was you and Khalid that brought her to me."

"Fuck you."

"Yeah, yeah, I know." He turned his attention to Shaheeda standing next to an opened window crying silently and said, "Look. You knew I didn't lie to you. You were going to be my main squeeze. My woman! I would have taken you in, but after your old man got killed, your momma stopped bringing you..."

"Why didn't you come get me, Craig! I waited! I tried calling and calling, and you would never call me back! Why?"

He held his head down, shook it, then said, "I had a lot going on...trying to run a Temple. I just didn't have time like that. I mean, I had the Temple pay for the funeral for Khalid, then on top of that, your mother acted like she didn't want nothing to do with us...like we killed him."

"Shaheeda, baby." Waseema interrupted, "I just needed you by my side. Without your father...it would have been..." her voice trailed off into a silence.

"There it is. You see, baby, I needed you too. It was really...all your mother's fault. She was being selfish"

"Fuck you, Craig!"

"Craig 3X to you...sister! You know what I'm saying is the truth. You allowed those devils down in Brooklyn to deter you away. We, the community, reached out to help, but you turned your back on us!"

"What the hell has that got to do with you raping my daughter; a child!"

"Naw, hell no, it wasn't like that. Tell her, Shaheeda. I didn't touch her like that. We kissed...maybe touched each other, but that's all."

"Oh, that makes it all right."

"C'mon, Waseema, you were in the Nation, you know how things go-"

"We didn't do that!"

Craig 3X looked up at her like she was crazy, and cocked his head to the side, then said, "Really, I mean, how old were you when Khalid pushed up on you? I remember you weren't much older than she was yourself."

Shaheeda stepped away from the window, closer to them, clinging to every word. "Ma...is that true?"

"It was different with me and your father."

"Why...you weren't married when you had those two boys out of wedlock, huh. Hell, I remember I had to convince your old man not to kick his ass!"

Waseema looked over at Shaheeda as she stared into his mouth. "It wasn't like that, Shaheeda." Her face contorted with different twists of guilt and shame as she searched for the right words, but then it clicked, just that quick, he was manipulating her, just like he would do at the Temple. "You did say he raped you, right!" She hollered as she pulled back the hammer. She realized that she was losing it, and that only pissed her off more, "He did, didn't he...Shaheeda!"

Shaheeda looked away from her and it was then that Craig 3X saw his shot. "Shaheeda, baby. We can still be close like we were. Waseema, come on now, listen to me. I can still make this right.

Okay, I'll marry her, Waseema, if that's what you want," he begged, but on closed ears.

"You're already married, Craig...to two other women!" Shaheeda screamed out.

"Come on, baby, you know I can still have up to four wives. We can make this work. It ain't got to go down like this."

"Shaheeda..." Waseema uttered as she started pulling the gun away from his head. "If that's what you want..."

"Hell yeah, that's what she wants." He yelled at her, but he sure as hell didn't want to incense her, she still held the gun to his head, so he switched gears. "But uh, she's been tested right? I mean, she ain't got that shit or nothing..." the wrong gears, "I can work through it, but, you know, I heard things about her. Hey, I got other people in my life to consider."

"You no good son of a bitch. You don't give a damn about her, she ain't nothing but another piece of ass to you."

"Fuck it. I can't make her whole again, she fucked that up herself. Remember, I didn't make her sell no ass in the first place, but hell, if she's gonna be a whore, she might as well help with the bills-"

"I thought you loved me, Craig." Shaheeda blurted out as the tears dived down her cheeks. "God! You're just like everyone else!"

"C'mon now, Shaheeda, you know what it is, girl, that's the best I can do. I'll make you as righteous as I can...least for my man Khalid." He looked up at Waseema with scorn in his eyes and said, "But, fuck you, don't know why he married you in the first place."

"W-What..." she said.

"You know what it was. Khalid was just feeling sorry for your ass. He really had his eyes fixed on that other chick...the Spanish girl. Shit, that's what he really wanted. Everyone knew, and you knew too! You were just a piece of ass to him, just like your daughter is now. You know apples don't fall too far from the tree. Now...untie me so I can get the fuck out of here! Had enough of this shit already," he said, then under his breath he mumbled, "And you better hope I don't fuck the both of you now, while I got the chance. Shit, Waseema, heard you had some good pussy yourself." He eyeballed her up and down, licking his lips.

"You piece of shit!" She couldn't believe what she'd just heard. That was the last straw for her. She had enough too, fuck it, she thought. Her mind was made. "May Allah forgive you," she said. She knew what she had to do.

"What the fuck are you babbling about? Untie me...now!"

She squeezed the trigger, maybe from fear, or from loath, but Craig 3X's surprised eyes widened as the hole in his head spit a stream of blood in her direction. She backed out the way as Shaheeda stared at her in horror, then voiced softly under her breath. "...and me too."

Waseema stepped over towards Shaheeda who started crying hysterically and uncontrollably and pulled her hands away from her face, then calmly slapped the pure shit out of her and said, "Shut the hell up! It's over with. Now let's clean this shit up!"

Waseema glanced over at the crumpled body of Craig 3X, thinking about what he had said about Khalid, about the girl. That wasn't the first time she'd heard it. She was tired of it coming back up to haunt her like a bad dream, in her mind; wondering over and over, if Khalid really loved her or not.

"Shaheeda, go outside and get the plastic bags out of the trunk. We need to chop his ass up and throw the pieces in the river before daybreak!"

"Ma!"

"Just do it...now!" She also wondered about Shaheeda as she stared at her while she ran outside to the car. What kind of twisted game was she playing just now? Damn, she killed a man for her; a man she wasn't even sure raped her in the first place, but fuck it, she did it anyway, probably more so because he knew things. Things she didn't want anyone else to know about. Not even her own children.

She pulled the Fendi bag she brought with her closer and rummaged through it. She pulled out what she was looking for; a six-inch, foot long carving knife and smiled.

The hidden figure watched them both as they meticulously took care of the body. The building was just dark enough to hide in, with the same streetlamp from outside providing the only light; unveiling the crumbling spackles of paint on the walls of the abandoned building from days gone by. They didn't even notice they were being watched. The lurking dark figure that peeped in on them had seen and heard enough.

The door behind them closed silently shut as the image that had shadowed their every move slipped off into the darkness of the chilled Harlem night, taking with it, yet another secret.

HIS MIND RACED AROUND as he opened his eyes slowly. He glanced up at the structure and could see bright, glimmering reflections of stars as they danced about the universe. It was beautiful and he smiled, then focused his attention to the man that stood over him with his hands outstretched, saying *'Come'*.

It was Khalid, his father, and Rasheed stood up after taking his hand and embraced him. He could smell his scent as he did; the strong masculine sweet odor of the Egyptian musk oil that he favored so much. His hand touched the nape of his neck and he ran his fingers through the soft trestles that were his dreadlocks. He let go and his father handed him a hammer and smiled.

Rasheed took the tool and turned and there were his brothers: Mustapha, Latif, and his sister, Shaheeda, standing off in the background behind him. He realized what it was now, they were building a house, their house. His father had started hammering nails into the structure and humming a tune Rasheed couldn't quite pick up on but was familiar with it.

The next thing Rasheed knew, the house started to shake; beams that held the frame together started to fall, and the nails started backing themselves out like they were possessed. He looked around here and there and it was the same all over. Bricks had literally started falling out of the walls. *"Bricks from wall,"* he wondered, where did they come from? It didn't matter. Grabbing at them furiously, Rasheed tried to put them back into place; his father did the same.

He worked the same frantic pace as his old-man, brick for brick, and could feel the hot beads of sweat as they popped off his face. Rasheed ran to the next wall, and then to the other doing the same, but it was too much.

The trembling continued, but finally he could see what it was that was pushing them in the first place. Not the shaking, but someone was pushing them inward on them, and laughing. An ominous disturbing laugh that rang around echoing in his mind. He peeped through the holes and saw what it was.

Some were tall, some were short, all long haired, and all Latino. Rasheed could see them as they looked at him and sneered. He tried to recognize who they were, maybe figure out why they were doing this to his family. They weren't bothering anyone, they were just building a place to live in, underneath the stars, the heavens. Maybe if he could just grab one of them, and question him, he could figure it out.

Rasheed needed help, his father turned, but it was too late. Khalid started to wobble, he tried keeping his balance, but couldn't. He fell into the pile of bricks that had started building up. Rasheed looked, there seemed to be thousands of them, quickly rising further upward, engulfing his father as he reached toward him. His father said something that he couldn't quite make out, it wasn't *'help,'* Rasheed tried in vain, but just couldn't figure it out.

Khalid pointed to his brothers and his sister. Rasheed turned quickly and watched as Mustapha fell into the rubble himself along with his father. He turned towards Shaheeda for help. She sat off in a corner across from him crying, seemingly fighting off a shadow he couldn't see. She was no use to him but there was still Latif. He dangled along the side of the structure, teetering dangerously close to the edge, frantically holding on to a beam. He reached out to Rasheed for help, but his father also reached out for him to pull him up at the same time to keep from sinking. Rasheed looked at him, then Latif, it was a difficult decision, but he grabbed for his father.

Just as he tried pulling him up, he looked back over at Latif. He was angry and he pulled back away from him. Rasheed reached out, but he wouldn't come. He turned his head and the bricks started opening behind him and he started crawling through. Rasheed continued holding on to his father, but he started becoming heavy, slipping out of his grasp. He fought harder to hold on to him, but it was too much, finally his father looked into his eyes and said, "Redeem me...son." Rasheed looked at him perplexed and screamed out, "What are you talking about, dad? Don't go!"

His attention was caught by the sound of his mother yelling at him in the background; screaming for him to hold on, he was getting too heavy, he couldn't hold him much longer. Maybe she could help, he turned to face her, and he could see her running towards him, fast but the faster she ran, she seemed to get further away, as if running in slow motion.

He struggled to hold on, but it was useless, Khalid fell out of his arms into the abyss that had started forming beneath them, and Rasheed looked up at the heavens as the walls started to close in on him and yelled, "Why don't you help me?" until his eyes closed shut.

When he opened them again, he was in bed, waking up in a cold sweat.

Mya stood in the doorway of the room he lay in with her arms crossed and said, "Still having those nightmares." She was changed now; smoking a cigarette, she reminded him of her mother, weight-gain and all. He looked up at her and said, "Yeah...but, these aren't the ones that haunt me...when I'm awake."

She sucked her teeth and left. He got up and stretched. Then, once he got his footing together, he stepped over to the mirror on the dresser, rubbed the stubble on his chin and said, "Damn...grey...getting old."

Rasheed walked over to the window after grabbing his toothbrush; brushing his teeth he paused for a second watching the little girl that jumped rope on the sidewalk in front with her little girlfriends and smiled. She caught him staring and looked up, waving and giggling.

Her small round dimpled face was reminiscent of her mother's. She would have been a spitting image, if not for one thing, the small gap between her teeth. That belonged to him. She mouthed some words, but he couldn't hear her because the window was shut, but he knew what it was. "Hi, daddy." So, he waved back and said, "Hey, baby."

She was a pretty little girl, and he knew he'd have to get her out of here and show her other things besides Brooklyn. He glanced over at the dresser and noticed the clock radio and the LED on it showed, 8:52 AM. "Damn, I need to pick up Ice!" He waved one more time at his daughter Khadija, turned and b-lined straight to the shower.

COMING DOWN THE LONG winding roadway adjacent to the Hudson River, the gates at the front door of the grandiose, stone-white, cave like shrine became magnificently ostentatious, for lack of a better word, at best. But that's what it was built for, to keep people away and keep them from coming to get people out. As Rasheed drove down the hill to the parking lot, he was glad he fit into the latter.

Sing Sing; maximum security prison. No way could he take that type of environment. It'd be hell for him, not that it wasn't for anyone else, he just wasn't built like that. He'd rather die than be locked up, and one thing's for sure, he didn't feel like dying, least not today.

Today Rasheed was coming to pick up a friend, a long-time confidant-his homeboy, Ice. The last time he spoke to Ice was sometime two years ago, and that was after all the years that had gone by. He did manage to inquire with his mother about Ice, and she'd tell him how he was doing, what he was up to, and when he was coming home.

Ice was crazy anyway to get knocked on a humbug, being careless, messing with the wrong people. A costly mistake that got him close to ten years. Granted, he was pissed right about now, but the revenge he was looking for could never be obtained at all, snitch-ass Kevin was dead, so he might as well move on.

Hell, one thing was for sure, he damn sure didn't need any money, he had plenty. And Rasheed remembered Waseema saying that they had plans on getting married. She said Ice even pondered the thought of becoming Muslim. Rasheed had to smile at the thought, yeah, Ice, a Muslim. Then he chuckled; if he stayed in the country, he'd be alright. He could see his militant ass flying off to Iraq or someplace on some old secret mission type of thing. Naw, he had other plans for him. Plans not made of money, but built on finishing what they had started. The only thing though, was Ice, after all these years, after not seeing him almost a decade, still down?

Well, he'd have to see. He parked the car by the gate and before he could turn the car off, Ice was already coming out counting his gate money. Rasheed waved at him, he turned his way and smiled, then peeped back at the officer who opened the gate and said," Hey, give the Warden something for me, please."

"Yeah, sure, what is it...convict?

He put his middle finger and said, "Here ya go...and by the way, break a piece off yourself," and started laughing. Looking back over his shoulder he hollered at him, "I did that."

Rasheed grinned, yeah, he hadn't changed much. He was built like a baby gorilla from the waist up. He always worked out, but prison gave him time to put in work damn near every day. He was a beast, his chest was barreled; huge, and he had arms the size of baby tree limbs. His hair was short, cropped, like he liked it with nice smooth waves laid down. His face was still youthful, hell, prison has a way of preserving in a way. His swagger was still that of a youthful thirty-something. He looked good, Rasheed thought. Waseema had a prize on her hand, and he was sure she was somewhere fixing herself up also. She wasn't bad looking herself, she still looked good too. They'd make a good couple, he remarked.

Waseema came to visit Ice on a regular basis, and whatever he needed or wanted, she got. She wanted to get married, but he didn't want to do it in prison, figured he'd wait until he got out. They'd take a trip to Europe, get married then spend some money traveling. Leave the country, she was down for all that. She didn't have any small children and he didn't have any either. Even though she asked him one time about adopting, he seemed to be okay with not having any kids at all; he was okay with just her, and him.

He made it into the car and Rasheed got out. He stepped in front of him swiftly, looked him up and down, then in his eyes, shook his head, and put out his hand. Rasheed grabbed his and shook it then he went around to the other side and threw in his duffel and waited for him to crank the car up.

Rasheed asked, "What was all that for?"

He grinned, then chuckled. "C'mon now, you serious?"

"Yeah, what was all that about?"

He turned towards him and said, "Man...I just wanted to see if it was really you. Remember...I was there." Then turned his head back towards the prison, glad he was out of that hellhole.

Rasheed shook his head. He was going to have to leave that alone for now, but he knew it wouldn't be for long though. He knew he had questions for him, and he, like so many others, needed and wanted some answers.

WASEEMA HUMMED A TUNE to herself that she couldn't quite shake out of her head. One of those catchy new tunes they called *"New Jack Swing"* pumping through the radio caught her ear. With a nice melody and a smooth beat; she danced from room to room in front of large vanity mirrors trying to get right for her baby. She was acting like a schoolgirl on her first date or something. Prancing around the large house. Ice was coming home and she couldn't wait.

It'd been at least eight years since he'd left. That cold embittered day was like yesterday to her as he told her going down the steps that he was headed to Brooklyn, Bushwick. Something to do with Kevin. She cringed when she heard the name, but regrettably didn't follow up on it. Ice knew Kevin's pedigree so Rasheed knew whatever it was; Ice was on point but the work was going to be dirty. She waved him bye and he drove off. That was the last time she would see him on the street.

The next time she would see him would be in court during his arraignment for a manslaughter charge three days later. She tried to get him bail, but they denied it every time. Rasheed knew it was something deep, and then, where was Kevin, the so-called confidential informant? They wouldn't even let her speak with Ice; talking she wasn't kin. He wouldn't say a word though, he even denied the paid lawyer she'd set him up with. Ice knew his fate was sealed, they knew too much, except where the money was; five to fifteen laying down he told her it had something to do with his past.

Rasheed still pressed him when he went upstate for answers and he wouldn't budge. The last time she pressed, Ice put her hands in his and said, "I have to pay for the rest of them...things...were done. It's Okay, that's the least I can do. Don't worry, I'll be home soon." She knew then to let go, just make him as comfortable as he could be in prison. Even though Rasheed felt that her sons had paid the ultimate sacrifice, Ice always had strong feelings about the situation so she left it alone. He'd be home soon.

Ice showed her true love; love for her family, her sons, and for Rasheed. He was no way like Kevin, why he fucked with him in the first place was a mystery to her. Anyway, Ice kept his mouth shut about the loot, like a trooper, it was what it was. He would have been home sooner, but his temper did him in, something about busting a C-O's ass made him eat another three on lock-up and killed his parole off. "That's the bid though," he'd say, "comes with the territory." Of course, Rasheed was pissed, but she dealt with it best she could.

She had the business that kept her busy; S&A's in Brooklyn; Rasheed, Shaheeda and Donna. It did well. Considering. They started out selling painted sneakers Donna would make. Taking out traffic going into the city and even Tom, Dick and Harry's shoe store on Broadway closer to the projects. Then, just like that, it exploded. Donna brought in some high end and designer goods, some Gucci,

Versace, new Air Jordans. The next thing you know, they were bringing in new money. Dope boys and hustlers started spending money. Rappers started spending money. Then the white boys started spending money and just like that they were making money in the six-figure bracket.

They were getting so large that they needed security. Donna brought in some people she knew. Waseema wanted the FOI to put in work, but after the Craig 3X incident, she changed her mind, so she stuck with the Columbians Donna dealt with from out of Bushwick against her better judgement. But, powered by a Jewish lawyer and a low-key Italian backer, they pulled it together. It seemed harmless enough, at first.

Shaheeda was doing alright though. She started living the life; parties, even a flashy new candy-red Beemer, granted she would have had that anyway, they had the money, but still she was living the life of the 'it' girl now. Donna, hell, Donna just showed her ass in the store, but one thing for sure, Waseema thought, she put in work.

Waseema ran the lip liner around her full sensuous lips. Hearing a sound, she spun around quickly; it was Shaheeda. She didn't even hear her come in. Shaheeda had a key but usually she'd at least call out to Waseema or ring before she came. Waseema looked at her and something about Shaheeda was different. Her face drooled, eyes dazed, and as Waseema got up closer, she smelled like alcohol; Shaheeda had been out partying again. She must have come to the house early this morning and crashed out in Latif's old room. "Shaheeda, I didn't know you were here. How are you? Haven't seen you in a while."

She pushed past Waseema and said, "Not long enough." Her voice was very dry and cold, and on top of that, she was coming down off a high.

Waseema followed behind her. "You alright, girl. How's everything in Brooklyn?"

Shaheeda shrugged her shoulders and the next thing you know, her mouth bloated, and she dived for the toilet, throwing up.

Waseema rushed by her side holding her as she violently convulsed, throwing up. The smelly clear colored spirits exiting her stomach. All Waseema could do was shake her head in pity. "What's wrong with you Sha-"

"Ma! Just leave me the hell alone!"

"What's going on with you!"

Shaheeda got up, went to the sink, rinsed her mouth, looked over at her mother and smirked, "You!" then brushed past her heading off towards Latif's room.

A tear formed up in the corner of Waseema's eyes as she wondered what was going on with her? She thought Shaheeda had gotten rid of those demons from her past a few years back, but evidently, she was wrong. The worst thing about it, unfortunately, was Rasheed was dead wrong, and at someone else's expense and life.

Shaheeda stomped off to Latif's room and slammed the door shut, causing Waseema to jump slightly. Damn, she thought, how could she let herself get caught up like this? She should have left well enough alone three years ago, but she had to show out. Prove to her little girl that she was tough, nothing to be played with. She pushed the issue by being nosey at first; Shaheeda never volunteered information about Craig 3X. In her own deranged mind Waseema could see that it affected her, especially in trying to establish any type of connection with the opposite sex. Shaheeda was untrusting, scathing, intimidating. Every time Waseema saw it, it made her angrier until it progressed to a point of misguided hatred and hostility. How could the man she trusted with her own child take advantage of her the way he did? How dare he? He can't get away with that. What would Khalid do? Waseema pondered? That's all it took; she didn't have to look far for a scapegoat- Craig 3X.

It didn't take much to lure Craig 3X into the trap Waseema set up for him. A promise of pussy. Muthafucka' wasn't shit. It also didn't take hardly anything for her to convince Shaheeda to go along with the plan. It's like that's what Shaheeda wanted all along. What started off as just putting the timb down, turned into a sordid discussion of castration. When Waseema reflected back on her and her husband's relationship with Craig 3X, especially hers, she had a pretty good idea where things would go as a result, but she played the cards out anyway.

The way Shaheeda acted towards Waseema since it all went down made her wonder now why she even bothered. Waseema had a body on her hands. She could go to jail for life easily. Shaheeda would plead out and take the stand against her and Waseema knew that, but, isn't that what she would have wanted anyway? Fuck it, he raped a child. She knew the courts would be sympathetic towards her. Maybe she'd plea out for some counseling and a couple of years' probation, maybe. Waseema had it all figured out, but she never would have imagined Shaheeda's response that night; that threw her. It's like Shaheeda enjoyed watching him beg. Like she took pleasure in setting him up and playing the role of the victim, she was so phony with it, but hell, who was really the victim here?

Waseema leaned back against the doorpost of the bathroom and shook her head slowly and sighed. Damn, a body. Prison. She'd lose everything. Sure, it hit her earlier on that Shaheeda was the only witness, and maybe she wouldn't say anything. Waseema grinned, and said, "Yeah right," then peeped down at the long sharp manicuring file in her hands, subconsciously stabbing the side of the doorway, continuously, wondering, would Shaheed really tell?

Shaheeda leaned back against her side of the door and turned slightly, listening, trying to get a bead on her mother's reaction. She didn't understand why she hated her mother so much, but everything Waseema did made her feel pain, ever since Shaheeda was a child.

She turned back around and rubbed on her stomach. It'd been a hell of a night. She still felt woozy and groggy on her feet. Staggering over to the bed, Shaheeda sat down, plopped back and sighed. Shit, she blurted out as she belched, hoping she didn't have to go again. It already felt like she threw her whole insides up the last time she went. Was it the champagne or her promiscuous lifestyle?

It was the same guy now for the last three months or so. Randy. She used protection and all, but lately Shaheeda had been slipping. Damn alcohol! He'd handled her rough, like she liked it; that's the only way she wanted it. That's why she kept him.

Hell, Randy would have worked out just fine, but he was much too greedy, for money, for the dope, and the sex. She'd end up verbally abusing him like clockwork; taunting him; making him fall to his knees and go to the 'candy store'. *He liked that though*, Shaheeda mused. But, when he wanted to do her, he couldn't get it up. When he finally did, she cracked on him about it being too small. The drugs had affected Randy's libido-big time.

*He just didn't know how to work it like Craig 3X did*, she thought back. Her face lit up thinking about him. Craig 3X was 'that dude' for her. He'd schooled Shaheeda well, and she let Randy know constantly. Craig 3X this-Craig 3X that!

Randy couldn't take too much more of being ridiculed all the time, just tired of it she guessed, that's when he pulled out the knife that day. Shaheeda tried getting him to back off, but she just wouldn't shut up about it; the fool tried to kill her ass.

Shaheeda couldn't tell her mother, and especially her brothers, the whole story about her sick perverse ways, so she made it look like Randy was the one that was crazy. It would have worked out, but when Felix heard about her erotic ways, it excited him and he kidnapped her. Her brothers thought it was all about money when all that time it boiled down to a piece of ass. Like he told her that day, *Randy told me about you...* that was crazy.

But her mother killing Craig 3X was *NOT PART OF THE FUCKING PLAN!* her mind screamed out. She tossed around the bed in a fit stressing over it-throwing pillows. Hell, what happened to just putting the tim down. Force his hand into marrying her. Now things had changed, her mother fucked around and killed him. And for what?

Shaheeda got up and stared at the door, then said under her breath, "I should let her ass rot in a prison somewhere."

"Shaheeda! Shaheeda!"

"What!"

Waseema paused, normally she'd have spazzed on her quick for that, but it'd been a rough morning so far for the both of them and she didn't want to make things any worse so she kept her cool. "Look, uh, if you don't want to talk, fine. But I just got the mail here... a statement from the bank about the store, and uh... damn; something ain't right. These numbers don't seem to add up... and they haven't for a little while. I haven't been mentioning it, figuring with the car, the cruises, partying, but uh... what's going on down there in Brooklyn?"

Shaheeda balled her face up, like, what the hell she was talking about? Things seemed fine to her. Donna always had plenty of money, and hell, customers and orders were coming in and out the door fast as all hell. "I don't know." It did get her attention though, she needed to play this one out and see exactly where it was going. "You need to call Donna. Remember, you put her in charge. You need to deal with that." Your move...Ma.

"I did that because I figured with you being my daughter and all, I didn't want to mix business-"

"I'll ask Donna, okay! Now, please, I need to get a little rest."

"Alright, I understand," Waseema sighed. "Before you leave, I'll make sure it's perfectly clear for you to speak on my behalf. We'll talk about it."

*That's what she wanted, power. Being able to control, along with her half of the business; flaunt some money, too, yeah, like Donna.* Shaheeda thought. "Sure, sure, whatever...I'm tired, okay." *Just be cool, girl, hold on. She'll be gone soon.*

Waseema stepped away from the door and hollered back. "And by the way, Ice is coming home today, too." She smiled hoping to get a positive response. Waseema and Ice were always tight like that, especially since her grandmother died and they all had to move uptown, but it was strange that Shaheeda didn't respond back, or at least, she didn't hear her as she walked away.

"Yeah..." she said under her breath. "Have a good day... Mom."

Waseema walked off with her head down, wondering what she had done to deserve that. The tear that held on for so long in the corner of her eye, swelled up and nosedived straight for the floor, bringing along with it a flood of others. She thought to herself, *Today is supposed to be one of the best days of my life...fuck this.*

# CHAPTER TWO

Albert Einstein sometimes said, "...The question that drives me crazy...am I, or the others...crazy?" That's exactly where this ride was going. Rasheed intentionally, and quite uncomfortably, kept his eyes glued on the road. At times even tried small talk like; "Damn...look at all these trees," and even, "...Didn't know there were that many farms up here." In which Ice would reply rather dryly saying, "Yeah...sure...uh huh..."

Rasheed didn't put any more stock into it than he already had. If Ice didn't want to talk, then the hell with it. But still, Rasheed was going to have to talk to him about some things. Things he wanted from Ice.

Too many years had gone by, and already the opportunities were slipping far from his reach more and more. Rasheed didn't quite know how to go about it, but he knew whatever he'd planned he couldn't do without Ice. Rasheed was the only one left who saw the vision, the big picture. Everyone else had moved on or was dead. He had to do what he had to do. Rasheed sighed as he thought more on it. Granted, it was going to be hard on everyone, but he had no choice.

"Man...where the fuck did you go?"

*Here we go,* Rasheed thought, *Finally.*

"What you talkin' bout-"

"Man, don't fuck with me! You know what the hell I'm talking about!" Ice turned towards Rasheed matter-of-factly and thought it through before he put it out there. "Evidently, you got out. How? I don't have a clue. I mean, I saw the explosion, Rasheed. Flames, hell, the building fuckin' collapsed!"

Ice started to shake his head like cobwebs were stuck in his mind as he thought way back when, then said, "I-I would have stayed, but..."

"I know man...I know."

"No...you don't know! You ain't got a fuckin' clue!" The brows on his forehead wrinkled as Rasheed glanced over, figuring maybe he should pull off by the side of the road, an exit. Hear Ice out. After all, he had a right.

"How the fuck did you get out? Giovanni said you handcuffed yourself to Felix, threw gas on the both of you and lit it up. How the fuck!"

"Allah was on my side."

"My ass!"

"A'ight! Be cool." Rasheed said, He cut an eye over, watched Ice ball up his fist and thought, *Yeah, maybe we better pull over, just in case.* "Hey, uh, I'm a pull over by the road over there...and uh, we can talk."

Ice turned back around with his hands folded on his chest, heaving and pissed off, "Let's do that."

The road off the highway pulled into a little gully past a patch of trees around a spot situated next to a sparkling running creek. Rasheed pulled the car next to crystalline waters headfirst and got out. He sat on the hood as Ice stood off a little way from him and said, "Well, uh...it's a long story, but I'll try to make it as short."

"Rasheed...I just did damn near ten years in the joint. Trust me...I'm a crazy patient," he said as he sat next to him.

"It was crazy. I mean, bullets were all over the place whizzing past my ears, and then Mustapha just died in my arms....Then Derek." Rasheed got up off the car, looked into the clearness of the running water and reflected. "Me and Giovanni were the only ones left standing after the smoke cleared. I mean, mind you. All hell had gone down in a matter of milli-seconds, it seemed. I looked around making sure Shaheeda was gone. She was. I was cool with that...then I heard a sound from behind me and it was Felix, so I tackled him...Then I guess, adrenaline just took over. Yeah, yeah, I fucked around and got on some bullshit with the gas, the lighter, bunch of drama, man."

"Yeah, Rasheed, that's your thing though, but the cuffs...the cuffs? How the hell did you maneuver that?"

"It wasn't about me. You see, Felix had a gun- I didn't know he was strapped. I mean he was shooting at us and all, but his boys had all the firepower. We, hell, we were loaded, but I guess after everyone went down, then the shooting stopped, and it was just me and Giovanni, I assumed that all the ammo was wasted. Know what I mean?"

"Somewhat, but I'm ex-military. You know if I was there, I would have maintained the cover until we-"

"You right... you weren't there."

"Not like I didn't try to make it back, Rasheed. I mean, I had to get Shaheeda out of dodge!"

Rasheed reached over and rubbed his back. "No man, it ain't like that, Ice. You did good, hell, damn good. I just meant that...you weren't there, and I didn't know any better. Of course, it would have been different if you were there, big time!"

That made Ice feel better, even though Giovanni had explained that fact to him over a hundred times already, it still sounded better coming from Rasheed himself.

"Okay, but still..."

"He pulled out the gun...think it was a little pee-wee .38 or something and aimed it my way. I reached and noticed I didn't have shit, not even a fuckin knife. Everything was scattered throughout the floor and hell, I was just plain fucked up, and then, I fucked around and handcuffed myself to him."

"But you had the lighter in your hand... the gas."

"Hell yeah, but he got the jump on me. Man, I don't know where that cat got his luck from...I swear, I don't. But he aimed the gun at my hand and shot. Somehow or another, he shot the fuckin lighter...I swear!" Rasheed showed Ice his hand and the burn marks on his fingers. "You see! Next thing you know he pulled the trigger again and I heard this loud rang and my wrist went numb. He shot the fucking cuff my hand, like in some old Western movie! Man, Ice, I didn't know muthafuckas really did that type of shit."

"Yeah...it could be done."

"Next thing you know he scurries over to a drain hole cover like a little rat, then pulls it open and dives in. I looked over my shoulder and the fuckin' lighter was still lit on the ground. It landed next to the gas can, like it was starting to catch. Then, I heard this loud ass 'sssss'-like sound and I just knew a gas line was broken somewhere."

"Hell, I bet he knew. That's why he hauled ass like that!"

"Man, Ice, I did what... it was just instinct. I jumped in the drain hole behind him and the next thing you know-*Kabooooom!*"

Ice looked him up and down and said, "But...you didn't get burned?"

"Naw. Some black nasty ass water was down there, deep as hell. I bumped my head falling in but I held on so I wouldn't black out and drown. Yo, it was nasty, and it stunk like all hell, but I dealt with it. I heard the sounds of water rushing in the background and looked up. It was Felix making his way towards a tunnel with water gushing out. I went after him; hell, I had no choice. The walls above me started trembling and the flames started shooting through the hole from upstairs. I knew then the building was starting to collapse."

"Then what?" Ice asked, all in his mouth, hanging on to his every word.

"I waded through the water and reached an open hole. Small. Tight. The roof caved in behind me and smoke was on my ass. You should have seen me crawl through that little muthafucka. When I finally came out, I was behind some buildings on Quincy Street."

"Where at? In the street?"

"Naw man." Rasheed got up and used his hands to describe the scene as he remembered it. "Right behind the buildings, Ice. You remember the little alley between the apartment complex on Gates Avenue around the back; you know what I'm saying. It's like, for electrical, sewage, all that."

"Yeah, Okay...I know where you're talking about."

"Anyway, I wound up behind there. I looked behind me and saw the building falling in and just ran."

"What happened with Felix?"

"I'm a get to that." Rasheed sat back down again. "I got up dazed and shit and started towards the street. I knew the cops were gonna be coming shortly, and that's when I saw him. Somehow or another, he gathered up some dudes, probably threw some money at them. Then, he saw me... pointed me out and they came running towards me. I dipped through the buildings and ended up back on Gates Avenue and then...just hauled ass."

"Why didn't you call us?"

Rasheed looked at the ground and kicked rocks. "I had to do it this way. I had to let them think I was gone."

"We had a funeral for you."

"I know...I was there...in disguise, of course."

Ice gawked at him, then shook it off. "Some of Felix's people did come by, but Giovanni's people had us covered. We were police deep. It was wild. Three caskets...your momma was going crazy. Hey, let me ask. Did she know? I mean...she had to..."

"Yeah, I called her afterward. Told her not to tell anyone, not even you, then I left town. Had to keep the heat off her...and you."

"Me? Damn, you should have called me!" Ice said as he stood up.

"Then what? You get some old cowboy shit. Go after him yourself. Naw...it had to go down like this! Trust me."

"I did Rasheed. I did...with my life, remember?"

Rasheed stared at him for a minute, then got up and put out his hand; Ice grabbed him, pulled him near and hugged him then whispered, "I did."

He nodded his head then gave him that old-well done homeboy look, then turned to get back in the car, satisfied with the way things went. Ice peeped over the top and asked, "Okay...now what?"

"Ice, my brother, I thought you'd never ask."

RASHEED DROVE OFF AS Ice waved at him until he turned off Amsterdam Avenue. Then he turned, picked up his duffel bag and looked at the three-story brownstone in front of him; home. The neighborhood: Sugarhill; still one of the best in Harlem. Proven; streets kept clean and the sidewalks swept. Not typical of Harlem.

Ice smiled warmly; it was a whole lot nicer than Sing-Sing. But anything was better than Sing-Sing.

He had expected to see Waseema rushing out the door. Running into his arms like he dreamed of over and over for the last ten years. But there was nothing like that. He stared up at the windows and saw that some were open. The drapes blowing pleasantly through. *Perhaps she just stepped out a minute and would be back shortly*, he thought. *Or hell, maybe, she just forgot he was coming home today altogether*, he thought again as he looked up and down the block. That couldn't have happened though, he'd just called Waseema the other day, reminding her.

Ice started climbing up the steps slowly then turned back around and spotted her car; a crystal-blue, 5-class Mercedes Benz coupe.

She was probably home. Guess things weren't that serious for her. After all, it was all his fault for getting caught up in the first place. She was probably still angry at him, pissed even, like she was in the courtroom the day he was sentenced. Waseema didn't cry or anything, just gave him the look, that, *damn you fucked up-should 'a stayed your ass home-with me,* look. Ice sighed, he knew she was right, then pushed at the door. It was open. Now, he thought, *Suppose something was wrong.* He pushed it wider and peeped inside. No one. Rasheed's rhetoric during the ride made him paranoid to say the least.

"Waseema!" he called out as he stepped into the foyer and sniffed. His senses exploded as the aromas they divided into danced in his head with delight. Lamb, barbequed something or another...biriyani? Something fried in a batter...quiche? And yes, finally something he was sure of; muffins. Yeah, her mother's kitchen bakery downstairs was still in full effect.

"Waseema...you here, baby?"

Now he was more than curious. Precariously cautious now, his mind started racing about with different scenarios. Like, *Suppose someone had broken in, tied her up, holding her hostage or something. Maybe, Felix's people-* "Hey, baby..." someone called out.

He spun around and his jaw dropped. In the dining room hall, spread out on the table, directly underneath the huge sparkling chandelier, a fantastically, fanciful, five-course meal had been set up. Waseema was dressed in silk lingerie; her long hair was spread radiantly off her shoulders. Her body seemed flawless as her long shapely legs were crossed and dangled off the table setting off six-inch stilettos that dripped *'sexy'*. The lighting from the miniscule glass mirrors on the huge globed light above her set off the color of her skin as Ice beamed. His favorite hue; cocoa.

The windows were slightly opened as the bouquet bit at his nostrils. His eyes gleamed with pleasure as he licked at his lips.

"Uh...you hungry?" Waseema asked as she sat on a gold platter then slowly, parted her legs.

Ice grinned and shook his head as he dropped the duffel bag on the floor and said, "Hungry for food...naw, but I'm starving...for something else."

There were no words to describe it, except, maybe: soft; smooth; silk-as he lay in her arms. His body just seemed to magically swim; float away even. Ice grinded against Waseema; his sex-starved organ digging into oblivion, all hers. The warm, but wet catalyst of insurmountable solace, racked his whole existence. Yet, at times he felt like passing out from the immense satisfaction. Even fantasizing-wishing, that he could make himself as small as an inch or so. Then he could have crawled inside of Waseema and just lay there in her vagina. Made that his abode. Instead of that cold, damp cell that was his home for the last ten years. But, as she let that low, audible, moan of ecstasy escape her plush, soft, lips when his pelvic hit hers, Ice realized that this was no dream; but in-fact true, real life, and certain words had to be said, Words he never spoke before sincerely. Right now, a grunt just wouldn't do it. Naw, not that. "I love you, baby." Yeah, that's what it was.

Waseema's slanted, doe-like eyes pierced into his, wandering, searching for his soul. She'd only close them slightly at times as the spasms of euphoria shot throughout her body in wakes, causing her legs to go numb and body shake. Making her long natural dark eyelashes flutter uncontrollably. Ice would slow down, ignorantly thinking he was hurting her, but she'd only pull him closer and let out a soft, "No, baby, more!" He'd then bury his face into her shoulders and kiss the nape of her neck gently. Holding her waist firm and slowly digging until she wrapped her long svelte legs tightly around his back. Raking her perfectly manicured nails softly into his flesh until he couldn't take it anymore. No holding back, Ice felt it all the way down to his toes.

It felt like he was having a seizure or something. Like as if his whole body had failed him. *Damn!* he thought, had it been that long? Ice felt like his whole insides were coming out. His dick was totally out of control now; bouncing against the walls of her pussy like a drunken monkey. He wanted to pull out so bad, spare himself some embarrassment but it was too damn soon. Something just wouldn't let him. He stopped-frozen, and she knew what it was. Waseema wrapped her legs harder and pulled him closer to her with all her might. Ice picked up his head, blinked, then it suddenly jerked backwards. He closed his eyes tightly and gritted his teeth, then yelled out, "*Oh my God!*" Smiling when she heard it, she thought, *No, not God. Me.*

It felt like it would never end as his body continued to jerk and his dick spit streams of the white sticky fluid inside of her. When it was full, it ran out like puddles of milk all over his groin. Ice's body gave way and he gently fell on top of Waseema, but still it wasn't over yet, it was just beginning...for her. Waseema's body started to jerk too; her vagina muscles grabbed hold of his dick and squeezed like a vice. She let out a cry. A low-pitched moan. And all of a sudden started to spasm. His dick was overcome and flooded with juices coming from her body that were warm, much warmer than his. "I love you, too!" managed to spew out her mouth as she grabbed his face and kissed his lips, hungrily. Waseema's tongue ran in and out her mouth like a snake. It was ugly. It was savage. They both collapsed in each other's arms, breathing heavily and panting. It had been ten years of wishing he was there for her-flirting in the visitation room-waiting by the phone for him to call-masturbating by themselves. It was cold. It was nasty. It was hard sex. The best kind. A fucking good time.

Waseema curled up in his arms afterward like she was trying to literally be a part of his skin. He didn't mind, he wanted the same, to be a part of her also. He rubbed his hands along her back as she cringed, ever so slightly, her body still sensitive to such pure passion. And every time he touched her, she'd cum. Ice's dick lay to the side like a soldier shot on the battlefield of love; backwards, head up high. But instead of blood coming from his mouth, it was the white remnants of sexual plasma. And along his shaft; chalky, white, hardened battlefield dirt. Dried up and flaky; the only remnants that a war had been fought. Ice looked over at Waseema, took a deep breath and said, "Glad to be...home."

She looked up at him and replied subtly, "Me too...me too." After all, it'd been some years for her also.

Once Ice finally found his lane, it was just a matter of learning how to press the gas again. Remembering when to every now and then switch gears to either go faster-harder, or just cruise. But he kept it going. They, for lack of a better word, screwed all over the house: the pantry, (*he felt like a snack*); the basement (*he was after the muffin's and she fucked around and bent over*) and the library (*just because*). They didn't mess around in Latif's old room or her mother's. It was about respect more than anything, but don't think that it wasn't thought about.

Finally, in her bedroom they cuddled in each other's arms, half asleep, half watching television. Waseema rubbed his chest and saw that he was drifting off, possibly to sleep so she started to ease out the bed. Ice grabbed her hand and she turned around and said, "What's wrong, baby. You alright?" Waseema moved closer and started fondling him. "Wanna go another round?" she cooed.

His face lit up like a baby in a candy store as he came alive in her hand, but gently pushed it away and said, "I'm good, baby, for now. But I wanted to talk to you about something."

"Sure...what?"

"Me and uh...Rasheed talked."

She rolled her eyes, sucked her teeth and said, "Oh god! Now what!" Her back turned to him, she pouted. "You sure know how to break the mood."

He started stroking her hair and said, "Naw, it's cool. We just had a serious talk. And...I want to share it with you, that's all. We're supposed to be close like that, right?"

Waseema felt bad when she heard that. Ice was right. They shared everything and if he felt that it was important enough for her to know about whatever he had to say, she should at least listen; 'cause he'd do it for her.

"Okay...bout what?" she asked as she turned around to face him.

"Have you ever thought about leaving?"

"Leaving? Harlem? And go where?"

"Arizona"

"Arizona? Why?"

"That's where Rasheed was. But I think you knew that though. And...why didn't you tell me he wasn't dead anyway? No, we'll talk about that another time. Anyway, he said he bought some property-bunch of land down there. Wants to take his daughter. You know, get her out of the city...somewhere nice." Ice moved closer and hugged Waseema. "He said he needed my help to help manage some property and ... I figured I could use you also."

Waseema looked at the sincerity in his eyes. The one place Ice couldn't hide; his eyes always told on him. That's why he always opted to just be truthful; 'cause he sucked at lying anyway. She smiled and said, "You know. That's what I always wanted to hear, Ice, really. You did change. Much more...mature." She kissed him, "But...use me?"

"Of course...a good woman...with me."

"Oh, so all I am to you is a piece of pussy, huh?"

"Well, the pussy is good." He laughed as she threw a pillow at him. "But better than that, I need a wife." He grabbed her and pulled her closer into him.

"Ice...you really wanna marry me?"

"Of course. C'mon now. This ain't nothing new. We talked about this, remember?"

"True, we did, but..."

"But what? You change your mind?"

"No...it's not that. I want to marry you. I do."

"Then, what's the problem?"

"You know, that's just it, Ice. There aren't any problems, and it just seemed a little strange. Know what I mean?"

He kissed her forehead as she peered out the window and said, "I do."

"Okay...I'm down, but tell me, how's Rasheed going to get Khadija away from Mya, or... Is he just gonna take her?"

"Don't know all that, but believe me, I'm sure he's got something worked out."

"I hope so. It'd be nice to be down there and watch my grandchild grow up...comfortably."

"I'm sure... He held her tightly in his arms. "Maybe, we should get in touch with someone down there..."

"But, Ice. I've got to take care of things here before I go. My mother's holdings. The brownstone...the store in Brooklyn, all that."

"I'm gonna help you get all that together. Cool?"

"Ok. Just gotta call Latif... Shaheeda."

"Now, that's gonna be the headache."

"You're right about that."

RASHEED DROVE DOWN Bushwick Avenue after getting off the Interboro Expressway coming in from Manhattan. It'd been a pretty comfortable ride, after all he was in Derek's old caddy. When he first came home, he was surprised it was still riding around, sitting in front of Waseema's place all those years collecting dust. She only kept it because Giovanni gave it to her after it was impounded. She couldn't quite figure out what else to do with it, so Ice changed the registration plates and kept it to drive it back and forth to Brooklyn. It was actually the car that he drove the day he was locked up. Afterward, Waseema just kept it parked until he could come home. What else would she do?

When Rasheed showed up, he needed to move around, so she gave him the keys. It was sentimental for him, because Rasheed was the one with Derek when he got the car. Besides, Rasheed needed to catch up with Mya anyway.

When he finally pulled up in front of Mya's place, she peeped out the door rubbing her eyes like she'd seen a ghost or something. The car had brought back a flood of memories, some pleasant, but mostly bad for her. *It's all good.* Mya thought as Rasheed got out. Then she watched the little girl come running out behind her. A small, tiny brown-skinned, knocked-kneed, chinky-eyed, cute little old thing. "That's your father," Mya said to her. Rasheed figured everything was going to be alright again, like it was before. His little girl jumped into his arms, and looked up at Mya, who smiled and said, "Knew you'd be back".

Things started out real decent at first. she asked where he was, and he explained everything best he could, let her know he didn't abandon her, but tried to keep her out of harm's way. The one thing that was really touchy for them, that they spoke around but never actually was about Derek. How Mya and he messed around behind Rasheed's back. There was a trust issue and it showed. He half-assed forgave Mya, but never fully did and she could feel it. In fact, if it wasn't for the little girl, Rasheed probably would have left for good.

Mya had been doing her own thing herself trying to survive with the baby while he was gone. Waseema asked her to come to Harlem hundreds of times right after she moved up there, but she was stubborn. Waseema was too overbearing, trying to stay up on her comings and goings. They argued all the time and Waseema figured it wasn't worth the headache or the irritation. Mya didn't want to stop Waseema from seeing her grandchild though, so she'd let things go until Rasheed came back. Told her anything she needed she could have, for the sake of the child and Rasheed.

Mya took advantage and started spending money wastefully and foolishly. She got busted one night by Shaheeda at the club. The baby was at home by herself. They fought and it got ugly. When Waseema heard about it she cut Mya loose. Had her accountants figure out what the child would need, and send it accordingly on the first of every month. Then Waseema put a trust fund in the baby's name and let it go at that. She would go by Mya's apartment whenever she'd go to the Brooklyn S&A's and Mya would catch feelings mostly because she felt like Waseema kicked her out. After that, Waseema said to hell with it and made Mya fend for herself.

Mya found herself a boyfriend, against Ice's wishes. A Mexican by the name of Chino; hung around the 'Vatos Locos' up in Bushwick, treated her like pure shit. Ice kept an eye out for her until he got locked up, then Waseema would send people down there every now and again. She had a pretty good idea Mya was mixed up in some bad dealings but she didn't know quite what it was. As long as the child was safe, taken care of, and not harmed, Waseema figured she could do whatever she wanted to do. Mya was grown.

By the time Rasheed had gotten back into the town she told him all had taken place, he figured he'd definitely stay close. He knew 'Vatos Locos' was bad news. Rasheed couldn't find a decent place for himself anyway so he moved in with Mya. She tried to patch up their relationship, but it wasn't quite working out the way she'd like. Then on top of it all, Chino tried staying in the picture. Rasheed had heard of him on the streets but never met him. Chino stayed out of his way, secretly trying to get up with Mya on the low.

Mya would try to throw herself in Rasheed's face, walking around half-dressed but he paid her no mind, she'd changed. She was heavier and had started smoking weed and drinking. She chained smoked cigarettes like her mother, and would smell of smoke constantly. That pushed Rasheed even further away until they became cold to one another. He wanted to move so bad but didn't want to leave his daughter in that environment. That's when he came up with the idea of going back to Arizona. That was the big plan he wanted to share with Ice. To leave the city for good, finally, just like they planned when they were younger looking out off the porch in the projects.

For Rasheed though, there was always something, something that just wouldn't let him leave his past behind. Constantly wondering and dreaming about his father's murder, the Cartel and even Felix. He wasn't satisfied with what Felix had told him that night. No, he knew there had to be more. He wanted to find out things, things he knew even his own mother was still holding back. Things that now brought him back to New York.

Rasheed turned the corner on Decatur Avenue; the block that Mya lived on, and got caught up behind the B-6 bus as it was picking up passengers. He chilled, listening to the radio and made a mental note to visit the store later on to talk to Shaheeda. Just plain old hang out. The bus moved and he peered over in front of the building. What he saw would be the beginning of the troubles he tried to avoid. It was always something.

Khadija was sitting on Chino's lap. He was laughing out loud, while Mya sat on the stoop directly behind him. He had a paper bag with a bottle of liquor in his hand, and he was drunk. He passed a bottle back to Mya and started rubbing on Khadija's back. Smiling, she giggled innocently. Possibly only because her mother did the same. Mya grabbed the bottle, took a swig and then another. Chino looked back at her, snatched the bottle away, sneered, pulled her by the collar and viciously back-handed her. Khadija tried to wiggle out of his arms, but he grabbed her tightly making her scream out to let her go. He swung her small body to the side and reached for his belt. Mya grabbed his arms but he swung her away as Khadija tried running up the steps. That was enough for Rasheed to see. He was already halfway out the car with it still in drive, because his right hand was already on the butt end of his .45.

The car crashed slowly into a hydrant and abruptly stopped. Everything after that seemed to move in slow motion. Rasheed had his pistol out with a bead on the already wide-eyed Chino, who didn't know Rasheed's pedigree, but he knew a big ass gun was pointed directly at him so it didn't really matter. He tried grabbing for Khadija to shield himself, but she was too fast, scurrying up the steps and diving behind the door. Chino drew back then tried to go another way but ran straight into Mya. He grabbed her by the throat in a yoke and pushed her out in front of him.

Rasheed paused for only a second to make sure Khadija was in the building safely. When she was, he now concentrated on the man who held his baby mama hostage. Cuffing his gun in his pocket he bulldozed into the both of them, knocking them down. Mya has enough sense to hit the ground rolling, get up and haul ass up the block. Now it was just him and Chino. Rasheed's hand came up out of his pocket. There wasn't much Rasheed needed to think about, the do or die was already ingrained in his blood. He pulled the trigger and Chino's chest exploded as he was blown back into the street with a reddish flush of blood gushing out. Rasheed watched as he tried to crawl. Then coldly, walked up on him, aimed the pistol to his head and squeezed the trigger.

Rasheed turned and glanced over at Mya, then up the steps at his daughter who hid behind the door. He waved at her to come down. Amazingly, as scared as she was, she ran to him, grabbing him by the leg. She was shaking like a leaf. Rasheed turned and looked over at the car. There wasn't much damage, more so because he was already stopped when he got out. "Go get in the car!" He told Khadija and she ran over to it and jumped in. He pointed at Mya and told her, "Go upstairs and get whatever you need now! We outta here!" She froze, then moved cautiously, slowly, then looked at the body in the street. Trembling, she stepped back and shook her head no. Rasheed's eyes narrowed and he frowned. He wasn't mad at her, he knew she was in shock, but he needed her to make a move before it was too late. He jumped in the car and backed up, stopped in front of her and hollered out the window. "I'll be back to get you. Run upstairs now!" Then he gunned up the street on Bushwick Avenue.

Mya stood motionless as she looked over at the crowd gathering around the sprawled-out body of Chino. She knew there was going to be trouble now. On top of that in the background the sound of sirens grew louder and louder with each passing second...*COPS!* Her mind screamed out, what did he do? Why didn't she go with him? Quickly she ran up the steps into the building, into her apartment and slammed the door behind her. Still shaking she tried to calm herself down and think it through. What to do? What to do? She grabbed a suitcase and started stuffing it with all kinds of identifying papers and clothes; hers, Khadija's and Rasheed's. Putting on a jacket, she ran to the door, looked down the stairs and outside the front door. All she could see were scores of police cars already out in front. They came so fast! She panicked and stopped in her tracks. Then she heard a deep husky voice say "Come on!"

She looked down to see the big, stocky built, dark skinned man that lived in the apartment below her. He was calling her. "You better come the fuck on before the police come in!"

She grabbed the bag and moved swiftly down the steps and into his apartment. He shut the door and said to her. "Now look. I'm gonna hide you. Just don't make a sound or say anything, not a word because best believe they're gonna be in here looking for your ass." He rushed over to a closet, then pushed some old bubble jackets and coats aside. He stepped in, put his fingers in a notch up top, kicked the door slightly and pulled out the whole back wall. He grabbed her and pushed her inside. "Remember, not a peep."

She nodded her head and tried to stifle her breathing, but it was hard as hell as her heart pumped straight Kool-Aid. After a short while she heard nothing then crouched down. She was so scared, she damn near pissed in her pants, and on top of it all, it was dark as hell. *Why was he trying to help her? He hardly ever spoke to them. He used to give Khadija candy all the time, that's all she ever knew...oh my God! Was he some sort of sick pervert?* No. She remembered Rasheed had spoken to him a couple of times briefly and they exchanged numbers. Maybe he was a friend of his or something. *Was he gonna come back for her?* Her mind raced like a son of a bitch, and only quieted when she heard the police come to the door banging and hollering out his name; "Kokomo!"

# CHAPTER THREE

"**H**E DID WHAT?" Latif yelled as he took the phone from his ear and put it down to his side, took a deep breath, then closed his eyes. *This has got to be a nightmare,* he thought to himself. "What the hell did he do? Damn!" *It is a nightmare. Yeah, that's it,* Latif thought. But it wasn't.

Maria was on the other end screaming her ass off. "You need to take care of this... Right now."

The phone was back in his ear again, this time his face grimaced as he listened, trying to get in a word edgewise to the craziest woman on the other end of the line, babbling in Spanglish. She had every right to be pissed. "Hold on...he managed to get in. Are you sure it was my brother?"

"Hell, yeah it was him!" she hollered

"I mean...how do you know for sure?"

"Come on now, you wanna play games? You know, and I know it was him. We have fuckin people down there who saw him, and hell, it was in broad fuckin daylight. The police are looking for his ass too and believe me they'll be coming your way asking questions soon. And, you know, we don't need any questions asked."

"Yeah, don't I know it." He sat down in a chair next to the phone and scrolled through the rolodex and said, "I'll make some calls and let you know something by the end of the day. Going to call my mother though..."

"You do that, but remember this. If you don't take care of it, and I mean soon Latif, then Cholo...will have no problems with hunting him down. And you know what that could lead to."

*Yeah,* he thought. "Tell him I'll help with the funeral cost."

"No. We got it. Chino was family. Cholo wouldn't want the brother of the man who murdered his own brother in the street like a dog to have anything to do with his funeral. Would you?"

"Got a point." He stared out the window of his three-story condo overlooking Sugarhill. He knew he needed to get up with his mother quickly, cause without a doubt she damn sure knew where he was. But, these days him and his mother didn't do too well, and he hated going over there. "Like I said, I'll talk to you later."

"Alright, Latif... It's on, you now. Take care of it. And I'll make a few calls and try to calm Cholo down a bit, Ok. Bye."

Latif leaned back in his chair thinking to himself. *Everything was going so smoothly these days for him, but now this. The thing about it was, what the hell did Chino do that was so bad? ca It had to be something real wild for Rasheed to just take him out like that in broad daylight. Right in the street in front of everyone, including his own kid. Damn. Now he needed to find him, and that in itself is going to be a task, especially now.*

Latif knew Brooklyn like the back of his hand, blindfolded, but that wasn't enough. No one in their right mind would say anything about nothing anyway. Folks down in Bushwick didn't deal with the cops. He had to rely strictly on the Hispanics and that was going to be tricky, at best. They didn't half-ass trust him, then on top of it all, Rasheed was his brother.

The first call he'd have to make after he went to his mom was Shaheeda. She was only a few blocks away, she had to know something. He picked up the glass of water he sipped on, then frowned and threw it at the wall, causing it to shatter all over the place. His phone lit up startling him; his partner Ra'Shon Lewis. "You alright, Mister Mohammed?"

"I'm alright. Just dropped something, that's all." He started to hang up, but he thought about something. "By the way, how is the schedule for the month?"

"Well, no court appearances.... Okay, a couple of client consultations but...other than that. It's clear."

"Good."

"You're going somewhere?" Her voice softened as she asked, concerned at best. She was smitten by him. Half of what she did in the office was more because of that than anything else. She was straight, college educated, smart, well-bred and from the other side of the tracks. Then, on top of that she was fine as all outdoors. But there was one thing that spoiled it all. "Are you going somewhere with, Miss Maria?" she asked, jealous. She got cold. Just that damn quick.

Maria, damn, he was tired of her ass already. Maria this, Maria that. Trying to run his life and so far, she seemed to be doing a damn good job at it. She fucked up his love life tremendously, and if it wasn't for the money. Hell, he didn't even want to start. "No Ra'Shon, just need to handle some business in Brooklyn, that's all, so I won't be available. At least, not all the time."

"But...you have your beeper on you, right?"

"Silly... Why would I lose it?

Another call came through and she patched it in. "Your mother. I'll talk to you later, Okay."

"Without a doubt." He took a deep breath and blew out, trying to relax himself before he spoke. For some reason he knew that this was just the beginning of the bullshit. "Yeah...Ma?"

"Latif. You heard?"

"Rasheed, yeah, I heard. It ain't good. Why the hell did he do that anyway? I thought he was chilling these days."

"I did too, but to what I understand it has something to do with the baby."

"Khadija."

"Yeah."

"So...you heard from him."

"No...but Ice did. He jumped in the car and drove down to Brooklyn. I couldn't stop him."

"Okay, I see. So, he's not up this way?"

Waseema cocked her head as she paused and looked at the phone, then said, "Why're you asking all these questions, Latif?" She paused thinking to herself. *He didn't even ask about Ice* "Damn! I should have known. Maria, right! I bet she's trying to find out where Rasheed is so she can tell her Puerto Rican buddies where to go get him, huh. Bitch ain't shit."

"No. Calm down Ok. But you know he killed one of their cousins and to be honest, yeah, they're gonna be looking for him. But, tell me this. Where are Khadija and Mya?

"Latif. I love you baby, but you're not playing ball on this side of the fence anymore. You've...changed. If I knew where any of them were at. I wouldn't tell you anyway. Even if my life depended on it. Bye"

Before he could get in a word, the phone clicked in his ear. He slammed it down. "Shit!" There went the whole ride over to Sugarhill to see his mom's plans. Now, he definitely would have to go to Brooklyn with the quickness, find Rasheed, and hopefully save his ass. But he had to deal directly with the man who would normally be his muscle down there, his Lieutenant, Cholo, and that was gonna be difficult.

THE ROOM WAS QUIET as hell, though there were at least a half dozen or so members of the notorious Vatos Locos gang hierarchy present. Not a word was said as they all smoked on fat cigars and

Turkish cigarettes. Careful not to flick ashes on the Brazilian hand-scraped wood floor, they waited for an answer. Cholo sat at his desk turned away from them in a high back, leather easy chair staring straight out the window at the view overlooking the piers in Williamsburg. Every now and then he'd frown and kinda winch his face like he was having a mini-stroke or something.

It was painful for Cholo, he knew his cousin all his life, was even the one who promised his aunt when he left Mexico that he'd watch over Chino, take care of him. Admittedly, it was tough, Chino had developed street behavior from the barrio that wasn't good at all. Bad, real bad habits. But, Cholo was there to help him along the way, guide him, even scold him if he needed it, like an older brother. He brought him into the Vatos Locos, against his family's wishes, he had no choice, Chino was close to him like his own blood. Cholo was already in charge of the notoriously deadly gang from his home country, controlling interest for the cartel at the peers and warehouses, as well as the drugs in Brooklyn Bushwick, Bed-Stuy, and all of Williamsburg. He was knee deep. The cigar he puffed on was the fattest.

Cholo started out riding shotgun for his cousin up in Harlem, Maria. She gave him charge over the exports coming in from the peers to the warehouses, all the drugs at his disposal, and even people. He did well for himself and her, but still she put someone in place to keep an eye on him, Latif. Hell, Cholo didn't mind much, he knew how she was, she didn't trust too many people anyway. Latif kept to himself, all he did was keep inventory on the goods and reported back to Maria about that, nothing else. The rest, he minded his own business. Cholo liked that, and on top of that he treated him differently, like a person instead of the way the Italians handled him. Greaseball they'd called him, but Latif kinda legitimized him. Taught him how to carry himself, dress, speak their language. He considered him an asset. But now... this.

Cholo didn't know how to handle this, *quote-unquote*, properly. What he did know was that he had to avenge his family's honor without a doubt, that's the way it was. It wouldn't have been major, but it was Latif's brother who did it. He'd wait though, at least hear him out, find out what really happened, if he knew. That would make Cholo look soft to his underlings, and he knew it. He wasn't feeling that. He'd always have to watch his back if he didn't play his cards just right, especially in this game.

Cholo glanced over his shoulder at the phone, spun around to face his people, found who he was searching for, took a deep breath and said, "Guillermo. Did he call yet?"

Guillermo was his right hand that ran the streets watching over things. It was he who told Cholo about what happened. It was he who ran over there to get Chino's body out the street before the police came. It was he who paid people to shut up, didn't need them in a neighborhood asking questions. He knew Mya was hiding out in the building, but he'd get up with that later. He needed backup to fuck with the likes of Kokomo.

So, after a good day of trying to figure this mess out, Guillermo knew it was time for his boss to make a move. Watching him as he slowly stood up, Cholo's short stocky frame of five-foot five, seemed weary from thinking too much. His eyes puffed, with black bushy eyebrows that almost met in the middle. These eyes seemed somewhat sinister; pitch black like midnight. Like little tiny dots in the middle of white milk, they searched; looking for that one weakness in people to exploit. He was dangerous at best. The small streaks of gray hair coming from out the sides of his head were the only significant signs of age on him. Otherwise he always looked the same, mean.

Guillermo wasn't Mexican, but Puerto Rican. He grew up in the Barrio in Williamsburg's South side. He knew how to maneuver stolen cars, drugs, and even people. That's what Cholo liked about him. "Yeah Cholo...said he'd be here in a little while. Want me to get the body bag?" The way he...did things.

Cholo didn't answer, but rather looked at the other members of his organization, his lieutenants, and waved them all out. Right now, he didn't need any of them, at least for now. They were of course loyal, and some of them even sympathized with him about his cousin. Though they didn't care too much for Chino, any of them would extract revenge for Cholo in a heartbeat. But this, this was way complicated. He didn't need them to know more than what they already had in this situation, it was personal, family. "Remember. Keep everything moving, be quiet," he barked, then turned back around to look back out the window again, towards Bushwick and said, "If there's any noise, squash it. Quickly." He frowned up his face, and that seemed to be their sign to leave.

"Guillermo. You don't go. Wait a minute."

Guillermo turned to face him. "Yeah. What's up Cholo? Want the bag, or what?"

"No. Wait until he gets here, I just want you to be here too."

"Okay. No problem, boss."

"No Guillermo." He sat down in his chair and reached for another cigar. "Actually, there is a problem."

"Come on Cholo." Guillermo said, he knew Cholo had some things on his mind he wanted to get off his chest, and he knew he trusted him finally, after all the years, and all the dirt. Guillermo spoke candidly. "You know how Chino was anyway. It was bound to happen."

"That's true. But now especially with the shipment we got coming in. We don't need all this...drama. Now, what do we do?"

"We handle the business."

"Seems simple enough, sure. But that fucken Maria. We need her to keep out of our business. This business. So now, she will be snooping around. So, you see."

"Yeah Cholo. I see. Latif doesn't know anything. And, we have to keep it that way."

"Yeah, it seems like he doesn't know, but I bet you anything... His brother knew something."

"Hmmm. A problem."

"No Guillermo. The problem."

REFLECTING BACK TO her younger days in Mexico, a place called Michoacán. Where her family was exiled to after a bitter and deadly turf war. Maria's father, Consuelo, only had minutes to flee the country. His rivalry sent the dreaded Zetas to kill his family and destroy all traces of them. Vividly remembering how she was rudely awakened in the middle of the night, told to pack some things quickly and get in the back of a box truck that awaited them. Closed tightly shut, the overwhelming darkness that surrounded her was unforgettable as she slid off into a corner holding the only possession she'd brought with her tightly; a picture of her mother. Maria listened to the whimpering sounds of her father as he mourned deeply over leaving his childhood country, as well as the gravesite of the only woman he'd ever loved, his wife.

Maria's mother had died when she was born. The primitive countryside doctors couldn't control the bleeding and she'd eventually passed away holding her tiny premature daughter in her hands. Her father had been broken ever since.

He seized control of a small bunch of rebels from the forest where he hid out and had campmates in the jungles where the cocoa leaf grew wild in abundance. The rebels didn't know what to do with it. Consuelo capitalized on their ignorance. He organized them, brought them guns, and after a few years of raids and pillaging of the much smaller tribes surrounding them, he became their lord; a drug lord.

Maria was sheltered constantly, chauffeured everywhere she went by bodyguards. Her father, still very much and rightfully so, paranoid, even of the very locals he controlled. They would have given Consuelo up to his rivals in a heartbeat if given the chance. So, he never gave them one. The ones employed by him where his cousins, his father's people. He had them by the droves. Family ties where bloodlines and their own debts contributed by underpay, made them indentured for the rest of their lives to him, for generations. Essentially, his slaves, and his new means of making thousands of dollars, easily.

Consuelo quickly garnished together what money he had stashed, and soon came up with the plan. Negotiating deals with the very same rival game, the nacarfantes that ran him off, shipping an important drug to the Americas, without them even knowing it. Tricky, but he still realized he had more control than them individually. He learned how to weld it wisely. Without him, any attempt to move product North of Mexico would be either met with resistance or disaster. All the work they ran through, would either be seized by the Border Patrol agents or the vicious gangs that rode up and down the border towns that just so happened to work for him. Ravaging the towns with guns provided by Consuelo, his familia, he became unstoppable. He used his people to negotiate power in the unsettled, volatile region and soon he became the largest importer of drugs into the United States with just less than a little of what was actually attributed to him. The only identifiable mark that was credited to his name, no logo used identifying the Cartel, was a distinctive capital letter *C* stamped across the crates coming in trucks profusely across the border.

Maria watched her father as he negotiated deal after deal, after deal. Watching his power, she quietly kept her eyes on him and learned. She used the field hand Felix as a scapegoat for her journey, against her father's wishes, across the border. He instead wanted her to go to Europe, learn how to legitimize the family business away from the unscrupulous world of drugs. But Maria wanted the America's. The glitter and the sparkle she heard about on the radio she listened to.

Consuelo was soon put in a precarious position when he heard the news. Maria would have been seduced by rivals if given this information. Paranoia poured through his veins making him move swiftly. He married Maria off to the field hand even though the allegations made about him were half-truths. It was his only out, Felix's too. An order is all it took. "Keep an eye on my daughter, or I'll kill you, he threatened, and your whole family, and anything related to them. It will be as if you never existed, do you understand?" Felix fell right in line and Maria got her wish, New York City.

She was sent to Carlos, Consuelo's exiled partner and was watched over by one of the many gorgeous American women he wined and dined as a young man. A gigolo in his getaway paradise South of Mexico, Cancun. A woman he met, and fell in love with by the name of Juanita.

Now she sat with legs crossed in thought, contemplating exactly how she was going to handle and work Latif. He was inside of her head, but she had too much to lose. She had to stay focused. For all the girls she had coming in from Mexico, $2000 to $6000 a day escorts easy. In addition to the flood of cocaine ravaging Bushwick and Bed-Stuy made her push him harder than a pimp on a rainy day in Boystown.

Maria remembered her poor *cousins* in Morelia, how she promised them the world by telling them she'd help them escape the bitter poverty and oppression from the warring Cartel's in Mexico to come to America. But they had to serve her, and only her. She promised them, but promises were made to be broken.

Everything was right at her fingertips, but now this foolishness with Rasheed. Why now? Felix was out of the picture. Why all of this? Him and his family were definitely well off from all the money she lost. *And, that damn Waseema,* she thought. *Strutting her ass around like she was the goddam Queen of England or something.* She knew they had it too, but that was the price of doing business and making things go away. It was well worth it, a measly couple of grand she could deal with. Hell, ten years had a way of letting things go away anyway. Out of sight, out of the mind. Like Juanita, dead and gone.

Still, for the life of Maria, she couldn't understand why Cholo would have the nerve to steal from her. After all she'd done for him and his family. She always knew something wasn't right. But proof is what she needed. Not word of mouth or assumptions, however accurate they may have been. Getting rid of him was the only answer. Away from all her father's people. *Snakes, all of them!* Latif had to be her way of using this whole Rasheed fiasco to find out about Cholo and his plans. The takeover of the docks downtown in Brooklyn and of course the warehouses over in Bushwick. She knew all about it. Yeah, he was the bait she'd use to work her way in. Maria would have to use it to get at Cholo from the inside because he had too much protection to make it personal. Especially without getting her own hands dirty. She knew he was planning something and she had to stop him. After all, he knew too much about the business, and her ...

Maria smiled and put out the cigarette in a golden ashtray on her desk. A present from the dealers that imported good weight from deep inside Puerto Vallarta. A present from a deal she made with the Cuchillos. Deals to not only ship into the United States, but all of the Americas including drug addicted ass Canada, she smirked.

She popped her feet down from off the chair and sat wide legged now. The thought of taking the business to the next level excited her. Expanding it into territories like her father dreamed and making her one of the richest women in the world excited the hell out of her. Maria leaned back her head, letting her long black silky hair fall, licked her lips, put her finger to her pouty mouth and slowly moistened those now extra glossy lips. After gapping open her legs the only thing that flooded her mind was not a man, but all the money she'd soon be making. Enough to fill a fucking medium sized swimming pool.

"YOU DID WHAT?"

"I mean...it, just sort of happened...like a reflex." Rasheed's raspy voice uttered as he sat with his hands clasped together rubbing them, and thinking back to the incident that just unfolded only hours ago. The woman that stood over him with her arms folded and face twisted up in a knot tried to decipher what was going on in his mind when he shot Chino. "Look at me, damn it!" she said as she kneeled down in front of him grabbing his hands. Her face had the look of deep concern as she stared at the floor then shook her head and asked him, "Do you understand exactly what you just did? Where is she now?"

"Yeah...I mean..." He shifted his body. She looked deeply into Rasheed's puffed up eyes that held back the flood of tears he'd rather be letting go of but he needed to put up a strong front. He'd just realized the magnitude of what he had done and she realized the same. "Okay... I'm a calm down," she said, then got up off her knees and walked over to a desk. An old, small schoolhouse type of thing that she had gotten from outside of PS-5 over on Hazel Street behind the dumpster. She figured she'd get a computer one of these days and set it off in a corner like a little office or something. Instead her purse ended up occupying the space. She reached in and pulled out a cigarette, let it up, then calmly walked over to the window and stared out across Bushwick. Watching the J train snake its way down Broadway as it moved closer towards Manhattan.

Rasheed peeped up at her and shook his head. He knew he'd messed up, in more ways than one. He wanted to get up from his seat, but he was stuck. All he could do was stare at the petite bow-legged figure across from him smoking a cigarette. He started to say something, but there was nothing to say. *Just keep your mouth shut. But it wouldn't hurt her to respond*, he thought. He knew she had his back and right now her mind was going over different scenarios trying to figure this crazy shit out. Or at least keep him and his daughter from getting marked, besides other things. So, he thought, *just be quiet*. At last she turned and said, "Okay, you blue Chino away because he was, as you say, fondling your daughter. Right?"

"Yeah."

"Well, I can see that. Freaking pervert. Hell, you should have shot Mya for even letting him get close to her like that." She flicked the cigarette out the window. "She did run back inside the building, right?"

"Believe so."

"Hell, I hope so. Kokomo got her then."

"I was hoping that."

"Rasheed. Right now, hope ain't on our side. We need to somehow get a meet up with Cholo. I can guarantee one thing though, he's got a hit out for you. That's his m-o." She walked over to him and lifted his head up. "Be strong baby, we'll get through this."

Rasheed stood up, grabbed her gently by the arm, pulled her close to him and hugged her. She was small, tiny, at 5-foot 5 and barely weighed a buck and a quarter. Her light bright skin was flawless. She was striking. Drop dead gorgeous. But her eyes are what did it. They were slightly chinked, like she was Chinese or something. Secretive, like she could stop you dead in your tracks with one glance. Hence her name, Asia.

Back in the day with his father, Khalid, Asia attended the Ansaaru Islamic community up on Bushwick Avenue, Rasheed was her first boyfriend. It was a secret of course and it had to stay that way. If the community found out they'd disapprove in a heartbeat, as well as the Imam at the time. He was supposed to be the only man that had rights to any woman in this community, those were the rules, his rules.

Asia was young, pretty, A target. Her mother didn't go for the okie doke though. After watching the Imam on many occasions, she knew he was planning to make a move so she packed their shit up and left. Her brainwashed husband caught her, paraded her back to the community where she was ostracized and beaten brutally.

She was estranged from her daughter for some time, a few years. When she did see Asia, or was allowed to see her, she was no longer her baby, but a woman. A woman every bit of 14 years old. Raped by the same supposed leader of their supposedly safe community. Their God. Things were never the same after that, especially Asia. A mother who couldn't look into her daughter's eyes after feeling like she'd failed her. But something about Asia wasn't right. Something just wasn't right about her daughter, her baby. One night, it showed itself.

By the time the cops had arrived Asia was sitting up in a corner, clothes bloody, rocking back and forth in the chair with a bloodied butcher knife in one hand. Her face was trembling and she was mumbling something inaudible to herself, like, "...I...I...Told...I don't..." Over, and over again. The police finally got her to let go of the knife or rather they pried it from her hands, and rushed her to the hospital. She vomited all over the place. They couldn't figure it out. After all she didn't have a scratch on her, nothing. She'd ball up, grab at her stomach, bending over the bed throwing up profusely. Then fall back like a rag doll, like she'd been possessed. She'd been at it for a while, a week. Her condition was about to go critical, at best. She suffered mass quantities of water dehydration and she couldn't hold on much longer. Her small body sucked down the fluids keeping her alive. The doctors mulled it over. Considering the vicious rape, she'd endured, they figured it was probably more mental than anything. Then there was a call from the nurse's station. Immediately they rushed in and had to restrain Asia. Then they actually started to induce more vomiting until her stomach finally released the vile poisonous obstruction that tried setting up shop in her guts, the problem. They finally let go of her, like a demon dead set on taking control. The doctor picked up the now full, stenched bedpan, and waded through the soup green, thick muck, until finally it showed up. A chewed up bloody penis. She looked up at them, her eyes dazed, sweat pouring down her face. They were ready for her to head to turn around 360 degrees. It freaked them out so bad. They wanted to leave, run, which at that point they were damn sure ready to do. Relieved, she grinned and said matter of factly, "Told that muthafucka...I didn't do oral."

Asia was never brought up on any charges. None, no murder, anything. What could you do? Even though her crazy ass did do a stint on Roosevelt Island at the State Mental Institution for a short period of time, after a quick minute, she was left alone. Eventually, her mother left the community for good. But her father stayed around. Trying to use the same insane, psycho religious rhetoric to justify the abuse that was prevalent there. Using the perverted twisted teachings that enabled him to rise up as a man of status inside the following sect. Making himself a leader. All of it he wanted to now claim, be his own demigod. Someone else didn't see it that way, nor shared his view. His body was later found in the sanctuary inside the mosque, his heart burst from a crack cocaine induced overdose. So they say. "Very mysterious situation" were the words they used. Her mother hauled ass to another state. A Pennsylvania city called Erie. She got herself together after some extensive therapy. She now resides there comfortably, away from any spiritual, sex, religious or otherwise communities. *Not even a goddamn YMCA*, she mused.

# CHAPTER FOUR

A sia became a notorious facilitator of a vicious gang known to rob and extort customers of the sex trade, among other things stemming from crack abuse in Brooklyn. It was well known that they were dangerous. Credited with at least 20 kills that were known, they played no games. Dope dealers paid to just leave them alone, and the prostitutes and pimps paid for protection. But now, laid back and older, she just watched how the neighborhood had changed for the worse; dramatically and she didn't like it. Granted, it probably wasn't that much better when she was coming up, but one thing is for sure, the Ansaah's damn sure didn't play that killing shit in the street. Unless they were, or any other man was protecting his own.

The Colombians and Mexicans rivaled and killed each other damn near for sport, and when they were tired of each other, the street was next. For control over a now upwardly striving Bushwick-Williamsburg, and Bed-Stuy neighborhood. But Asia still had pieces of her old crew, at least the ones that weren't dead or locked up. Kokomo was one of them, and he was always ready if she was ready to make some sort of move. She looked over at Rasheed and smiled, she knew of his reputation from back in the day. Asia had thought maybe the whole shooting incident was a result of that, but most of those old ass Bean-yos were dead or either long gone. She never crossed their path though. She fell back when they robbed Felix and Carlos. It was her score and she was the one who put Derek on to them all along. She was the so-called source, and Derek never told the fellas about her. Asia was cool with that.

"Asia..." he said softly as she fell into his arms. "I... I..."

She pushed away softly and stepped back. "Rasheed..." Asia turned to see Khadija standing in the doorway, awakened from her sleep. She picked up her hand and pointed her finger at them and said, "*Bang! Bang!*"

Asia cringed in horror as Rasheed rushed over to her and started scolding her. "Don't ever do that!"

Little Khadija was confused now. She started whimpering as the tears gushed down from her eyes like twinkling, sparkling waterfalls, "I just want to be like you, daddy." Rasheed's mouth gaped open as Asia rushed over and got in between him and consoled her. "Oh, you do little lady. Well, let's start with a little bit of cornflakes. Okay." She peeped over at Rasheed and smiled reassuringly, then picked her up and went into the kitchen.

Asia knew what it was from her own experiences, so she played her role like her mother. She also knew that later on in her adult life, that moment would come back to hunt Rasheed, she'd seen it before. All he could do was hold his head down in gloom at the thought of it. Asia put another bowl on the table and called him over. "She won't eat it without...her father." His face lit up like a candle as he rushed over. She whispered in his ear. "We'll talk later, Okay." She rubbed his face and said, "Everything's gonna be alright baby...I promise."

It was a promise she knew she'd have to keep. After all she was the one that Cholo was looking for all the time. The one who was hitting his spots, the one who made plans on getting the box truck that imported the exported tons of Maria's dope at the Navy Yard, and ripping it off. It was payback time. She had a smile as she sipped on hot coffee watching Rasheed interact with his daughter. Asia couldn't be mad at him, after all he did her a favor. Chino was on her hit list anyway. Cholo was next.

SHAHEEDA HAD MADE IT off the Interboro driving down Bushwick Avenue from Hylan Park towards the store erratically. Taking all the usual short-cuts. S&A was her normal hangout anyway. But her reason for going there today was specifically to confront Donna about some money. She didn't have all the facts, but she knew her mother played no games when it came down to money. And if Waseema said some money with short, then it was.

Shaheeda also wanted to show her mother that she knew how to run things, instead of Waseema being over her shoulder all the time. She could handle things on her own. Shaheeda figured she'd let Donna know, and they'd both confront the managers together. Rosario, or Rosie he was called for short, and Carlito, Cholo's boy. She never did trust them and was trying to figure out why she let Donna talk her into letting them work there anyway. Donna damn near put herself on the line for them. She didn't know for sure, but if they fucked up some money, or were caught stealing, then they'd have to go. Waseema probably would make Donna cover the loss knowing her. Even though she didn't need to. "But after all, they were her mistake," she'd say.

Shaheeda pulled up in front of a slim, squirrely looking Spanish boy outside who ran to open the door for her. *"I got it Miss Shaheeda."* Probably the after-school help, they were paid to valet the VIP customers. It was a decent school kid hustle. She smiled at him politely and peeped inside. Things were busy. More of a mature crowd today, she thought, instead of the regular school kids. The high school and college age traffic that came through and spent money really didn't have on the newest styles, clothes and other accessories. It seemed that it became synonymous with the store.

They'd get calls all the time exclusively from designers at first rate manufacturers. They had clothing no one else had or would even carry for that matter. No one wanted a store full of blacks and Latinos all over the place. Walking through their place loose, well maybe Macy's, but still, that was the allure of the store. Danger. That part of Broadway hadn't been that hot since Moon's tailor shop back in the day. At any given time, Nike would be on the phone pitching a fresh new pair of Air Force ones, and the next day the UPS truck would deliver. Exclusively to the hood, and throughout the hood. One could only imagine the type of loot that came through. No price was too high cause even if the school kids couldn't afford it, the dope boys could. Rappers and everything else that came along with them, money.

Waseema told them about the idea about safeguarding the money months ago, but they didn't listen. Too much of it was coming in. Things got pretty rough at one point, someone actually tried them. Guns were pulled. A shotgun blast was fired in the air, customers hitting the floor, and all that. Hell, they gave well over a couple of 'G' from the registers and out their own pockets behind that bullshit. But once it was published in the newspapers, the publicity it brought was priceless. It was on every newspaper's front page in New York City.

They soon after reinforced the doors with bulletproof glass. Adding plexiglass windows with blowout netting embedded inside. In addition to a layer of thick concrete and rebar inside the walls. Smart move they thought, but never figured on being robbed one night from up top the goddam roof. That was enough. S&A's needed muscle and some pull in the hood to keep the thieves up off of them. That's when they bought in Cholo.

Latif introduced him. He gave them the whole song and dance about Cholo being in the know in the neighborhood, like a greaseball Don or something. They bought into it, *needed protection*. And hell, they could afford it, so why not pay him a little something-something? The cost was probably anywhere between eight to ten stacks a month on the side to get right. After that S&A's became a safe spot. Hadn't been fucked with since.

As the door opened in front of Shaheeda, by way of an electronic device they had installed, she thought, *Maybe Cholo, or maybe the money that went to Cholo, wasn't added in or figured right.* Maybe she'd bring that up. She put on her best face as she spotted Donna coming from out the back, and said, "Hey girl!"

"Hey Sha!"

Donna was thinner these days. She spent a lot of time at the gym over in Flatbush where she stayed, and it looked good on her. Her svelte five foot six made the buck-105 package she carried look good as all outdoors. She sported a two-piece brown-beige ensemble. A sleeveless blouse, revealing toned arms and luscious coco brown skin like honey. Her hair was cut in a loose Valley girl bob, but styled fashionably in an uptown loose curl. Yeah, she wore her money, and it looked like a million bucks, easy. "Didn't expect to see you here today. Why didn't you call? I would have arranged a lunch...or something."

"Well we can still do...something, Was uh-," Shaheeda glanced over and spotted one of the managers she didn't like, Carlito, and sort of gave him that half assed fuck you smile then looked off like he didn't exist. His was the same, except, she was the boss, so he had to put on a fake smile. Grin and bear it. She knew it, and approved of his fakeness. He couldn't stand Shaheeda. Hated her guts. "Hello, Carlito. How's things?" she asked in the coldest, driest voice she could muster short of her going hoarse.

"Fine, Ms. Shaheeda...Ma'am"

"Good." She had waited for that, and it killed him to say it.

She met Donna and hugged her with open arms. Then they did the fake kiss on both cheeks thing that was big at the clubs where they rubbed elbows with celebrities and athletes' wives spending plenty of money. Donna escorted her towards the back as something different caught her eye. "What are those?" She asked, looking at the wall sized sneaker rack.

"Don't really know. Something Nike wants us to introduce. That guy Jordan, the basketball player. He wants us to showcase them for a minute, then give him some feedback.

"Yeah, Michael... I remember him. Fine."

"Alright now, back off. I already invited him to dinner when he comes back into town."

"Know that's right."

"I think they're called...Air, or something. "

In the back of the shop, things were set up like a regular office building. The managers offices, production offices, a conference room next to Donna's office, and a much cleaner seldom used office. That belonged to Waseema and she shared it with Shaheeda. She was hardly ever there though. When she was there, she stayed in Donna's office most of the time.

Along the backside of Donna's office was a door that remained locked. It was the stairway leading to the basement downstairs. There were two. One had stock, shoes, clothes, etc. The other one, the biggest safe next to a Federal Reserve. Donna had part one of the combination, Shaheeda the next, and lastly Waseema. Hers was the tricky one. Designed to be the last. No one knew or had a clue as to what line of code she used, verbal or numerical. She had it set up like that. No one could move any money without her knowing, coming or going. That was the one day she came to Bushwick, her and a Brinks truck. Yeah, a Brinks truck. In Bushwick. You better believe many people wanted to hit their spot knowing that the money was there. Cholo's people kept them away, along with the help of the New York City Police Department.

Shaheeda sat down in her favorite loveseat, a plush white padded glove leather thing Donna flew in from Italy. "I went by my mother's this morning."

"Really. I thought you an old boy toy had other plans."

"Come on girl. That was a done deal in the ride over. I sent him home. Didn't want no extra drama from my mom's."

"I feel you. How's she doing anyway?" Donna asked, sensing Shaheeda and her mom had gotten into it already. Her body language told on her. Nothing new. In fact, when Waseema came to the store everyone was a target, including her. She had to show her the stock, the inventory, the books, everything. And she knew, even though it wasn't verbalized, Waseema didn't trust her. But hell, she didn't trust anyone. "Hey! Did ice come home?"

"And I'm so freaking glad."

"Now she can calm down. Get some."

"Know that's right."

They both giggled, then straightened up when they heard a knock at the door. It was Carlito. "Miss Donna. Uh, Cholo's trying to get in touch."

"Ok, tell him I'll get with him in a minute. "

"Okay."

The door closed and she focused back on Shaheeda, "So, what's up girl?"

"I need to check the books." Shaheeda said, "My mom's got a receipt or something that didn't jive with her numbers. Just wanted to check it out."

"Damn, she doesn't trust me! She could have called. I know she ain't sending you to do her dirty work!"

"Calm down." Shaheeda looked at her oddly. "I'm sure everything is good. Hell, I just want to prove her wrong that's all."

Donna got up abruptly and reached in her desk drawer, then threw a set of keys her way. "Yeah, sure. Here's the keys. You know where they are." She walked by her pouting. "Don't see why she doesn't trust me."

Shaheeda was dumbfounded as she slammed the door behind her, but now also more curious than anything. She wondered, *Why did she act like that? I knew her for years almost forever and she always held her head, especially when it came to my mom's.*

Shaheeda picked up the keys and opened the locked drawer, took out the books, and started opening them. *Hmmm, wonder if things are straight?*

"Bout tired of this shit!" Donna fumed as she hastened towards her office. Carlito was already there waiting with the phone in his hand. "Would you believe this shit? The nerve of her!" she said as she snatched it away and huffed into the phone. It was silent for a second, then she sucked her teeth and said, "Hello! Ms. Waseema?"

"Cholo..."

She stepped on the brakes as his heavy rest voice lingered in her ears. Carlito smirked as he watched her whole demeanor change. Embarrassed, she caught him staring and turned away abruptly, trying to keep what was left of her already compromised composure. "Yeah. What's up, Cholo?"

"Donna."

"What's going on, everything alright? I mean, we took care of our business on time, right?"

Everything is okay. With that."

"Well, what's going on?" She hesitated, waiting on him to answer. She knew it couldn't have been anything else going on, but money. They had no other type of interaction with each other except for the store. It was clockwork. He came by every month to check things out. When he left his people had the envelope in hand. He himself never touched any money, never made it look like a payoff of any kind. Just business. Just one security consultant checking out the premises for any breaches of any kind and giving his input on correction or any lack of, therein. Of course, it was bullshit, but the bullshit kept things safe. Now she wondered why in the hell was he calling this late in the afternoon, this early in the week. "Hello?" She thought he'd hung up.

"I have this problem." You could hear him choosing his words carefully. Even though she was already in his pocket he didn't want to alarm her with what he had to say. Besides he didn't know what she knew. She might nut up. "You heard about...Chino?"

"No. What about him? Well, I saw him drunk, uh excuse me. I saw him the other night at a club over on Broadway."

"He's been killed."

"Killed. What! How!"

"Gunned down. Over near you."

She glanced over at Carlito, who evidently knew what they were talking about all up in her mouth, shook his head yes. "Okay, but uh...what does that have to do with us?... Me?"

Now she was getting smart. Yeah why was he calling her. "The person who killed him was a guy you may know named Rasheed."

"Rasheed? You're kidding me. It had to be about something then," she said,

"That black bastard murdered my cousin in the street like a dog!"

Donna pushed the wrong button and sure as hell didn't want to push anymore. One thing she knew for sure, that wasn't Rasheed's pedigree. She knew if he killed someone it wasn't over money. It sure as hell had something to do with family. And, as she glanced over her shoulder at the door, for what she saw of Shaheeda when she came in, everything was cool. Or maybe she was like her, clueless. "I understand, but like I said, What do you want me to do?"

"If you see him, call me. That's what you do." She couldn't believe he'd ask some shit like that. Hell, his mom owned the store. If he did come by, and as much as she didn't like Waseema, if she had to choose a side, it would be with Waseema.

"What do you mean?"

"You know what I mean!" His voice was starting to become incensed on the other end. His patience with her was running thin. She pulled the phone away from her ear, and Carlito walked towards her and pushed it back. "All the extra little...deals you made. The money you skimmed from-"

"Okay. Okay. If I see him, I'll call." She glared over at Carlito and said, "Or I'll let...someone know." Now she had no choice but to choose his side.

"Do that. And.. We'll keep an eye on you." With that Carlito pulled back his jacket revealing the handle of a 40-caliber tucked into his waistband and smiled. "I'm sure you'll do the right thing," he said, then hung up the phone.

Donna hung up her end of the phone, slowly putting it down and backing away. Carlito smiled and opened the door slightly glancing his thin warm eyes at her and said, "Oh yeah. We're low on those *FUBU* loose fitting shirts. You know they seem to be selling good these days. You wouldn't mind fetching a....damn my bad, getting some for me out of the stockroom. Would you mind? Damn, my bad again...Miss. Donna?" His mouth twisted into a smile and he grinned as she backed out the door with her head down. She could hear him laughing as she beelined her way back to her office. Shaheeda was still looking down at the books. "Girl. Yeah, there's just a few entries here that's off, that's all. Couple of dollars. No big-" She glanced up at her and gasped. Donna had tears running down her cheeks. She got up and raced over. "What's wrong Donna? What's wrong?"

Donna slid down to a heap on the floor as she held her close and said, "Rasheed."

"What about him?" Shaheeda asked as she stared at her, eyes wide open hanging on to every word, hoping that those words would produce better fruit instead of the bitter sweets she'd been getting all morning.

Donna looked up, still in her own little world herself. Her mind back and forth between her own dirt being uncovered, and her loyalty towards her people. People that set her up. People that gave a damn about her. She grabbed her hand and said, "We got to warn him." Scrambling to her feet she blurted out, "before it's too late." Donna hurried to her desk and started flipping through her Rolodex. "Come on now. What's the number? R...Rasheed..."

Shaheeda had seen and heard enough of the drama. Suspense was never her strong point. Marching around the desk she grabbed her by the shoulders and slapped her. "Donna. You better tell me right now. What the hell is going on with my brother!"

Still out of it, she looked up at her and said, "Oh my God, Sha. You really don't know." Donna snapped out of it, and it dawned on her. "Chino." Trembling, she took her by the hand and they moved toward the sofa to sit. She stared up towards the ceiling before she blurted out in no particular way, "Sometime this morning. Rasheed killed Chino."

"Killed Chino. Where?"

"Over here...near Bushwick Avenue...somewhere."

"Over...I thought he was supposed to pick up Ice...from prison."

"That's what Cholo just told me Sha. He also said..." Taking a deep breath she paused before she continued, knowing that what she was going to say next would set her off. "That he was looking for him...to kill him."

"Kill? What!" Shaheeda snatched up her purse and started towards the door. "Oh, hell no! If my brother killed him it had to be for a damn good reason!"

Donna ran behind her and grabbed her by the arm. Shaheeda tried shrugging her off, she put her finger on her lips and said, "Shhh. Come on now. Be cool. Trust Me."

"What the hell is going on Donna?"

"That crumb ass Carlito is his earpiece. So, we need to keep it cool."

"Okay. Okay, I hear you. Now, what exactly did Cholo say?"

Donna walked over by the phone on her desk. "Something about Rasheed killing Chino like I said, and that he wanted revenge."

"Hmm. The number you need to find is Mya's. If he was over in this neighborhood, he was most likely at Mya's." Knowing what she was hunting for, Donna searched through her clutch bag and pulled out a small black book. "Here it is. 4-4-3-5-0-6-8... Got it."

"Yeah." She dialed the numbers and put the phone up to her ear. "Good. It's ringing." She smiled. "Someone picked up. Hello?"

"Who is this? Where is Mya?" The voice was strange to her. Even though she and Mya weren't close, she still, by word-of-mouth from Shaheeda, Waseema, Latif and even Rasheed himself, had a good idea of her comings and goings. Plus, anybody that would have been in her rather small circle.

"She's not here. Who's calling."

Donna covered her mouth piece and whispered to Shaheeda. "Someone picked up and it sure as hell ain't Mya...or Rasheed."

"Then hang up...now!"

Donna hung up the phone and looked up, then they said at the same time. "Man. Something ain't right." Then the phone rang again. Donna jumped at first, then cautiously picked it up after some coaching by Shaheeda. Obviously, they had just read out the number that came up on the callback, but Donna figured she didn't want whoever it was to think her or Shaheeda knew anything so she switched it up this time. "Hello. S&A. How may I direct your call?" It was dead silent on the other end, then they hung up. Donna shook her head slowly. "Well, we know one thing..."

"What is it?" Shaheeda asked.

"It's not the police. They just hung up. The damn cops would have been asking all kinds of questions."

"Shaheeda heard a sound in the hall and rushed over to the door and put her ear up to it. "Someone is in the hall..."

"Probably that damn Carlito. Stalking us."

"Knew he wasn't shit. We gotta get outta here."

"Damn right, but how?"

"Somehow we need to get through him...then haul his ass... call Latif or something."

"But how, Sha. He was strapped."

Shaheeda pulled out a small pearl handle .25 from her bag and said, "Me too." They huddled together as Shaheedah grasped the doorknob. "Just call Carlito inside, and then we handle the business."

The door pushed and instinctively they both pushed back against it.

Shaheeda braced herself as Donna stood off to the side with her fist balled up in preparation for a serious throw down. Feeling confident in her newly developed skills learned from her workouts. The person on the other side pushed at the door harder and they let it swing open so they would catch whoever it was off balance. It swung open. Shaheeda stepped to the side and aimed her gun. Donna was up on him with a straight unforgiven right jab. "MOTHERFUCKER!" She punched the shit out of him. He fell to the floor holding his face, yelling "Ow! What the fuck!"

They backed up as the person got up holding his nose. "What the hell?" He was standing back against the doorway holding one hand over his nose and the other in front of him. "Hold up!" He looked at the two crazy women in front of him, one holding a gun and said, "For some reason I think I know what the hell is going on, and if you don't. Then I advise you...layoff the fucken coffee!"

"Latif," Shaheeda said as she put her arm around him. "I'm sorry."

Donna rushed over with a towel and put it up to his nose. "Here. Hold your head up. In case it starts bleeding."

"Damn! What the hell was y'all gonna do?"

"You don't wanna know. Donna just spoke to Cholo."

"Oh yeah. I was just over here to warn y'all. Rasheed, right?"

"Hell yeah. What happened, Latif?"

"Let's sit down. I'll explain. It's complicated at best, but one thing's for sure."

"What's that?" Shaheeda asked.

"He sure as hell fucked up."

HE SAT BY THE PHONE contemplating on the move. How to set up a safe meet with Cholo. Where could she get the advantage? She thought maybe somewhere crowded so no guns could be openly used. A mall maybe, then disappear out of sight, unseen. Naw, didn't want that. She must set up somewhere with her back up against the wall. Well possibly if she picked a restaurant, but then she'd be trapped off if something went down. She'd have to fight her way out. Much too risky. She couldn't quite grasp her head around things as cool as she'd like to because at risk was someone she cared about dearly, and that was Rasheed.

His presence around her made it all too difficult for her to concentrate. She was thrown by him all the way to the left. But the thing was, so were a lot of other women. Mya was the only woman that he publicly paraded around Brooklyn now that had changed. And not for the better either. Rasheed stayed around her for the sake of the child, but after this situation here, it would be just a matter of time before that changed too.

She looked over as he played with his daughter wishing that she was the one who had his child. They wouldn't be in this predicament now. Thinking about Mya only made Asia angry and jealous. She sucked her teeth, got up, walked over to them, smiled, then stepped over to her purse to get a cigarette. Her mind now preoccupied that quick with hating the fact that she smoked and thinking of a way to quit. Suddenly, there was a knock at the door. Rasheed stood up and pushed Khadija gently behind him. "Were you expecting anyone?" he asked.

"No..." Asia said as she made her way to the closet for her gun. Rasheed eased slowly towards the back room, put Khadija inside, pulled the door shut and put his finger to his lips, shushing her. Then, he and Asia slowly moved off to the side of the door and she called out. "Who is it?"

No sound came from the other side, except for some rumbling around in several movements. Asia nodded her head and raised her gun. Rasheed reached for the door. "I'm just stepping out the shower." Asia hollered out, then he swung the door open and she leveled the gun right smack into Mya's face. Damn near pissed on herself, her eyes crossed as she looked up the barrel of the 9-millimeter. Pointing dead at her mouth. "No...." She uttered.

Kokomo stepped out from the side of the door off to the side of Mya and slid to Asia's right, cutting her off, then he grabbed her gun with both hands and lowered it slowly. "Be cool Asia. Didn't know what was up. Had to be cautious."

"Damn Koko! She could've blown her brains out!"

"I know. I moved to the side. She was the one who stayed," he said as he brushed past her.

Asia smiled and lowered her gun. "That was stupid," she said under her breath as she glanced Mya's way then looked both ways down the hallway saying to her, "Get your ass in here!"

Kokomo smiled as he gently peeped inside then looked over and saw Rasheed. "Figure you wouldn't be far." He grabbed his hand and hugged him. "What's up, homeboy!"

"What's up man. Thanks," he said as he looked over at Mya.

"That's nothing. That's what we do."

"Yeah. I would have done it for you."

"I know."

Rasheed walked over to Mya and asked. "You Okay?"

She was still nervous, dazed, and now even more confused as she looked around the house then spotted her daughter's shoes then went ape shit. "Oh my God. Where's Khadija? Where is my baby?" She turned back around and ran towards Rasheed and started punching him in the chest. "Where is my baby? What did you do to her?"

"What the hell are you talking about?"

"Did you kill her too? Did you?"

Rasheed pushed her off of him. "You think I would hurt my own daughter?" He looked at her awkwardly in disbelief that she would even have twisted her lips to say something like that. But she always had the tendency to say and do stupid shit. He knew her pedigree, so he just stepped towards the bedroom door and opened it. "Khadija." She came running out towards her mother who swooped her up and said, "You alright, baby?"

That was way too much drama for Asia. As far as she was concerned, Mya had crossed the line. "Of course, she's alright. Hell, she's better here than with that damn bean-yo you had her around!"

Mya shot her a glance and put Khadija behind her back. "Who the hell are you?" Then at Rasheed. "One of your whores?"

Asia was like lightning as she stepped towards her and smacked the shit out of her. "Don't you ever..." And was just about to raise up again when Khadija jumped in front of her and yelled out, "No! Please..." Asia looked down at the little girl who had her hand up, eyes focused on her with her fist balled up by her side, ready to protect her mother. Asia looked over at Rasheed, then back at Khadija and moved away slowly saying. "Oh my God. I am so sorry." She reminded Asia of herself when she was that age and it struck a nerve.

Mya reached down and hugged her then looked up at Asia. She saw it in her, and said, "No, I'm sorry. We've been through a lot today. Let's just try to relax. Figure this thing out. For one..."

She peeped over to Rasheed and asked, "Why? Why'd you jump so fast...you didn't ask anything. Kill him?"

Rasheed stared off at the ground. If there were any rocks, he'd damn sure been kicking them. Then Mya glanced back over at Asia and said in no sort of way, "Don't ever...slap me...again...please."

Asia shot her a look that Kokomo had picked up on. He then stepped in between them and said, "Trust me...y'all two are more alike than you think. Let it go." He turned and faced Rasheed, "Yeah Rasheed...what's up?" He changed their direction quickly because he knew from experience that Asia didn't take too kindly to threats. He only knew Mya from what he'd seen of her, and how she reacted today damn sure wasn't the norm. All she did coming over was talk about Rasheed and knew how Asia felt about him too. That brought him to the conclusion that this wasn't over with between the two of them. But right now, this wasn't the time, or place. When that time and place did come; all hell was gonna break loose. And by the way Asia stared at Mya, fuming, Kokomo knew that time and place would be one day soon.

# CHAPTER FIVE

"Look...the muthafucka' pushed my kid. In my book, that's wrong, and in his case...dead wrong."

Kokomo sighed as he listened to Rasheed's bravado, thinking to himself that this cat hadn't changed much, still on that old school bullshit from back in the day. Then he turned toward Khadija and asked him, "Okay...did they see you bring her over here or what?"

"No....went through the back way. Dipped on some side streets behind Broadway...the cut, it came straight here. Only place I knew to come that would be safe." Rasheed turned towards Asia and said, "I see you keep a car in the cut just in case for this type of shit, huh."

Kokomo said, "Look. This ain't back in the day. They are looking for you, us! Police got lookouts. Snitches everywhere. You could have been followed."

Rasheed shook his head and started stroking Khadija's hair. "True. But," he glanced up at Kokomo, then Asia and said, "I know I messed up." Asia nodded her head in agreement. "But, trust me, I ain't new to this."

"Alright." Kokomo walked over to the window looking out over the street. "Cholo will probably want to talk to you."

"About what?"

"Hell Rasheed, that was his family. Probably thought you killed that dude because of some sort of plot aimed at him, or something."

"Plot? What plot?"

Kokomo turned and faced him. "Man. Cholo is dirty...And hell. Why your mother chose him to do some sort of security over at the store is beyond me anyway."

75

"Always said that, but mom. She's too headstrong."

"Well, maybe it's not about your moms. Shaheeda...Donna?"

"Couldn't have been Donna and Shaheeda ain't that heady. He shot back."

Asia grinned. "Got that right. Hell, I heard she was fucking around with the help."

Embarrassed, Rasheed looked down toward the floor. It was all in the streets, common knowledge about Shaheeda's behavior, gossip. "Yeah...I heard that too."

Kokomo walked over to where they stood, rubbed his chin then pondered. Finally, he looked over at Asia and said, "We need to tell him."

"Damn..." Asia sighed, "It's gonna put too many people in our business as it is. And in danger."

"Hello! We are in danger now." Asia turned towards Mya and said, "On one condition." And pointed at her, "You tell anyone. You're through." Mya eased close to Rasheed. "And believe me. He won't be able to help you."

"What's going on Asia? Tell me." Rasheed pointed Mya toward a chair. "She won't say anything." She got up and grabbed Khadija by the hand and said, but not before frowning at Rasheed. "No, that's cool. We are going in the back. Maybe, it's good I don't know. Just like before."

Asia nodded, "Good." She came closer to them, sat, turned towards her purse, grabbed a cigarette then sucked her teeth and put it back in there. "Fuck it...now look. This can't go nowhere, Rasheed. Matter of fact." She glanced over at Kokomo. "We really wouldn't mind your feedback anyway. Maybe even get down."

"If you are about to talk on shit I used to do. I'm out of the game now. Going straight."

"Well. We'll see when I finish telling you what's up."

MARIA TOOK THE CALL in her office, a four-room, five-bedroom, three bath, 4500 square foot, 50-story high-rise penthouse enclosure. Dark oak floors, acoustic features, floor to ceiling windows, and an eye-popping view overlooking Williamsburg in Bedford Stuyvesant. She just came in from a meeting and was slapped dead tired. Feet kicked up on the desk and high heels tossed on the floor. Every bit of half sleep when her assistant patched the call through.

After years of struggle, paying off people, securing old lots and abandoned property that crack heads had vacated, putting the right people in the right places, she'd come up. She solidified deals for ownership of many warehouses off of Bushwick Avenue, as far as Grand and Metropolitan Avenue, way up to the old Williamsburg projects. It was all good. They'd soon make a way for the many upscale properties, and of course more office buildings, just what Bushwick and Bedford Stuyvesant needed, more office space.

Space. Smiling at the thought of it. Who would have thought that Juanita was in on it all along, right in Harlem? Finally, she herself was the legitimate business professional. No more rubbing elbows in dark alleys with grease balls, pushing girls off on the politicians for a favor, corporate was her new thing now.

She picked up the phone. "Yeah. Did you take care of it?"

"Not yet, but I know where he is though."

"What's the problem? Do it."

"You sure you want me to kill..."

"No! Don't tell me no details, fool! Just get the job done!"

"Got it. Call you when it's done."

"No. Not me idiot. My assistant." She hung up the phone in his ear. It was all set-in motion. Kill Rasheed, tip the police Cholo's way.

Then, clean up the mess and solve her problem with the rampant stealing over on the docks on Flushing Avenue.

Yeah, for real, corporate was her new thing now, no more getting her own hands dirty, after all that's all it really was.

SHAHEEDA TRIPPED, "YOU'RE sure Latif?" She couldn't believe what she just heard.

"Positive."

"We need to find out where he is then."

"Yeah. Least let him know what's happening. But. Y'all might have to close up the shop for a minute. It's going to get really ugly around here."

Donna sighed as she sat down behind her desk. "Right, but we got to let your moms know what's up to. "

"Oh man." Shaheeda said, "She's gonna want to raise all hell. Ask too many questions."

"You know she is."

"But." Shaheeda sat on the side of the desk thinking out loud. "Maybe, if we can get to Ice first. Then."

"I see what you're saying sis. Ice would definitely know where he's at."

"I think I might know where he's at," Donna said.

"Who? Rasheed? Where?"

"There's this woman that comes through every now and then. Ask about him every now and then. Hell, I asked some questions too. Found out it was an old girlfriend."

"Mya?" Shaheeda asked.

"Come on Sha. Think. No. Someone else. Say, about my height, long hair, damn near down her back. Chinky eyes. Good looking...really."

"Oh hell. Not her. Damn. Thought she was gone."

"Who? Sha..." Latif was puzzled.

"Back in the day, we used to go to this Mosque on Bushwick Avenue. Daddy would take us."

"Don't remember that. "

"You were too little."

"Really? I thought maybe it was because my mother shipped me away. Didn't want me." His voice trailed off. His quip with sarcasm gave away too much emotion and Shaheeda picked up on it. She walked over and started to massage his shoulders. "No. Wasn't that. At all. And, when we all get together, we need to work through that. I can see it still bothers you."

"Through what!" He got up and pushed her hands away. If she wanted me to stay. She would have kept me with her!"

"Whoa you two," Donna said to them. "Focus. Y'all work that out later."

"Yeah, later. Should he decide to do so. Anyway, this girl was damn near kidnapped by the so-called Imam there. Corrupt muthafucka. He raped her." She stopped cold then sort of walked off in a trance, prompting Latif to ask. "What Sha? What's wrong now?"

Remembering her own ordeal, it pricked her skin at the very thought of it in her mind. Was this a trend with everyone back then? "Sorry Latif. Thinking...about something." She responded.

"What?"

"Nothing. Nothing at all. "

"No sis. It is something. Something that, eventually, we all, this whole damn family needs to talk about, one day. Soon."

"What the hell are you talking about Latif I'm alright!" She shook her head back into the moment and continued. "Anyway. Her name is Asia."

"She must live close by." Donna said, "Don't know where she's at now."

"I hear you, but I tell you what. If you know, and now we know, then I bet one of Cholo's people know too, at least by now."

Carlito's ear was damn near through the wall listening. He heard all he needed to hear. Now, he needed to find the woman they were talking about, Asia. Then, he'd have Rasheed in his reach. He put the panel back up against the wall that he'd move aside so he could hear what they were saying, then quietly backed up out of the utility closet situated next door to Donna's office. Closing the door gently behind him he tiptoed his way towards the front of the store, and picked up the phone. He dialed Cholo's number. "Hey boss... I got some news."

"What is it?"

"I might know where she is."

"Where?"

"He's with a girl...someone named Asia."

"Where's she at?"

"Don't know exactly where at...yet."

"Don't know! Then find out!"

"But, hold up. She must live close by because I heard them say that she comes to the store all the time."

"What does she look like then?"

"Like any other black chick, I guess...but one thing. She has Chinese people's eyes."

"What? Chinese people's eyes? Well, it's crazy, but...okay, that's a start. Find her!"

Carlito hung up quickly as Latif, Donna and Shaheeda approached. "Yes." He looked over at Donna and asked, "Did you get what I asked?"

"Yeah right." She shot back as she took out the keys to her car and walked past him. "Get you something? And I'm paying you? Yeah...okay. Picture that." She glanced back over her shoulder and said, "Or picture me walking the fuck out. You get it yourself!"

Carlito grinned at the remark slyly and said under his breath. "Yeah, Senorita...I'm gonna get it alright." He eyeballed Donna's shapely ass switch back and forth out the door. "Yeah, one day...I'll do just that."

RASHEED WAS ALREADY at the door opening it when they finished explaining to him what they were into, saying "Naw...not me. Count me out." And yelling for Mya to get Khadija's things as Asia tried her best to persuade him to join them. "Look Rasheed...we could use you. I mean...you know how to handle those types of situations. We need your help."

"Well...we could use your help. Ain't like we really need you"

"Come on now Kokomo. The last time we made a lick that deep we almost got popped. You know we need another man to watch our backs."

"Hell...Ray-Ray was there!"

"That's why we almost got hit. We need someone on point. Ray-Ray froze when that dude rolled on him with that Uzi. Barely got out of there."

"What?" Rasheed stopped. "You mean Ray-Ray, from Bushwick Projects? That Ray-Ray?"

Asia looked at the ground inside. "Yeah... That Ray-Ray. We needed someone."

He shook his head as he headed towards the door with Mya and Khadija in tow. Should be glad y'all still alive then he said as he opened the door, "Damn...Ray-Ray." He snickered.

Kokomo stepped in front of him. "Look man this is serious. We not gonna beg you, but damn...you owe us one." He looked over at Asia. "I mean...you just gonna walk out on us like that."

Rasheed pointed Mya and Khadija to the elevator, then turned around and said to them. "You're right. I do, but...not like that. Y'all talking some serious shit. Look, let me take them to Harlem. Stash them somewhere safe," he walked over to Asia and stroking the side of her face said, "I'll be in touch, baby-girl."

She smiled then looked over her shoulder at Mya scowling at her, then turned towards Kokomo and said, "We can live with that. But the job is going down soon, so you need to let us know something. That's what you owe."

"Cool," Rasheed said as he scurried over to catch the elevator.

"Kokomo, I believe he will do it, but he's the type you can't twist his arm. He's also the type that's not gonna have anything hanging over his head either."

"I can dig it, Asia but I don't want him to have the impression that we are some two-bit thugs or something." He walked over to her and grabbed her hands and caressed them. "I see how you looked at him. I know you like him, but we need to keep things business...or we can get fucked up, quick."

"I know...I know..."

"Alright then." He smiled then started towards the door. "I better get back to the crib and see what's going on. Cholo's people are probably all over the place by now-" *Pop...Pop...Pop!!!* "What the fuck!" he said as he ran over to the window and looked out. "Oh shit!!"

Asia pushed him to the side. *Damn...not that... she couldn't believe it.* "Oh no!"

The blue, four door sedan skidded up Broadway going towards East New York as they stared out the window. Mya was lying sprawled out on the ground with blood pouring out of her as Rasheed kneeled next to her yelling, "Somebody call 911!" Poor little Khadija hunched over her, stunned, and in a state of shock, still holding on to her hand.

Asia had already bolted out the door when Kokomo turned around. He thought about gunshots, *they might come back and want to shoot it out*, he thought, but his gun was at his crib. He did remember that Asia kept a Glock in the hall closet with an extra clip in case of emergencies, and this was definitely that. He got it out, then was right behind her running downstairs.

Asia was out the building first pushing people out her way, running towards Rasheed. "Oh my God," she said as she stopped dead in her tracks.

He looked and said, "Call an Ambulance."

But Asia just stood motionless, still. It was already too late. Mya was dead. Two shots to the head. When Kokomo came out of the building, he glanced up the street towards the direction the car had gone trying to remember if he'd seen it before, but it didn't look familiar. There were no plates on it, no distinguishing marks, nothing that made it stand out. But still, there was something quite not right about it. He tried lifting Rasheed to his feet, saying "It's too late bro...it's too late."

"No!" he cried out; the pain evident all in his voice as he did.

"C'mon now, Rasheed...she's dead."

Asia prodded Khadija to finally let go of her mother's hand, then walked her over to the benches in front of the building. The air was now filled with the whine of the police sirens as she sat her down. Dazed, confused, eyes wide open welled up with tears; she'd seen more in one day then any little girl should see in her lifetime.

Rasheed finally stood up and screamed out. "Do you know who it was?"

"Naw man..."

Angrily, he grabbed at him. "You sure!"

"We'll find whoever did it."

"You damn right we will!" Rasheed looked over at his daughter. Her mother was murdered, right in front of her eyes. Her father had just killed a man earlier in cold blood, right in front of her eyes. A lump welled up in his throat as he tried to swallow, he couldn't come up with words to say to her that would ease the hurt she was going through. His slanted eyes grew to a slit as he glanced over at Kokomo, he was mad, then he said quietly under his breath, "I'm in." He had tried his damnedest to do the right thing, but the right thing just didn't want anything to do with him. Just like in his nightmares.

Kokomo walked over to where Asia was consoling Khadija on the bench, trying to play the background as much as possible. A small crowd was gathering, a couple of people were already pointing fingers at him and he had the Glock cuffed in his waistband. It wasn't going to be good.

The cops arrived and were all over the place, but mostly surrounding Rasheed asking questions. He knew it's be a matter of time before they approached him too. He leaned over and whispered to Asia, "I gotta go, but who do you think did this?"

"Hell, Kokomo...couldn't have been Cholo's people. Too close to home," she said.

"I think so too."

"To tell you the truth. I think it got something to do with those warehouses we hit. I think someone's trying to send a message...to us. Think those bullets were meant for you. I mean...that's just what I feel."

"Yeah...I got the same feeling too."

Rasheed fended off questions as fast as he could, hopefully before they'd realize that he fit the description of the man wanted for the shooting of Chino. He tried backing away, but they kept him under close watch. He glanced over at Asia; she knew what it was. He was gonna have to take the chance and dip into the crowd that had gathered and cut the hell out. She'd have to handle the rest on her own. Take Khadija to his mother. A nod was all it took, and on top of it all, he needed a distraction.

He put his plan in motion by easing off into the swarm towards the street when suddenly a car screeched in front of him and stopped. Maybe, they'd come back! Maybe, the drive-by was for him. Bullets don't have eyes! He stood fast.

In that stilled moment, he eyeballed his surroundings. It just might work to his advantage, to get away. He'd have to yell something to the effect like, *here they go!* Yeah. That would turn their attention to the car. And as hype as they were already just by being in Bushwick, guns would be drawn, all that, then he'd make his escape. Who knows he might even have enough time to snatch Khadija. But as he felt the still warm blood of Mya's on his shirt, the thought quickly receded itself. He'd stand out too damn hard. Glancing over in the lot at his Caddy, parked inconspicuously, he thought to himself, *make a move Rasheed*, but it would only be a trap-off at best. The car was probably hot as all hell, A-P-B's up the ass. Damn, he cursed, he didn't need this shit today.

The car window rolled down and a man in a black Kangol reached over and waved him closer, then hollered out. "Come on. Get in!"

Hesitating at first, he didn't recognize the car and couldn't get a bead on the face. "Come on man! Ain't got much time!" he said again. Rasheed reached cautiously for the door and snatched it open, not knowing what to expect. But it couldn't have been any worse, at least he hoped. He dipped his head in first, relieved, he gasped, "Oh shit...you!"

"That's your daughter, right?"

"Yeah."

"Call her over...quick! We ain't got much time."

Rasheed quickly did as he was told. He got Asia's attention, she picked Khadija up in her arms and ran to the car and put her in the backseat. She reached over and asked, "You gonna be alright?"

"I will. Y'all just be safe. I'll be in touch this week."

Glancing over his shoulder, she looked at the stranger behind the wheel, mean-mugged him and asked him another question. "You know him...or what?"

"He's family."

"I don't know him," she replied coldly.

The man inside the car yelled at them. He was tired of it already and he let them know. "C'mon man. Ain't got time for that shit!"

Rasheed waved at Kokomo then closed the door. The car pulled off and Rasheed turned towards him. "What brings you to Brooklyn?"

"You. Heard some bad shit."

"Look..."

"Look hell. You might have been the one that got that little girl's mother killed with the bullshit you pulled earlier."

Man, I didn't...

"I thought you had changed."

"I am..."

"I can't tell."

"Look! It is what it is!"

"Don't yell at me Rasheed. Don't you dare!"

They were silent as the car raced towards the Williamsburg Bridge on their way to Harlem. Rasheed peeped in the back at his daughter, sleeping hard. He tried to find ways to explain this to her, then he looked at the man who drove the car. He wasn't expecting to see him, but he was glad he did. It wasn't the first time he backed him and his family out of a jam. He glanced up at the cards on the dashboard and asked, "What's this?"

"For one, stop being nosy. And they're my business cards."

Rasheed read out loud the thick printed ink on the undersized slits of cut paper, something that he possibly made from a copy machine.

"Okay...Okay...it's about time. Mickey Giovanni. Private Detective."

"Yeah...That's me these days."

WASEEMA COULD ONLY hold her head down as she listened to the details of Rasheed's account. It was all happening again. The same old bullshit. After ten years of peace, the violence that would become family history with her, would rear its ugly head again. She peeped up at Ice then walked out the room. Ice glared at him. "Damn...we were just together this morning. Man, I ain't been out the joint a hot minute and you get caught up with all this shit. That's crazy!"

"Ice, man, it...just couldn't be avoided..."

"What! Couldn't be avoided? You shot a man in the street in cold blood because he...might have, what... touched your daughter? I don't understand..."

"That's my kid! No man ain't got no right to touch my kid!" Rasheed stood up and banged his fists down hard on the table in front of him causing the chandelier to sing a tune as the crystal mirrors touched and danced around each other. It also caused Waseema to stomp back into the room. "Look god-damn-it! This ain't the streets, you hear? Don't raise your voice in this house!" Rasheed dropped his head. "And, Ice is right. You didn't have to kill a man because of that. That's not a reason..."

"But ma..."

"Ma, my ass! Mya is dead. And to be honest, you ain't got a clue if it had something to do with you killing that boy or not, Rasheed." She kneeled in front of him. "I wish you would have left earlier; I swear. That's why I never wanted you to go back to Brooklyn...Tried to get Mya to move up here. Bushwick has a curse on us." She stroked the locks of his hair and said, "You gotta leave...get out of here, now."

Giovanni was sitting across from them observing, and had just picked up his Kangol, ready to leave and she caught him staring. "You gotta help him."

"Oh, hell no." He stood up and put his hat on. "No way, I'm getting caught up in this. Hell no!" He started walking towards the door. "Y'all know how much I love y'all, but this...this is just too deep."

Ice stepped past Waseema and said, "Hold up. You keep saying it's too deep all the time...like..." Pointing at him he said, "You know something don't you?"

Rasheed thought back. How was it that Giovanni Just happened to show up at the right time? "Yeah...you do. Damn, what's really going on Giovanni?" He asked.

*Damn,* he cursed as he took his Kangol off and marched back into the room. "Rasheed. You blew into a major case."

"Major case?"

"There's a big federal investigation going on about activity on the piers. Large shipments of money coming in and going out across the borders around Mexico. Drug trafficking, money laundering... All hinging around the whole neighborhood in Bushwick."

"What are you talking about?" Waseema asked.

"You see. We all know Bushwick, and even Williamsburg is starting to grow. New businesses, banks and all of that. Which is all good, but it all comes from laundering drug money. And, that's what the Feds are investigating."

"So, Giovanni. What's that got to do with Rasheed? Mya getting killed?" Ice asked.

"There's a certain gangster down there they're looking at. Think he's involved. Name is Cholo. Well, they know him, but they're looking for his people too. His boss. They just can't seem to figure him out yet, so now, Rasheed, you killed the person of interest they were looking at. Probably a snitch. Now, you are a person of interest.

One thing though, you both have one thing in common I hate to say. Mya. She might have been tied in one way or another.

*Damn,* Rasheed thought, that hit probably was for Mya then, not Asia. But still, her and Kokomo are involved in something bigger than they think. Much more than a heist. "Shit!" he said then looked around. "Ice...we need to talk"

"Oh, hell no, Rasheed!" Waseema grabbed Ice and pulled him closer to her. "We don't want no parts of it."

"But ma...it's not..."

"No, Rasheed. I don't want him to end up dead too!" She pushed him behind her. Tears streamed down her eyes as Ice looked over at Rasheed and nodded. He'd talk later. He escorted Waseema out the room and glanced back at him. "Clean yourself up and get some rest. We got a lot of shit to do. For one...we need to bury Mya."

Rasheed nodded back. He was right. He needed to have his mother strong. There was work to do. Claim Mya's body, bury her, then explain to his daughter what happened. What could he tell her?

Damn, he pondered, it was all going down again just like before, real fast. He didn't want no parts of the plan Asia and Kokomo laid out, but it seemed like it was sucking him in more and more. Feeling Giovanni's hand on his shoulder startled him. "What's on your mind Rasheed?" he asked.

"I think you know what it is." It all made sense now. Someone else was pulling the strings, he thought as he got up and walked toward the stairs to the bedroom upstairs. "Fact is, I think you know more than what you're letting on. Goodnight. Let yourself out."

Giovanni stood there by himself feeling some sort of way. Those words had cut through him like a knife. Turning slowly towards the door, he thought. Hell, he didn't want any part of this either, but there seems to be no way around it. He frowned up as the cold wind hit his face opening the door standing him up straight. A chill ran up his back causing him to shiver.

Stepping into the air he glanced upstairs at Waseema's window. Catching his eye as she glared at him, it was unnerving, but still he couldn't help but think. She knows what it is too, I know, but why didn't she just cut it loose ten years ago when she had the chance? And, why won't you say anything about it? Why won't Khalid's memory just leave her alone. She knows things.

# CHAPTER SIX

C holo mulled over the events of a few weeks ago. It was still not sitting right with him, at all. Mya getting killed, much less in a drive by not ordered by him or his people just didn't seem to fit. He paced around the patio of his ranch style, baby mansion in Rosedale, Queens stretching. The place, small for the money he was making, but nevertheless, comfortable. He purchased the out of the way haven for himself years ago while still nickel and diming in Bushwick. Back then he was just a small street level thug with ties to heroin, cocaine, petty gambling, and muscle at the social clubs located behind the bodegas was his come up. Most likely what put him in the game were his ties to Felix years ago, way back then.

After Felix's odd disappearance, he worked his way into the then empty slot and along with Maria's blessings became her main man. Trying to maintain her holdings in Bed-Stuy off of Broadway that Felix left wayward was his thing. But the local gangsters wouldn't give as easy as he thought. Still, he tried to test the waters and he was met with resistance. His spots robbed; people killed. It wasn't working for him nickel and diming drugs. Economically it was supposed to have put him all the way in financially and with Maria. But it was shown that he wasn't ready to make moves on her level then. So, he laid in the cut. Keeping control of the properties and the shares of the newly structured boutiques and store fronts coming up on Broadway kept him occupied, new construction, new money. But it was Maria's not his.

Right now, his whole thing was, who was knocking off his warehouse connects these days? It had to be the same crew, the same people, consistent with the same m-o. Granted, it was small potatoes at first, and he paid it all no mind. Then, gradually it moved over into Maria's personal warehouse properties where she held most of her personal earnings, payoffs, and some cocaine. Though he himself never actually saw any dope, he was positive from his sources that that was what she moved with the muscle from his people. Not wanting to get her own hands dirty.

Based on that, he asked her for a cut for his, quote-unquote help, but she ignored him, paid him no mind, returned no calls, all that. Like he was an underline, under her, her help, and he resented that wholeheartedly.

Instead, she opened the doors for him to move product for himself, even control some of the property she had locked around in the area of Broadway. But that was pennies compared to the money she pocketed. So, he did what most greedy people would do in that situation, skim. She, so he thought, wouldn't miss it, but his skimming amounted to thousands off the take. Maria was no rocket scientist, but she wasn't no fool either, she took notice. He didn't give a damn, and since then, their relationship had weakened.

Somehow, he knew she had something to do with Chino being killed, Mya in the drive by, somehow. It damn sure wasn't his people, but it sure as hell made it look that way.

He walked over to the edge of his mid-size 6-foot-deep pool and dipped his toes. Water was much too cool, but he needed to calm his nerves. He threw his robe off to the side and started to walk towards the small ladder in the water, then he stopped and thought out loud. *Damn, suppose she knows about the meeting with the Mexicans? That would make her hot as hell, no telling what she'd do, but fuck it. I could move the product much better than her anyway. To hell with her, who cares if she knows.*

He glanced over at the perimeter 12-foot-high cement wall that loomed over his yard and sneered. *I need to keep an eye out for that bitch, she might try me. But hell, maybe I should try her.* He snickered, and belly flopped into the water. The cool 50 something degree water opened up his pores and senses as he tensed up. The coolness warmed his body. He closed his eyes as his temperature adjusted to it, then leaned back and relaxed. He might as well enjoy the peace and serenity now he figured, because after this, he'd go ahead and call Guillermo, cut him loose, send him on a few missions. Missions that he'd been waiting for anyway, just from this moment. It was time.

"YOU SHOT THE WRONG person, you idiot!" Maria yelled into the phone. Banging her fist on the glassed marble countertop caused her maid to come running into the kitchen, asking frantically in her broken English if she was alright. She shooed her away, but not without some hesitancy. After all she'd seen Maria succumb to chest pain, shortness of breath causing her to rush to her physician's office more than once. As always, the same misdiagnosis, she'd say, it's just gas, indigestion, her own denials. In all actuality she was diagnosed as having heart disease from all the stress, anxiousness, lack of sleep, and her four pack a day cigarette habit wasn't helping any either. She wasn't trying to hear it but her ambitions were driving her to the brink of killing herself. Possibly going insane but, here she was anyway early in the morning, not even finishing up a cup of coffee, on the phone screaming at the hit man she hired to take out Rasheed.

"When he came out, I couldn't get a clear shot."

"You're a fucking professional...or so I thought. What do you mean you couldn't get a clean shot?"

He had a child, a little girl in his arms. So, I waited until he put her down and I made my move. I didn't expect the woman to suddenly step in front of him and pick the little girl back up. It was unfortunate. I tried to get at him again, but he ducked behind some benches. Couldn't get off a clean shot."

"Damn! You should have shot him when he had the girl in his arms!"

Look Maria. You wanna butcher, then you get someone else."

"No, no. Calm down." Maria sat on a stool by the dining room bar fixing herself a drink. She poured herself a Bourbon and took a sip. It's Okay. Still it looks like Cholo did it right?"

"I used a rifle, and bought an old used beat up Chevy. Made it look local...crude. Like Cholo's people would do."

"Okay...I'll work with that."

"Anything else?"

"No...I'll call you soon. Uh, you know where the money is?"

"Of course. Same place, right?"

"You know me well. Good doing business with you." She hung up the phone and finished her Bourbon. It was tragic that Mya was killed, but it would only put more kindle on the fire. Rasheed would definitely go after Cholo now for killing the mother of his child. She glanced back at the phone. Maybe she needed to call Waseema, convey her condolences. "Yes," she smirked as she reached for the phone. "I'd love to hear the pain in that bitch's voice".

The trigger man turned away from the phone booth, and sneered, to him Maria was a piece of shit. He reached into his pocket and pulled out another number and dialed. "Hey. The girl is dead."

"Are you sure?" the voice said from the other end.

"Very much so."

"Good...its set-in motion. Does Maria know anything?"

"Naw...She's as arrogant as she's always been." The phone was abruptly hung up. The hit man stuffed the number into his wallet, but not after looking around, making sure no one caught wind of his I-D, his badge. Edward Gonzalez. Special Agent. Alcohol-Tobacco-and Firearms.

"HELL, I HEARD THE GIRL was a snitch."

"What? A snitch?"

"Yeah...worked for the ATF...informant, I think. Heard also, she was trying to pimp Cholo's boy Chino for information."

"You sure?"

"Believe so, Giovanni."

Giovanni walked out the Fed building in lower Manhattan, rubbing his chin, then stopped, still dwelling on what was just said to him by a buddy of his that worked for the Feds...ATF. Damn. He thought out loud to himself, *Still don't think it could have been Cholo's people that did that drive by? Hmmm...straight fucked up. Don't even think-damn Giovanni-what the hell you got yourself into now?* He scratched his head and readjusted his Kangol then continued up Church Avenue thinking of a hundred different reasons to let it all go. But none of them good.

HIS MOTHER CALLED THEM all together, Latif, Shaheeda and even Ice. She wanted to talk, discuss something she felt they needed to know. Really, Rasheed didn't feel like being there, but it would be a good opportunity to tell them all he was leaving, with Khadija. He straightened his shirt and stared at the reflection in the mirror, paused, then stared at the image looking back at him. A much older version of himself, but he sure as hell didn't feel that way. He rubbed at the stubble on his chin, then ran his fingers through his thinning hair and twisted it when he spotted a streak of gray on the sides of his temple. He started to frown, but instead he chuckled. Hell, after all he was starting to favor his father, and he was okay with that.

He was starting to have regrets shooting Chino. Too much had transpired, and none of it good, headaches, all of it. Now he had to run, and cut tail as a result. Something his father wouldn't have been okay with, at all. "Rasheed!" He spun towards the door, his mother, everyone must have arrived. He peeped out the window and saw his sister's Beamer and Latif's ride parked out in front. He heard a sound that startled him. The door opened suddenly behind him, his daughter stood there, grinning from ear to ear. Oblivious to his surprise, she stood naively elegant in a pretty bright pink and white velvet dress, and little girl knee highs with white shoes. She looked every bit like her mother as she beamed at him. He walked over, kneeled, hugged and squeezed playfully until she started giggling. He then swooped her up in his long arms and walked towards the stairs on their way to the library downstairs to see exactly what was going on now with his family. Hopefully, a welcomed change of pace.

Waseema was majestic as she stepped into the room with a dress glittering of gold lace flowing like a waterfall from off her long shapely cocoa brown legs. Her long silky hair masterly done in a whimsical Eton cropped-French braided chiffon, highlighted her high cheekbones on a still youthful face. Her sexy doe like eyes fluttered her long natural thick eyelashes that could easily zero in and stare a man down, as well as take his breath away at just the sight.

She walks regally over to where Ice sat, a high back plush red velour armchair, and Rasheed could only admire how stately they both looked together as a couple. Ice handed her a chalice of wine he had waiting, then turned towards everyone she held it high and said, "For Love. For success. For family." Shaheeda, Donna, Latif, Rasheed all responded in a lush *"Here, here'*.

"So ma... what's up?" Latif asked as he glanced casually over at Rasheed. He made it his business to come over. He needed to talk to Rasheed about things too. Maria was on his back, and he had to warn him that Cholo was ready to make a move of some sort. He couldn't divulge her plans without exposing himself but he damn sure had to tell him something. During Mya's funeral he had heard him speak to Ice about leaving. Where he didn't say and he felt it was better that he didn't know anyway. He owed his brother an out and he felt it was a good time for it. He looked at his mother again. "Ma..., he checked his watch, I'm kinda pressed."

"Hold on now, will you, Latif?" she said as she frowned at him. "Slow down."

"It's all good ma, I just got things to do, that's all."

"Maria can wait," she replied coldly, causing Latif to furrow his brow. She tried understanding his hostility, but she didn't care too much for it either. It was time for the both of them to hatch things out. Bring all of whatever it was out into the open, but just not today. "Okay Ma...sorry about that."

Rasheed and Shaheeda took their bickering with each other all in stride. It didn't seem serious, so far, besides, as far as Shaheeda was concerned it didn't hold a candle to her own beef with her mother. Giggling, she glanced over at Latif and said, "All right now. Don't let her get the belt." She chuckled along with Rasheed and Latif turned his head and shot back. "Forget y'all." Yeah, it was definitely all good. Family acting like family, but with secrets.

"I called you all here for a good reason. Not to waste your time. It's about time I'll let you know some things. Things I should have told you all years ago. She turned towards Donna and said, "Donna. It's nothing personal, but what I'm about to say to them is exclusive, it may even be uncomfortable. For them. Would you be so kind as to take Khadijah, for a little walk?"

As awkward as she felt, she complied, she understood. And besides, if she really needed to know Shaheeda would tell her what was up anyway. "Oh...uh, yes ma'am." She got up and clasped Khadija's hand to walk out. Then she turned around and asked, "'Bout what time is good...to come back?"

"About an hour or so. You got some money?"

"I'm okay."

"I'm sure...thank you."

As she walked out Waseema sat on the other side of Ice. She sat and crossed her legs then peeped over at him. "You, uh...might want to go too."

"Me?"

"You might think...differently of me."

"That serious?"

"Yes."

"Then, I should be here."

She held his hand and smiled as they all sat up waiting to hear what she had to say, and hopefully satisfy their inquisitiveness and expectations.

"Ma...what do you mean this might hurt us? What the hell is going on?" Rasheed sprung to his feet, "You're holding...secrets?"

"Yeah ma...what the hell?" Shaheeda followed him.

"Hold up!" Waseema bellowed at the both of them. "Sit down! I'm about to tell you things about our family and you should be at least adult enough to hear me out." Embarrassed, Rasheed sighed, then sat quietly. Shaheeda sucked her teeth stubbornly and only after Waseema glared her down did she sit, too. "Alright now." She continued. "It's about your father, Khalid. About how I met him. You see, I was introduced to him by Malik, a small-time hustler back then."

"He damn sure didn't change much."

"C'mon Rasheed, just listen. Anyway, he was from Bushwick and he'd come up to Harlem to buy heroin and bring your father along with him, mostly for protection. The both of them used to run with a gang called the Tomahawks and your father was considered a warlord. But he broke off later from them because he wasn't with the drug thing. He helped organize a gang called the Black Spades from out of Brownsville, which wasn't much better. He was a straight up thug.

"Damn ma...Dad was pretty low down huh?" Latif said.

"Yeah, but something changed them, him and Malik. One night, they had this big argument, messed around and got into a gang war over territory... and drugs. Khalid felt that moving heroin into Bushwick and Brownsville wouldn't work for them or the people that lived there. Malik thought differently, he wanted to make money."

"Right up on Bushwick Avenue past the cemetery, around where East New York meets Brownsville they fought, both gangs. People got killed...close friends. Police picked them up and they both ended up going to Rikers Island awaiting trial. Murder charges. Malik ended up taking a plea. Khalid wouldn't snitch. And ended up doing time. Malik walked."

"That's why Dad went to prison...looking out for Malik." Latif said.

"Yeah. But Malik made sure Khalid was straight while he was away Elmira, I think."

"Hold up ma, you knew Malik from Harlem? I thought you met him in Bushwick Projects." Shaheeda asked.

I'd seen him a few times in Harlem. Hell, back then no one came up to Harlem to cop dope on their own. And they...him and Khalid didn't know anyone. They stood out like sore thumbs. They had to deal with my cousins or risk getting robbed and that applied to even the white folks that came uptown to buy dope. It was something serious, that's how it was back then."

"Anyway, after Khalid went to prison, he'd still come up every now and then, but it wasn't to cop dope. He'd messed around and got into the Nation of Islam Temple number seven on 125$^{th}$ street where my family went. Looking at it now I think it was my cousins that kinda pulled his coat, because it was just around that time that they started to slow down too. Started going to the Temple and all. And that's where I met him."

"Daddy...or Malik?" Shaheeda asked, this time her demeanor a whole lot humbler.

"Malik...first. He'd come into the temple trying to fit in. He was crude, thuggish but the brothers helped him out...especially one, Craig...3X."

"Yeah old Craig 3X." Latif said, "Haven't seen or heard from him in a minute...got missing. Nobody don't know where he's at. No trace of him...nothing. Just vanished. It's crazy huh?"

"Yeah... sure is." Waseema replied but only after taking a quick glance at Shaheeda did she say. "It's a shame, but you know how it is. People go missing all the time in New York."

"Well, like I was saying he hooked up with Craig and they kinda...got him right. He wanted to start his own thing in Brooklyn, a temple, but they, the Minister, wouldn't give him the blessings. So, he did his thing in Brooklyn anyway. But doing his own thing cost money. The kind of money an honest man doesn't normally make. He ended up trying to rob a supermarket. That definitely didn't work out, so he gave up the robbery thing and became a full-time activist. Still he needed money; donations, anything, something; he was desperate, that's when he got caught up with a drug dealer in Bushwick by the name of Carlos."

Rasheed's face twisted up at the sound of his name. He hoped the connection she was making wasn't going to pan out with him and Derek from back in the day. He was still trying to figure that one out, and as much as he desperately wanted to ask hundreds of questions about Felix, he stayed quiet, and nodded his head, listening.

"He borrowed some money from him and in return Carlos asked him to front his face for some property. Old lots, abandoned buildings, all types of shit, and before you know it, Malik's name is all over Bushwick and Bed-Stuy. Granted, he did some good. He put people in apartments for little or nothing, but that wasn't the direction Carlos had in mind...nothing good. All he wanted to do was set up shop for his drug dealing enterprises. Malik turned a blind eye and Carlos let him shine. Fronted him cash, cars, political pull; he was the man. Then the money left or he couldn't pay it back. I mean after all he was a bought man, but his prices were getting too high. He ended up being in his pocket. It was crazy, but it was just about that time Khalid came home...from prison."

"Didn't they open up a Mosque together?" Latif asked.

"They did. He was changed. He'd accepted Islam while he was in prison, and he would come uptown to the Temple and offer his prayers. The Ministers, Captains...they loved him. Offered him the world but he turned it down to do his thing in Brooklyn. Maybe, it would have been better if he had stayed uptown. She smiled as she looked up in remembrance, a small twinkle revealed a tear off the corner of her eye. Wiping it away she peeped over at Ice and apologized. "I'm sorry."

"No. That's okay." He pulled the handkerchief from out his pocket and wiped her eyes. "He was good. Hell, if I can only be that good to you."

"You are." Without a doubt Ice was that dude. He took care of her. The one thing that they all did agree on.

Latif, he still wanted to know more. He knew there had to be more to the story. He could feel it. "But ma...where are you going with this?"

Turning her attention back to them she said, "I fell in love with your father, but I knew Malik...first."

"Hold up. What are you saying?"

"I was with Malik, first."

"Oh shit, I mean. You know what I mean. So, you dated him, then met dad."

"Yeah, but it's more complicated than that."

"So..." Shaheeda grinned ear to ear, about to draw blood, picking. "You're not a goody two shoes then, huh?" Ice put it up his hand to hush her. "Alright Shaheeda. That's enough. Don't disrespect your mother like that. Ever!"

"Okay Ice." Stepdad. She snorted sarcastically, "You know, ...we all got secrets, too."

Rasheed turned towards her. "Secrets? We all know about those Mexicans in Bushwick, trust me."

"Trust you? Yeah, Okay, picture that. Let's talk about this then, since you are putting people's business out there. Why did you kill Chino then, huh? I heard he was screwing Mya. Maybe, you got jealous. Mad." She got up and made the mistake of pointing her finger at him, "Maybe, it was you who got your own baby mama killed!"

Rasheed rushed over towards her, but Latif managed to get in the way and stop him in time. He sneered and said, "I don't know what your problem is, Shaheeda, but you've changed lately! If you know like I know, you better get right!" He snatched away from Latif and walked towards his mother and said, "Look, maybe we can finish this another time. I ain't in the mood. "

"Rasheed baby. Don't pay her no mind. I need to finish what I'm saying."

**BAP! BAP! BAP!**

"What the hell was that? Gunshots!"

"Where!"

"Outside the window. In front."

Waseema screamed out. "My God, wasn't Donna and the baby downstairs?"

Rasheed was at the window first, then spun around and hollered back at Ice. "Get the guns!"

Eddie Gonzalez crouched down in the front seat of the tattered interior of the old beat up Chevy and pulled the sun visor down off to the side, so as not to be seen. Glimpsing up and down the street he saw no one walking, stirring, except for maybe a few nosy ask people in their window idly staring, but not anyone in particular, definitely not at him and that's all he was concerned with. Reaching beneath the seat he pulled out the clip for the 40 Glock he had warming in his lap. Picking up the gun, he held it down low in his left hand, twisting it around, inspecting it, feeling its weight, its power, making sure it, and himself was ready for the task at hand. Once he was satisfied, he jammed the clip up the butt producing the sharp but quiet snap.

Maria told him just to send some low-level gunfire at the building, not to shoot anyone. Let them think it was Cholo, a drive by. Hell, they already had that idea based on the make and model of the car. That the shooting of Mya had something to do with him, anyway. This, if anything should push it right over the edge. Prompt them to make a move, especially from out of Rasheed. Along with the killing of Chino, it had all the makings of a small feud, and that's what she wanted.

He watched as they went inside earlier, giving them a few minutes to settle in. To pass time he drove up the street, parked, reached into his pocket and peeled off a couple of dollars. Figuring he'd have time to get a pack of smokes. Stepping out the car into the open, he pulled down the brim of his hat and popped the collar on his jacket so no one could get a good look at him. Then headed for the corner bodega. Opening the door, he glanced at a pretty brown skinned woman coming his way and grinned. Being more flirtatious then friendly, he waited and opened the door for her, and also the small little girl that was with her.

Walking to the counter he pointed out a pack of Newport's and laid a twenty-dollar bill on the counter. He felt a nudge on his coat and looked down and the little girl was staring up at him. He moved off to the side out of her way. She pointed to some candy licorice she couldn't reach so he grabbed some for her and laid them on the glass top and motioned to the man behind the counter that he'd pay for them. The woman she was with walked up behind her and said to him. "That's alright...I got it."

"No...It's okay, really."

Donna wanted to resist, but Edward had one of those die-hard smiles that wouldn't quit. "Thank you," she replied. Edward shoved the change back into his pocket, nodded and stepped to the door, stopped then turned back around and said to her. "Hope I, uh...see you around."

"You never know." She answered back.

A passing sort of thing, perhaps. The type of thing that happens more times than any one thing in life, at least in New York City. Small thing. Edward got back into the car and opened the cigarette pack, pulled one out and stuck it in his mouth. He pushed the lighter in the dash and wiggled it. The car was an old beat up Chevy that barely ran. The same car that he used in Bushwick a couple weeks ago. This time he would fire a couple of rounds, lay low, let them get a good look at the vehicle, then pull off. They of course would notice it was the same car and according to the plan, they would also assume that it was Cholo's people. They'd go after him, just like Maria said they would probably do.

He took a deep breathy drag off the smoke and cranked up the car. Deliberately, he drove up the street, parked in front of the three-story brownstone, rolled the window down, pointed the gun and started shooting. Three shots, good enough. The white Jaguar was the victim this time, Latif's. He waited, peeped up and watched as they got out the window. Letting him get a good look, he tipped his hat down over his eyes, rolled back up the window and gunned it up the block. Turning the corner, he raced toward the other side of town, but this time he made plans to ditch the vehicle, in Queens...Rosedale. Right where Cholo's house was. Parking right in front, just like Maria had told him to do

When Donna heard the shots, she covered Khadija and threw herself to the ground shielding her. Once she heard the car screech away, she peeped her head up and looked around. Not seeing any imminent threat, she picked Khadija up and ran back inside the store. "Call the police!"

"No-no. Not me. It's none of my business. I don't want no trouble."

Donna mean mugged him and glanced back outside the door. She eased herself out cautiously with Khadija in tow and could see Latif as he ran outside. She yelled for him, and he looked up and waved her on. Once she made it up the block and was safely inside, he pulled her off to the side before the others ran outside and asked, "You see anything? Was it Cholo's people!"

Knowing the threat Cholo had put down on her earlier, and knowing that she'd have to work around Cholo and his people, she figured quickly that it was in her best interest to think this through before she opened her mouth. She answered saying, "No, I didn't see no one like that." Her mind clicked back to the man at the store. She felt shame. She was no better than him. Karma's a motherfucker.

# CHAPTER SEVEN

"**A**lright...I'ma need...Yo! Grab some of those filed down .357 hollow points over there." Rasheed pointed to a canvas satchel full of miscellaneous ammo. Ice picked it up and started rummaging through it. "Got em."

They were both in the basement of the brownstone, in an enclosure in a darkly lit backroom located towards the rear, separate from the vast wine cellar that already had established space. Behind on the far right was an old wooden and steel encased door with a large brass handgrip. Somewhat rusted around the trim, it still worked even past the repair. It did what it was supposed to do, and that was not to expose the arsenal that hid behind it. Some of it dating as far back as the time when Rasheed's grandfather was still living, to as recently as when Waseema stashed guns there for herself shortly after Ice had gone to prison. Now here it was, Ice found himself leaning back against the wall and thinking out loud, in a moment of clarity. *What the hell am I doing?*

Rasheed paid him no mind as he continued to dig through the shiny projectiles of different calibers. "Whatever happened to those pumps we had Ice? The shotguns! Where are they at?" He finally lifted up his head then glanced over at him and asked, "You alright?"

Ice looked around at the guns scattered about the floor, a shiny black nine-millimeter, five blue steel 38 snubs, an AK-47 with twin 30 and 50 caliber banana clips. He backed up and asked Rasheed, "What are we doing here?"

"What?"

"I said, What are we doing? Here?"

Holding a handful of 38 grain bullets, Ice walked over to him and slowly one by one dropped them to the ground, slowly and saying. "Man... I can't do this anymore."

"You can't what? You going soft on me or what?"

"Rasheed, I'm just not trying to get caught up with this type of shit anymore."

"Alright. I see." Rasheed said, nodding his head, then casted an eye over at him. So... It's okay for them to just kill my people then. You gonna to let them do this... to us."

"If we go down there shooting. It's only gonna get worse and on top of that a whole lot of people gonna get killed, for nothing. Hell, Mya was one. Who's next?"

"Whatever!" Rasheed turned away from him and said, "You go then. Go, but remember, if you're gonna be a part of the family. Either, you all the way in or you all the way out. You call it."

"Hold up!" Ice grabbed him by the arm. "I spent 10 years of my life for you and your family. What the hell are you talking about! I'm down with y'all. Forever! You know that. But this, this is foolishness. We grown, we ain't kids!" He turned away from the guns and said, "I ain't trying to do no more. I want better things for my life."

Rasheed turned toward him and said, "It's cool man. I understand. Really, I do. But me, I'm still obligated."

"But, can't you see it though, 'Sheed, it's deeper than this. Bigger than us. Now, we gotta do things differently. We just can't go in a place shooting them up anymore." Rasheed still didn't seem to be paying him any mind, but he knew his next statement would prick his ear. "No one said anything about it. But, I'm your main man. I'm not gonna talk behind your back. But you really didn't have to shoot that guy in the street like that. I know you got to see the can of worms you opened."

"I don't care what everyone thinks. Like you said ice, it was deeper than that. What I'm feeling is that somewhere down the line it seemed like we never finished the job."

"Job?"

"Felix. My old man. All that. Things were left undone."

"Undone? You tripping."

"No... He's not tripping." Waseema said as she stood by the doorway with her arms crossed. "He's right."

"Right? Where's this going now?"

"Ice, baby. I never did finish what I wanted to tell y'all."

"Oh, come on mom. We ain't got time for those old stories. Some other time, alright!"

"Rasheed close your mouth for once, shut up and listen!" Suddenly, she clutched at her chest. The dust and excitement were too much for her. She felt faint. Ice rushed over and propped her up against the wall while he grabbed her a chair. After a while she was settled, calm, then she continued. "Ice, he's right. It's not all about his father...Khalid. Malik, my father, mother."

Rasheed stared bewilderedly at her and asked, "What's going on?" He got closer to her face and said, "Ma, if there's something you need to say, then say it."

"My mother told me before she died what to do. What properties to watch. At first, I didn't understand, but now it's starting to make more sense. I see why your father, Khalid, said years ago that it would go down like this one day. That's probably why he went back to Bushwick I'm guessing."

"Come on now, mom. You're losing me. What did grandma say to you? I mean, I know she owns some property up here in Harlem, couple of buildings and stuff, restaurants, but what they got to do with us?"

Like you said earlier. It is bigger than this. Your grandmother was a gatekeeper so to speak. She held on to certain deeds. These people were rich and believe me not everything we own, yeah, we...is in Harlem. She ran her hands through her hair and twisted to get comfortable in her chair. "Need anything water or something?" Ice asked her but she shook her head no.

"Your grandmother met this guy from Mexico named Consuelo when she was young, she'd go on trips to Cancun. They had an affair, then he followed her back home, made his way up to New York by way of the ports... Smuggling, bringing thousands in cocaine to New York with him without her even knowing. Then, he just disappeared. Years later, he showed back up, but this time running scared. He needed a place to duck out, so he sought out my mother, but she didn't want anything to do with him. She found out he was using her. Besides, she was married by now. Still, she helped him anyway, after all, he wasn't by himself. He had a kid, a little girl named Maria with him."

"At the same time, my father was still doing his thing with the property he held onto, but business got slow up in Harlem, club life got quiet. Mostly, when I was coming up it was all about heroin and cocaine, pimps and pushers. My father wasn't down with none of that. He was old school. But business got slow, and the taxes on the properties kept coming. He needed some money; big money. He didn't know which way to turn. Hell, people were coming at him left and right trying to buy him out, but he wouldn't budge. He didn't know no one he could trust. He was just about to give in, but my mother found the way just in time, Consuelo. She got in touch with him and some deals were made from a partnership sort of. My old man wasn't really with it, but my mother talked him into it. My old man, for the first time, he was desperate."

"Consuelo had set up shop in Brooklyn and he was feeling out Harlem. He wanted to grow. But Harlem ain't no Mexico. He didn't know how to navigate black folks up this way, but my father did, and that's how we maintained control all these years."

"My mother was frugal with money. She kept records and recorded everything. Every move that Consuelo did with us, she wrote down. He didn't like that, he wanted out, but he made a deal and my old man held him to it. He left Harlem and went back to Mexico."

"Oh shit." Rasheed said as he glanced over at ice. "That's deep."

"There's more. Before that, Consuelo messed around and got down with some of his Mexican buddies, and that's when things got ugly really quick. They started importing thousands of pounds of dope in... Using mules, women. Well, he needed a place to stash his dope, money, and a place to put all these women coming into the city while laundering the money. Remember, he didn't know the people. He went underground, but he couldn't trust the Italians. The Irish in Hell's Kitchen wanted too much of a cut. And his own people in Brooklyn, he couldn't even turn his back on them."

"He got back in touch with your father. That's why we own all those whore houses."

"Brothels, Rasheed. Look, it is what it is. My old man didn't want nothing to do with prostitution, but he needed to do something, remember the partnership worked both ways. My mother started financing brothels and social clubs on the other side, Spanish Harlem. She held them in bogus names, names she knew would stay in the family." She lifted her finger and pointed at Rasheed. "My father wanted to use the names of you and your sister and brothers. Khalid wasn't going for it and that's when my old man and he had a falling out."

"The only other person up for the job was Maria. Granted, she didn't have any kids, but she had a grimy ass husband, Felix. I'm sure you all remember him. He got the names and faces, and Consuelo gave him his blessings to push his dope as a result of. But there was this other guy, part of Consuelo's partnership in Mexico. He was the real go-to guy. Together they came up with the front. Some Moors out of Williamsburg helped them form a company. A newspaper or something.

"Goddamn Carlos, I bet."

"Yes. How would you know, Ice?"

He looked over at Rasheed and said, "Damn. You might be right."

"Right. Right about what? What are y'all talking about?"

"Nothing. Yet. Just finish, ma."

"It was Malik that daddy sent to keep an eye on things in Brooklyn-the warehouses. He couldn't do nothing on his own. The Nation of Islam was breathing down his neck pretty hard about...his quote-unquote, business practices."

"This new minister...named Craig. He'd stay on my old man all the time, watching him, accusing him. Then, when he saw his chance, he blackmailed him, extorted him into giving him money. Money that continued to be funneled to him...until he died. The last part she said under her breath."

"Died? Craig 3X...that's who you talking about, right ma? I didn't know he died. I mean, I heard he was missing."

"I just assumed." Waseema butted in. Ice cut his eyes her way. Something about the way she dodged that wasn't right. "Somehow or another a lot of money was stolen and Consuelo blamed daddy for it. He swore revenge and the old man didn't like that; Consuelo got missing. I mean you can read between the lines with that. Daddy stayed really low after that up here in Harlem. Up until the very end, mama never spoke on these things until she told me that I had to do the right thing."

"The right thing?"

"Yeah, it was strange to me too. I asked her, what was the right thing? She said to clean up the family name, my father, Jamar."

"To do that, you'd have to figure out who stole the money."

"I believe...we already know who did."

"We?"

"It was Felix."

"Then if it was Felix that means Maria's money..."

"Half of it is ours!" Rasheed spit.

"One thing for sure, you can bet on it! She damn sure ain't gonna give it up easy." Waseema smirked.

"So damn, 'Sheed. It is bigger than us. But, how did we just happen to pick this guy, Consuelo, to rob? It couldn't have been a coincidence. Waseema did you know all about this before?"

"Some of those things, but not at this level. But I do believe Malik did, and maybe that's why he was killed, I guess."

Rasheed walked off to the far end of the room in thought. He paused, then looked at the floor, the guns, then turned around and said, "Then, we got to go after...Maria."

"That's what your father would have wanted."

"Well Ice. What do you say?"

He looked over at Waseema and sort of shook his head, then said to her. "Is this that important to you?"

"Yes baby. It's about redemption. Khalid's. My father's. We can't leave until this whole mess is cleaned up."

Ice pounded the side of the wall causing dust and old spackle to heat up around him. "Damn, what about the police? Can't they do this!"

"They might be in on it." Rasheed answered back.

"Great, just fucking great."

"I spoke with Giovanni. Waseema added.

"Don't tell me he's in on it too."

"He's with us," she said as she wiped the dust from around her face. "He knows some things too. Right now, he's poking around the Police Department asking questions. I mean Rasheed, why do you think they haven't found you. He's been feeding the wrong information all this time. Putting his own self in jeopardy."

Ice sighed loudly, then he glanced black over at Rasheed and said, "Well. We're definitely gonna need more people. Guns."

"I think I know just the right people. Rasheed said as his mind drifted off to the last thing him and Asia spoke on. *Hope they're ready*, he thought. Because it was all going to come crashing down real fast, just like in his dreams.

Latif had his head pressed to the black metal vent on the floor, eavesdropping on the exchange downstairs. He couldn't hear everything, but bits and pieces were just enough to form his own interpretation, however incorrect it may be. "Oh shit! Knew it was something she was holding out on!" He got up from his knees brushing himself off saying to himself. "She's about to make a move on Maria. Damn, should I warn her or what?"

"Warn who?"

It was Shaheeda and pulling up the rear was Donna. "Who you talking to Latif?" She asked. Peeping around him, she spotted the vent. He tried to cover it, slowly trying to slide away off to the side, but there was no overlooking the small specks of the dust on his pants, his knees. "What's going on?"

"Nothing," he said as he brushed past her. "I'm going to find mom, then I'm out of here. Too much drama here for me."

"You're just gonna leave? After everything that just happened."

He looked over at Donna and said, "She's alright. Khadija's alright. Look. This is Harlem. Gunshots are the norm. Trust me. Ma ain't gonna let it happen again though."

"Where she at anyway?" She asked as she walked over to the vent and peeped in. "Matter of fact. Where is Ice... Rasheed?"

Latif walked out the door and glanced over his shoulder. "Downstairs. I guess."

Donna walked over to where Shaheeda stood and peeped into the vent also. "What's up?"

"Don't know yet."

"Where does the vent lead to?"

"The cellar."

"Let's go down there then."

She glanced up at her. "Yeah. Let's go."

On the way out they could hear the door leading into the cellar opening. It was Rasheed, her mother, and Ice coming out, with Latif lurking by the door. Waseema turned, blocking his view, and took out a key, and locked it behind her. He tried spying the key trying to find out which one it was on her vast key chain. She almost caught him. Averting his eyes, he said, "Hey mom. I gotta go." He kissed her on the cheek. "I'll call later, Ok."

"Ok... Just be careful." Waseema knew of his dealings with Maria and she knew if the plans they made were to go down he would be in danger. She'd let him in on things later, once the pieces were all put into place. She watched him as he stepped outside, then rushed over and yelled out. "You want me to handle the damage to the car?"

Latif shook his head. He totally forgot about the bullet holes on the side door. "Damn, forgot all about that."

Ice caressed Waseema's back and moved her aside gently, "I got it, baby." Then called out to him. "Yo, Latif. Let me handle that." He shot an eye over at Rasheed, and said under his breath. "I need to get a look at the casings."

"You're right." Rasheed whispered back then stepped outside the door and handed Latif the keys to Waseema's car. "Here, take ma's car. Least until we handle the damage. Cool."

"Damn. How long is it gonna take?" Latif didn't figure in on the angle, to him the car didn't mean anything, just another toy. In all actuality he'd rather not be seen driving his Jag with bullet holes on the side anyway. "Alright then." He caught the keys Rasheed tossed at him and said, "See y'all later."

From the upstairs window, Waseema watched Latif as he pulled off. Guessing that he was running off to tell Maria something. Or ask about the things he heard her speak on earlier. Hopefully for his sake and Maria's, her guess would be wrong. Sighing, she thought about the events that brought her and her youngest son, her baby, to this level of uncertainty and skepticism anyway. She really just wanted so bad to sit down and touch base with him. Find out what was going on between them, the rift. But lately time never seemed to be there, it had been lost to the both of them. By Allah, would there ever be a tomorrow, she agonized? One thing for sure, she'd definitely have to eventually confront Maria and get the ball rolling first.

Glancing over toward the phone, she thought that maybe now was the time, today even. Instead, beyond the phone she looked up and found herself staring into the eyes of her daughter, Shaheeda. She knew that this wasn't going to be one of those conversational type moments. Her arms were crossed and her face twisted up in a smug. It would just have to wait though. "What's going on now Shaheeda?"

"Mama. We need to talk."

"I hear you, sweetheart, but now is not the time. I need to make a call."

"You never have the time!"

"Shaheeda. Please."

"Please, my ass!"

"Shaheeda!" Waseema lashed out as she stood to meet her defiance.

"Don't worry about it, mom!" she said as she stumped off. Waseema was fuming. Shaheeda was agitated over something, but what, she didn't have a clue. She figured she'd deal with her behavior, however brazen, however foolish, later, on her own time. Waseema was just glad to get rid of her for now, she didn't need the drama. Finally, there was peace, at least she thought. She reached for the phone and Donna came through the door, holding Khadijah who was rubbing at her eyes, apparently awakened. *Hungry*! She whined as Donna asked, "Miss Waseema. You mind if I take her downstairs and whip up a little something? I'm kinda hungry, too?"

"Of course not. Thanks, Donna."

On her way out, she turned around, pausing for a brief second, as if she wanted to say something. Carefully she selected her words. Waseema stared, waiting patiently, at this point for anything, giving her a moment. Hopefully, it wouldn't be about Shaheeda, she wasn't up for that anymore today. "Oh. You won't have to worry about...the books anymore."

"The books? Oh yeah."

In all the drama, she'd forgotten about that. Actually, it was the last thing on her mind. "It's okay darling. I'm sure it was oversight."

"Yeah. An oversight, but, please. Next time you see...an oversight. Call me, directly."

She heard that loud and clear, and respected it. She should have called Donna herself personally. She was dead wrong. "Next time," she said as she watched Donna leave out the door. *S&A's. Have to get on that*, she thought as she exhaled, tired and weary. Then, swinging her feet up on the couch, she kicked off her heels. Maria would have to wait for now, she needed some rest. It'd been one hell of a day, and it still had a whole lot of bite left in it.

DONNA WAS TRANSFERRING from the F to the J train on Delancey Street when she thought of calling Cholo. Looking around to make sure no one had followed her she used the subway phone far off from the tracks. But still, she waited for the trains to clear before she died. "Hello...Cholo?"

"Hey...Donna, baby. What's up?" Cholo was still kicked back by the pool contemplating, smoking weed, starting to get paranoid thinking about the threat of an invasion coming over the back wall of his yard. Too much surface and weed for him. For whatever reason anyone would want to get him it would be justified though, but all they really had to do was come in through the front doors. He had cheap, measly gates, and no real security. Besides that, he wasn't that big of a deal. But he thought so and his people around him did too. That's what mattered to him. "Everything good? Or what?"

"Did you send someone uptown to shoot up Waseema's place?"

"Shoot? Waseema? No. Why would I do that?"

"Well, someone did. And they think you had something to do with it."

"What?"

"Yeah, I saw the car too. Beat up type Chevy. Spanish guy behind the wheel."

"Oh, because he was Spanish, they think I had something to do with it."

"I'm just saying. Look. I did what you asked me to. So, we're good, right?'

"Sure senorita. Sure."

"Ok, gotta go." She hung up the phone just in time to see the J train rolling into the station. Hurrying up the steps to catch it she felt a whole hell of a lot better with Cholo off her back. For now, at least. She made it through the doors before they closed. Finding a seat, she plopped down in it. The next thing you knew she felt the vibration of her beeper. Checking the numbers, it was Shaheeda. *Damn... now what?* She saved the number and stuffed it back into her pocket. Leaning back, she stared at the waters as the train stormed across the Williamsburg Bridge. Briefly closing her eyes in a daze, she thought back to the face of the man she'd seen earlier in the car. He looked vaguely familiar. But she'd see him again anyway if Cholo was involved. She didn't mind sooner, *after all,* she smiled, *he was kinda cute.*

DRESSED IN A BLUE SWEATSHIRT and gray running tights, her long muscular but shapely legs were crossed comfortably as she admired the view through the large floor to ceiling window of the Williamsburg Bridge. She smiled as she caught the slow-motion slug of the J train as it creaked lethargically across. Thinking back to a time when she herself would have been on the same train, cursing its sloth and unhurried creep as it slid its way into Manhattan. If she had a nickel for every time.

She glanced around the room she was escorted to by the receptionist when she came in, a carpeted, large, but somewhat empty space with a large mahogany desk and high back plush leather chair, all placed middle ways in. Mammoth in size yet seemingly if there were anything else in its space it would have seen out of place. She admired its simplicity through its ambience and breathing room in a place where you could think.

Her eyes stopped rolling long enough to get stuck on a grouping of an array of pictures that gave it a gallery-like feel towards the sides of what would otherwise be a colorless room. A large catchy 11 by 24 black and white, overhanging several other styles which were arranged neatly in a collection. The mostly deco wall they hung on, gave them bright vivid colorations, in an array of tropical liveliness of different hues. Giving the black that stood in the middle, a hauntingly 3D like appearance.

Entranced in her eyes was the image of a tall, six-foot three or so, brown skinned, and well to her, strikingly handsome man caught up in a moment of mirth, laughter, and fun.

A beach; from the look of the thick, lush and healthy bright green palm trees in the background, blue waters and blue skies, it had to be somewhere south near the islands down off the alluring coast of Florida, the Keys. The Gulf of Mexico perhaps. There was a woman that shared space with him in the photo and from what she knew of her, it was probably Mexico, Cancun, she figured.

Complimenting the young man by her beauty, long jet-black hair cascading from off her shoulders, flawless mocha chocolate skin and ravishing smile she stood out, literally stole the show as he held her in his arms amid the splendor and magnificent, magnificence of the white pearly sands. *One hell of a picture*, she mused. The time of their lives they were having, all immortalized by a cheap Kodak 35-millimeter camera bought at the beachfront bodega.

The woman in the picture was of her mother, in her youth. The bronze handsome young man was Consuelo, Maria's father also in his youth. Waseema favored Juanita in beauty, but her adventurous spirit, lively exotic personality and grandiose lifestyle was in contrast to her own. Staying close to family, and the homebody type she adhered to was more akin to her father. Juanita admired her for that, not being fickle, and never once trying to push her persona on her. She was venerated, very much content with her being her own woman, independent and strong. She would sit her down and talk to her frequently for hours at a time and they became close. So, what Waseema lacked in travel, and flamboyant lifestyle, her mother made up for it with her wisdom.

They spoke about Consuelo in many a conversation. Reminiscing, telling her all that she needed to know about the situation, her involvement, romantically and financially. All of that. *Why didn't you ask me? You ain't got to go nowhere else! Always keep it family, keep it close!* Her mantra. Waseema kept that very declaration as she matured. Grateful, because armed with that, especially in Bushwick during the dark years amid the rumor surrounding her family, it allowed her to deal with it unemotionally. Unattached, from all the bullshit. It was also an opportunity for Juanita to expand to her, her knowledge of men, of the world, the dunya. She'd say that however difficult it was to leave Consuelo; she was content with the fact that she did. She confided in her that she'd witnessed a very dark side of him that she'd seen in too many a men. It made her realize that she would not have a healthy, normal life with him. Based on all of what she'd seen of Maria, she was glad that she did.

# CHAPTER EIGHT

Waseema felt some cool air on her neck. Startled, she jerked her head around towards the source of it; the door. Maria had just stepped in. She stopped momentarily in her tracks as well. Waseema held her glare on her, like a deer stuck in the headlights of oncoming traffic. She straightened herself back around, allowing Maria to adjust to her composure, and hers too, once she saw who it was. Now, it dawned on her why her furniture was situated the way it was, clearly so she could have the advantage coming into the room. Clever of her, she thought, since no telling how long she might have been standing there, watching her.

Maybe she was just trying to see what she was so caught up on, which picture? But, why would it even matter to her anyway, she pondered, or maybe she was just reading into it too much.

As she pulled out the chair from her desk to sit down, Maria was glad to see her. It had been awhile since they had a social visit and she'd really hoped that this would be one, but she knew it was just wishful thinking on her part. So, before they started clawing each other's eyes out like they normally do, she might as well at least get the chance to say, "It's good to see you."

"Same here." Waseema answered. "Been awhile." She added.

"That...it has."

"I couldn't help but notice the pictures you have hanging," she said as she pointed over towards them.

Maria got up from her chair and walked over to the black and white Waseema was staring at earlier, rubbed the sides of the frame tenderly, then blew on the side of it where she had touched earlier, and wiped it clean with a sleeve of her blouse, saying, "I can imagine the fun they were having." She turned around and faced her. "Good days, huh."

"Yeah. Guess so." Waseema answered flippantly, confirming now that she was indeed being watched.

Maria nodded then walked back over to her desk and sat. Picking up the phone she buzzed her assistant and asked her to bring in some coffee. "I wonder what could have happened?"

"Happened? What do you mean?"

"Coffee?" The assistant brought the coffee, and offered Waseema a cup. She seemed a little scary, nervous even as she poured the drink. Maria kept her eyes peeled on her, and when a small drop hit Waseema's hand, she frowned her disapproval, and the young lady rushed out of the room. Maria sipped on her cup and said, "Sorry about that. It's hard to get good...help, these days." She glanced back over at the photo. "Suppose my father and your mother would have stayed together?"

Waseema shifted in her seat, picking her words carefully. It seemed like all of her other photographs had been framed around this one picture. So, it meant more to her than just mere idle talk. It was personal. "By that, I'm sure you mean if me and you grew up together. Well, I guess it would depend on exactly where we would have been raised. Harlem? As opposed to Mexico? I guess."

Maria leaned back. "I guess so. I never thought."

"I'm quite sure Mexico would have dealt both of us the lifestyles we have now." She gestured her hands towards her, then of the other images of her and her father enjoying themselves as well as the glamorous resorts they were photographed at to make her point. "Money, property...I believe, even an antique dealership of sorts."

"Ah yes. Williamsburg. You've heard. Quite proud of that."

"I've been. Even bought. But like I was saying. Do you think that Mexico would have been so generous?"

"Quite observant, Waseema. Quite."

"You have to also remember; your old man needed a front once he got to New York. And that front came in the form of...my father."

"True. True." She took another sip of coffee. There was silence between them for a few as they both drank and stared out the window, then Waseema grew tired of it all. She thought by now Maria would have picked up on the fact that she was aware of her dealings by divulging the antique store or something, but she didn't catch on she guessed. So, she'd have to use the direct approach and get right to the point, after all this was personal. She said, "I really do feel like we can work out our differences, but..."

"Always a but," Maria cut in.

"Right now, we need to. No, I need to stop you. Perhaps, even warn you." Waseema lowered her cup, and hunched forward.

"Warn me?"

"Let you know that whatever business you're trying to conduct in Brooklyn that it involves my family's interest..."

"Hold up."

"That, whatever dealings you got going on with Cholo. And, if you had anything to do with Mya's...murder...and," She got up and moved towards the desk. "The shooting up of my home." Then she slammed the cup down spilling the contents of her drink on the table, and then reached for her jacket. "My home!" She exhaled loudly. "I will put you down! Do you hear me?"

Maria chuckled. "God, you're so much of a drama queen." She stood up too. "Do you think I would try to hurt anyone in your family? Do you?"

"I don't know Maria. You've changed. You really have."

Maria's lips quivered as she looked off and said bitterly. "I had no choice!"

"But. You did."

"How dare you point a finger at me? You don't know how hard it is!"

"Perhaps, but it's not hard anymore, Maria. Let it go."

"Let it go? Never! I want what your family stole...from us."

"Stole?"

"Yes...stole."

Waseema twisted her head around glaring at her in disdain. "Wow. You really...really need help. Look. I've been nice, but you heard what I said, and know one thing, sweetie. I don't play cards, so there's not a whole lot of, uh, bluff, in me. Okay."

Maria laughed softly at her mockingly, then said, "You're right, you're so right. You are straight up. I will say that much about you. Just like your mother was, but."

"But?"

"But. If you're so straight up. Why don't you let Latif know? About himself?" She turned around slowly and cut her eyes.

"What are you talking about?"

"Ah, come on. He has every right to know! It's his own flesh and blood!" She turned and glared at her.

Waseema stepped in towards her, saying. "If you mention anything to him..."

"Maybe, I will. Maybe, I won't. Like I said, I only want what belongs to me and my family. If you don't give it back. Then." She clenched her fist grinding her teeth and said, "I will take it! And. Whatever gets in my way." She crossed her throat with her finger.

Waseema opened the door and slammed it shut behind her on her way out, echoing across the room. Maria took a sip from her coffee, sneered, then opened her drawer and took out a cigarette and let it. She blew smoke up in the air, turned and sat down on the edge of her desk looking towards the same picture they spoke of earlier and spoke maliciously under her breath. "I will get it back, father. I promise. The property, your money. And, your honor."

Stretching up in his seat he laid the mug of coffee he had in his hand in the holder on his right trying to get a good view. Rubbing at his eyes he tried to focus in on what he was seeing. *Who was this woman coming out of Maria's office building? And why did she look so familiar?*

The car he was driving was dirty on the outside and he'd done everything he could to keep it that way, except for the windshields, and he used it to his advantage before. He grabbed at a cloth and started wiping, being able to see out with the tint he had on the passenger side windows preventing people from looking in. At least from a distance so he continued to stare.

Waseema marched out of the building's doorway buttoning up her jacket dipping her head into the breeze coming off the water, it'd gotten windier since earlier. Pausing for a second, she looked back at the tall, glass building, upstairs toward the window of the offices she'd just been in. Still pissed off at Maria. She backed up against the wall by the doorway contemplating on whether to take a cab as opposed to the train into Harlem. She didn't feel like being bothered with the hustle and bustle of the subway or footing it to the el. She turned back inside the doorway and asked the doorman if he could call her a cab. He asked if she wanted to wait inside, but she declined content with standing outside of the building fuming over Maria's words.

The nerve of her, Waseema thought. Trying to bother her, extort her even. She'd kick her ass if she ever told Latif, but she also knew deep down inside that it was time to tell him anyway. He was grown. Get it from her conscience, at least. She should have done it before her mother died, like she'd told her, but she put it on hold, thinking that maybe it wouldn't matter. That it would just go away. And then there were arguments between them. Even now she contemplated whether it would matter or not.

She frowned up at the thought.

No one knew. At least not any of her other children, and those who did would have been older. Folks up in Harlem that knew her mother and father from way back in the day had since died with her secret, all except Maria. And with that, Maria always held it over her head, so yeah, it was time to tell him. Time to tell Latif that Khalid was not his father.

The man in the car kept dibs on Maria and was scrutinized by his people in every possible way as a result. He remembered what Giovanni had said about her and how she may have been innocent of any dealings in or around Bushwick, just inherited some bad crops. He looked at him like he was crazy, and said the hell with that and kept her under his radar. She was dirt and he knew it, and anyone that had any dealings with her would come up dirty too if they were to put through the wash. Maybe, he thought, she might have more of an interest in everything than what his Department thought, and so happens, he was right. But he needed someone to go deep inside, get intel, info, dirt. He just didn't volunteer for the job, he jumped at it, convincing his superiors that no one could do it better than he could. Maybe questions so far.

He cranked up the car and put on his baseball hat. He pulled out in traffic towards the building and continued to watch the women as she glanced at him. Waseema couldn't make out his face through the tint, but she could feel his eyes on her. Lowering her head, she turned away as he passed, she felt uncomfortable, but continued to look, she thought for sure there was something inherently familiar about that car.

Edward Gonzalez crossed Broadway going crosstown, opposite the Williamsburg Bridge. He had one more stop to make before he dropped the car off in Queens. Bushwick. To see his snitch and possibly find out more about the woman standing in front of the building.

Gonzalez turned up a side street off of Bushwick Avenue and cruised to a stop in front of the three-story house. Getting out of the car he glanced paranoid up and down the street looking at the same scenario, a couple of kids playing, old men on stoops drinking liquor, cussing, playing Domino's while a couple of women chastised them from the sidewalk. Normal scene. Smiling, he was content. He bounced up the steps to the green and white colored screen door and knocked. A couple of seconds later an older Spanish woman with gray hair and scraggly lines around her eyes answered the door. Ola.

"Como esta usted?"

"Mubein, gracias."

After the formality she pointed to the back door of the house. He took off his hat out of respect and smiled as he scrolled through the foyer to the back door, where he could hear loud sounds from outback. The old floor creaked and groaned as he walked, the house was old, late forties at best, pipes, plumbing, the whole nine. Going past the kitchen he slowed just briefly enough to get a good smell of the subtle aroma that danced throughout the air. Peeping at its source, the oven, he licked at his lips. Peeping over his shoulder he saw the older woman nod her head as she turned into the kitchen saying, "*ropa vieja.*" And in cracking broken English she said to him, "Roast beef, care to join us?"

Gonzalez's stomach grumbled as he smiled politely then said, "We'll see." His stomach continued to voice its opinion as he continued walking until he reached the back door.

Outside there were three men standing around a metal stake dug into the ground reddish clay with about twelve inches or so sticking above ground. Gonzalez scanned the whole yard, a spacious 1,700 square foot enclosure. A wooden split picket fence around in it, still fairly new, put up on his orders, for privacy.

He chuckled as they argued. Evidently, from what he could gather, in between the cussing, broken English and Spanish. It was over a game of horseshoes. On the end where they were standing where two horseshoes wrapped snugly around the stake. Apparently one of them had thrown the latter and it bounced off of it and made the other shoe jump on it, on the stake that is. A one in a million shot, which probably would or couldn't happen again, but when you're paying for something as serious as bragging rights, the odds didn't matter. The word cheating had come up and it was on.

The smaller of the two, a wiry man with more age than Gonzalez could imagine, considering his mind state, was also the owner of the home. His wife was now cooking a roast beef to die for. He argued his point like a seasoned attorney, pleading his case like a pro. Pointing down at the stake, motioning into the other side of the pit, hand movements, gestures, *actually making a point*, Gonzalez thought as he raised an eyebrow. The other between the two, his cousin, who refereed the situation, at least as best he could, could barely hold back his laughter. He wasn't any good in the situation at all. In fact, it only incensed the loud barking that came from across him that boomed all the way to the other yards, and Gonzalez quickly took notice. It was time for him to intervene. He stepped through the door and hollered "Hey. Come on fellas. Too loud!"

The big bellied man with a loud mouth turned towards him and said, "Can you believe this little shit?"

"Come on now, it's not that serious."

"Like hell it ain't. This little shit's trying to weasel out of giving me the game." He turned and waved his hand flagrantly at him. "I don't believe this!"

Gonzalez shook his head trying to distill his own laughter. Then he jerked suddenly, his instincts kicking in. The old woman was right behind him. He didn't even hear her as she walked up. It threw him. "This is all they do. All day along. They'll stop, don't worry," she said, "They eat, drink, play some more, then do the same thing all over until it gets dark and they get tired. Then they sleep like little babies. Crazy."

*Yeah crazy.* Gonzalez mused.

The older man looked up and shouted. "Crazy? No! He's fucking crazy. I'm not giving him shit." He turned towards him with his lips frowned up and said, "We'll play another one."

"Oh, hell no!" The big belly one screamed, and spit bad curses in Spanish as he did. The man who refereed had sat down and lit a cigarette. Gonzalez walked over to the big bellied one and pointed at him towards the back of the yard. The big belly man complied, still talking shit as he did. Gonzalez winced as he noticed the scars on his arm and back when he passed by. Old burns; he'd heard the story. He pulled a couple crates out from a beat down old shed and they sat. Gonzalez kept silent, observing the men as he reached back in his pocket and pulled out a paper bag bottle of whiskey and took a swig and offered it to him. He waved it away. He was all right now, so Gonzalez cleared his throat and said, "Hey, I got some questions for you."

"You always have questions. I must be your answer man, or something."

"Calm down, will ya."

"I am calm. I'm just tired of you asking so many questions. You have enough information to do whatever your people need to do. I think everything."

The man Gonzales was speaking with was his snitch. His eyes. The man who the whole operation was centered around. It was his information that opened the door for the ATF, DEA, and pretty soon to be the FBI, to operate. Right now, though, Gonzalez was the lead man, and he was that dude. After all, it was his snitch. He found him.

He had needed to find the source of the money running in and out of Bushwick, via drugs, prostitution, and now, real estate and properties. A huge operation, run by, as far as he knew, Maria. He found her flunkeys, Cholo, his boys, but he couldn't put his hands-on Maria, the prized trophy.

Yeah, this guy in front of him was the real deal, but he had to deal with him with kid gloves, damn near kiss his fat ass. He was getting tired of it all, but nevertheless, the game had to be played. "Look, Felix. I know you're uncomfortable with me asking all these questions, but-"

"I'm tired of this! I can't go anywhere." He glanced around the yard and spat. "Except this freaking backyard!"

"Yeah. I feel you. But, Felix, do you really want people to know where you are? Especially The Cartel?"

Felix's eyes grew wide at the name. A marked man for sure. The only thing that kept him alive was the fact that everyone thought he had either disappeared, or was dead. "Okay, Okay. What is the question?" he glanced over his shoulder at the old man who cleared the horseshoe pit and said, "We play, we play another one in a few. You cheat this time, I'll kick your ass!" The old man looked over at him and gave him the finger.

Gonzalez reached into his pocket and pulled out a cigarette and lit it then offered him one. They puffed and Felix took a few more totes before Gonzalez spoke. "I saw a strange woman coming out of Maria's building today. She looked familiar, but I couldn't quite make her."

"What she look like? Got a picture?"

"No."

"Then, how the hell am I supposed to know? Come on now."

"Yeah. Long legs. Pretty brown. Long black hair, brown skin. What else? Oooohhh yeah. Real cheeky, Chinese type eyes."

Felix nodded. "Oh yeah. She's fine."

"Then you know."

"If she was coming out of Maria's building, then she's involved with something. Either that, or you played your card well with it, or another. Well enough for her to move about. She's hard to get next to."

"Who is she?"

"God-damn! You just killed her freaking daughter-in-law, shot up her house, and you don't know?"

Gonzalez lowered his head. "I just couldn't quite get a look, Okay. And, who told you about the shootings!"

"You guys are crazy. I know everything about you too. Anyway, the cocolo bastard that put these scars on me. That black fucker Rasheed, his mother...Waseema."

Gonzalez nodded. His old buddy, Giovanni's people. He wondered, why the hell would she be involved directly with Maria, but then he thought out loud, *isn't that Maria's right-hand man's mother?*

"Latif? Right." Felix's eyes narrowed as he took another draw off the cigarette. "You get her. And the rest will buckle, even Maria. She's the rock."

Gonzalez grinned as he took a drink, warming his chest as it made its way down. Now, he remembered where he'd seen her before. Yeah, that wasn't the first time he'd seen her around Harlem. His mind wrapped around several different scenarios. He took another swig and now it dawned on him. *One missing black activist, Muslim leader, now presumed dead, Craig 3X. Used to hang around and do crime back in the day. Find him, and he might be the missing piece to this puzzle. But where?*

"OKAY, SO YOU'RE SAYING that she's got, what, 8 to 10,000,000 set up in a boxcar at the Navy yard?"

"Right up front. And, we have the numbers to it so it won't be difficult to find."

"Ok, so why can't we just walk in and get it?"

"There is a level of security around it."

"More than the norm."

"Yes." She stood up from the table she sat on and walked over to Rasheed. "You have regular security. That's easy. But there's always the around the clock guys that hang out there while any shipment is being made. Now, I noticed that it's heavier when certain shipments are brought in and out. That's when I noticed. That's when it happened, Maria's cargo was in motion. All the crates were marked with the letter C."

"Cartel." Rasheed rubbed his goatee and walked over to the window to look out. They'd come to play in this upcoming event, whether they were ready or not, especially for a job of this magnitude. "Pretty serious stuff, as well as dangerous. Who are we working with again?"

Asia sat back down at the table going over a blueprint of the Navy yard. She found the best possible in and out strategy, so there was no problem there. A serious undertaking. When asked, she didn't mind being asked because she knew who her right hand man was. "Kokomo, of course. Me, you...Ice?"

"We need one more man. A backup. Someone good with a gun."

"I figured that too. So, I called someone."

Rasheed walked over to the table where she was sitting and stood behind her, stroking her hair. "So soon? Is he that good?"

"Yeah. I wouldn't have given him an invite if he wasn't." She turned and looked up at him and said, "Besides, you're the one that's going to do the, let's say, interview. "

Rasheed nodded, "Yeah, interview." She gently rubbed his hands and got up from the table, then snuggled in his arms rubbed his back.

Not much shorter than him, she was able to lean her head on his shoulder. "What about us?" She asked.

"What about?"

"When this is over. Do we have a future?"

Rasheed squeezed her, kissing her on her forehead and said to her. "That's something I'm willing to consider, but."

"But?"

"We'd have to leave. This place."

She backed up a little and pushed away from him, frowning up. "Oh, you don't like the projects anymore."

"No, little mama, it's not that. I'm tired of it, for Khadija sake. I want to go where it's safe and comfortable." He glanced at her, "And pretty."

"You figured out a place?"

"Yeah," he said as he walked her over to the window and pointed out. "Way out. Out of this state. Arizona."

"Arizona? Way out there?"

"Way out there."

"Ever been there?"

He nodded his head yes as a grin came across his face. He reminisced. "That's where I went, right after."

"After. Everyone thought you were dead."

He pulled her close. Her lips sparkling from the gloss, a scrumptious wet glow like water in the moonlight. The softness, he wanted to just dive into them. He felt the urge hit him, a lovemaking urge. He glanced towards the room. "What's up?"

"We are expecting someone? Now?"

"They won't be here that soon, will they?" He grabbed her hand and led her towards the room. She was more than willing. She finally had him to herself, but then there was a knock at the door that killed the moment. "You see. There he is."

"Damn!" Rasheed said he let her hand go and stomped towards the door straightening up his pants. Tugging and pulling trying to conceal the hard on he just worked up. She fluttered her long full eyelashes seductively his way. Her full round ass not making it any better, then he opened the door. "Hello."

Standing in front of him was a brown skinned voluptuous woman, sculptured eyebrows, long eyelashes, lip gloss, and long auburn-brown hair that fell to the sides off her shoulders. With a nice handful of tittie, she wore a tight fitting, colorful t-shirt and tight faded denim blue jeans. Her long legs and four-inch pumps only accentuated her heart shaped ass. Rasheed said, *damn* under his breath and turned towards Asia. "It's for you." He moved to the side and peeked out the door, asking. "Excuse me miss, did you see anyone else...downstairs?"

She nodded no and walked over to Asia. "Ok, I'll go downstairs and wait for our friend. I'll be out front." He started to grab his jacket but Asia stopped him. "No need."

"What?"

"No need."

He stared over at the woman, then chuckled. "My bad, baby, I thought you said it was a dude." He walked over to her and put out his hand. "My apologies."

"No need."

Rasheed frowned his eyes. "What did you say?"

"No need...to apologize."

He looked at Asia dumbfounded and she said, "This is...him."

Rasheed turned around and threw up his hands. "Oh, hell no you've got to be kidding me, right?"

The woman, now identified as a man, spoke up. "No, she's not. Now, why don't we go over the job. Really, don't want to waste your time...or mine."

"Hell, you can go now. I don't need no he-she type dude. I need a real man for this job."

He put down the Coach bag he was carrying and stepped into the center of the living room and into a fighting stance. "I could put you down in three moves...with heels."

"Man, back up! Number one. I'm not even gonna get caught up in no damn wrestling match with no faggot. And two, I'd just blow your brains out. Don't even try me, you're barking up the wrong tree!"

Asia moved in between them and looked at him. "He's right. We don't need this drama."

"Well then, I better go." He went to pick up his bag and Asia stopped him. "You're the right person for the job." She turned towards Rasheed and said, "You need to at least hear him out."

"No, I'm not dealing with that."

"No, you're not. You need a good man that can use a gun, you said that. Not someone you need to have sex with. So, his sexual preference has nothing to do with you, you understand? If I say he's good for the job, then he is."

"Why did you tell me?"

"So, you know off the jump what you're dealing with. And besides. What difference should it make? I believe it can work to our advantage."

Rasheed stared at her for a while, then turned his head towards him and pointed towards the couch. "Have a seat."

"By the way. My name is Cookie."

Rasheed chuckled and sat down. "Well then...Cookie. Have a seat, please."

Asia said, "You don't need me, do you?"

Rasheed looked over at Cookie, and said, "No. It's cool."

# CHAPTER NINE

**"I** told you one day you'd be kissing my ass!" The velocity of the slap delivered echoes around the room as the receiver's head was bounced against the wall. "Now, didn't I!" The hand was held high again for the backward momentum, then came down. But, this time, missed. "What the..."

Donna kicked Carlito hard in his nuts as she rolled around on her stomach and sprang to her feet. Dazed from the unexpected carnage of blows inflicted by him, she managed to pull herself together and back up against the wall, hands up, to defend herself. At least as good as she could.

"I see. You want to fight back, huh. Okay. Okay." Carlito put up his hands also and staggered toward her. "I will teach you something, huh." He threw a right jab. Donna ducked, came up and punched him hard in the stomach. "Aw!" He screamed. Bent over, his legs buckled just long enough for her to push him to the side and bolt for the door. She grabbed the doorknob and swung it open. Face swollen and wet from the tears she tried to stay focused, but suddenly she ran straight into a figure standing in front of her. Scared, she froze, then put up her hands in front of her face. It was Shaheeda. "What the hell is going on here?" She shouted as she looked at Carlito trying to straighten himself up in pain with his hands between his legs. Scanning the room, she spotted the knife on the floor he'd used earlier to try and rape Donna. He lured her into the basement under the pretense of needing help bringing up some merchandise, then tried using his ties to Cholo as a way and a means to scare her into taking that ass. But Donna wasn't going for it. Sure, he groped her here and there a few times. She didn't like it, but dealt with it. She figured she'd take the issue to Waseema at a time when things were right. Lately, there had been so much chaos she just never got around to it. Carlito used it as a weakness and continued on until he figured he'd take it to this level knowing full well that her back was already up against the wall dealing with Cholo.

He wouldn't dare play that foolishness with Shaheeda though. Not only would she die before another man put his hands on her without her permission; her brothers, her mother, would raise hell. It came with too many dangers involved and already Chino was a casualty. He damn sure didn't want to be another. So, *Donna*, he thought. But he thought wrong. Donna was not a weak link.

When Shaheeda looked over at him, then at her friend as she stood by her side crying, she decided to let him know he made one hell of a mistake. "Donna. Get behind me. Okay." She stepped forward inside the room and reached into her purse and pulled out a shiny stainless-steel Glock 40. "When I shut this door, go upstairs and call this number." She pulled out her pad, wrote down a number, then peeled off the paper and gave it to her. "Here."

"Shaheeda. No, come with me. He's crazy. He tried to rape me. We can call the police."

"No! I got this."

Donna could see it in the face, her eyes. There was no way she was talking her out of it. "Just do it!"

"Okay. Okay." Donna ran up to the stairs and only looked behind her once and that was when she heard the door slam and Carlito yell. "No. No. Don't do it!"

Waseema had already closed up the store while Donna busied herself with the receipts trying to tie up the loose ends of the day on the cash register, making sure everything appeared normal. "You took the security tapes out? Right?"

"Yeah. Replaced them with the dummies."

"Then, dated them?"

"Damn!" Donna rushed back over to her computer. Cholo will be here before the day was out and by that time Carlito would have come up missing. Tracks would have been covered. Waseema whirled around suddenly when she heard a sound at the back-stairway door. "Shaheeda! Stay down there!" She called out.

"But mom."

"I'll be down there in a minute. Just do what I say!"

"Ok."

She hurried over to the back stairway where she had a green army type duffel bag by the door, then waved to Donna that she was going down. Donna nodded her head back at her, not really paying any attention, still into the security tapes, still a lot to do.

Cholo would do his walk-through and check the security cameras. If not for nothing more than to see how many people came in and out, and made purchases. At least that's what he'd always say, but Donna had an idea that it would be bigger than that today. Today he'd be looking for something more, specifically Carlito's comings and goings. Waseema swung the heavy bag over her shoulder and grabbed the rail steadying herself as she timidly stepped down the stairs. Blood spatter was visible on the wall, partly on the floor leading towards the door. You could tell there had been a struggle.

She eased her way around, carefully not to get any on the bottom of her shoes, or even her clothes. She glanced over at Shaheeda and said, "Stay where you are, so that we don't get any blood tracked all over the place. The less we have to clean up."

Shaheeda was sitting in a chair leaning her shoulder against some file cabinets with her arms tightly crossed in front of her chest. Crying, blood stains on her hands. Sad, puppy dog like tears ran down her face. She looked over at her and said, "Mom. I'm sorry. It just got. I couldn't control it."

Waseema knelt down in front of her, kissed her forehead gently and said, "Don't worry baby, will take care of it."

"Like before."

"Yes baby. Like before."

The before she referred to was the night they, her and her mother, disposed of Craig 3X, and his body. The night Shaheeda had deliberately lured him into an abandoned building on the outskirts of Harlem's Riverdale section on the promise of giving herself to him. Her love. The night Waseema grabbed her gun and shot him. The night she helped to hack up his body into pieces, and enjoyed it. And, the night her and her mother, dumped him into the Harlem River. The night where she'd never be the same again.

Donna eased her way down the stairway and peeped inside the door, watching her step over the blood and gore that was once Carlito's body. She thought of the noise, and the hollering she'd heard from behind the door then turned and threw up.

For Donna, it was reminiscent of the night she peeped her head into another ghastly scene. A sight that she couldn't get off her mind; the nightmares that came with it. It was unexpected for her as her eyes watched as Craig 3X desperately pleaded for his life. She regretted being the one who followed him and Shaheeda uptown that night. She also would regret witnessing what would forever be known by all those involved, as the secret.

Waseema didn't have a clue then about the events with Donna. But when she glanced over at her, her own eyes gave her up. Somehow Waseema knew. It seemed to all come together. And if all things she put together in her mind were true and things pointed towards her, she knew that there was a witness, Donna. Waseema definitely would have to do something about it. Protect the family at all costs, protect her daughter, her baby, at all costs, by any means necessary. Someday, but hopefully, not soon if any, for Donna's sake. She needed her. She had to ask Donna to help slice up Carlito's body.

Shaheeda was getting hard to control. She was getting worse, and Waseema didn't know how long she'd be able to help clean up her mess.

"YOU KIDDING ME OR WHAT?"

"No. Dead serious."

Ice stared at Rasheed like he was crazy, but the only thing, he knew he wasn't. "Okay...but. Why are we dealing with this bullshit anyway? We can get someone else for this job. Hello, it's nothing to find a real man for this. I know mercenaries that would do this for chump change. Maybe not chump change, but you know what I'm saying. Why get caught up in this drama?"

Rasheed thought about what Ice just said, licked his lips and glanced over at Asia, took a deep breath, then said, "Well, Asia recommended him. And, to tell you the truth Ice. That's good enough for me."

Ice cocked his head to the side, glanced at Asia, then at Rasheed. He threw up his hands, then sighed. "All right, but know this much. Any bullshit and it's on your head Rasheed. Your head!" he glanced back over at Asia and Cookie. "Ain't got no problem with the gay thing, really don't, but understand, this is some serious shit about to go down. If these people get a hold of any one of us. No telling what they'll do. So, just know what you're getting into, that's all. They won't give a damn if you're straight, male, female. Hell, no telling what they may do if you're gay."

Asia stepped up to him and snapped. "You're right. But he's good to go, trust me."

"Hell, looks like I ain't got much of a choice."

"So, it's on. Asia, where is Kokomo? Rasheed asked.

"He'll be here in a little while. Remember Rasheed, he caught hell from his landlord behind that Chino shit. Cops are still messing with him. Might be needing a place to stay, soon."

Rasheed peered out the window staring towards Decatur Street, where it all went down. "Yeah. I got him."

Cookie sat down saying, "Damn, then it was you."

"Yeah, it was me. What do you know about it?" Rasheed barked.

"Hey, don't get crazy with me, but I'll say this much."

"What!"

"Them damn Mexicans want your ass, bad."

"Don't I know it." He looked over at Ice. "Story of my life."

"Well." Cookie crossed his legs. "Pretty much the same ones we're about to hit. Me personally, I really ain't got no love for none of them, but then, that's me."

"Right, right." Ice pondered, "Tell me, Cookie, right?"

"Right."

"What do you know?"

Cookie smiled then turned towards Asia and winked. "Well I know this much, and this is why Asia wanted me in." He reached in his bag digging, Ice assumed it was for a cigarette and reached into his pocket for a lighter. Cookie looked at it and said, "No thank you I don't smoke." He continued to dig until he pulled out a pad, then opened it and started looking at some things that were scribbled down. "Let me give you some background first."

Rasheed stepped away from the window and sat next to Asia. "I'm. No, we're listening."

"I wasn't always...like this. I was a dude. Played ball and all that. Granted, I might have had some tendencies, but that was all it was, tendencies, until." He started to breathe hard, like he was ready to hyperventilate.

"Look, Cookie, you don't have to." Asia said as she put her hand out towards him.

"No. I got to. These guys are putting their lives on the line. They should know." He continued. "I used to run newspapers back in the day. Had a paper route and everything. But, during the early crack years, hell, they just made me an easy victim, riding around with a pocket full on a bicycle. Anyway, I was finished for the morning doing a Sunday newspaper route. Made my money and was about to take it in. I had to go down Myrtle Avenue. That's when it was straight Latino. Puerto Rican's, Colombian's, everything."

"I remember it well." Ice said,

"There was this gang. Crazy Angels I believe they went by. Half ass organized, pushing secondhand dope down Broadway towards Bushwick Projects."

"Had to. We stuck up most of the big boy spots up here, right Ice."

"Damn right. Back in the day with Derek."

"The Mexican that ran things." Cookie continued. "His name was Cholo. You know him I'm sure. Anyway, he was a two-bit thug. He had his boys rob me. Hell, I didn't give a damn about the cash, no biggie, I'd make more, but..." Cookie sneered. "He had...tendencies, as well. He had them drag my ass in a basement that morning, then made them leave. Hell, I figured he'd just beat me, put this extortion game down, but he didn't. He didn't."

"What?" Ice asked.

"He raped me."

"That's so messed up."

"No, that wasn't what was really messed up. What was so messed up was...I liked it."

"Oh snap," Rasheed gasped.

"He became my lover. Of course, it was undercover though." He frowned. "I really wanted to come out. Like I am now." He glanced over at Rasheed, impressed with the fact that he didn't know he was actually a man earlier. "He'd give me money to get the treatments and everything. He liked me, as long as we were somewhere no one knew. He'd come to me when he wanted to be satisfied."

"Damn, so... you're Cholo's lover. Cholo's a faggot."

"I'm not no fagot. I resent that."

"Then what, then?"

"I'm gay. A tranny if anything. I don't have the full package, yet."

"You mean, your dick ain't cutoff, then."

Asia stood up. "That's enough. You ain't gotta say anything else to them!"

"No! Don't you see, I've got to. That man messed me over. He promised to love me! Promised. But they found out about me. His people. He beat me. Then, he had his drunk ass buddies rape me. Made me do...things. Laughed at me when they were finished. Kicked me out in the street. I swore I'd..."

"Right, right. You're justified, but where did you learn how to use a gun and all? Learn how to fight? I'm only assuming that you actually know how." Ice said as he also stood up.

"Asia?"

"Hold up. Asia, you taught her-him?"

"She's my student and...informant."

"What...informant?"

"She was close enough to him to find out about the stashes. The Navy Yard deliveries. Everything. I mean, she did her thing."

"Yeah. I see. A person will tell you anything when your head is between his legs."

"I wouldn't know. So, that little book has what?" Rasheed asked.

"Dates, names, places."

"Ok, but how is this helping us on this job?'

"Because. We don't have to just sneak in. We almost literally walk in. Hell, she knows everyone that Cholo knows." Asia said.

"But, doesn't Cholo know that, too?"

"He does, but he won't tell his partners."

"Why not?"

"Too ashamed. A Mexican thing. They'd kill him. I stayed low enough so that he thinks I'm no threat to him. I'm just a cross dressing punk."

"And...to us?"

"A cross dressing...threat."

Ice stood up and paced the floor for a minute then looked around at everyone, and punched his fists into his hand. He walked over to his backpack, reached in and pulled out some blueprints. Looked over at Cookie and asked, "Okay. So, what you got?"

After a good hour or so of brainstorming back and forth. Scrutinizing every miniscule detail, and going over every item to its last, at least known items, all detailed. They finally came up with a plan. "So, if we attack this entrance, then, according to the schematics I got, we should be successful. In an out."

"Ok, Ice, I see that, but."

"But, what?"

"Suppose that entrance gets locked down. In other words, suppose they fuck around and get there before we get there?" Rasheed asked.

Ice pointed over towards Cookie. "That's where he comes into play."

"Cookie? I don't see it." Ice Rasheed said as he hunched his shoulders. "Now, don't get me wrong. The plan was to utilize Cookie to get in, Okay, I see that. But, getting out will require firepower on a serious level."

"You're right. Now, Cookie." Ice looked his way, and with steely grey eyes and direct emphasis asked, "Are you ready for that?"

Abruptly, Asia got up and brushed past everyone, disappeared into the backroom, came back out with a case and tossed it on the table. She looked over at Cookie and said, "30 seconds. Tops."

He quickly grabbed the case and opened it. Nimbly he slotted together the top slide into the shiny metallic steel .40 cal. slab and inserted the spring firing mechanism with the barrel; in that order. Rasheed checked his watch at eighteen seconds and sneered, "Still don't work without the clip."

By the time he'd gotten the last word out of his mouth, Cookie had already notched the silencer into the barrel. Asia tossed him the clip, and with one fluid motion chambered a round and aimed at an image on the refrigerator about thirty feet away. The image was a photograph of Cholo. He kept his eyes dead on as he hissed out the side of his mouth. "Thirty seconds...tops."

Rasheed checked his watch, glanced over at Asia as she said, "Tops."

"On point."

With respect Ice said, "It's there but Cookie, with no disrespect; I hope you are ready to pull the trigger when it comes down to it. You understand?"

"I'm ready." He answered. Ice nodded discreetly. He was, if Cookie wasn't.

There was a knock at the door and Asia went to answer it. Ice rolled up the plans and Rasheed put the block on Cookie long enough for him to put away the weapon. She opened the door. It was Kokomo.

They exchanged greetings and filled him in on what was going down. Rasheed pulled him to the side afterward and said to him. "Look man. I know you're catching hell on my account. I want to set you up with a crib up in Harlem. Moms property. Real nice."

"That's cool. Appreciate it, but I'd rather stay down here in Brooklyn."

"Well, least let me help you find something down here then. I got you."

"Ok, fair business. I never got to tell you, but I'm sorry about Mya. She was alright. Liked her. How is the little girl?"

"Khadija. She's cool. As long as she can be in the situation. She's hanging out today. Going shopping with my moms."

"But I was just with your moms and them."

"When?"

"Right before I got here, that's why I'm late."

Ice turned towards them. "Sorry to ear-hustle, but you said you saw Waseema."

"Yeah. Help her load a couple of heavy ass bags in the trunk. Hell. Looked like they've been working pretty hard. That dude Cholo was there, too. He looked pissed. They argued back and forth for a little."

"Argued?"

"Figured, because she wouldn't open the store back up, or something. But yo man, it really wasn't none of my business. I just wanted to help out your mom, that's it. After that, I dipped."

"I understand."

"But, one more question. Did you see Carlito? You know him, right?"

"Yeah, the tall, lanky Spanish dude."

"That's him."

"No, ain't see him. But I'll tell you what was strange. It looked like there was a fight."

"Why do you say that?" Rasheed asked.

"Donna and Shaheeda were dirty as hell, scratched up. And to be real with it, that girl Donna looked like she had a couple of bruises on her face. I mean, she had makeup on, heavy, but you can still see through all of that."

Ice put on his jacket, grabbed his bag and turned to Asia and Rasheed. "Look, I gotta go see what's up. We'll get back and have another meeting around... let's say next week." They all nodded as he grabbed a doorknob and glanced over at Cookie. "I need to do some one on one with you. You look good with the weapon, but I need you sharper, you understand?"

"I understand."

"Alright, see y'all. Rasheed...I'll call you."

Asia locked the door behind him and turned towards Kokomo. "You hungry?"

"Damn right." He looked over at Cookie, then Rasheed and said to her, "Yo, everything alright?"

"It's cool. "

"How come that dude Ice is so hard on me Asia? Damn, it's not like I need to be on some old military shit or something." Cookie whined.

"No. You do." Rasheed said as he turned towards them. "You see people can get killed. Real quick. And, the one thing about that even when you do all the planning, when people get killed, you can never bring them back. You can always train. You know why?"

Cookie looked down at the floor, sheepishly, and asked, "Why?" Rasheed walked over towards Asia and kissed her on the forehead then walked over to the door before saying under his breath. "So, you won't end up like my brother, Mustapha, or my friend...Derek."

Ice pulled into traffic towards the store. When he got there, it was closed. He looked around and up the street and caught the tail end of Shaheeda's BMW as it turned up Bushwick Avenue. He followed. As he made the turn, he spotted another car right on their tail. Pulling up closer to get a good look, he could see three men. Two in the front, one in the back. The one in the back turned his head ever so lightly and he recognized him. Cholo.

He pulled back another car length so they wouldn't notice him following closely. He tailed them all the way to Atlantic Avenue and racked his brain trying to figure out where they were heading. He couldn't think of anyone Waseema knew in the vicinity. And, it got even crazier when he thought about Red Hook, because that's damn sure where they were heading. But, for the life of him he couldn't figure out. Why the canal? The docks?

Waseema drove the car down the dark and gritty streets past Red Hook Projects. Past old duplicated buildings, and ruined abandoned storefronts attached to the one-time thriving docks. Donna fidgeted around in the back seat sobbing quietly while Shaheeda sat up front with her mother, motionless, staring out blindly into the waters as the sun set off into the all to distant West. She spotted an opening behind a warehouse off to the side, near the abandoned desolate piers. Waseema stopped and put the car in park for a second, scanning the area. If anyone was in there; Mob, dope dealings, or otherwise, they would have been on their way out by now looking to see who she was. An easy vic or the police. Waseema was neither.

She glanced over at Shaheeda. "This is it." Then looked back into the rearview mirror at Donna. "It is what it is. What you're about to see, cannot go nowhere. You hear me."

"Y-y-y-es ma'am."

"It's real simple, and I'm not gonna pull any punches. If you tell anyone about this. I'll kill you myself."

"I-I-I know. I never said anything about before..."

It was too late. She couldn't take it back, she owned it now. She blurted out what Waseema had long suspected. "So, you did know about...Craig 3X."

Shaheeda snapped out of her spell and measurably turned looking into her direction. "You knew. All these years?" The words came out with venom.

Donna's body started trembling as sweat drenched her face. She was scared as all hell. "I did. But I never said anything. To anyone. I swear."

Waseema turned around and said, "Get out of the car."

"Please. Don't kill me."

"Get out the goddamn car!"

Donna did as she was told. Waseema got out, walked towards the trunk and opened it. "We're just gonna get rid of this...trash. The canal will take it all the way out to the ocean. Eventually, it'll disappear. The only people that will ever know what happened to Carlito, will be me, Shaheeda, and now...you." The trunk opened and Waseema pulled out the first of three bags, and it burst on the ground. Donna flinched. "It's just blood. Let's hurry before we can't see anything, or worse all the bags bust. Come on!"

Shaheeda stepped in front of her, shoving her to the side and pointed to the last one spitting in her face, "I can't believe you held out!" Donna was reluctant. "Go on!" Shaheeda barked. Hesitantly, she did as she was told. Picking up the bag she was amazed at just how light it actually was, but feeling the bones scrape against her legs made her grimace. She whimpered, still following close behind Waseema as she got to the edge of the pier and she said, "Ok, this is it. Remember the plan we made."

They nodded their heads, yes.

"No one will ever know."

"No one will ever know. What?"

Waseema turned around to see Cholo and his men staring them down with guns drawn on them.

"No one will ever know what, Waseema? What's in the bags!"

She swept the area to see if there was anyone else there. No one. She had her .380 in her jacket that she bought just in case. She thought she might have had to use it on Donna, but, even if she reached for it, they still had the drop. She needed time, and a distraction.

Donna dropped the bag and her jaw dropped as well. She looked over at Cholo and started babbling. "I swear. I didn't do anything! She made me come here!" She screamed as she pointed at Waseema.

*Damn, I should have killed her in the car*, Waseema thought. But still she needed to get Shaheeda out the way. Glancing behind her the water was green, dirty and murky. One of the one things she knew from Bushwick Projects was that Shaheeda could swim. She might have enough of a chance if she pushed her into the water and dived in right behind her. It sounded so good, but the bags, the evidence, damn.

She'd have to go out firing. No other way. Donna's begging ass would have to be her diversion.

Cholo kept his eyes peeled on Donna as she crept towards him crying with her hands out. "What's in the bags!" He spit as he raised his gun towards her.

"Carlito! She killed him!"

"Who! Which one!"

She stared into the face of her friend. Her childhood friend. A friend who would have given her life for her if she had to, but today, right now, she wasn't going to give hers. "Shaheeda!"

That hurt. Shaheeda dropped her bag too, turned towards Donna, and was ready to go at her. Fuck the guns. Choke her black ass out at best. But Waseema wasn't having none of it today. She pulled her back. "First, your fuckin' brother kills my cousin, then you kill Carlito. Was I next?"

Waseema spat back. "No, the question is, were we next? I know you and that bitch Maria were trying to bring me down for the longest!"

"HEY, JUST BE PATIENT little girl. She'll be back in a few." Latif said as he winked his eye at Khadija. He smiled, but deep down he was worried. It was unusual for his mother to leave so abruptly, much less in the middle of the day. She said it was important when she called, and he could hear how pressed she was by her voice.

No questions asked he came over to babysit Khadija until she got back. She said she'd only be gone a good hour or two, but now it was half a day. He tried calling the store and it was closed. He tried to call Shaheeda and she wasn't home. He paged them both and received no calls back. He was worried. If he didn't get a call within about 15 minutes or so, he'd call Ice next. Maybe, that's who she's with anyway. Maybe, she got stuck in traffic. Too many maybes.

"You want to get some McDonald's?" he asked Khadija. She jumped up and was at the door in seconds. "Yeah, I'm hungry too." He put on her coat and took out his beeper and checked. No calls. If he didn't hear from her at McDonald's he'd have no choice but to call Ice. And probably Rasheed.

He put on his jacket and was just out the door when his pager went off. He snatched it out his pocket and looked at the number. Strange, it was Maria. He hesitated at first, then stepped back inside and called her. "What's up?"

"Hey, when you get free, I need you to come by."

Sensing the strain in her voice he asked, "Sure. Something wrong?"

"I don't know, yet. We just need to be prepared."

"Prepared? Prepared, for what?"

"Anything. I just got a call from a good source. I heard things about that Cholo. Bad things."

"Yeah, bad dude. Been told you to stop messing with him."

"Is Waseema there?"

"No. She stepped out. Went to Brooklyn. Something important came up. I'm babysitting Khadija until she comes back. Hey look, I gotta go. When she gets back, I'll call you. Ok."

"Ok. Latif?"

"Yeah."

"Be careful."

"Yeah, sure." He hung up the phone and stared at it strangely. Crazy day. He looked over at his niece and said, "Let's go get some McDonald's."

He locked the door behind him, and they walked hand in hand up the street to his car. He forgot and left his beeper. Sure, as hell, it started beeping like crazy the minute he pulled off in his car.

# CHAPTER TEN

"No, it was all about you! I know!" Cholo pointing his gun to her head.

"What the hell are you talking about?" She sidestepped trying to avoid his aim. She walked closer to him. His hand trembled and she didn't want to be the recipient of a sticky trigger. "What?"

"Oh, don't play dumb, I know you told your son. That black bastard." He shook the thug's arm who stood next to him. "What's his name again?"

"Rasheed, boss."

"Yeah, that's it. Rasheed. I know you told him to come after me."

"Why the hell would I do that?"

"Because, you knew I was skimming loose ends from Maria over at the Navy Yard, a couple of 100 grand here, a couple of 100 grand there. You also were the only one who would know we were moving product in and off of the docks. The drugs. I didn't know that, but you knew it, so you sent Rasheed to knock off Chino. Make him tell where the next delivery would be." A sickly distorted grin started to grow across his face as he continued his rant, "That's why we kept getting robbed. Hit us there, hit us here. All of them around the same time of our shipments. Too quick! At first, I couldn't quite figure it out, but now I see it." Waseema looked at him like he was crazy. Shaheeda stared at Donna, remembering she'd heard something like that she'd said before. She turned towards her mother. "What's he talking about mom?"

"Shut up! The both of you!" Cholo shouted. "You think I'm some kind of fool!"

Waseema put up her hands, trying to reason with him, but it seemed useless. He wasn't trying to hear anything, but she tried anyway. "Look, just be cool. We really, I really don't know what the hell you're talking about. First off, I don't have a damn thing to do with Maria, and what she does. You need to be dealing with her on that level. Matter of fact. I thought you did. But I will tell you this. If I were you, I'd replace the money. And, the dope. I really don't think either belongs to Maria. I know that much about her."

Cholo looked over at Donna. "You. Tell them! Tell her what you told me!"

She looked over at Waseema and took a deep breath, sighed, then cut her gaze downward, and said under her breath. "It was a lie."

"Speak up!" Cholo shouted

"Damn it! It was all a lie!"

"A lie!" Cholo lowered his gun and walked toward Donna. "You lie? Lie, about what?"

"The whole thing. I just made it up."

"Why!" He raised his clenched hand high and when it came down it found its mark. Donna dropped in her tracks to the ground. He reached down and picked her up by the neck. "You freaking lie. Why! You bitch!"

"Yeah. Why?" Waseema asked.

Donna looked over at her and grinned, a grin more repulsive than Satan himself. The origins of it, deranged and all of them sinister at best. "Because, I hated you. I did!" Her eyes zeroed in on Shaheeda. "You think you're so high and mighty. Every time I needed something, I had to humble myself to you, and your daughter like a straight junkie, a fuck up! Hell, Waseema, you didn't even have the decency to offer me half the business. After all I've been through with your family! It was all my idea! Laundering money, that's all it ever really was. So, yeah, I lied! And, it would have worked out well too, if it wasn't for that greedy ass Carlito!" She got to her feet and kicked the bag. "I'm glad he's dead! And, thank you Shaheeda. That little act I put on, yeah, I knew you'd fall for it. With your sick ass. So, thanks, but I hope you both are next!" She snarled at them before backing up towards Cholo and his men. "Cholo, I swear it wasn't all a lie. I'm telling you, kill them before they run to the goddamn Police. Or worse yet, Maria!"

Cholo glanced at Guillermo, his number one man. He knew what it was, someone was going to die. He smiled like he really enjoyed his work and raised his gun towards Waseema and aimed. She reached over, grasped Shaheeda's hand, looked over at Donna and hissed. "See you in hell, bitch."

"Well, let me know what it looks like when you get there." Donna shot back.

She said a prayer. She knew it had been awhile since she'd prayed. It'd been even longer since she'd been on her deen too, the straight way. Supposedly, her way of life, Islam. Maybe, this was her punishment for going off the path. She could only hope that Allah would have mercy on her soul. As she looked at Shaheeda, her daughter, she snapped. "Just make it quick!"

Ice pulled up in time to hear what Cholo was babbling about and listened to Donna. If what Cholo said was half ass true, Ice knew for certain that the spot they were about to hit was definitely a sure thing. Money. A big stash of it. Damn, all that money coming in off the ships from God knows where. Eventually, Cholo would do some investigating on his own and Asia and them might come into his sights. Eventually, he'd have to be stopped.

But, now, this wasn't the time to reflect. That was for later. Right now, there was a gun held to his woman's head, and he had to take a shot. He was working with a spike tactical custom AR-15 with a 13-inch rail, Magpul milled, special series. The rifle of snipers worldwide, thanks to the United States Army. His aim wouldn't stray if he was blind. He was about to fire, then something else happened.

Guillermo turn and pointed the gun to Cholo's head. Cholo looked at him and his eyes got as wide as golf balls and screamed. "What the hell are you doing, Guillermo?"

Guillermo said, "You don't just steal from Maria. You steal from us."

"Us?"

"Yes. The Cartel. They send you greetings." He pumped two holes into Cholo's head. He was dead before he even hit the ground. Guillermo leaned over him and then turned towards Waseema. Her and Shaheeda both flinched, and closed their eyes. "I have no beef with you. You can go."

Waseema was shocked, but Shaheeda pulled her out of it. "Let's get out of here!"

"One more thing." They froze in their tracks. "Throw those bags into the water. Please."

They did and hastened towards the car. Guillermo looked over at Donna and said, "You better go with them. I don't want you."

Donna looked over at the car as they got in. It cranked up, and they started to pull off. She was downcast, despondent, and dejected, only for a minute. The brake lights came on and the rear passenger door opened up. She ran for it and jumped in. The first thing she did was babble on and on, copping deuces. "Miss Waseema. Shaheeda, I'm sorry, I didn't know what I was saying. I don't know what got into me. Please. Forgive me." Waseema turned the rearview mirror aside from her sight, not wanting any dealings with her, ever. If it wasn't for Shaheeda she would have shot her a long time ago. Waseema reached for her gun but couldn't find it. She figured she might have left it back at the pier, and she definitely didn't need any evidence lingering. Might as well stop, pull over and look for it. Slowing down she pulled into a cut off to the side. It was then, she saw Ice. He nodded and she nodded back. He showed her his rifle and smiled. All that time, he had her back. She put up her hand and waved him away from the car.

Ice just cranked up, turned, then sped off. He was there for her, the rest was none of his business. He was sure they'd explain everything to him later, especially that bullshit about Cholo.

She was alright, and it wouldn't be good for Guillermo to know that he was there anyway. Besides, she was going to have a stern talk with Donna, and she didn't want him to see what was about to happen. *Bap! Bap! Bap!* It was too late. Shaheeda had already turned and unloaded three shots to Donna's brain from the .380 she'd stashed.

Guillermo was still by the pier when Waseema backed up the car. Him and the other thug, most likely another Cartel operative, tossed Cholo's body into the water. He already knew what it was. He said, "I would have done the same thing." He walked past her car to his. "She never would have made it to the car. Good luck. Miss. Waseema. Maybe, I see you around."

Shaheeda drug Donna's body towards the edge of the pier, and Waseema looked over at Guillermo and said, "I hear you, but I hope not."

"Me too, for your sake." He got into the car and sped off. They tossed Donna's body into the water and watched as she bubbled down to the bottom. Shaheeda shed a tear and clutched onto her mother and said, "I thought she was my friend, mom."

"She was, baby. She just didn't know it."

LATIF SAT IN AN OLD colonial, brown, calfskin leather arm chair. Slouched with his legs crossed and hands clasped across his lap watching Khadija as she slept peacefully. On his right a night table built into a glass frame where he held his pager at one point, vibrated like crazy on the glistening surface. Playing a tune that shook at his senses. Crazy, but it only dawned on him to turn it off when he thought it made crack the delicate crystal. Checking it he found that all the numbers on it belonged to Maria, prompting him to call back. He was tired of her paranoid rhetorical bullshit. He'd get there only when Waseema got home, that was all there was to it.

Dirt was starting to sprout underneath his fingernails. The brothels that he ran for Maria were starting to get muscled in on from gangs coming in from Russia. That was a major problem. The tenants he managed were being threatened with gentrification by developers looking to make a quick buck. Harlem was on the verge of change. The old way of doing business was getting old. Latif figured with his smarts, he could get in on the ground floor of the pursuits and march straight into the next century with a focus. A much better plan for his community, and him.

Maria stood in his way, or so he thought. Why was he obligated to her anyway? This was the question that arose over and over again; tossed around in his brain like cleaning dirty laundry in a linen factory. She spoke empathically about legitimizing money that had been grimy for years. But, how could she? He didn't see it.

Using his political clout, and business savvy, he could help out his own family's holdings and properties. Make money doing it too and leave Maria alone. Latif just couldn't vibe with his mom's though. He couldn't for the life of him, figure out why either. Yeah, questions were popping up and he needed answers to be able to move forward one way or another. It was crazy, too many things were going on with his mom that he needed to know about. Why wasn't she telling him everything anyway? She was holding out. Of course, she didn't trust Maria, he didn't blame her for that, but why not him? He was loyal and he'd proven that. There had to be something more to it. His thoughts were interrupted by the fumbling of keys at the door.

Checking his watch, it was well into the late evening, about ten or so. She was supposed to have made a quick run. *Yeah right*, he thought. The door opened and so did his mouth. "Mom! Where the hell have you been!"

Fatigue in the face and hair tossed all over, she glanced over at him as she came into the foyer. Bags underneath her eyes, and for just a tiny inkling of a second, she looked her age. It was late and she knew where he was going. She put up her hand instead. "Not now Latif, not now."

He jumped up. "What do you mean, not now! You owe me an explanation. You said you were just going to make a quick run. Ok, I can dig that, but all day? You don't think I had something to do?"

"Damn it, Latif. She's your niece! Was it really a bother to look after her? Hell, I did it all the time. For you, your brothers. Something important came up. That's it! I'm your mother, I'm not married to you, or your father, for that matter." She stopped herself, sighed and walked off. "Never mind..."

"Hold up. What do you mean by that? Not married to my father. What was that about?"

Shaheeda came through the door right behind her and slammed it. She too was all weary looking in the face. Walking into the light, he saw that her silk blouse had spots of blood all over and her pants were stained at the knees and her hands were dirty. She gave him the look that told him she didn't want to be bothered either and to go on about his business. He did. He continued the rant directed toward his mother. "What the hell happened? Where the hell did y'all go?" He caught up with her in her bedroom, walked up behind her and grabbed her by the arm. "What the hell is going on? Tell me, now!" Waseema snatched away it and snapped. "You ain't my daddy!"

"I'm your son! And, you owe me an explanation!"

The look in his eyes, the pain, she was still his mother and he was still her baby. Understanding his woe, she let up, finally. She did owe him an explanation. "You're right Latif, I do, but please, just let me get right, take a shower, at least. Please." Waseema reached for him and tried hugging him, she needed one bad, but he pushed her hands away and stepped off sulking. "Latif...I'm sorry," she said under her breath as he slammed the door shut behind him. "I don't mean to hurt you."

Grabbing his keys and beeper out of the living room, he stepped through the archway of the door and called upstairs. "Mom. I'm out. Khadija's down here sleeping on the sofa. I'll call later." He turned to go out and ran straight into Shaheeda. "What the hell..."

"Latif. If you run into that bitch Maria, tell her, she's next," she said as she ran her hands over the blood on her blouse.

"What the hell are you talking about? What happened to y'all?"

"You're on the wrong side, little brother. Trust me." She snarled then walked off.

Waseema walked in the door, as he mulled over what she just told him. "I'm sorry about what I said baby. I'll explain everything later I promise." She picked up Khadija then looked at him. "Thank you, but just please. Keep all this to yourself."

"You think I'm running off to tell Maria something? This is my family." He stumped off towards the door. Least...I thought." He slammed it behind him.

Waseema watched through the window as he walked up the block to his car and got in. She knew he had to know everything but she couldn't tell him. Right now, she just wanted to get Khadija off to bed and call Ice. She needed him for some good loving.

Latif drove past the house and watched as his mother closed the blinds. *This is bull crap*, he started thinking. Maria kept blowing up his pager talking about something that was about to go down. Crazy. But it all had to stop now he was going insane trying to figure this shit out. His mother, Shaheeda, what happened to them? This has something to do with him, he bet. He knew it. Him. Or his old man.

MARIA PACED THE FLOOR in her office, waiting on Latif to show up. Worried, her sources had just informed her that Cholo was dead. Someone had killed him. They didn't know who or where, just that he would no longer be a part of her team. She didn't really care about Cholo, hell she couldn't stand him. He was a headache at best. She was worried more about who killed him. Whoever it was, was clever enough to get rid of the body and any witnesses, if there were any. And smart enough to lure him away from his people in the first place. It was an inside job. It had to be.

So, now she needed to speed up the process to this genius plan she had brewing. Let Edward know more than she really wanted him to. Instead of dragging it along, milk it for what it was worth. Once you put him in on everything, it was going to tilt the scales his way dramatically. Well she mused, it was what it was, time to move on. Maria had done as much as she could do in New York anyway, especially Brooklyn.

She knew one thing for sure though, it had something to do with the Cartel. They were the only ones that could pull off a hit like that. She figured out their money laundering and drug shipping routes coming out of Mexico and the money coming through the Navy yard. Hopefully they didn't know that, but suppose he told them about it? Damn she had to find out, cover her ass. The beeping on the intercom from the lobby caught Maria's attention. The security guard downstairs was letting Latif upstairs on the private elevator.

Latif stretched his lean, slender, six-foot four, 195-pound frame up against the back of the elevator. A ballplayer. That's what it was. His one-time dream, pro basketball. It was in him, the topic through his entire life. A Riverside Church AAU basketball team standout. Georgetown University expressed interest, but in light of what happened in Brooklyn with his family and his grandmother's death he chose to stay and play ball in New York at Saint John's University. He attended. He excelled. He played one hell of a game.

Pro teams wanted Latif. He was the Harlem success story. Local boy went good, but there's always a but. He ended up hurting his knee playing in a game, eventually ending his dream. Granted, he could have had the surgeries needed and still played, but he knew he'd never reach the pinnacle of his game. He'd never reach All Star status. He opted out while he was still a winner with another dream. A degree in political science and economics. It was a smart move, real smart.

The reason he dealt with Maria was mostly because his grandmother Juanita had put him on to balancing books. Eventually, he began to manage all of Maria's property and her dividends grew to a point where he handled her personal accounts also. Maria had included the accumulated shares from her husband Felix's percentage of the dope game in Brooklyn. Latif had advised her to let it go, but the money was too great and she was much too greedy. After Felix disappeared, she took it upon herself to use the capital from her father and Latif's grandparents' trusts to scheme and buy up more property in Bushwick.

There was however prime property that she wanted, instead of the broken-down walk-ups she possessed. Property she couldn't touch. Latif checked out those properties. Large depots; huge buildings that incorporated volumes of encased raw material and commodities exclusively. All privately owned buildings. All off limits and converted low end real estate worth millions. Maria wanted in. Drugs had lost their flavor and appeal in Bushwick and Bed-Stuy. The economy was starting to grow in other directions. The future was in big businesses, real estate. Real commerce. Move the junkies out. Move rich white folk from middle America in. Money-money-money. But she needed a front and Latif had it all figured out.

Maria's father, Consuelo had owned a company with a silent partner in midtown Manhattan back in the day. A partnership that was obviously to Latif, created as a front. He dove into it and found out that she'd found the paperwork for ownership rights while rummaging through Felix's belongings. 493 West 27$^{th}$ street, right off Eight Avenue. Moors Science Institute was the name. What pricked at his inquisitiveness was simple. Why the hell would a half-crazed, illiterate, Colombian illegal, drug lord want with a publishing company? That was the way in. That was the way he used to legitimize his affairs. A straw company. It would be Maria's ticket also. But, as always there's a but; the silent partner just happened to be the Cartel.

Latif remembered crying himself to sleep, wanting so bad to be with his brothers and sister but Juanita wouldn't let him in. His grandmother told him to be patient, how one day he was going to own Bushwick. He wasn't into that, and it hurt him to the core. It caused a rift between Latif, his siblings and his mother. But to Juanita, he was much too valuable a commodity to get caught up with all the foolishness that was going on in Brooklyn. He just didn't realize it then. He didn't realize now either.

The elevator door opened and the double glass, crystal glass doors stared back at him in the face. Reaching for his ID card he unlocked them by swiping the security slide. The door slid open smoothly and he walked through to knock on her office door.

"Come in...Latif." She was waiting.

Sitting behind her desk with both legs kicked up she fluttered her naturally thick, long eyelashes. As the sun glistened off her brown Latino skin, she looked up at him and smiled. Maria was a very attractive woman. That's the one thing Latif always noticed. Seductive too, but she had every right to be in her line of work. Deceit and treachery, he mused, bringing a much-needed grin to his face. She tried him on occasion, but he kept it business, kept moving, and for a good solid reason. He'd lose, he didn't have any wins.

He looked up and down at her legs and her thighs, catching a glimpse of that fat ass cat that stared back at him. He wondered how long he could keep saying no. "Have a seat." She purred.

Latif sat down and reached for some papers in an envelope on her desk that eventually would have made it to his hands anyway. He flipped through them. Bills. "This is what was so important?"

"Of course not." She put her feet down and pulled up closer to her desk. "Do you ever wonder why I kept you near all these years? Why Juanita allowed you to deal with me? Why your mother never did?"

He leaned back and crossed his legs. "At times."

"Well... I'm going to tell you."

His eyes arched as he got comfortable. "The truth?"

"The whole truth. Are you ready for it?"

"Well, I guess we'll see. Tell me. The truth."

SOMETHING ABOUT GOOD love making that relaxes you. Taking you on two different levels of consciousness, a pleasure beyond the body. Spiritual. Mental. That's where Waseema was as she laid in Ice's arms. Bliss. She needed to go somewhere, in his presence, his arms, his embrace, his solace was where she found herself. She held on tight as their breathing morphed into one and their heartbeat unified. She let go and he held onto her, as if her life depended on it. That's where she wanted him to be, in full control.

He knew what she needed, and he had it for her. That good love, the escape she was looking for. Kissing her body from head to toe, slowly, allowing her time to cherish every single kiss. Her body exploded in rhythm, in motion as her orgasm heightened. Moaning gutturally, almost animalistic as the fruits of their lovemaking grew more intense, their wet, limp bodies seemingly morphed into one another. The embrace, just one more, a done deal, the euphoria, rapture, ecstasy taking over.

They spooned. They kissed. They got up and walked to the kitchen hand in hand and fixed a sandwich. They drank wine. They ate. They showered. And like good lovers they celebrated each other. They didn't talk, nothing was needed to be said, lest doing so would spoil the moments, not yet, at least. Afterward she laid in his arms, stared out the window for a while, then she took a deep breath inside. It was over with. "Ice, maybe I should have gotten her some help. I saw the signs, but I didn't think she was out there like that. Then, the kidnapping made it worse. She was never quite the same and Mustapha's death didn't make things any better. "

"Yeah. I know it. I saw the darkness in her eyes at the funeral myself. I knew she'd never be the same. I think she blamed herself."

"Huh, huh. I bought the business just for her. Tried to get her mind off of it. Granted, it was a money-making opportunity for me and Donna too, but still it was hers. Hell, I was being greedy myself. I really didn't need the money. She knew that though, and she acted like she didn't care. She just started to...I don't know, change, I guess. Staying out late, drinking, being promiscuous...crazy things. I had to keep my eye on her, she became paranoid, she thought I was being nosy."

Switching gears Ice said, "So...he was already dead? Carlito."

"Yeah, that was a bad episode. I just had to dispose of...the body, best way I could."

"I can't say I blame you, but I wish you'd have let me know. It could have gotten dangerous, ya know."

"I know baby, I know. Everything just happened so fast."

"But. That Cholo thing was crazy. Do you know anything about that?"

"No. Ice, I can only guess that somehow Maria is involved."

"And, the Cartel?"

"And the Cartel."

"Back in town, huh."

"To tell you the truth, Ice baby. I don't think they ever left."

"MARIA, SO, YOU THINK the Cartel is still in town, really?"

"Like I said Latif, I don't think they ever left."

"Why do you say that?"

"Latif. They have interests that keep them here."

"What?"

"Not what...who."

"Who...what do you mean?"

"Someone that they have their eyes on. Someone that's an unknowing key player in their crazy game."

"Key player. Unknowingly...who?"

"Latif..." Maria leaned forward, and stared straight into his eyes and said, "You".

"Me?"

"LATIF!" ICE EXCLAIMED. "How?"

"Not how...who. You see Ice." She sighed again, then looked off, away from his eyes. "Latif is not Khalid's son."

Ice pulled himself up and staring intently at her replied, "Then...who?"

"Malik."

"Malik?"

"Yes. It was a bad time for me and Khalid. He was barely around, all the kids, responsibilities, I felt neglected, and he, Malik, took advantage of me. We'd rendezvous uptown, and that's how Craig 3X knew."

"So, he's dead too then."

"Yes.

"You killed him?"

"Me...Shaheeda."

"Wow." Ice blew as he leaned back and stared at the ceiling. "Does Rasheed know?"

"No."

"Okay, Okay...you need to fill me in."

"YOUR FATHER, MALIK, fell out with Khalid at one point. My husband Felix, and his partner Carlos was on him, hard. Paying him off for political aspirations, money, property, but only by the orders of the Cartel. They were the ones really pulling the strings. Carlos played by the rules, but Felix, Felix just didn't do right. At first, I was with it, but he got too damn greedy."

"Funny, your brother Rasheed and his crew of wayward stick up kids just happened to be the catalyst that changed the whole destiny of events. I mean, Khalid's son...who would have ever thought..." her voice trailed off as she reflected.

"But still Malik is my father. That's... So, that's why my mother sent me to Harlem."

"Somewhat. You see, Juanita knew of the Cartel's interest in Malik too. you were sent up to Harlem so you'd be safe. Malik was in a sense working for them and if they knew about you then...no telling."

"But Khalid still treated me like a son."

"You were, in a sense. Hell, he knew he was wrong for leaving Waseema in that situation. He blamed himself. But he also knew about Malik's dealings and he knew it would have been dangerous for you to stay in Brooklyn. But he did something that was amazing...he looked ahead. He had foresight."

"Foresight?"

"KHALID HAD ENOUGH FORESIGHT to make Malik put all the property titles and land ownership in Latif's name as beneficiary."

"Oh shit..." Ice said as he stood up in the bed with his back propped against the headboard. He turned towards Waseema and grinned. "So, you're saying that..." he said, still trying to get a grasp on the enormity of the situation, "All the money, property..." he said as he rubbed at his eyes and spoke again. "Latif...owns..."

"EVERYTHING? I OWN...everything?" Latif uttered, as Maria stood up and leaned over him and answered.

"Yes."

# CHAPTER ELEVEN

ATF Special Agent Edward Gonzalez drove around the block for a while trying to get his head right. He pulled into a lot off Broadway and parked, stuck in thought. He'd gotten the call he knew was one day inevitable. Even though it was too soon, he now had no choice but to pull Felix in. Orders. He'd been their number one mole for years. All Eddie had to do was keep an eye on him. Make sure the point A to B synopsis was achieved, with maximum surreptitiousness, and minimal dissipation his bosses said, Real simple it seemed to his superiors. At least for the most part.

But with Maria in the picture, it got really complicated, real fast. He was sucked into a perplexed situation and he had to deal with some real grimy types along the way. Cholo was one, and Chino the other. His number one snitch. His inside man. It was his desires for the passions of a woman that got him killed. Hell, a woman that wasn't even his. Eddie was glad Chino was dead. He couldn't keep his pants up and his mouth shut. He should have killed him his damn self. But he still had to kill the girl though. She already knew too much. She knew who he was. Had seen his face.

Revenge was what he really wanted all along. The dish best served cold. For years, he bided his time. Chilled. Schemed. Made all the right moves. Went to school. College. Pace University over by Chambers Street in Manhattan and studied Criminal Law. Then, when the time was right, he took the test for the Feds; the AFT. He passed, moved up the ranks out of Washington D.C., and made his way back to New York, his home. Back on the brow-beaten path to his plan. To avenge the murder of his big brother, Ali.

Big Sam was the bastard that had sent the man that murdered his brother years back. The memories still haunted him. Eddie's brother worked as a janitor in a building in Midtown Manhattan. He remembered when he got the job; dude from out of Bushwick Projects looked out for him. Cat by the name of Khalid Muhammad. All in all, it was a good gig for him. He needed the money. Not for the gambling habit he'd kicked, but for him and his little brother.

Edward wanted Ali out of the neighborhood. Gangs were breathing down his neck way too hard, and their mom had just died of cancer. They had no one else to turn to but each other. His brother had called Eddie earlier that evening and said something about a lick. Said it was going to be a big pay day. Talked shit about hauling ass back to California. Get him in one of those good schools near the beach. Yeah, Eddie was down with that. It sure sounded a hell of a lot better than Bed-Stuy, the Bronx, or even Harlem. Choices were slim next to none for the both of them back then, at least the good ones, but it never panned out after Ali was killed.

Killing Big Sam was easy. But, just before Eddie jammed the shotgun into his mouth he babbled on and on about this...Cartel, said it was their fault. Eddie didn't care, he died anyway, but he did do the research later and found out that the Cartel he was babbling about was a huge crime conglomerate that dabbled in everything from the girls to dope. From one end of the coast to the other. Mexican, Columbians, Puerto Ricans, Brazilians, all Latino. Big, real big. He didn't know who was running for them. In New York City when he was coming up, it was Carlos. Then it was Felix. Now, he wasn't quite sure who it was. He'd hit a dead end with that.

The only direction he had was Cholo, and now he was dead. Edward thought briefly about Maria, but she was much too greedy. Way too out there to be running something on that level. Now Cholo was dead, and he was sure the Cartel done the hit, but for what? They normally didn't show their head to someone that close by. He had to know who it was.

The only way to sniff whoever it was out, was to bring back Felix. Put him out there. He knew the Cartel would rear their head once they knew he was out. But Edward couldn't let Felix know he was bait. So, he had to come up with something. A plan. A life.

He glanced up the street at the store, pondering on a good deceit and he caught the storefront ads on a bodega. The analogies hitting close to home. Times were changing, fast. The nineties, late nineties at that. Pretty soon the year two thousand would be in. Close to twenty years for him on the job. He needed to find a nest egg, some retirement money instead of the pocket change he was getting. Cigarettes were up to two dollars now. Two dollars for a pack of damn smokes, he sighed. Yeah, times were changing.

He cranked up the car and made a few quick left's before he pulled up in front of the safe house where Felix stayed. He looked up and down the street like he always did, and it was the same old same old. Though he did notice a van down near the far end. It was a plumbing company, seemed harmless enough so he shrugged it off.

He got out and walked up the steps and knocked like he always did. This time it wasn't the old lady that answered, but instead a very fine, demure Spanish woman in her late twenties or so. Shoulder length hair, nice full and bright brown eyes, the type you almost always fell for. He smiled and said, ``Uh, is, uh Mr. Torres here?'' while he steadily looked past her trying to get a peep inside. She stepped in front of him blocking his view.

"No senor. He took his wife out of town." Her accent dripped with the dialects native to the indigenous tribes south of Mexico...smelled like the Cartel, for sure. There were two things though she didn't have a clue about. One. The government sure as hell didn't pay the old man and woman enough money to haul ass and leave a slob like Felix alone in their home, besides, Eddie mused, he was their meal ticket. And two. Their names weren't Torres.

She looked out the door past him up the street, then grabbed it with two hands like she was going to slam it, but instead asked, "Who are you?"

He could expose himself by taking out his badge or take the stubble way out and go with it. But she was clueless and he wanted her to stay that way, for now, "A friend...of the family." He had to get through to find out if Felix was in there, or even still alive. "I normally play horseshoes with Mr. Torres. Matter of fact, my shoes are in the back. If he's out of town, I'll need them to play somewhere else." As he spoke, he pushed past her and b-lined to the back door. She was right behind him. "Sir!" He noticed that there were dishes on the table, and he could still smell the warm brisket coming from out the oven as he walked by the kitchen. When he reached for the doorknob to open it, she grabbed him by the arm and yelled. "Stop!"

He swirled around and she had a gun pointed to his stomach. He had to think quickly. "All I wanted was my horseshoes." He pressed his back up against the screen door and it opened slightly, enough for him to look out. He glanced over his shoulder at Felix sitting by a table near the far side of the horseshoe pit with another gentleman that he didn't recognize. Edward then, turned all the way around and called out. "Hey...Tony" He had to pump fake Felix's name in case they didn't know who he was either. Felix went with it, waved. Now Eddie knew without a doubt that something was up. He had to make a move. "Hey. I thought we were supposed to play today. Where's Torres?"

Felix didn't speak, but eyeballed the man that sat next to him who stood up and reached slowly into his jacket. He had a gun. The next thing he knew the woman jabbed the gun in his back and said, "Down the steps slowly." He complied. "Now over to the table." He did as he was ordered and sat next to Felix. "What's going on?" he whispered.

"Hell, I thought they were friends of yours."

"Where's the old man and his wife?" he asked.

Felix nodded his head towards the cellar at the back of his house. "Dead."

"Damn," Eddie sighed. They didn't have shit to do with anything.

"Okay...just hit the ground when I..."

"What are you going to do!"

"Just do it, will ya!"

The man and woman walked off a bit talking to each other discreetly then stepped into the house and came back out both staring at Eddie and Felix. She nodded and then the man grinned, slob damn near came from out the sides of his mouth. He pulled out his gun. A shiny blue steel nine-millimeter. It was time for Eddie to act because he knew what they wanted to do.

He reached into his jacket and pulled out his own gun, a government issued Glock .40. He was lucky she didn't frisk him earlier or she'd have caught it and things would have gone wrong, very wrong, hopefully not for him. Very fluidly, he aimed and with the pristine precision of a trained professional. The kind that spends most of his time at the gun range. He squeezed the trigger twice. The man's head exploded like a cantaloupe as he targeted the stunned woman next. It was like clockwork. He'd hoped she'd just give up, perhaps he could at least find out who sent them, but it was never that easy. Whoever sent her, she was committed to them and only them. And well, to hell with him. She reached for her gun too, and like him, aimed. More shots were fired and Felix hit the dirt like Eddie told him to.

The smoke cleared as pigeons overhead scattered about and flew off in all directions like they were dodging bullets themselves. She squinted through the hazy blue gun smoke and dust blown about, then fell to her knees. She was hit, but not fatally. Eddie eased towards her cautiously; she still had the gun in her hand. He pulled out his badge and ordered. "ATF-Drop the gun!" She sneered at him, and spit into the dirt "Fuck you...traitor!" and he pointed the gun to her head. Eddie frowned then pulled the trigger, it was, what it was, loyalty. He turned around and ran towards Felix yelling. "Let's go!"

Without hesitation they hauled ass towards the back door, but Eddie stopped, pulled Felix to the side, and said no, not yet. He peeped out front and spotted the same van from up the street, the side door started opening. They damn sure didn't call the plumber. "They were watching the house. Probably heard the shots," he said as he looked at the back fence and ran towards it, then leaped, climbed over, and jumped. "This way!" Felix stared up at the eight-foot-high picketed boards and hollered back. "I can't make it."

"You can't make it?" Eddie lunged at the top of the fence again and pulled himself up. Peeping over he looked at the woman and the man dead on the ground in a pool of blood. Then, he heard the sound of people coming through the house and shouted. "You better."

Felix sighed and jumped at the top of the fence and grunting, started pulling himself up. It took everything he had, but halfway over Eddie reached up and pulled his fat ass over, headfirst, plummeting Felix to the ground on top of him. It hurt like hell, but he pulled him up to his feet and they ran towards the street. Eddie was sore as hell from the fall and was still seeing stars. He was a little disoriented for a while, but one thing for sure he knew he couldn't go back to his car. He knew they had to get out of dodge, quickly.

Eddie pointed towards the elevated train on Myrtle Avenue, and with everything they could muster, hauled ass. They made it upstairs in time to catch the J train express to Manhattan pulling into the station. Once inside, the doors closed and they looked out the window as the train pulled away. Three men with black masks and holstered shotguns got back into the van and screeched off towards Bushwick Avenue. Exhausted and tense, they finally plopped down in the seats across from them. Eddie looked over at Felix and asked, "Cartel?"

Felix looked back at him and said between breaths. "Probably...but, the question is...which one?"

Eddie nodded his head, for once Felix made sense.

ICE STOOD OVER BY A kitchen window peering out over the tree lined street towards Amsterdam Avenue as Waseema cooked breakfast. Rasheed had just come in seated and himself at the table. Quiet. Another morning, but Ice couldn't help but shake his head thinking back to the conversation he had with Waseema about Latif. He didn't know whether to share it with Rasheed, his best friend, or let Waseema, his woman, continue to hold it in and let it fester inside of her. It mattered.

Rasheed in his own little thoughts, contemplated the heist. Were they ready? Did he and Asia have everything in order? This was a dangerous undertaking. The most dangerous he'd ever encountered.

Tired of it all, he was ready to leave New York and call it quits. Live life like a normal man. Watch his daughter grow. Share a life with Asia hopefully, comfortably. Was it too late for that even? Maybe, this was his time. He played with his eggs then glanced up at Waseema. What about her? He looked over at Ice; he'd be there for her. He knew that, but why was there this nagging at him still? Could it be the Asia factor? The Khadija factor? He sighed deeply and Waseema turned towards him and asked, "Rasheed. What's wrong? You haven't touched your food. You sick or something?" She leaned towards him with her hand and touched his forehead. "Fever?"

"Naw, ma," he said as he kissed her hand. "I'm alright. You?"

She rolled her eyes over at Ice and replied, dryly. "I guess"

Ice snickered. "What I do? Okay then...here goes the morning." He walked over to the table and pulled out a chair and sat. "Let's put something out on the table, besides food, huh."

"What?" Rasheed asked as he pushed his plate away.

"I think we should-"

"No, Ice." Waseema interrupted. "Let me tell him."

"Tell him? What are you talking about?" Ice turned toward her. "All I wanted to do was say..." Waseema tensed up. Waiting for Rasheed's imminent outburst. She knew she should have already told Rasheed about the whole Latif thing. "We should have been told Rasheed about the whole Latif thing. We should let you take the money to the store. Keep it safe."

Rasheed pushed back from the table some more and asked, "You mean...we take the money there, or something?"

"Naw. She needs to be right there. Hands on."

"Hell no. Anything can happen-"

Excited about the idea, and at the same time relieved that he didn't divulge anything about Latif, Waseema exclaimed, "I can do it, Rasheed!"

"I said no!"

"Hold up, dammit! You must have lost your damn mind. I'm grown." Waseema banged on the table. "I can do what the hell I want to do!"

"But ma," Rasheed sighed. "It's much too dangerous."

"Look." Ice cut in. "True. But we'll have eyes on her. And she doesn't have to be exactly in the mix. We just need her to transport the money and to be honest, she's available. Look, the store is probably the quickest place to go, and the safest."

"He's right, Rasheed. Think about it for a minute. It wouldn't look out the way. You know I got people over there to watch my back once I make the drop. Hell. She gestured as she turned towards Ice. It'd just look like a merchandise drop."

"What? A merchandise drop...at three-four in the morning?"

"All the better, less eyes." Ice said.

Rasheed got up and paced the floor. He stopped and stared at Ice. "Ice I lost my brother...my daughter's mother...Derek, I, I don't know."

Ice walked over to him and put his hand on his shoulder. "We...we lost them. I understand and believe me. I ain't trying to lose the woman I love, Rasheed. But...we need her right about...now...for real."

Rasheed sighed again, then said, "Okay...set it up." He glanced over at his mother. "I need to let Asia know."

Just then Shaheeda came rushing through the kitchen doorway. "Let her know what?"

"Uh," Rasheed averted his eyes and said, "Nothing... Nothing. "

"Okay." She walked over to the table and sat down, then pulled Rasheed's plate towards her? "Whose eggs? Somebody want these?"

"Baby. I can make some more. Those are cold."

"Thanks ma."

Rasheed kissed his mother, dapped Ice, then walked towards the door when Shaheeda called out to him. "Oh yeah, bro."

"Huh?"

"Ma's gonna need some help unloading the money once she gets it to the store. You think so?"

"Damn you Shaheeda!" Rasheed said as he stormed out the door.

THE SQUEAL OF THE BRAKES from the elevated train rose high above the shrieks, yells and shouts of the small delightful children running around in the stone and steel playground amidst the brown and orange bricked, project building.

The air was crisp, cool, but not yet cold; autumn had just set in. The wind was just heavy enough for a sweater to be worn on top of a loose-fitting shirt, or maybe even a wife beater in cardigan typical gangster, ghetto, GQ etiquette. The streets were seasonal. Trash swirled around on the sidewalks like paper winds whirls, caught up like flies in a trap in the gutters off the corner blocks.

Brooklyn, New York. 1995. Times were changing. The stores were all being redone into super shopper, retail marts mostly Colombian owned. Corner Bodega's were now outdoor veggie marts; Korean owned. The streets repaved, no more potholes, and old shiny blue-steel rails with cobblestone bricks running up and down Broadway.

Kokomo stepped across the street and looked over towards the stores. One in particular, S&A's. He nodded reminiscing back to the time when it was just a small, Jewish owned, sewing machine repair shop. They cleared out, left after the blackout in the mid-70s. It stayed abandoned then open for a time when the drug pushers manufactured crack cocaine and heroin. Later, it was overrun by the drug addicts. Then, left to rot into the mid-80s. Soon after, similar shops moved away with the renovations going on Broadway, from Bed-Stuy to Williamsburg.

The store stayed closed most of the time now. Waseema's flamboyant Brinks truck coming in and picking up money, no longer. The neighborhood was going through another change. Hopefully, a positive one. It was gentrification, but in this case, it needed it.

Kokomo knew his time had come. No more gangsta. Hell, no more drug pushers to shake down or dope boys to rob. It was time for a change anyway though. He rubbed his well-groomed goatee and smiled as he remembered how he picked out a few grays earlier this morning. Getting older now, he had to change his game. Either go legit or come into some serious money. And going legit was not happening. The job at the Navy yard would be his biggest, but also his last.

However, there was still one thing. Asia. He thought about when he first met the broad. Doing stick ups, robbing the Colombians and Mexicans. Crazy. He'd covered up for her when she was way, way overhead at one time. When the contract was offered for her body, dead, not alive, that's how much damage she had done. He went straight to them. Negotiated for her life. Never told her. That's the least he could do for the woman he loved. But now, this Rasheed thing. Why now?

He turned and looked at the building she lived in. She had called him earlier and told him the date was set for the heist. It was time. It was also time to let her know where he stood. He had to. He had to fight for the woman he loved. But the man he had to fight against was a man known for fighting, today even. Rasheed. Was it a fight he was ready for? He rubbed the chill from his hands and pulled down his cap over his eyes and nodded. Then he snarled an ill-tempered, throaty, "Yes".

THE FLAMES FLICKERED, embers snapped and crackled as the small fire blazed. The brown marble mirth kindled warm into the large room and soothed peace into the sofa that sat in front of it. Latif had just finished his third glass of nouveau and had been sitting now, thinking for the better part of an hour. His mind going over and over throughout the centuries of his still so very young life. The memories that haunted him. The good of it, the bad of it. Never would he have fathomed such a theory as told to him by Maria. He thought about confronting his mother, but why? Why should he?

Why would Maria conjure up a tale like that if it wasn't true? Besides he couldn't, he didn't know how, and he wished he just didn't have to. He wished she'd let him know a long time ago, maybe.

He felt like he was being played. Made a fool of. He thought maybe Rasheed was in on it. But thinking back to the days when he and Mustafah would come and visit him, that was way out of the question. So far as they knew he was their brother from the same father. But Juanita, his beloved grandmother, why did she hold back?

It was after all the emotional turmoil that spun around in his head did actual common sense and reasoning come into play. It was brilliant after all. Of course, it was. He soon realized that he owned a good portion of properties in and around Bed-Stuy and Bushwick. He was a rich man. But what really put a dent in the bottom he was drinking on was the fact that he was also powerful. More powerful than Maria even. Hell yeah, he poured another drink, then gulped it down. The smooth, vintage, 76-year-old dry Ammasso burned at his throat, and soothed his mind. The flames continued to dance, causing his head to swirl. The door to the bedroom swung open and the sweet softness of a voice sang out to him. "Sweetheart. Are you coming back to bed?"

"Yeah baby. In a second."

"You alright?" Ra'Shon asked as she stepped through the door. Her Filipino reddish, brown skin glistened from the fireplace; silhouetting her voluptuous shape against the soft cues of the large, duplex living room. Her bright, great, doe like eyes and thick sensuous eyelashes showed some concern when she came through. Standing in front of him she leaned over seductively and kissed him tenderly along his face. She wore his shirt. His old college basketball warm-up jersey. The good old days he thought as he slowly ran his fingers across the embroidered letters Saint John's University. He stopped as he traced his fingers slowly across her nipples and played with them, caressing her breasts gently. She giggled from his touch and asked, "You want to talk about it, baby?"

"No. I'm good," he said as he guided her hand towards his crotch. She responded by squeezing the now hard muscle between his legs.

Ra'Shon, his partner, but right now his lover. He'd eventually have to pull her in and let her know what was up. She was smart though, knew a lot about commerce and where to put money. He'd need her. Right now, he needed her for something else, and she was coming through like a champ. She pushed his legs wide and knelt down. Reaching for his glass he offered her a drink. She swallowed it down, smiled, licked her lips, then reached into his silk boxers and pulled out his dick. Tenderly, she touched it, watched it in rapture as the long, large organ obtained its peak. "We'll talk later Okay. All I want to hear right now is..." All that Latif could muster out of his mouth, "Oh baby...don't stop." The only words she wanted to hear.

Latif leaned back and caressed the back of her head as it bobbed up and down, grinding his hips in unison. His fortune was now changing. He didn't need Maria anymore. He was that dude now. How to get rid of her was another thing. Maybe she could end up as a bargaining chip for the Cartel.

With his hand he gently pushed Ra'Shon's head off of him and motioned for her to stand. He mounted her hips on him and thrust inside of her, then pumped deeply as her long brown legs swung wildly out from the sides of the chair. Kissing her full, ruby red lips he whispered in her ear, "I got you baby. I got you."

"I know you do, Latif," she purred.

The fire continued to flicker and sparkle as they continued the passionate love making throughout the night. Leaving Latif to wonder if he was getting off on Ra'Shon, or the fact that he would now and forever be one of the richest men in New York City.

MARIA SAT AT HER DESK staring at the phone, trying to figure how the whole Latif thing could work to her advantage. One. She knew more about the properties that belonged to Malik and her husband Felix than anyone. Two. She knew more about the Cartel's dealings as far as the properties were concerned. And three. She already had control of the properties physically. She figured, she could easily let him have that and keep everything that she had in her name. Including all the money that was made from them. It was lucrative enough to keep her wealthy for years. She'd be out of the filth that covered her in shame and gone legit. Let Latif have the headaches. That's why she told him.

She almost fell out of her chair as she pulled away from the phone when it rang. She started to slowly push away from the desk. Glancing outside, searching the rooftops. Straining her eyes to see if anyone was watching. "Ma'am, are you going to take the call?"

She stared at the phone again. That name. She knew that name. it couldn't have been him. As far as she was concerned, and everything she knew, he was dead. Gone. Damn, why now? "Ma'am?"

She took a deep breath and reached for the phone. "Yes...I'll take it." She picked up the receiver and said, "Hello."

"Ah, hello, pretty lady."

"Who is this?"

"C'mon. you know who this is! The fucking man you shared your bed with. Your fucking husband...Felix."

"Felix. Where are you? I was worried about you. I'm so glad to hear from you."

"Shut the fucking lies up! Listen to me! You have my money. I know...most of it, at least."

"Uh...some."

"I will call you later. You will come to me. You hear me."

"Felix...I have a lot to do..."

"You will come! Alone!" *Click.*

The phone went dead. She hung up the receiver and started breathing heavily. Why now? Tears came down from the corner of her eyes. She couldn't turn back now. Damn, she was almost out! She picked up her coffee mug and turned towards her father's picture, the one she and Waseema had admired, the one with Juanita, and tossed it. Damn you to hell!

Reaching into her drawer she pulled out a bottle of brandy and a glass. She opened the bottle, poured a drink, then took out a cigarette and lit it. Pressing the intercom button, she took a drag. "Yes, Ma'am."

"Tina...call Latif."

"Yes, Ma'am."

Maria had no choice. Felix was coming for her. Once he squeezed everything, he could out of her, Latif would be next. If he was really alive, then he was definitely back into the clutches of the Cartel. That's why he needed the money. He still owed them, "And Tina..."

"Ma'am?"

"After that...dial Gonzalez...Edward."

"Yes, Ma'am."

She needed someone in her corner, but was he the right one? She didn't care, taking out Felix was her main objective.

SPEAKING BABBLED, INCOHERENT broken Spanish at a highly, accelerated, rapid pace. Spit flew from his mouth uncontrollably. Sweat poured down the sides of his face as his arms wailed about in a not really telling anything-nondescript dialog. The Spaniard did his best trying to convince Guillermo that it wasn't his fault that Felix had gotten away.

"So...hmmm. That's all you have to say then." Guillermo asked him.

"Si, senor! That's it. It wasn't my fault. They ran out the back...jumped the fence!"

"But, you, uh...saw this...so called man...go into the house and help him escape."

The Spanish man looked around at his comrades, reached into his shirt pocket, pulled out a handkerchief and wiped his face. When he'd finished it was soaking wet. "We all did!" He spat as he pointed at the two other men that were with him.

"Oh! So..." Guillermo looked at them all, then turned back his way and glared. It was their fault? He pointed to a man by the door and gestured. He walked over to the two and casually, but very quickly pulled out his gun and shot them both in the head. They dropped and blood oozed its way out their brains onto the floor. Guillermo said, "Okay, well...that's what you said, It was their fault, right?"

The man looked at his deceased partners and instantaneously, very wisely nodded his head. "Si, senor."

Guillermo smiled and stepped towards him putting his arms around his shoulders patting him on the back. "Oh sure. I know you tried, too. I understand." He pointed to the bodies. "Clearly, it was all their fault. Of course, you had nothing to do with it."

"Si, senor," he said eagerly. He felt bad for his buddies but was damn sure glad it wasn't-*BAM*. Guillermo reached into his jacket pocket and pulled out his gun and in one swift movement, shoved it into the man's mouth and squeezed the trigger; blowing it wide open. He wiped the blood off his face and shirt like it was no big deal and said, "His mouth lies...he won't be needing it anymore. "Papi! Papi!" He hollered out to the man who had shot the other two. "Go get me a new suit. Now."

Guillermo wiped the blood off his gun with his shirt tail, then glanced at one of his men. "Get this shit cleaned up."

"Okay, boss."

He took off his t-shirt, threw it on the floor by the bodies and pointed to his assistant Omar, who'd just walked through the door. "Boss...you hear that?"

"Boss? Don't make me laugh. Guillermo, you shouldn't have killed them. They were good men. We don't have too many as it is now."

"You doubt me?" he said as his brow glanced up from the corner of his eye.

"C'mon now Guillermo. I'm not one of your flunkies."

"One day, Omar, one day."

"Yeah, yeah. Fuck you, too."

Guillermo laughed. "I like you. Since we were kids. I like you." He walked into the bathroom as Omar followed behind him. "We still have to find that damn Felix."

"Of course. That was the plan, but how do we flush him out now? He knows the Cartel is looking for him...not us."

"What do you mean, Guillermo?"

"Well...he basically knows it's a hit squad from the Cartel. He really doesn't know about us. As far as he's concerned, we could be the liaison for getting back into their good graces."

"But we were."

Guillermo smiled as he glanced at him. "True, but that was until we found out that he had access to a nice size of the Cartel's money."

"So, you're saying, go at him a little more...diplomatically."

"No guns blazing. It doesn't work."

"Sounds much better. But, Guillermo."

"Yeah."

"Who was the guy with him?"

"You know. I was thinking of that myself. I've got people working on that. When we do find out, we will kill him."

"That bitch Maria too?"

"Of course...Maria, too. She knows way too much."

"Yeah...about us."

# CHAPTER TWELVE

E dward sat in a chair at the kitchen table of the small walk-up studio apartment, a safehouse. One of those spots provided him with compliments of the DEA. He managed to keep the place on the books in case he ever needed it. Today, he was glad he did.

He watched as Felix whipped up something to eat in the kitchen. They'd stopped by the Bodega and bought some ham, grits and a couple bags of plantains chips. What could he ever do with that was beyond him? He didn't feel like eating anyway, he was pissed. He almost lost his life this time playing both sides of the fence, and almost didn't make it out.

There was no one to call, and he damn sure couldn't tell the people in his agency what he was doing. He was in too deep. He couldn't trust anyone. He knew Giovanni, his old police department buddy, was somewhat trustworthy. But since he killed the girl earlier in Bed Stuy, he knew that that would even be a stretch. It was a message provided by him that did her in. She was just in the wrong place at the wrong time. She was about to get done in anyway, just not at his hands.

Maria was out of the question. Hell, he wanted to take her out so bad, but he wasn't quite ready yet. She still held the cards. But now, with Felix out in the open, he could accumulate more information. Tie it all up in one little neat bow. Bring down the Cartel once and for all and get the millions that went with it. But, at what cost? His life? Right now, he needed to concentrate on the ones, or one that was trying to kill Felix. Safeguard his meal ticket.

"So...these guys were...what, Cartel?" Eugene asked.

Felix nodded his head humming a tune as he maneuvered around the small stove sizzling something up in the cast iron skillet. "Huh, Huh."

"Why didn't they kill you when they had the chance?"

Felix didn't nod this time. He snickered. Once he was satisfied with whatever he was cooking, he turned towards the table where he had two pieces of sliced bread waiting. Stirring what was in the pan he slid it on the bread. Edward had to admit, it looked half-assed good, smelled good too. Felix offered him some. Edward pulled out two pieces of bread from the small fridge himself and Felix put the rest of the cooked meal on it. He pulled up a chair after he put the skillet in the sink, ran water on it, and was about to eat when Edward posed the question again. "Felix...the question. Why didn't they kill you when they had the chance?"

"Oh yeah. How do you know it was really me they wanted?"

"Hell, if it wasn't you, then who?"

"Who?"

"Well...who were they shooting at, huh?"

"Me! What the hell would they want with me?"

Felix poured himself a glass of the cheap bottled wine they bought, and looked up at him, then said, "I don't know. But, maybe...you do."

Edward's jaw dropped. No way could they have known about him. He was too careful. Hold up, maybe they weren't the Cartel. Maybe, they were someone else. "You sure they were Cartel?"

Felix snickered again, put the sandwich down and licked his fingers, then said, "Look. I play no games. I don't. But they definitely were Cartel. I really suggest whatever business you need to handle." He took another bite off the sandwich and said, "You'd better do it...now!" He reached for the wine and offered him some. "Have you some...you look like you might need it."

Edward let him pour him a cup full. He swigged the whole thing down as Felix laughed in his face.

WASEEMA HUNG UP THE phone slowly, then sighed deeply, guttural. Somewhat depressed, and tired, she slumbered slowly towards the upstairs lounge. A cup of tea in hand she plopped down on a plush, velour sofa that faced outward towards the large ceiling to floor window. Looking through, she pondered deeply about whether she was doing the right thing. Was it all really worth it? She sipped her tea and breathed out a composed, yet relaxed reply. "Yes."

She told Latif to come over to talk. Divulge it all. At least what was left to be told. By his attitude over the phone, he knew much of it all already. Somebody had told him some things, and it was no secret who. She reached around her neck for a key, a gold key that looked more ornamental than functional and held it in her hand. Crossing her legs, she played with it between her fingers. Patiently waiting for Latif to come.

Latif crossed Lenox Avenue and headed up towards 145th street to Sugarhill. He looked around the old historic, black neighborhood as he drove through; it had changed so much. Now white just as much as it was black. But, was that a good thing? Perhaps. For his business ventures, it'd work well in his favor. Now he saw why much of this property had meant so much to Maria and them. It'd be worth the millions. It was already worth that now. Yeah, he definitely wouldn't mind having all that old money at his fingertips. He'd accomplish much.

By the time he made it past Martin Luther King Blvd., he opened up his glove compartment and pulled out the 9mm. It was tucked discreetly out of view behind some papers towards the back. The clip for it was hidden out of view, underneath the spare tire in the trunk. Just in case Khadija was in the car by herself and found the gun was a good enough reason for it being under there. With the shots fired at the house, Mya's murder and the death threats on his brother, he needed something. He needed bodyguards too but that was something he'd work on once he acquired the funds.

Latif turned up the street towards the three-story brownstone and eased into a parking space up front. A quiet, reserved street it always was, except for the drama his family brought about lately. For the most part, everything was cool. Most everyone had known his grandmother, his grandfather, and the old timers remembered his mother when she was just a little girl. Sometimes, he mused, they even treated her like one. It was all good. They spoiled the hell out of her, and for that matter him too. He opened the trunk and lifted the spare tire exposing the clip, put it in his pocket, then slammed the trunk shut.

Assuming his mother was sitting in the lounge and waiting on him, he bounced up the stairway to the door instead of coming in through the living room downstairs. The lights above the big oak door were brightly lit, and he could see deep inside the foyer because the curtains were pulled aside. She was home. Opening the door, he called out but no one answered. He called out again, and still no one answered. He reached into his pocket and pulled out his gun, reaching for the clip. Sliding it into the butt end, it produced that distinct snap and he stretched his ears around waiting for a response or a sound. Any movement.

His paranoia kicked in high gear. Maybe, someone might have gotten to his mother. He wanted to change everything. He slid a round into the chamber and walked slowly towards the lounge. He called out again, but still no answer. Latif walked into the room and raised his gun. His mother stood by the window with her back facing him and she said, "Unless you're thinking about shooting pigeons...put that away." She never even turned his way, she didn't even budge. Right then, it was like he had just seen a ghost. She reminded him of his grandmother.

He lowered the gun. "You could have at least answered when I called out!" He yelled before shoving the gun onto his jacket.

Waseema calmly walked over towards him and threw out her arms. "Your mother can't get a hug anymore?"

"I'm just saying you could have said something." He hugged her. "I thought something was wrong."

"I'm sorry...deep in thought. I really didn't hear you." She reached into his pocket and pulled out his gun. Holding it low she pointed it towards the chair and unchambered the round, then dropped the clip out the butt into her hand. "Khadija is in the house...can't be too careful."

"Oh yeah...sorry."

Waseema pointed towards the seat and said, "Please, sit down. I have something for you."

His attitude was mulish, a little defiant, but nevertheless he was still a little boy, obedient. He did as he was told. Latif took off his coat and tossed it across the other end and sat down, crossing his legs. Waseema had walked to the table across from him and picked up an envelope. She walked back towards the sofa and sat by him. "Here...read this."

"What's this?"

"Your father...he left this."

"Yeah, that's the problem. Who...Malik...Khalid?"

Waseema just smiled at the remark. She knew she deserved that. She got up and said to him. "You figure that one out yourself. Read it. You'll know...I'm sure."

"Hold up. What does it say?" he asked as he looked inside the envelope and pulled out the letter with his name on top.

"I don't know, it was for you," she replied. Her hands are still stroking the gold key. For your eyes only. She walked out the room, then called out to him. "I'll be in the kitchen...if you need me. I love you, son."

Latif didn't respond, but not out of disrespect. He was just too entranced by the letter, already the heading had intrigued him.

*Dear son*

*Asalaam alaikum.*

*I hope and I pray that this letter reaches you in good health and blessings. Ameen.*

*Latif. If you're reading this, then you are aware of three things. One I am not your biological father. Two, I am not with you in this life, and three, there's a whole lot of money coming to you.*

*My dearest son, when your mother told me she was pregnant, it didn't take much to figure out you weren't mine. Of course, I was upset, mad, but I loved your mother. Son, I was not there for her, so don't blame her. I was always busy working different jobs, in and out. A slave. it's still like that for me even now as I write this letter. I just want the best for you all.*

*Your biological father, Malik. I wasn't so forgiving with him. He's doing his own thing now. Involved with a slimeball named Felix. I hope he changes his way, but I thought ahead, for you, just in case he didn't.*

*I hope that Juanita, your grandmother kept her promise. The best schools, away from the streets. That's why we sent you to Harlem. To get away from Bushwick. We had to separate you. You weren't safe here. Forgive me, and may Allah have mercy on me!*

*I hope everything turned out well for you for all of you, your brothers and sister: Mustapha, Rasheed, and Shaheeda. I love you all so much. But son, I have to redeem myself. I have to make things right.*

*I found out some things that may help. Clear up to the family name, your mother's family. Mine. If things are still going the way they are by the time you receive this letter, then this will help you to set it right. It was always about you, Latif.*

*Your mother has a key. Engraved gold. By the time you receive it, keep it guarded. It opens the lock to a safe, and in the safe there's a ledger, and a couple of deeds to some property in Brooklyn that should be worth a lot of money.*

*All of it yours, son. It all belongs to you. Manage it well. Do the right thing. Stay in the deen, and if for some reason you're out, return! Remember this.*

*Qur'an 2:226: they who have brought the life of this world at the price of the hereafter. Their torment shall not be lightened, nor shall they be helped!*

*Latif, my son. Stay away from the...DUNYA!*

*I love you, and may Allah reward you.*

*Khalid. Your dad.*

*Asalaam alaikum.*

Wa alaikum asalaam...dad.

Latif folded the letter up and put it into his pocket. Looking out the window he smiled. He could see a little bit more clearly now. It wasn't his mother he was angry at. It was himself. His own ignorance. It was starting to come together.

He got up from the sofa and walked out the lounge to the stairway leading to the kitchen. On his way he heard the pitter patter of little feet running up behind him. He turned and Khadija had jumped up into his arms. "Whoa little girl...you almost knocked me off my feet."

"Sorry, Uncle Latif."

"Where're you on your way to in such a rush?"

"You don't smell it!"

"Smell it?"

She sniffed at the air and so did Latif, he knew immediately what she was talking about. He continued his way to the kitchen and when he made it through the doorway his mother said, "I know I couldn't keep her off the trail, but how's she digging you up?"

"Aw, ma..." he walked over to her and kissed her on the cheek.
"What was that for?"

He stepped back and beamed. "For being a wonderful mother who sacrificed...much." He put Khadija down and she raced for the bowl that was being used to make the sweet, smelling chocolate cake that lit up the air. "Thank you," he said as he put the envelope in his pocket.

"Okay." She pushed a big spoon over to Khadija and let her go to work. She held out the key that she had earlier and said, "Well then... I believe this belongs to you...right."

He nodded his head as he reached for it. "I believe so. Where's the uh." He glanced towards Khadija and whispered. "Safe?"

"Don't worry. She doesn't have a clue about any of it, and besides she's too caught up in that cake bowl."

"Yeah, like we used to be."

She led him over to the stove and checked the cakes that were in the oven, then said to him. "In the basement, but we have time. Besides, there are other things you need to know."

"Alright."

"Latif," she reached out and caressed his hands. "It's gonna be alright."

He pulled her closer and hugged her. "I know it will. Besides, my...dad said it would be."

"Oh, so you figured that one out."

"Yeah...I figured it out. You know ma, it really wasn't that difficult after all."

"I know, baby, that's usually how things work out."

GUILLERMO HELD THE phone in his hands so tight his knuckles had turned white. Controlling his temper, he was angry, but in no way as irate as the man on the other end of the line. He'd been cursed at. Called every derogatory name in the book. English and Spanish. His family threatened again, as well as his own life.

He wanted so bad to lash back out at him, but he dared not. On the other end of the phone was a spokesman for the Cartel, and he'd better be right, "What do you want me to do?"

"What do I want you to do! What do I want you to do!" Guillermo could hear some shouting in the background, then he came back." I ought to kill you! You have the nerve to ask something as dumb as that!"

"No disrespect. But I did everything you asked me to do so far!"

A pause. "You did." Another pause. "You found Felix, right?"

"Yes."

"Okay...okay. I'm sorry but you know this whole New York mess is getting out of hand." Guillermo nodded at that. He'd finally said something that they both agreed on. "You need to interrogate Felix and find out about the properties." There was a pause. Then, "You know Guillermo. We sent you up to New York to handle this. I handpicked you for this because of your abilities to, uh, take care of business. Granted, I should not have disrespected you earlier. I apologize, but this New York connection is a strong vein in our arm. Millions of dollars and someone, someone, is stealing at least a million from us every time we move. Someone we don't know."

"I may have a good idea."

"We do too, and we know it involves Felix. So, look, I'll give you the room and the blessing to do what you have to do. Then I call back."

"When will you call..."

"Soon! Have everything in order before the next shipment. Okay. Do you hear me Guillermo?"

"Yes sir."

"Good. Oh, by the way. Check your account. There a little bonus for taking care of the matter with that scum, Cholo, okay."

"Yes sir. I appreciate it."

"The Cartel appreciates you. Bye."

"Bye." Guillermo hung up the phone, much more relieved than he was earlier. He had to lie about Felix. He couldn't tell them he had him in his hands and he got away. He had to knuckle down and find him.

Omar walked into the room interrupting his thoughts and said, "Guillermo, we have a lead on Felix."

"Good." He grabbed his coat. "Let's go get him."

"No."

"No? Now what?"

"He's being protected by some guy with the ATF."

"ATF huh?"

"Yeah. We're getting info on him as we speak. We're on it. Be patient."

"I don't have much time Omar!"

"Guillermo." Omar walked over and guided him to a seat. "Calm down. Trust me. We have a good lead on Felix, and his wife Maria."

"Hmmm, you know what, Omar. That Maria, hmm, there may be something to that. After all, she's direct lineage to the Cartel. Yet, they never ask about her."

Omar sat next to him. "Guillermo, I've been curious about that link too. Hell, even Cholo was nosey about that."

"Yeah, all of a sudden Felix pops up. You think she might know where he may be? Yet, the Cartel is busting my balls about Felix... And not her." Omar got up and started walking towards the door and Guillermo called out. "Where are you going?"

"To see if this ATF guy had any dealings with this Maria lately, and if so...."

"Deposal Omar." Guillermo laughed out loud. "The puzzle gets solved. Ha!"

Omar walked out the door and said, "Until we get to the next one."

Maria was packing boxes in her office and got a call from her secretary. "Ma'am, the realtor wants to show the condo. "

"Okay, Tina. Tell him I'll be there for at least a couple hours."

"Yes ma'am. I'll tell him."

"Thanks Tina. "

She was moving out to the Hamptons and wanted to start a whole new life. Legit. That's what she wanted. She even thought about changing her name. Something more American, clean. She'd already sold Latif out. Telling him everything, at least everything she wanted him to know. Now, he was on the Cartels bulls' eye, and not hers. Maria was going to acquire counterfeit names and use them to manage her properties and accounts. It was over with. She was tired of it all.

She had enough information on the Cartel anyway, so they'd back off of her. Besides, she still held her father's stake in the Cartel. They wanted that too, but no way would they get it without a fight.

"Ma'am. The realtor is on the phone. "

"From the Hamptons?"

"Yes ma'am. "

She still needed a little more cash to secure the property she wanted. "Tell them I'll be out to see the property next week." She was about $1,000,000 short to her dream lifestyle.

"Yes ma'am. "

She knew about the Cartel shipment coming in. Pick up some money, drop off some drugs. The only thing was these drugs weren't meant for New York, but for Canada. New York was just a stopping point of sorts. The money they dropped was cleaned, and the new money shipped back.

British Columbia was the starting point on one end, then Québec. Once it hit New York it was exchanged for clean money. Then the dope split in half and distributed. Next it was on to California by way of freight train. The Cartel fronted trucking companies. From there, Mexico. The process is then repeated again, but in reverse.

Maria stopped and sat down at her desk, taking a breather. She looked around the room at the boxes, then glanced at the pictures on the wall. She'd pack them last. Smiling at the photos of her father she mumbled the words, "time to get out dad," affectionately under her breath.

Latif would eventually get full rein over all the properties that Felix had wrangled for the Cartel. For her troubles, she'd receive percentages from any dealings stemming from the transactions of the properties and of course the skimming would stop. She had gotten them for millions, and had already put the money up in an offshore account.

The only one who could stop anything now was Felix, at least so he thought. But she knew what to do with him though, kill him. Really easy. She was tired of him already. Maria had done all that she could for him. She just couldn't believe that he actually tried to be a witness against the Cartel. That was crazy cute. They'd eventually find him, then kill him.

Maria disassociated herself years ago. The phone call bothered her. He was up to his old tricks again. All he really needed to do was lay low, but now he was trying to twist the Cartels arm behind their backs. Playing games with the cobra.

But Felix had no bargaining chips to work with. He no longer owned the property flat out. Years ago, she took over his share and now since she gave Latif his share, or at least made him aware of it, that was a rap.

She slid open her drawer and reached for a folder, pulling out a card, Edward Gonzalez. Her personal hitman. Don't know what type of game Felix was playing, but for sure she wouldn't be the one he'd be meeting with. She'd send Edward to take him out.

Maria leaned back in her chair while holding the card above her and smiled. Who knows, after this job she might even take him along with her. He was a handsome man, and after all a little eye candy wouldn't hurt.

Tina scanned her eyes around the office making sure no one was watching. Maria just told her to hold all her calls for a while, she'd be on the line making a personal call.

Tina knew what time it was. She had to act swiftly. She already dialed the number she needed on another phone. A private line, and was waiting for the person on the other end to pick up. She didn't have to wait too long though. "Hello, Omar?" The Cartels operative in the United States, Guillermo's right hand man, and her boyfriend. He'd gotten her the job.

"Cor'tina, believe it or not, I was just thinking of you."

"She's on the phone now."

"With the guy!"

"Yeah, the ATF guy."

"Okay, okay. Then, she must be planning something with him. You would be able to listen in, right."

Of course, she could. She had it down to an art, a science even. How else could they have known most of all Maria comings and goings as well as her dealings, business and personal, AT&T?

She was the perfect plant, Maria's receptionist, Maria's secretary, Maria's personal assistant. All because she was just too cheap to pay anyone else. And Guillermo, by way of the Cartel, Cor'tina, her real name, and her family were paid well.

"I'll be on it. I'll call you back, Okay."

"Okay, señorita, okay "

Tina picked up her phone like she did many times before, and held it in her hand, placing the dampened handkerchief to the speaker. She lightly pressed the button for the line Maria was on while her other hand started writing down the information that Omar wanted. However primitive it was, it worked.

She snickered to herself, this was too easy. Maria, always the loudmouth flapping her gums, never had a clue.

"What the hell do you mean?"

"Look, Maria. I can't kill him! Hell, he's probably being watched by the Cartel. I'll be spotted, I know it!"

"Spotted?" Maria banged her fist on the desk. "You fucking kill a woman in broad daylight. In a crowded nigga neighborhood. Surrounded by cops! You weren't fucking nervous then."

Edward paused. She was taking the bait, but he had to sell the whole thing. He knew she would probably call and ask for Felix's head, but he needed more information. "Not enough money."

"Not enough, you're kidding me, right? "

"No, I'm not. It's a dangerous job. It might as well be my last because if I do this then they'll be after me for life. I'll need papers, a new identity, the works, and that costs money."

Maria leaned back in her chair and kicked her feet up on her desk. "Yeah. You may be right. Matter of fact." She twirled the telephone cord around in her hand. "I might just have the thing for you."

"Like what?"

"Well. I'm about to get some money."

"Cartel money?" Damn, he hoped he hadn't let on too soon. He had to be patient. Let her put it out there.

"Let's just say... money accumulated over the years, huh. A lot of money."

She was a braggart, and that would be her downfall if he had anything to do about it. She talked way too much, and was always trying to shine. "Where? Tell me."

"There's a load coming in through the freights."

"Where?"

"Brooklyn Navy yard. I got a copy of the manifest and the cargo bill."

"Yeah, okay, so you know where the cargo is held?"

"We go in. Get what we need... a little extra, maybe and then disappear. Maybe...hmmm, even, together." She drug that out softly, then paused, waiting for his response. A very crucial response.

"Hmm. Sounds good." Edward pumped his fist in the air. He'd hit the jackpot. The Cartel's load. All of it. And, she had a manifest. Hopefully with names. "Deal."

She almost fell over," Deal?"

"Yeah, a deal. Just tell me where to meet you."

"Sure." She jumped up. "Can I call you back in a few hours? Make sure I can have the papers you need ready." She headed for the door then stopped. "By the way, how much were you looking for?"

Edward paused for a second, then thought, "100 grand."

"100,000?"

"Yeah, that's what I want! "

"You got it."

Edward thought. Did she have that much of the Cartel's money? 100 grand sounded like a drop in a bucket for her. "Okay, call me later."

"Bye, bye." Maria headed for the door and swung it open. Tina had just hung up the phone and turned her way. "Tina. Call the realtor in the Hamptons and tell him we don't want it."

"You don't want it? The house?"

"Yeah. The Caribbean sounds a whole lot better right about now." She turned and closed the door. Tina picked up her pad and ripped out the papers, then scrambled the information she had just heard down and called for a Messenger. She knew Omar had to have those new developments right now and Maria was going to be calling her any minute. "Tina!"

"Yes ma'am."

"Come in here. We need to make new plans. "

"Yes ma'am, on my way."

Tina stuffed the papers into an envelope and hastily wrote down an address on the front. She spotted one of the messengers and called him over. "Delivered this asap."

"I got some other..."

She pulled out a fresh one-hundred-dollar bill and shoved it in his face. "Will this help? "

"Hell yeah." He snatched the money and the envelope and jetted out the office. Tina turned around, and with pen and pad in hand, stepped into Maria's office with a smile on her face. Maria asked arrogantly, "What the hell are you fucking smiling about?"

"Nothing ma'am. It's just a good day."

"Damn sure is. Now, come over here and help me with these boxes, quickly."

"Yes ma'am...yes ma'am, quickly."

# CHAPTER THIRTEEN

Waseema blew the dusk of the keyhole of the dungeon vault door in the cellar. Behind her was Ice holding her steady as she stepped through. The lights from the flashlights lit the bright room as she spotted circles of light probed around the inside of the old room. "You know, one day I need to come down here and clean this place," she said.

"For real. Why is there so much dust anyway?" Latif asked.

Ice looked at the walls and felt them. "The walls are all dirt, that's why. They were never forged with brick, concrete, or anything for that matter. It's really just a cave."

They all chuckled, and Latif added. "Seems kinda haunted."

"Eeeek!" Waseema screamed. Ice jumped in front of her and reached for the knife he had tucked in his pants and hollered. "What's up!" Latif was propped up against the wall laughing hard as hell. Waseema reached around Ice and punched him on the arm. "Stop, boy!"

Ice sighed, "You need to quit playing!"

"Damn. Ice...just having a little fun."

Ice pointed his flashlight around the ceilings and walls and questioned, "Where is it?"

"I don't know for sure. Mama hid it. At one point she said before she passed that even Malik had a key to it."

"The same key? Damn, how did he get it?"

"He stole it, made a duplicate."

"Stole it?"

"Right from under my mama nose. But that's another story. She eventually got it back and gave it to me, the original."

"You know, your family is one big mystery. All these stories." Ice grabbed her by the hand. "Is this one real?"

She pulled him closer and kissed him. "What do you think, baby? "

Latif pushed past them saying. "Get a room for God's sake." He pointed the flashlight around the wall and spotted a light switch, then walked over and flipped it. No light. He flipped it again, and still no light. "Hey ma... Didn't these lights work before?"

"Yeah," Ice said as he walked over to him and flipped the switch himself. "They damn sure did the last time we came down here a few weeks ago."

Waseema stared off then scanned the room and walked over to the far side and pulled a chained light switch on a fixture that stood off from the wall. The lights came on. She went around the room and turned on the other three. "No. These were the lights I used."

"Then, what is this?"

"Shhh, be quiet and be still." Ice flipped the switch again and they could hear a crude sliding sound that led them straight to a corner wall, where they pushed aside some old books, boxes. There it was. "Oh shit!"

Towards the backend opposite of where they stood and along the bottom base of the floor. Small mounds of dirt were built up, and clay trailed heavily along the foundation of the floor. It was a brick, and on it, what appeared to be a latch. A very small latch with what seemed to be a spring attached mechanism behind it.

Years of damp gave way to rust, and without the proper maintenance-oil. It produced the loud squeaking sound that they now heard. Latif pushed aside the dirt and muck and brushed at it. As he did, it turned out to be a brick of a pattern of sorts. About twelve inches tall and five to six inches or so wide. It was a door for an opening. Ice flipped the switch again and in tandem Latif yanked it open. Behind it was a grey metal box. A small box-the safe. He blew at it and the dust revealed a keyhole. He looked up at his mother.

Waseema quickly took the necklace that had the key from around her neck and handed it over to him. He put it in and started to twist it but before he did Ice stopped him. "See if the whole thing can come out first."

Latif glanced up at him and answered. "Yeah...okay. Let's see." Working his fingers on the side of it he pulled hard, but it was stubborn, after all these years it wasn't going to be jerked out of what had now become its home, that easily. Ice looked around for something to dig at the clay that had molded itself to it and saw nothing. Waseema kicked off her shoes, picked them up and broke off the long stiletto heel. "They weren't expensive, anyway," she said as Ice shook his head and handed it to Latif. He dug around the sides and finally it started to give. He pulled, it came out, and more dust came right along with it. "Damn, cough, cough, hope this is worth it."

"Must be. Somebody sure took the time to keep it secure." Ice said as he wiped his face.

"It was probably a spot my father used at one time." Waseema said, "No telling what else is in here." She added as she eyeballed the dimly lit dark cellar. "No telling."

"True, but right now we need to get this box out." Latif jerked and it came out, causing him to fall back. Ice helped pull him up and he took the box, which seemed a little heavy for its size out the cellar. Then they all went upstairs. Waseema cut off the lights, shut the door, then locked it, vowing to come back down another day and clean it up. Maybe even look for some more little cubby holes. See what else was there. Ice pulled at her hand and said, "C'mon baby. I know what you're thinking, and I'll come down here with you."

"Yeah...real soon."

They made their way to the kitchen putting the box on the table, but only after Waseema grabbed a couple of sheets to cover it. Latif blew the dirt off the lock, then very carefully inserted the key and twisted it. It didn't open. He slid it back out and angrily exclaimed, "Now what?"

A woman's touch, Waseema took the key and placed it in her mouth wetting it. She stuck it back in and gingerly twisted it. It opened. The top popped and you could hear the rush of a seal being opened.

Latif cautiously lifted the long metal top. It was filled with papers. Curled up at the ends a little, but real crisp. He lifted one out and observed it. It was a document showing ownership, a deed. "Oh shit!" He looked up at his mother. This is a location for 142nd Street and Lenox Avenue.

The Cotton Club.

He reached for another. This is somewhere in Brooklyn. Latif handed it to Ice.

"Hmm. Let's see. Okay...Okay...Gates Avenue, Halsey Street, Chauncey Street, all the way up to damn near Eastern Parkway. Wow, a bunch of scattered stores all the way up Broadway, including yours. He looked up at Waseema. You all...own them."

Latif grabbed more, and it was all the same. Deed after deed. All prime property. All worth thousands, if not more.

"No wonder Maria wanted you around all the time. You were worth millions to her." Ice blurted out.

But Latif looked over at his mother and sighed, "She paid me peanuts." He shook his head in frustration. "She played me."

"She played us, son." Waseema rubbed at his back comforting him.

"But...we'll get ours." Like your father said, "We'll get our redemption..."

"And his, too!"

HIS LONG FACE DWINDLED downward as his mouth twitched below his short-cropped mustache. His eyes; narrowed. His shoulders hunched as he concentrated. Something devious was on his mind. It was like a vulture to its prey, biding its time.

Omar had just verbalized to him the information he had gotten from Tina. And it was championship good. Maria was planning to steal money from one of the Cartel's main sites. Daring. Bold. A bit ostentatious, perhaps. But it was nothing to her, she'd been doing it for years.

Licking his lips as sat in the padded leather seat in front of a hardwood oak desk that once belonged to another occupant who'd been since evicted; Cholo. If only he knew at the time. Guillermo had been sent to New York by the Cartel a few years back in the early nineties to find out about some missing capitol; the books were short. His standing orders were easy. Eliminate the problem. Cholo got hip to him, his plans, and played with his life. At any cost, was the Cartel's declaration, and his sentiments.

But now, he too was trying to figure out how this whole thing could work in his favor. A double cross indeed. The only ones who knew anything so far were him, Omar and Omar's girlfriend, Tina. Hell, he thought, easy enough for him to just start eliminating.

"Guillermo! Don't even think about it! I can literally see it brooding over your head." Omar had snapped him out of his dastardly plot and bought him to a stark reality. An actuality that didn't play to his licking. Omar knew his pedigree. He was not to be trusted. "The Cartel wants her alive...and me too."

"I know, I know, of course. You! C'mon now...but, what if..."

"There are no what if's, Guillermo, just dos." Omar walked over to his desk and stood. He was a short, stocky, solid man of stature at five-six, two hundred thirty pounds. The build of a man that had put in a lot of work, hard work, physical work. The kind of work he no longer desired.

He grew up dirt-poor and knew the value of an education, working tirelessly to put himself through school. To be more like the American. The gringo. His mother however, knew the value of a dollar. She worked hard herself for pennies on the dollar on her back for one of the Cartel's henchmen. She overheard him saying one night that he needed a man, a trusted servant, loyal and smart to do a job for him. Her son fit the bill.

Omar's mother was no longer poor. As a result of Omar's loyalty to the Cartel, she now had her own domestic help.

Omar was a very devoted man to the Cartel, and Guillermo knew that, but he was going to test him anyway. See if he was really committed or if it was an act of genuineness towards the American dollar.

"Hey, look, suppose we...don't inform the Cartel just yet?"

Omar's mouth curled into a grin. He knew he was going to try him and was ready for it. "Talk to me."

Guillermo thought maybe he might have to cut his compatriots throat. Literally. He was curious, he could see in his eyes, small it on his breath. This was a new chain of events. "Are you sure?" he said as he glanced down towards his desk drawer where a .38 revolver laid inconspicuously in the cut.

Omar walked over to where a small chair was and drugged it right over up in front of Guillermo. Guillermo couldn't see where his hands were, unless he got up and leaned over. Which would pose a serious risk if something were to evolve. Omar knew this, so he asked, "You got a plan or what?"

What was there to lose? Guillermo knew what page he was on. He knew he was going to find out if they were both reading from the same newspaper. Fuck it. "We go in behind Maria. Find out exactly where the money is."

"And drugs"

"And, the drugs. Kill her. Kill this ATF guy...frame him for the murder. Take the money that's washed, all that."

"And, the other money that's coming in to be cleaned?"

"Use that to capitalize on the properties that we'll be taking over from her. Business, my friend."

"And, the Cartel?"

"Omar, give me a break. If they sent us, then they really don't know too much about the broad anyway. Or what she was doing. Now do they? Now...any more, questions?"

"You've got a point." Omar got up and paced the floor, then scratched the hairs underneath his chin, saying, "Okay...okay, then, when do we do it?" He turned and stared at him, then asked, "And...do I have to watch my back, Guillermo?"

Guillermo looked up at him. "What do you think?"

"I think it's a good plan, but perhaps." Omar walked over to the door and cracked it. Guillermo still hadn't answered his question. "I think I'll take my share to uh, let's just say. California...you stay here with the New York thing."

Guillermo stood and reached out for him to stop. "Hey! I got a better idea. You do know how deep the Cartel is in California, property, drugs, all that? Look, a truce. Me and you, no bullshit. I've been looking at another spot. Just as lucrative, if not more. Hear me out."

"Where?" Omar was intrigued enough to take notice. He stopped and listened.

"Arizona."

"Arizona?"

"Look, think about it, it's right in the main vein. In and out of Mexico. A straight shot into California, and a b-line up into Canada by way of Detroit."

"What about New York?"

"What about New York. Who needs it anyway? We can still have our people here handle the business. I just might even have the right man in mind."

Okay, Guillermo. He walked back over to his desk and extended his hand. "Deal?"

Guillermo extended his, but not before he eyeballed the .45 Omar had so conveniently exposed. He nodded his head. "Deal."

"Okay then Guillermo. We meet when? Where?"

"The end of the week. According to the info your people got. That's when they're supposed to go, right? We'll get up with each other tomorrow at the armory to get what we need. The right supplies. Maybe, a few men."

"Not too many. Only the ones that can be trusted."

"Men, that are tired of the Cartel, you mean?" Guillermo looked at him and smirked.

"Yeah," Omar walked to the door and swung it open. "That's exactly what I mean." Then closed it shut behind him as he stepped through.

Guillermo sat back down pondering over what he had just done. Of course, it would be a good thing if Omar was genuine, but he knew it was just a scheme. He was a Cartel for life. He knew once he got the money, he was going to have to take his ass out too. The Cartel would be on him too hard, and he'd fold under the pressure. Unmask him. Yeah right...a traitor. You won't betray me though. After all, dead men can't talk.

ASIA GOT UP FROM HER bed walking into the bathroom singing a song she'd heard over and over again on the radio. One of those popular little hooks that you just couldn't shake. Not exactly knowing the words she made up her own and came up with what she thought was a rather catchy number. Feeling good this morning, and not as sluggish as she'd been going through lately. In a couple more days she'd be a very rich woman. The biggest cash payday she'd ever had. Enough to do other things besides killing and robbing. She knew she was nothing more than a thief, the only thing was, she was far from petty.

Rasheed had just left her bed and she felt like exploding. He was her greatest love and by far one of the best lovers she'd ever had. And hopefully, she would ever know. She finished brushing her teeth and examined the roots of her hair line; still thick, vibrant. She ran her hands through her slick, black curled mane and smiled her teethiest in the mirror. Looking and feeling every bit of twenty-five. Feeling ever so good she ran the water for a nice hot bath before she set out for the day.

She dropped the t-shirt she had on to the floor and stepped in the steamy water laced with perfumed, aromatic oils and then the phone rang. She started to ignore it, but it continued on. Maybe, it was Rasheed calling. Curious she put the t-shirt back on and rushed to the phone. "Hello?"

"Hey wassup, baby."

Asia took the phone away from her face and shook her head, not out of disgust, but she knew Kokomo was on some drama shit that she wasn't trying to feel right now. It'd spoil her morning. "Hello, hello?"

"Hey, what's up, Kokomo."

"Nothing, baby. Thinking about you, that's all."

"That's nice."

"So, uh, we're still gonna meet up today?"

They were supposed to get together and make a run uptown to the Bronx. Check out a dude they knew, an old Italian wise guy. Their plan was to pick up some special armor for the job. It was routine. Not like it was a date or anything, but evidently, he took it that way. "Of course. I was just thinking about that. But look, uh, I'm just about to step into the tub."

Yeah. Okay. You want me to come over and wash your back?" Kokomo shot that out there. He was feeling that way anyway. At least he'd see where her head was at. He was tired of the games. Mostly the ones she was playing.

"No...that's alright." She giggled. "But, thanks for asking."

"No, Asia...I'm serious."

"What?"

"I'm serious. I...want to be with you."

Asia pulled up a chair. Here it comes. Wasn't the first time, but it would have to be the last. She had to let him know. She glanced into the bathroom and noticed the steam coming off the water less and less. Now she was pissed. "C'mon now Kokomo. You know we don't get down like that."

"Why not. I ain't good enough for you?"

"No. It ain't that. You're a nice guy, but..."

"But, what? Ever since that dude Rasheed came into the picture you've changed."

"Why are you going there? We're friends, right?"

"Who, me, or him. Look, Asia." The tone of his voice diminished some, but the intensity of the matter hadn't. "I have feelings for you. I want us to go legit. Do some positive things. Maybe. Even raise a family."

"Family? You're kidding me! What the hell are we gonna do with kids? Me? You?" She laughed. "Look at Kokomo. I'm sad you feel that way towards me, and I'm sorry. I love you, but only as a friend. "

He bit the bottom of his lip hard enough for a trickle of blood to spurt. As bad as he wanted to slam the phone in her ear. As bad as he wanted to race over there, bust the door down, snatch her up and take that ass. As bad as he wanted to, he didn't. Instead, he did what he'd always done. "Damn." He laughed back. Played it off. "You know I was just joking. You're alright by me."

"Why are you doing that, Kokomo?"

"What?"

"Playing around like that. I thought you were serious or something. You need to stop. You know how I feel about Rasheed. Hell, he just left from here. I'll tell you the truth. I wish you were the type of man he..." She caught herself. "I mean, you and him are so much alike." She tried to put some straightening on it, but it was in vain.

"I get it, Asia. You don't have to explain." There was a silence on the phone, then, "Look. I'll be there in a couple of hours to pick you up. Be ready, alright?"

"Kokomo. I didn't mean to sound..."

"A couple of hours. Be ready." He hung up.

"Damn." She hung up the phone and walked back to the tub and got in, thinking about what she had just said, She knew it was wrong, but what was she to do? She loved her 'Sheed and there was nothing Kokomo could do or say that would change that. She just hoped it wouldn't affect the way he did the job.

She looked underneath the sink towards the back to retrieve a hidden pack of cigarettes. Sure, she thought about her promise to Rasheed to quit, but she needed one. He wouldn't know anyway. She slid deep into the hot steamy water and took a smooth pull off the cigarette letting the warmth burn her chest. It soothed her. She started to moan as she fondled herself all the while thinking of Rasheed. She found herself purring and letting out a throaty euphoric sound saying. "Oh. Baby."

Kokomo slammed the phone down. He was pissed. He had to get it off, let it go. He walked over to the weight room and stopped. No that wouldn't do it. He walked towards the door and stepped onto the railing calling downstairs, Shante! Shante!

The pretty, petite brown skinned, young woman came out her door and looked upstairs at him, "What!"

"Come up here!"

"I'm doing something!"

"Now!"

She sucked her teeth and stepped back inside, then came out with her keys and locked the door. She stomped up the stairs to his door and peeped in. "What's wrong?"

Kokomo was in the bathroom when she called out. "You know what it is."

"Come on now Kokomo. I was doing something. Can it wait till later?"

"Look!" He peeped out the bathroom and pointed towards the table. A fresh $100 bill. She sucked her teeth, and walked over to it and stuffed it in her bra. "Now what?"

"You know what! Don't play stupid!" She walked into his bedroom and started undressing. She turned to climb on the bed and was roughly grabbed from behind. "Come on now. That hurt."

"C'mon now, that hurt." He mocked as he bent her over across the bed and started rubbing up against her ass. She squirmed trying to resist, but his weight kept her subdued. "Now, you know what to say right."

"Right." She kicked her pants on the floor and raised her ass up high. "Kokomo, please, fuck me hard," she said as she felt him harden up and as he continued to rub his dick up against her; faster, harder. He wasn't gentle. Not that he ever was, she thought to herself, but he must have had a bad morning, and she somewhat knew who this whole thing was directed at. All she could do was let loose and let him have his way. It wouldn't last long, it never did. It'd be painful without a doubt, but he always paid extra.

A tear came down her eye. It was hard for her. School was hard. Paying the rent was hard. Kokomo looked out for her. She just had to play the role he wanted for her. She did. He wet his dick inside of her moist pussy, then pulled out and rammed it hard into her ass and started stroking wildly. It was rock hard, and she dared not to tighten herself around him or she'd risk damaging herself more than she already had. But this was his thing, punishment. "Yeah, baby. Yeah...Asia. Yeah. My dick good, Asia?"

More tears came down from her eyes. She really dug the hell out of Kokomo. This whole scenario was aimed at some stinking ass woman she'd only seen a few times. She knew she was cute and all, but she wasn't nowhere near as pretty as her. She'd treat him better than Asia could though, and she meant that. One day, she'd tell him. For right now she had to play the game. So, just like in the movies with the scene played over and over again. "Yeah, baby...it's good."

"Is it good, Asia?"

"Yes, it's good! Yes!"

He continued to pump harder and harder inside of her, until she felt something watery splash on her back. He slowed. Maybe she thought, it might've been pre-cum dripping. Good, he's just about finished. Then she realized he was still inside of her. More and more it continued to come, then she finally realized what it was. Tears. His. "Yes, baby...I love you too," she whispered under her breath. So yeah, it was just like in the movies. A real live script.

EDWARDS OLD BEAT UP Ford smoked its way up the Avenue, stopping across the street in front of the steel and glass framed building. In contrast to it, the edifice not only dropped it in size, but appearance.

Indifference to him, however, he was wearing a black custom fitted suit. ATF attire, but he only wore it on occasion. This was an occasion. He needed to play the game. Maria wanted him so he needed to draw her in. Make the package more attractive to her. He didn't normally do the dress up thing. He was, thinking of finishing the knot on the tie he had strapped around his neck, but changed his mind. Tossing it to the seat, he instead pulled up the collar on his crisp white shirt, took a deep breath, and strutted towards the front of the high rise.

The security guard told him he was expected. Even so, he did look him up and down to see if he was the right man. The features were correct. The clothing threw him off. After all, Maria had never seen him in a suit. Whenever they met, he always had on some grungy, tattered jeans, and a T-shirt with either a hoodie or a jacket on.

He pointed him to a private elevator. Edward stepped in and pressed, penthouse. Dang, he thought, this chick was living the life. He leaned back. Not knowing what to expect, he reasoned that it couldn't be that bad. Couple of more moves and this whole scheme would be over. But he had to be patient, let her lead first, then he'd go with it. His mission was twice as fast. One, find out where the money and drugs that the Cartel had shipped. Two, find out when the date was set to go in.

Everything else was irrelevant. He did need one more thing, though. That was to keep her alive long enough to find out more about the properties she had control of. No way would he turn her over to his authorities. No way. She'd sing like a bird. Figure he'd kill her to make it look like she was trying to escape. Or she'd try to kill him. He reached for the personal weapon he had strapped to his ankle and patted it. Easy enough. The elevator dinged and stopped. The doors opened and he took a deep breath. It was on.

She was standing at the receptionist desk when he came through the glass, double doors. The long, soft, mahogany wood console with light streaming across the top and bottom showed brightly in contrast to her two piece, pinstriped, pants outfit, and radiant, pink blouse. Her long hair was down well past her shoulders covering the long plunging cleavage she exhibited. Nails, a hot pink, and matching lip gloss. Edward stopped in his tracks. She picked up on it, and struck yet another, more seductive pose, then licked her lips wet. He felt his lower half stiffen, but he maintained his cool. Thinking about the business and all the plans he'd made just a measly five minutes ago on the elevator coming up. He couldn't be that weak and expose himself like that. "Maria. How are you?" He extended his hand.

In response, he also struck a pose, robust, masculine, after all he was supposed to be her hired hitman. His tall, strong, muscular body had fit well in the suit, and she noticed. She licked her lips again, and felt herself get horny too. But she had to keep it business, for now. "I'm fine. Why don't we step into my office."

She led the way and walked past Tina's desk and said, "Tina. Things are rather slow. Why don't you, and everyone else leave for the day? I won't be needing anything." She turned and looked at him up and down like a piece of meat. "I'm good."

"Sure you are. Excuse me. I mean. Sure. Everything is good. I'll." Tina peeped over at Edward and cut her eyes downward. "Tell everyone." He let that action boost his ego and fed into it. "And, your name is?"

She glanced at him, but turned away sharply as Maria cut her eyes towards her. "I'm her assistant." She picked up her bag and started towards the office area with the other employees. "I'll be letting everyone out, ma'am. "

"Thanks, Tina." Maria opened up her office door and said, "Please, come in."

Tina watched as the door closed. She doubled back to her desk, opened the drawer, and grabbed her phone book. She turned and rushed back out behind everyone else, making sure she locked the front door. She piled on the elevator and couldn't wait for it to get downstairs. She'd be calling Omar first thing as soon as she got to a phone. It was a shame she thought. That ATF guy looked rather handsome. Too bad he'd have to die, but that's life, she thought, his, not hers. Maria walked around her desk and sat down as Edward got comfortable on the sofa, looking at the pictures she still had on the walls. "Nice, who are they?"

She spun the chair around and said, "My father, and a friend...of the family."

"Hmmm. The family friend looks familiar."

"Maybe. But I don't think you know her. She's dead. "

"Okay. I get it. It's none of my business. "

"Well...you said it." She turned back around and crossed her legs. "So, did you consider my offer?"

"Of course, I did. But where's the papers I asked for."

Maria slid open the desk drawer and pulled out a manila envelope. "Right here." And tossed it to him. He opened it and thumbed through it. "Is it all there?"

"Yes, except."

She pointed to the briefcase she had posted by the sofa.

"Damn...didn't see that." He picked it up and opened it. Stacks of bills. Thousands, he guesstimated. "What...about one hundred grand?"

"One fifty. Lil extra."

Appreciate it." He sat it back down. "Now, what else is uh...up." He unbuttoned his jacket and let her observe and ogle over his chest for a sec.

She took that as a go and smiled. She stood up and swung her hair over her shoulders revealing her breast. "Let's...negotiate some things."

He nodded, then stood up letting her check out the hard on between his legs that had risen. "That's about the size...of matter."

"Yes, I see." She walked over to him slowly unbuttoning her blouse and allowing him to observe the low cut, hot pink bra she had on. Once she got up on him, she reached and popped the clip. Her titties sprung out. Edward grabbed her by the arms and pulled her closer, starting at her soft, luscious lips and said, "We'll talk later, okay. Right now, I'm going to fuck the shit out of you."

She purred. "I hope so."

Maria lay silently sleeping, curled up on the sofa in a little ball like a baby while Edward leaned against the windowsill looking out towards Manhattan. Watching the sunset, he observed how the shadows fell off the skyscrapers casting a darkness on the brightly lit, urban streets. The ambiance and flow of the sprawling metropolis changed once the sun went down.

He walked over to another window of her spacious office in glance eastward at Brooklyn. A clear view of Williamsburg, Bushwick, Bed-Stuy, and Fort Greene. The warehouses and the canals, all about to be remodeled into condos, steak houses, sushi bars, and yuppie playgrounds. She was smart to have chosen this building, it gave her a clear view as well.

He turned, faced the door, then wondered. Did she have this whole floor? He didn't even bother to look behind him when he got off the elevator. Once he walked into the office area it just never dawned on him. He figured he'd explore, check it out. His investigative instincts kicked in. He looked over at Maria, she was still asleep. He tiptoed towards the door, grabbed a doorknob, and twisted it.

"Where are you going, darling?"

It was Maria. She was awake.

"Just looking for a bathroom. Have to take a leak," he said as he grabbed his crotch. She pointed towards the door located on the other side of her office.

"Over there."

"Thanks," he said as he walked over, opened it and gasped. A marble floor and sink with a polished glassed, stand-in shower. He gawked at the eighteen-karat gold, sink fittings; the highly burnished, glossed porcelain toilet and goose feathered, padded lid top. At least she spent money on the comforts, no doubt. He picked up the lid and was just about to pee when his attention was diverted towards the shower area.

The back end. A window. A captain's window like the one you'd see on ships, a porthole. He strained his neck trying to get a glimpse outside, but after pissing on the floor, he figured he'd just wait.

Once he finished and wiped up his mess, he stepped towards the shower and looked in. Sure enough, a window. But to where? He couldn't get his bearings, so he stepped into the shower and looked out. It was the Brooklyn Navy yard. Wow, this chick didn't play any games, he thought. The door opened behind him. It was Maria. "Oh, so you want to take shower."

He had to go with it. Besides, he'd be able to look out some more, see more. "Sure, why not." He started undressing, then looked her way and said, "You are joining me. Right?"

She smiled and started undressing also.

They washed. Made love. Washed again, then Edward questioned. "So...why do you want me to kill your husband again?"

Maria grinned and pulled a towel off the rack. "Why not?"

"I mean, it's a lot of money for a, "why not". Hell, why not watch him die of old age first."

She giggled. "You are funny." She stepped out of the shower and there was a small closet. She opened it, grabbed a robe and threw it over to him. "Let's just say he comes into the way of our plans."

"How?"

"Well. He's still my husband. He would still be entitled to half...if not everything."

"Why not divorce him?"

She glanced his way and smiled. "You are a thinker, that's for sure."

"The work I do requires a man to think, otherwise I wouldn't be successful. I'd be locked the fuck up instead."

She giggled again. "Got that right. Well, if I divorce him, then all of what I have as well as the little he has becomes a public record. He'd drag everything into court. I know he would. But if he was just to...hmmm, perish, then all I would have to do then is to bury him. Everything he has becomes mine. You know, the poor, grieving widow thing. And if anyone asks questions about the business finances, then I can disclose what I want to disclose. Use my people, accountants. You do understand?"

Edward slipped the robe on and walked towards her and hugged her, then sumptuously kissed the nape of her neck. Fully. They walked out the room into the office and he asked, "How do you know I wouldn't do the same to you?"

She slipped on her pants. Picked up her drink, turned towards him and said, "Then, I guess I'd have to kill you too," then giggled.

Edward nodded. He thought to himself, don't I know it.

"But, there's still a matter that needs to be handled."

"And, what is that?"

"This property has other partners. A partner that needs to be eliminated. Soon."

"Is that so?"

"Yes." She reached into her desk drawer and pulled out a manila envelope, opened it, pulled out a photo and shoved it towards him. "His name is Latif."

Edward looked at the picture. He recognized the face but couldn't quite place it. "You want me to..."

"Kill him." Maria grabbed the photo and threw it on the desk. Then, she walked up to him and kissed him. "Then, everything will belong to us...darling.

# CHAPTER FOURTEEN

The latex, Kevlar gloves weren't as heavy as first expected, but were still smooth and nimble enough to handle a gun. The trigger finger had all the flexibility in it to do the job, and that was what was needed. However, the full, black body suit that they donned seemed a little heavy in comparison. It was all due in part to the Kevlar vest sewn into the front and back. Rasheed picked up some goggles and tried them on. "So, this is what they wear in the Army?"

"It's new technology. I'm borrowing all of this stuff from a friend of a friend over Fort Dix. Maybe one day it might be a standard issue."

"Standard issue. Dang, that sounds really dangerous, and sexy." Waseema blew a kiss at him.

"Come on guys. Get a room," Rasheed sighed.

Ice turned his attention back and continued. "It's still the 90's. But I guess by the Millennium..."

"Whoa...hold on." Latif interrupted. I'm in as much, uh, awe, as the next man on all this GI Joe equipment, but shouldn't we be focused on the task at hand.

"You're right." Rasheed said, "Now, we all know our roles, right. Any questions? We need to come clean now. This is serious. People can get killed. Hopefully, God willing, none of them will be us."

Ice put his hand out. "We are all in this together. Are y'all ready?" He looked at Rasheed, then Latif, and finally Waseema. "Are you sure you want to do this?"

"Yes," She looked around at them. "I do. I know how to handle myself."

"Mom, just be careful, that's all we're saying." Rasheed said, "You're still our mother. The only reason we're letting you come into this is so you can keep a lookout. So, do that...that's all. You hear?"

"Yeah...yeah."

"Baby, we're serious. This is very serious. The last time me and your son did this..."

"Yeah...the last time people died." Rasheed spit.

"I'm sorry Rasheed." She reached out and grabbed him by the hand. "I'll do whatever you say. You got it."

"Okay then." Ice rapped on the side of the truck and Shaheeda opened up a sliding window attached to the backend of the half-ton truck they were in and said, "Ready?"

"Ready." Ice responded.

"Alright."

The truck cranked up and after a few turns, and bumps from pothole laden streets, Latif lamented on a memory. "You remember Rasheed, when dad would take us to you and Mustapha's basketball games in the summer. The ones at the old Boy's High in Bed-Stuy."

"Yeah, I remember."

"He used to teach us a dua. He said you needed it the way y'all played."

"Yeah.' Rasheed snickered. "It worked though."

Latif raised up his hands and said, "Allahummaa tahli abwaabil rahmatika."

Waseema reached over and kissed him on the forehead. "O, Allah! Open the doors of your mercy for me."

The truck stopped and Shaheeda opened the window back and yelled out. "Alright. We're here. The corner of Adelphi Street and Myrtle Avenue."

"Fort Greene projects...C-Town supermarket." Rasheed said under his breath.

Ice pulled up the door, peeped, then jumped out. He came back a few seconds later and motioned everyone out. "Let's go. Coast is clear."

They got out and hit the sides of the building where it was darkest, blending in. They ducked and slowly, stealthily made their way down the street towards Park Avenue. Where they would then wait in the cut for Kokomo and Asia to signal them on.

ASIA PULLED UP IN FRONT of the apartment house and honked the horn. Kokomo stuck his head out the window upstairs and shouted. "Be down in the second!"

She sucked her teeth, and yelled back. "Hurry up! We got things to do!"

Kokomo stomped down the steps and banged on Shante's door. She opened it up and spat. "Yes. What do you want now? "

Kokomo frowned up. He deserved that. This girl was nothing but good to him, and he dogged her out. Never really told her how much he really felt. "Who is it, babe?" A voice hollered out from the back. Her bedroom. She turned her head and said, "Just a friend, from upstairs."

"Well, tell him to come back later. You got company!"

"Chill out!" She turned back towards Kokomo. "I can't do anything for you. Anymore." She held her head down and started to close the door.

Kokomo reached into his pocket and pulled out a set of keys. "Look, I'll be away...for a while. If you don't see or hear from me in about a month. Take everything in the house." He handed them to her.

"And, go where?" she asked.

"It's all yours."

"Mine? What's wrong?"

"Just do it, okay."

He turned and took a step towards the door, but she grabbed him by the arm, pulling him towards her, then kissed him. "I got you."

Kokomo kissed her back, and said, "I know you do." He pulled away and opened the front door, glancing back he saw that Shante had tears in her eyes. He didn't know his future, but he knew if he made it back, he'd made changes in his life, and maybe even hers. For now, this was the present. He turned and focused, Asia was in the driver seat with Cookie in the back. He opened the door and said, "Sorry about the delay. Had to handle something."

Asia nudged him. "I know you got a little thing for that old hotty toddy downstairs. "

"Yeah, whatever." She pulled away from the curb and turned to look out the window. Shante had just put their head out the door, and Asia sneered at her, "Skeezer."

Kokomo looked over at her, and smirked. "I guess there's a lot of that going around, huh?"

She stomped on the brakes almost letting a bus ram them from behind, and hollered at him. "You got something to say, then say it!"

Kokomo's face frowned as she leaned back, she had never seen that look before. She had touched a nerve. Slowly she started reaching for her gun thinking he was going to slap her. She'd have to shoot. No man would ever put his hands on her again. Cookie thought also, and leaned in between them. "Now stop this! We got work to do, and we damn sure ain't got time for this. Y'all handle this another time!" Kokomo leaned back in his seat and spit. "Yeah. Other times."

Asia mean mugged him, then turned on Bushwick Avenue. "Where are you going?" he asked.

"I'm going to turn on DeKalb Avenue, make our way to Myrtle Avenue and drop Cookie off on Vanderbilt Avenue. If that's Okay with you." She added sarcastically, but Kokomo ignored her, and asked Cookie, "That ain't too far away?"

"No, that's good. Gives me time to get my mind right," Cookie pulled up the mini he was wearing and showed him two razors. "And my tools are right."

"Cool. Just thought I'd ask."

Asia made a right turn on Tompkins Avenue, then a left on Myrtle. She turned towards Kokomo and said, "Look. I'm sorry. Nerves."

"We're good."

"You got the walkie talkies? Batteries good?"

"I hit Rasheed up just before I left out. They should be in place by now."

"Okay."

She turned onto Vanderbilt Avenue approaching Flushing Avenue and pulled over. Alright, here we are. She put the car in park and turned around. "You be careful. Remember, will be right there. Right behind you, okay."

Cookie crawled out the back seat and Kokomo grabbed him by the arm. "You can do this right?"

"I told you I got it. Stop worrying. Trust me. "

"I'm alright. But, damn. All that ass you got hanging out." Kokomo laughed for a while before you made it to the Navy Yard. "You can make a little piece of change before..."

Cookie smiled. "Your ass."

"Kokomo, let him go, and quit playing," Asia laughed.

"But serious. We are right behind you."

"I know. Come on now, let me go, boy. Touch me again and you're gonna have to pay."

"Get your punk ass out of the car. "Kokomo teased.

Cookie smiled back and said, "Yo mama."

"I know right!"

Asia cranked up the car and drove up Flushing Avenue and parked. She parked up the street and, in the shadow, she saw Rasheed and them. She flashed the lights, letting him know everything was in motion.

Then her and Kokomo opened up a black duffel bag in the backseat, and started loading up the guns. Asia touched Kokomo tenderly on his arm and said under her breath. "I just care for you, you know."

"I know you do."

"Just be looking out for you, that's all."

He turned her way, smiled, then kissed her on the cheek to her surprise and said, "But, I gotta look out for me now. You and Rasheed...do your thing. It is what it is."

She reached into the bag and came across his hand, and gently squeezed it, saying. "Yeah. I love you, too. Now...let's do this."

MARIA SWERVED THE SKY-blue Jaguar into the slow lane, passing the driver cursing her out, almost sending him off the road. She was a rude driver by all sense of the word. Approaching the exit fast, Edward pointed up to the sign and said, "Alright, slow down."

"I got this," she said as she sped abruptly onto the exit ramp of the BQE, Tillary Street. Fort Greene projects. Downtown Brooklyn. Albee Square mall, all that. Edward reminisced fondly of his days as an agent. Remembering how wild it was over there then. The streets that were once ravished by crack, dope fiends and prostitutes were now fast becoming part of urban regeneration. Slowly moving, but still Edward could see changes. More white people. Less trash. Not too much lingering, and much more activity. As she turned onto Park Avenue, he glanced over at Central Booking, the 84th precinct. He nodded, then adjusted his jacket snug, tapping slightly at his chest. Maria shot a look over and asked, "What are you doing?"

"Nothing."

"Nothing." She smirked. "Oh, the Police station." Edward tightened up a bit. Maybe, he gave himself away. "Your heart skips a beat or something." She laughed. "I can imagine. A man like you. The trouble you've probably been in." She reached over and grabbed his hand. "But no worry. After this sweetheart. I'll take you somewhere where all you have to do is worry about me, baby."

Edward smiled. A small bead of sweat came off his brow. She didn't notice the wire he was wearing, and she damn sure didn't pay any mind to the black van that was parked under the overpass that blinked his headlights, twice.

Giovanni looked up. "You think he saw it? You think the broad caught on?"

"No. But, he looked right over here at us."

"Yeah, but he looked worried. The broad was reaching for something near him. You think she found the wire?"

"Don't think so, Giovanni. If she did, the car would have stopped right about now, but now it's making a turn on Washington Avenue."

"Good."

"Relax." The cop turned towards Giovanni and snickered. "You act like you're still on the job."

Giovanni laughed it off. "Yeah... I know."

Another cop in a van looked at the other, puzzled. He said, "This is New York City Police Department detective, Michael Mickey Giovanni. The famous. He's put more Cartel affiliated bad guys behind bars than anyone." Giovanni nodded his head. He was right but he didn't get the main man. Hopefully this time, with Edwards help, he would and perhaps Maria could lead him to the one that got away, Felix. He was guarded by the ATF, used as a snitch, but still he wanted him back. Just one piece of evidence was needed before he could snatch him right from under their noses. The evidence ties him to the death of Malik. Then, he could rest easy.

"OKAY, BABY. WE'RE COMING up the gate. Pass me that paperwork."

Edward reached into the back seat for a leather book binder that had contained some documents. He handed it to Maria trying to get a glance of what they were.

"These are manifest papers. A bill of lading, so to speak."

"How did you get them?"

"Oh, I have my ways, and the money."

Okay, Edward thought, this chick has enough pool to buy phony documentation for the Brooklyn Navy yard. Definitely a federal offense, but the question is. How far up the letter did this corruption lead? And, was the Cartel involved?

"Oh yeah, also." She smiled. "The Cartel's hands are really deep here."

That answered his question.

"You see anything?"

"Not really."

"Let me see!"

"Wait!" Guillermo pushed Omar's hand away as he grabbed for the binoculars. "There's nothing going on right now." He turned towards him. Get me another coffee.

"What? I'm your slave now?"

"Come on. Please." He turned back and said, "I know this is taxing, but it'll be well worth it."

"Yeah, yeah, yeah, but suppose she's bullshitting and may be out of the country by now."

"I doubt it."

"We should have grabbed her, and the ATF guy when we had the chance. "

"Then what? Kill them?" He watched Omar fix him his coffee, then eagerly reached for the hot brew when he came back. "Be cool. They'll be there shortly. Will go after them, and take everything they got for ourselves."

"You've told me that one hundred times already. Make it seem like they were robbing the money, blah, blah, blah. Least, that's the story we tell the Cartel, right."

"You got it." He took a sip, got up and turned to look back out the window. "Damn, this coffee is terrible! Hmmm."

"What? You see them?"

"No...no. just some...strange activity. That's all."

"Like what?"

Guillermo handed the binoculars over to Omar and said, "There's this prostitute; I watched her go up and down the block a few times, then she stopped, spoke to the security guard."

"There's more than one, right...security guard?"

"Oh yeah. But he let her in...the gate."

"Nasty muthafucka. They should hire better help."

"Yeah, you'd think that. Anyway, it's been a good while since she came back out of the guard house."

"So, they're all getting fucked and sucked. What the big deal is?"

"Don't know yet. But one thing for sure. I haven't seen hide or hair of either one of them. Yet."

COOKIE WAS CALLED OVER to the gate. He strolled by at least three times already, and according to a hooker friend of his that worked the area, she said it would take just about that long.

The security that worked the night shift and graveyard hours, as well as the weekends, were mostly Spanish, Mexican, and Colombian, some Blacks, but they were more comfortable with the inside perimeter. Real dead, more time to sleep. Easy money.

The guards learned to supplement their income by allowing the dope dealers, and smugglers to come in and grab their wares from the cargo. Maria was one such person. She had a contact that provided her for scan phony documents. Easy in and easy out. Security was paid a couple of hundred for the trouble. To her, it was a chump change.

The only thing though, they had a vice. Drugs and quick, easy pussy, and Cookie's girlfriends provided for them. Cookie paid the ladies off for the evening, and Asia provided them with dinner at a high dollar restaurant in Brooklyn Heights to secure the area for the night.

The guard at the gate watched Cookie hard. He knew something was off, but Cookie's walk, stroll, high heels, thick legs and fat booty made him think otherwise or he thought with the head Cookie wanted him to think with. "Hey. Prostitute?"

He took the bait.

"Cuanto dinero?"

Got him. He wanted to know how much, but Cookie already knew what they were giving up. His girlfriends filled him in on everything. "Not cheap."

"Come on." He opened the gate and let him in. The guard shack stood to the right of the long, tall gate. A gated opened door was off to the side of that. Operating electronically from the inside, it was only after one of the guards asked for paperwork, then once it was examined and confirmed true, the gate opened, and the party or parties were allowed through.

Under no circumstances did anyone just walk in off the street. That was done through a separate entrance. A building behind the long stone wall. There, they went through a metal detector and was scrutinized heavily before letting in. The building was only open Monday through Friday, from eight to four, business hours. This was a different type of business going on.

"I want my money up front." Cookie said as he strutted up the steps to the booth. Stepping through, it was all that he was told about. Two large windows. One facing the front, the gate, the wall. The other facing the shipyard cargo area, and the Hudson River. They had a view of it all.

The back of the space they occupied had a bathroom with the sink. A desk filled with scattered papers, Spanish newspapers. Old uniforms stuffed in a steel, rusted locker. On a table off to the side of it was a microwave and remnants of days old food. It was a dump.

He pointed Cookie to the back of the room. His buddy's mouth was already watering as he bent over to drop his bag. He turned around and with all the attitude he could muster, and with his hands on his hip said, "Who's first?"

Running over each other, Cookie put up his hand to stop them, and smiled. He had them right where he wanted. "Okay, I can do two at a time." Cheesing, they licked their chops and shook their head yes. Cookie backed over to a corner out of view from a window thinking to himself. These are the horniest...what the hell did they do to them? Then, he motioned them over and pulled up a chair. "Okay. I do one head, and the other from behind, and then switch. Okay." Again, they shook their heads like they were crazy.

"But first I want my money."

They stuff their hands into their pockets and pull out a wad of bills. Small denominations, 5, 10, and they messed around and peeled off a 20. "Oh no. You know better than that," he said as he snapped his fingers. They frowned up but dug deeper. Between them all it came out to 300 dollars or so. All for a few minutes of work, Cookie mused. No wonder his girlfriends were on them so hard. It was an exclusive pay date.

"And, we give more to. If we like."

Exclusive.

Okay, Cookie thought they wanted an all-nighter. He smiled and felt his blades. Razor sharp. They get their wish forever, an all-nighter.

By the time he sat down, the first one had already dropped his pants. Rock hard, swinging all over the place, he was outrageous, if not enthusiastic. The other one was more obedient, he positioned himself right behind Cookie, waiting patiently. Cookie turned to the other one who looked on and said, I can't do three. The others gave him a look that said burn up the road. "I got you, though it'll be well worth it, sweetie." Frowning up he walked to the door, and slammed shut. Like a chump he sat down on the bottom stoop pouting.

Everything was in place. It was on.

Cookie snapped the blade open nimbly and soundless. He opened it up, and with one swing, the guard's dick was cut clean off from his nuts. His face turned to horror as he watched the downward strokes slash deep into his throat. Gagging, he fell to the side while the other one who was already on all fours with his pants down tried to stand up. Easy. Cookie drove the stiletto of his heel, all six inches inches of it, into his eye. He fell backwards holding his face in pain. Cookie got up calmly, walked over to him, bent over, and slashed his throat, ear to ear. Blood leaked all over the floor.

Not wanting to prolong things anymore, he drugged them into the bathroom and shut the door. He opened up his bag and pulled out his nine-millimeter with a silencer attached. Like Ice had shown him, he put the muzzle right up to the temples and squeezed, it was over with, quickly.

Hurriedly, he glanced out the window, time was rapidly moving. The other one was pacing out front, impatiently. Looking up at the window he stopped and saw Cookie looking down at him. Taking that as a sign for him to come up, he started for the steps. Cookie had to think fast.

Suddenly, the guard rushed through the door, and looked around. He didn't see his buddies, or Cookie, who was behind the door. Stepping up from behind he started feeling on the guard's crotch arousing. He got the response he was looking for, the guard quickly forgot about his people. Cookie slow walked him away from the window then whispered seductively in his ear, "I'm ready."

"Where are..."

"They're in the bathroom getting cleaned up. It was good for them. You want that, too...right!"

"Yeah, yeah!"

"Okay. Move over towards..." when he stepped away from the window into the shadows Cookie put him in a choke hold. He tried to fight, but he clamped down hard, like a vice grip, until he didn't move. His eyes fluttered and then Cookie snapped his neck. It was done. Now all he had to do now was flip the light on and off to notify Asia and...a honk. Someone was at the gate, damn. Now what! He peeped his head out. A man and a woman in a sky-blue jaguar. The one on the passenger side looked edgy, like he was ready to explode at any second. Cookie couldn't have that. Not tonight.

He started undressing the guard and putting on his clothes, then ran to the bathroom, stepping over the others, and wiped the makeup off his face. He found a hat laying around and stuffed it on his head. He manned up and walked through the door, opened it, and hollered out. "Yes. Can I help you?"

Maria looked up and said to Edward under her breath. "That's not one of the guys I deal with." She shouted out the window, "Where is Alvarez?"

Cookie thought. He didn't need them to get out of the car. The place was a mess. Blood was all over the floor, and he never got the chance to pull the other one out the bathroom. "He's doing rounds. The boss called him and told him to check out an emergency."

"Who are you?"

"I work here. The piers most of the time. Hey look. Who are you? What do you want here?" Cookie asked with a bit of irritation on his tongue.

Maria was growing snappy already. "Okay, okay." She turned towards Edwards, and said, "I paid the other guys already. Now I'm gonna have to give him a hundred bill or something." She put the money in the paperwork and waved it out the window. "I have papers. I was scheduled to be here."

"Okay." Cookie looked at the control panel. He had no choice but to let them through. He had to find the right switch to open the gate. Studying the control panel hard, he said to hell with it, and hoped he was right. He flipped the knobs back and clicked at them. He got lucky. He opened the door and stepped out all the way. "You said you have papers? "

"Yes. Here they are."

"I can get out and give them to-" She was cut off.

"No. I got it." Cooking grabbed the binder and opened it. He looked through the papers, and a hundred bills fell to the ground. He bent over and picked it up. He studied it for a second, then looked at Maria. A test. Hell, they weren't legit either. Should he give it back. He tried her. "Go ahead." He smiled as he glanced out at the money. Wait till Asia hears about this, he mused.

Maria waved at him as she drove by. Edward mean mugged and said to Maria. "Damn. Something about him."

"No, don't worry about him. Probably from the projects. Hell, I wouldn't be surprised if the other ones were somewhere getting their dicks sucked."

Edward looked at the side view mirror at Cookie and shook his head saying. "Still, something just ain't right." His police instincts were on full blast.

Cookie ran up the steps, and pulled the other body into the bathroom. He ran to the window and looked out. He could see Asia in the cut. Rasheed and them wouldn't be too far. It was a go. He flipped the light switch, twice.

Maria drove up to a four-way crossing and stopped. Pausing for a second, she looked right, then left. Edward was confused by her action. "What's the matter?"

"Oh, nothing."

"You know where to go, right?"

She looked left at a warehouse situated towards the back end near the farthest reach of the pier, and turned towards Edward and said, "We go to the right."

"Okay, then. Let's go," he said as he tapped on his chest. The action Maria had expected. She noticed earlier that he kept tapping on his chest and she also noticed how he kept his chest thrust out. Something wasn't right, and she hoped her intuition was wrong. She traveled West all the way around the old warehouse shops, shipping containers stacked three to four stories high, and underneath the huge bowleg cranes that towered over them. Edward asked again, "You sure you know where you're going? "

She stopped the car. "You know. I might need to make a call."

"A call...now?"

"Yeah. I thought the container was..."

"You thought!" He sat up straight and she noticed his collar. His action was stiff, and there it was again. His chest, deliberately, prominently poking out. Then he tapped on it. "So, you're saying that the money, and the drugs aren't here."

It was obvious. She couldn't let him know. He was trying to set her up. She grabbed at his shirt and pulled. The buttons popped off opening up and exposing the wire that crawled up his stomach to a microphone taped to his t-shirt just below the neck. "I knew it!" she yelled.

Edward was exposed. Pissed off, but more perplexed than anything. The jig was up. "So, who are you? The police! FBI. What!"

Edward just sort of nodded his head. Calmly, he reached for the wire and continued ripping it off his shirt he put the microphone to his mouth and said, "Nothing happening here. Everything's Okay. Lay low."

Maria pulled back away from him. "Who are you! "

He reached into his pocket and pulled out his badge. "Edward Gonzalez; Alcohol, Tobacco, and Firearms."

"Hell, I don't deal with any of those."

Tired of the charade. He wanted answers. "No! Not you. The Cartel, and your connection to them. Now, either you tell me where they keep their stash, and cooperate with us about their supply routes, and maybe, we might save you! Now, what is it? "

Maria curled her lips into a smile, and laughed out in his face. You're kidding me right. You think you can butch kid me. Do you know who you're fucking with!"

"Yeah, a low-life, slimy ass bitch."

That did it. "Okay, I'll take you where you want to go." Ditch him. Call her people. Have his ass snuffed out. In that order. "We go then."

"Alright, no funny stuff."

"No, no, no...sweetheart. And, uh by the way. I wonder what your people will say about the girl. Remember, the one you murdered."

He covered up the mic. "Don't worry about that." Easing closer towards her, he started lifting up his hands to her neck. "Sorry you had to know about that." Maria pushed him back and yelled. "You can have it all! I won't say anything... Please, just don't kill me!"

He paused, thinking. This phony chick. I'll just get the money, then let the ATF kill her off. They'll be here shortly, anyway. "Okay."

She made a U-turn and drove past the crossroad again. If they would have bothered to turn their heads left, they would have noticed a shadowy figure that hid in the near darkness behind the guard shack.

Cookie watched as Asia ran through the gate. A little less than a minute later Rasheed rushed in. He counted. Someone was missing. He turned around watching as they squirreled their way inside, and made them out on the way they walked. He thought out loud Kokomo!

"What!"

He turned around and looked down the stairs. Kokomo had just come through. He looked back out both ways, then nodded at him as he dashed past. Cookie hurt him inside to close the gate.

"What the hell was that?" The cops in the van were stirred up as they watched the black catsuit figures run inside the shipyard. "Who the hell are they?"

"Don't know." Giovanni said, "But something's going down."

"Damn right, something's going down." The senior agent turned towards his men and said, "I'm gonna call it in, headquarters will probably give the okay to go, but...after we get back up from the guys at the eight-four precinct. You got that Giovanni." He looked around and he was gone. "Giovanni! Giovanni! Where the hell did he go?"

Giovanni was dead set on making his way to the gate. He watched as the guard inside the shack turned to go inside, and it slowly started to shut. He heard quickly and made it just in time before it closed. He ducked behind the steps as Cookie came out and looked to make sure it was shut. When he saw no one, he stepped back inside.

Cookie turned towards the guard he had killed. His body sprawled out on the floor. A good time now to clean up the mess that was now made. He walked over and grabbed his ankles and started dragging him to the bathroom. All of a sudden, the guard kicked at him, jumped up and started coming at him. Damn, he thought he'd killed him. Apparently not. All he managed to do was crack his back, hence the popping sound. What he actually did was choke him out. But it was too late for all of that now. He grabbed him and they wrestled, fell to the floor. He was kicking Cookie's ass as he fought desperately for his life.

He tossed him into the table. And falling hard against the microwave oven he knocked his head and a nasty gash opened up right above his eye. He grabbed at him again. This time Cookie tried to maneuver, and threw two jabs to his grill, but the guard feeding on adrenaline shook it off. He kept coming. Cookie dodged, and tried to run around him, but he was too quick. He grabbed him by the waist and threw him backwards against the table, again. Crashing to the ground half dazed, and half conscious. He got a good look at his face. Then he stepped backwards. "You?"

Cookie struggled through the darkness that tried to overcome him and glanced up at him. Maybe, he had a chance while he was stupefied. He reached for his blades, then realized he was wearing pants. It was all messed up, he had to drop his pants to get to his knives. Forget it. He reached into his pants in the guard took it the wrong way and screamed. "I'm no faggot!" He ran over and tried to stop him. Cooking managed to grab one of the knives. Pulling it out, and the blade cut deep into his leg and he grimaced in pain. He had no time for it now. He swung, and it hit paydirt. Blood mushroomed across his chest. It stopped him, even staggered him, but it only seemed to make him angrier.

Cookie struggled to his feet with his knife thrust out in front, screen off. It was do or die, who made the first move? Cookie launched. The guard dipped out the way, and right crossed him straight across the jaw, staggering him. Then, he caught him again, and blackened his eye. He was hurt, but not out. His eyes swollen and hand trembling, but still he kept the knife in front of him. "Come on, come on!" He shouted.

The guards sneered. "I'm gonna kill you!" He launched and Cookie had enough in him to sidestep out the way, causing the guard to slam into the bathroom door. It burst open, and he fell backwards over his buddy's bodies. A horrified expression came across his face as he looked up at Cookie. He jumped to his feet, and tackled him to the ground. The knife had jabbed him in his chest, but it wasn't deep enough to inflict any damage. He still had to fight. He grabbed Cookie's neck and started to securely squeeze tightly, tears came to his eyes, he didn't want to die, not like that. The guards shook him furiously as the air wheezed out of his lungs. He choked, and convulsed uncontrollably. Then out of nowhere, the guard fell forward on top of him. His hands were loosened from his neck and he fell face forward on top of him. Cookie gasped for air. Something happened. As far as Cookie was concerned, a miracle. He pushed the guard over and started to get up the next thing he knew a 45-caliber revolver was pointed right down to his face. "Don't move." If it was a miracle, he sure as hell wasn't Jesus Christ. Cookie stood motionless but managed to ask. "Who...who...? Are you?"

"Right now. The person that probably just saved you. "

Cookie looked over at the guard laid out on the floor next to him. The back of his head bashed in, then back at the man with the gun, who looked over at the body, too, then said to him. "Mickey. Mickey Giovanni. Now. Where are they!"

# CHAPTER FIFTEEN

"We go now." Guillermo said as he put away the binoculars, getting up away from the window. "Tell the driver to crank up the car."

"What?" Omar asked as he peered out the window. "Did you see something?"

Guillermo shook his head. "Of course. That's why we're leaving now. Tell the driver to get ready." He sucked his teeth on the last part. Omar started to buck, but decided against it. Since there was no real reason for it, except for his own arrogance, it wasn't needed for the task at hand. He simply replied, "Okay."

Guillermo closed the blinds and stepped away from the window just as Asia and then went through the gate. Not aware of the events that took place after." Omar came back in. "The cars are ready, but we need time to load the guns, okay. Give us a second."

"No need."

"No need? What the hell are you talking about?"

Guillermo stepped over to the phone and picked it up. He started calling some numbers, then looked up at Omar peeping out the blinds. "I said...no need."

MARIA DROVE TOWARDS the peers and cut a quick left into the warehouse area. Mostly maintenance shops and cargo holds with private docking bins marked hazardous. Edward kept his peeled. He told her to stop as she approached the chain link, fenced in the parking area. He looked around. An old half ton truck, and three tractors.

The front end of the warehouse had three doors, all rollups for cargo being delivered or taken out. To the right side were doors to offices and a stairway, two stories high, to the shops."

Edward pointed her towards the back. The Hudson River and the pier only a stone's throw away. There was no boat anchored, but two hundred yards away there was a ship moored to the back dock. Edward stared at it. No movement, it appeared to have been there for a while. He couldn't tell how long, though. Maria followed his view, and said, "The rope is relatively new, so it just got here. Also." She pointed. "There's running lights on. Somebody's probably aboard. Most likely, the crew. Don't think there's any threat there."

"Yeah, well. Can't be too careful."

"Right," she said as she rolled her eyes. "You don't know who to trust these days." She smirked, then continued to drive around the building.

She pulled up alongside the first roll up door in the park. Edward scanned the area, again, and there were no cars. "This is the place?"

"Yeah." Maria said as she pointed to a sign-up top. "Bay seven...this is it." She undid her seat belt and started to get out. He grabbed her by the arm and flashed his gun. "No funny business. I'm right behind you."

"Of course not...sweetie." She grinned as she got out of the car. Walking over to a buzzer she pushed it, then continued to smile at Edward as they waited.

"Who are we waiting for? Who's inside?"

"Didn't you listen to the guard at the gate? Security is still on the premises. For God's sake, stop being so paranoid. I told you we had papers."

"Okay-okay!" He kept his hand on the gun. A minute later the gate slowly started rolling up and Edward backed up a little. Maria continued to smile. It rose head high, and out of nowhere a shotgun was stuck in his face. "Damn."

Maria said, "Yeah. You can't be too careful. Miguel. Take him out back and lock him up."

"Then what?"

She walked over to Edward who held his hands up high. Reaching into his waistline she pulled out the gun and said, "We'll deal with him. Later."

Maria walked towards the crates in the warehouse and started surveying them. She walked up one, then back down. Edward watched her as the man kept the shotgun glued to his back. "Keep walking!" He pointed to him in a gated cage and opened it. "Get in!" He did as he was told. The guard locked it, then caught up with Maria. They disappeared out the view down another aisle.

Edward's eyes searched around the small damp room for a way out. There was none. He shut the door and it was secured. By the protrude smell he can tell that this was probably a hole for some sort of animal coming in from overseas. He continued looking frantically outside the gate for Maria, then he yelled out. "Remember. My people are waiting for me to get in touch with them!" He got no response.

Maria walked back towards the back of the smelly, dimly lit warehouse, and found what she was looking for. Two huge dark, and dusty crates. On top of both was a spray-painted white symbol. A big letter C. She pointed to it and Miguel shook his head. He whistled and three other men came into sight out of the shadows. They hurried over with tools in hand and started working feverishly on the containers.

One had cracked open pretty easily as Maria looked on. Once the top was taken off, she looked in. A canvas cargo sack. One of the men cut it open and ripped into it. Money. She sniffled at the fresh ink, beaming as she did. "Pop the other top." The other one was busted open and she walked over to that one. There, another cargo bag was being ripped open. It was full of wrapped aluminum bundles of what appeared to be drugs marked with a capital C on top. She picked up, and one of the men handed her a dagger. She stabbed at it, and a white powdered substance caked the tip. She tasted it. "Yaa-yo." She smiled and put it back inside. "Thirty bundles is good enough."

Miguel pointed to the other cargo bands. "There's more." Behind them was a wall of more than two dozen.

Maria smiled and said," Of course there is. This is the Cartel's hold. There's always more, but I only need a little." She walked off towards the back into the warehouse where Edward was being held.

RASHEED CAUGHT UP WITH Asia while his mother, and Latif hugged the side of a container. Ice examined the area and asked, "Which building is it?"

Rasheed looked over at Asia and she said, "In the back. It's an old warehouse." She reached inside of her pocket and pulled out a piece of paper with some writing scribbled on it. "My inside man said this was the place."

"Bay seven," he said as he watched Kokomo take out a crudely drawn map, then looked up towards the back end of the pier where a large warehouse was, and pointed. "That one."

They started on a trot towards it, ducking in and out, staying out of sight as they did. Halfway there, they dipped into a gully, and Kokomo started digging into his bag. "Alright. We need to check these walkie-talkies."

Asia asked, "Cookie has one, right?"

"I gave him one." Kokomo said, "He's good. I saw him when I came through the gate."

"Well, call him, anyway." Asia was about to call when Rasheed stopped her. He pointed towards the warehouse. "Look, there's someone coming out."

It was Miguel. His mission was to pull the car around back. Meet Maria, then load up the money.

"Who's that?" Ice asked.

"Don't know," Asia replied.

"What do you mean you don't know!" I exclaimed, "Didn't y'all case this joint out?" He looked over at Kokomo.

"It was her job," he said, Then frowned bitterly at Rasheed. "Maybe, if she would have spent more time on the job, then in his bed."

Rasheed jumped at him. "That ain't none of your business."

Ice held Kokomo back." Hey, come on you two. This is bullshit."

Waseema stepped to Rasheed and pulled him aside saying. "Keep your focus, son."

"I'm alright, mom," he said as he walked off from her. She started to go after him, but Latif held her back saying. "He's okay, mom. Let's get back to the plan, y'all."

"Yeah, the plan." Ice nodded his head. "Okay then. We know there's a man inside. So, you can damn sure believe there's more, but how many more we don't know." He turned towards Kokomo." I need you and someone else to do surveillance around the back. Take," he scrutinized them carefully, "and said, Latif."

They started jogging towards the warehouse, and looked over at Waseema "I need you to play the front."

"I can go in. I can handle myself."

"I know you can, but somebody needs to hold down the front. Keep a lookout."

Waseema sighed, "Okay."

"Rasheed. You, me and Asia. We go inside." He gave Rasheed a walkie-talkie "Make sure we're all on the same frequency, alright."

He turned the frequency knob to one, and started to run off, but Asia stopped dead in her tracks. "Kokomo and them know what frequency we are on right?"

"They're cool." Ice said as he turned towards Waseema. He held her hand, then kissed her tenderly on the lips and whispered in her ear, "Be careful, okay."

"You too baby." She waved at Rasheed and Asia. "Be careful." They both nodded and turned and along with Ice started towards the warehouse.

Maria stood in front of Edward laughing in his face; clowning him. "You honestly thought, I was so naïve that you could just charm, little ole me off my feet."

Edward scowled at her.

"You say you're an agent. ATF, at that, and you really didn't see this coming."

Miguel came to her and whispered in her ear. She smiled, then nodded. "I'll be right there in a short."

She moved closer to the cell. "Remember the papers. Well, I got them. They'll be here when your people arrive. Along with the evidence that you killed the girl in Brooklyn. Also, that you conspired to murder my good friend Waseema and her family up in Harlem. You do remember that?"

"They'll never believe it."

"Maybe, they won't, but the Cartel sure as hell will."

"What?"

"You see. The mole you were looking for, was not me. He's inside your circle. Once he gets hold of this information, like you said, if your own people don't get you, believe me, the Cartel will." She threw the papers on the table next to the cell and said, "God, we could have been so good together." Walking off she said to him. "You slimeball. "

Edward banged and kicked at the gate, then yelled at the top of his lungs. "Maria... I'm gonna kill you."

She laughed and said, "Yeah. Yeah. You should have done that from the jump, after all I would have. Bye."

Miguel pulled the car up to the back of the rolled-up hanger door. His men would take the money and drugs that Maria told him to get, and then travel to LaGuardia Airport where a private jet would be waiting. He didn't know where she was going, or if she'd even be back. He didn't care. All he knew was she was paying him and his men, his cousins, good money.

As he put it in park, he couldn't help staring at the half ton truck that was parked only a few feet away. Strange. Something. He shrugged it off as one of those things, then, just out of curiosity, because it was killing him already, he needed to peep inside. Empty? He could have sworn he saw someone. He got out of the car and was on his way to investigate, and Maria stepped out. "Where are you going?"

"The truck." He pointed.

"Fuck that truck. You'll have enough money to buy your own fleet of trucks."

"But..."

"Look, have your men hurry up and load the car." She looked at the watch on her arm. "I gotta go."

She turned to go back inside and the back of the truck door opened up. "What's the rush?"

She stopped in her tracks. That voice, she knew it. It couldn't be, she thought.

"I told you I'd be in touch."

She turned around and looked. Him. Her anxiety kicked it, panicking. She took a deep breath, her composure. She damn sure couldn't let it show, especially in front of him, not now. "What are you doing here?"

The big bellied, fat man wobbled as he got down from the truck. The side of it shook as he stepped off the lip. "I see you're planning a little. Trip."

"No, I was just collecting some merchandise. For someone."

"You're still stealing money!"

"Maria snided. Busted. "So what! It's nothing you haven't done a hundred times yourself, Felix. I know, remember."

"You're right." He started walking towards her. His stomach made his gait swagger from side to side, making him appear larger. Scary. It intimidated everyone he came in contact with, including her. "But this time it's my money you're stealing."

"Your money? Yeah right. Who are you now? The Cartel." She laughed.

He stood for a while, and let her get off. Then he said, "Yes."

RASHEED AND ICE STAYED low and made their way to the door. Asia pulled up the rear. They both ran to the corner and peeped around. "How do we get in?" Rasheed asked.

"Right there." Asia said,

"What? Right where?"

"I think we're going to have to use the torch I brought." Ice said,

"It's too bright." Asia said, then pointed at the bottom of the gate. "That little space."

"Yeah. It's small as hell. We can't possibly get through."

"I can." She gave Rasheed her gun. "I'm small enough."

Rasheed looked. "Yeah. She might be able to do it."

Ice grabbed her backpack and said, "Hell, it's worth a try."

"When I get in, I'll find the button that controls it, and hopefully it's quiet when it rolls up. I'll raise it up just enough so you guys can get through."

Rasheed looked at Ice and shrugged his shoulders. "Sounds good to me."

"Let's do it, then."

Asia ran to the door and got on her back. It was only a good eight inches or so, but she managed to ease her way through. Her body was halfway in and all that was left was her head. She turned it to the side and then was gone. A couple of minutes had gone by and they hadn't heard anything. Rasheed started to get worried. "You think she got caught."

"Don't know. But...have your gun ready just in case."

Without a doubt. They moved closer and then, it jerked, and rose two foot higher and stopped. Rasheed held out his gun and Asia peeped her head out from underneath. "Come on."

Quickly, without a sound they were on their backs creeping underneath the gate.

Latif and Kokomo couldn't believe what they were hearing. He was ready to confront her but glad he didn't. Especially since he saw the back of the truck doors open and all those guys come out. Kokomo counted them. Seven. All carrying heavy weaponry.

Something was going down. He didn't know who the fat man was, and Kokomo didn't either. But they were getting an earful, and Maria definitely wasn't too happy. They agreed to lay low, wait and see how it was going to play itself out.

Ice crept with Asia behind him and Rasheed pulling up the rear. Creeping salt inside of the dust driven building. Lights from the rafters above glistened off the scaffolding that stood at least four stories. Platforms full of cargo and merchandise. Rasheed paused to check the crates. Most had sheets posted four to five pages with manifests and faint descriptions of the freight it held. Company names were present on some, but Rasheed didn't recognize any. All written in languages he couldn't discern anyway. Asia tugged at him. "Come on..."

They walked another fifty feet and saw an opening towards the back. A white double door with splitting plastic hanging from the stopper to the bottom. The type that allowed for trucks to come in and out possibly keeping out the draft and moisture coming off the dampness of the River behind. They hug the side of it more closely and Ice was about to turn towards the opening, when. "I wouldn't do that if I were you."

He pointed his gun in the direction of the voice. "Whoa hold up!"

It was Edward. Ice kept his gun raised as Asia got closer towards the cage. "Be careful." Rasheed said,

"I'm not the one who's dangerous."

"I can't tell. You're the one in a cage." Asia shot back.

"Look. It's not what you think. "

Ice came over. "Tell us what to think, then. And, it better...be quick."

"There's a woman out back who kidnapped me. "

"Woman?" Rasheed started to walk closer to doors, and Ice stopped him. "Hear him out, first."

"I mean? How serious..."

"Her name is Maria. She's part of an organization called the -"

"Cartel" Rasheed finished his sentence and stepped back away from the door.

"I see. You know the name."

"Know it. You'd be surprised at what we know about Maria. And, the Cartel." Ice answered. "Now, who else is back there?"

Edward stepped back away from his confinement and asked, "Who are you guys?" Confused now, with all the firepower they had on them, and after what was said, "Look, I don't know anything."

Ice picked up on his movements, and said, "We're not here to hurt you, at all."

Asia stepped up and lowered her gun. "All we need for you to do is be quiet." she smiled. "We just want to alleviate the premises of some merchandise, that's all baby."

"Oh." Edward shot. "You mean, rob the place." He laughed. "Well hell, I think she's beat you to the punch."

"What?" Asia gawked.

She's outback loading her, what do you say again, merchandise. Right now."

Asia rushed to the gate, and screamed. "What do you mean by that! What are you saying!"

"Hold up, Asia." Rasheed said to her. He put his hand over her mouth, gently, and got closer to the cage. "Look man, I know what Maria is about. Now, straight up, or" he pointed at Asia, "she's gonna blow you away. Now, where is their stash?"

Edward kept his eyes fixed on Asia. "What stash?"

Asia turned and started to walk off. "Okay, okay!" Edward blurted out.

"Okay, what!"

"The other aisle. The back wall. Loaded. But I wouldn't mess with it."

"Just for the sake of asking," Asia asked as she pulled her gun down away from him. "Why not?"

Edward got closer and said, "I'm a cop."

"Damn. That's not good," Ice exclaimed.

"In a few, this place will be crawling with agents."

"Agents?" Rasheed interrupted "Who are you with...FBI?"

"ATF. Alcohol, Tobacco, and Firearms."

"We got to kill him. He's seen our faces. Asia said, "We don't have a choice."

Rasheed nodded his head at Ice. "She's right."

Ice looked his way, shrugged his shoulders. "Sorry."

"Hold up!" Edward said as he backed off. "Look I'll tell you where the money is."

"You already have. Remember." Asia said as she took aim.

"Damn." Edward said as he dived into a corner and curled up. "Please don't kill me."

Asia was about to squeeze the trigger and a ruffling came from out back. They took cover underneath a scaffold. It was two of Maria's men. One of them said, you know who that guy is.

"No, but it doesn't look good, though. We need to get Miguel and haul ass."

"What about the money?"

"Fuck the money? Hell, we'll just take a few stacks from the crate we opened up before we leave."

"Yeah sounds good. Get Miguel."

"Okay."

One of the men stepped back through the curtains, and Rasheed stepped behind the other and cracked him over the head with the butt of his gun. He dropped. Ice pulled him underneath where they were and pointed to the back. "We need to take out the other two."

"And, grab the chick."

"Maria. Damn." Rasheed said, not too happily.

"You know her, Rasheed? Asia asked.

"Unfortunately." Ice answered for him. "We'll grab her from behind." Ice pointed towards Edward." Like he said, "His people will be here in a short time."

"We still kill him, right?" Asia implored, putting the silencer to the muzzle.

Ice eased over to him, and said, "What do you think, huh?"

Edward got up and called Asia over. "Put her in the cage too. As far as I'm concerned."

"Yeah... That sounds good, but...we don't really give a fuck about you...or her. Just the money. You can do what the hell you want with her. But you never saw us...right."

Edward nodded. "Third row over. Whole crate. Wide open. Money. Thousands, even more, but remember. Be quick."

Ice backed up near Asia. "You're sure."

Ice lowered his gun and looked over at Rasheed. He nodded him over. "What's your name?" he asked." I mean. You sure know a lot about...the money."

Edward stared at him, then said, "Edward...Edward Gonzalez. Special agent."

"You know we're saving your life... Agent Gonzalez. Maybe even...your job. If...and just if, we let your ass out of there."

Edward looked towards the ground, frowned up, then back at him, and not it. "Yeah...It's funny how that works."

"See you around, then...Agent Gonzalez."

"I'm sure."

They moved towards the back door, and the next thing they knew. BAM!... BAM!

Gunfire.

"What the hell did you do Felix!" Maria screamed.

Felix stood gloating over the body of Miguel, and the other one that ran out to get him, his cousin, Maria's men. Smoking gun in hand, he looked at her with a sickening grin on his face, and said, "Now, we go get the rest of the money, yeah. Or, your next." Maria froze, the fear evident in her eyes.

Kokomo jumped out from behind the barrier where he and Latif were crouching. Sliding a round into the gut of the Mossberg he brandished, and called out, "Hold up, fat boy!"

Felix turned his way. "Who the hell are you!" Walking backwards sluggishly towards the truck, he turned and dived. Kokomo, thinking he had a bead on him, let off a couple rounds.

Pow! Pow! Pow! Missed. Felix got up and hauled ass around the far
side of the vehicle. His men fired a barrage of bullets at the back
door. Maria ducked and ran inside the door. She made it through
just in time, falling face forward on the ground. Realizing she wasn't
hit, she tried to get up and scrambled straight into the muzzle of a
nine-millimeter. "I'd advise you to chill the hell out."

Asia pulled her up by the arm and drug her over to the scaffold
where she cowered. Shots were still fired at the back door by Felix's
men, and ricocheting inside. "Stay low." Ice shouted

Outside, Latif and Kokomo had to figure out a way to get around
the truck, to get inside. Right now, it was impossible. One of Felix's
six men tried to run towards them. Kokomo reached into his bag and
pulled out an Uzi, and with fully clipped rounds of 30, he sprayed.
He down him instantly. Felix peeped his head from around the side
of the truck, and hollered out. "Who are you? What do you want?"

Latif called Kokomo closer to a crevice he'd dipped in. "We need
to get inside. At least from being pinned down."

"You think Asia and them made it in?"

"Don't know. That's why we need to make it in. If they are
waiting out front, we can let them in."

"Wonder where that broad ran to? You knew her?"

"You can say that. We need to catch up to her, too."

"And, that fat fool. So, I have some time to scheme up a plan."

"Alright."

Rasheed started ripping up shreds of cloth to gag Maria so she
wouldn't be able to let her people know where she was, and at the
same time trying to stay out of sight. Asia helped to hold her down,
facing towards the cage where she could also watch Edward. "You
had something to do with this?"

"It was smart. But no, actually, I didn't," he got closer. "This is
your mess."

Maria jerked away from Asia and tried to run, but Rasheed grabbed her, and that's when she saw his face. "You!"

"Damn...you shouldn't have done that." Edward said.

"Where's Waseema! I know she's got something to do with this! She wants to kill me anyway, but...but...I'll let Latif know."

"Damn...she knows your whole family or what." Asia butted in.

Rasheed was about to stuff the gag in her mouth, but Ice stopped him, and said, "No need. Change of plans." They both know us. He looked over at Edward and shook his head.

"Hell no!" Edward bellowed. "We had a deal."

"We did." They looked at Maria. "But, her seeing our faces wasn't part of it."

Edward cursed under his breath. He paced while Asia spun the last ring of the silencer on her gun. "Put her in here with me then."

"Still, you both seen-"

"Trust me! Put her in here with me."

Rasheed looked at Ice, then walked over to the cage and called him over. "You're people will be here soon. She's already seen our faces. What guarantee can you give us to not kill you?"

"Get you out of here clean."

Ice thought then, and snarled. "How do we open the lock?"

Maria dug into her pocket frantically. "Here's the key."

Ice snatched it, opened the lock and threw her in. "There you go."

Asia shook her head, but not in agreement. "I swear, this ain't my style."

"Look, it's complicated. I'll explain later. Let's get this money first."

"What about Kokomo and them? What do we tell him?"

"I'll go get them. Ice dipped underneath the plastic awning, while Asia and Rasheed bolted to the next aisle.

Ice moved slowly towards the opening, peeping outside he saw the truck, Felix and five of his men were loading up their guns. He turned toward the right and caught Latif's eye. He nodded. He needed to lay some ground cover to get them inside.

Latif yelled out to Felix. "Look, we don't want no trouble. We just here to pick up a couple of products. I think all of this is a misunderstanding, that's all."

Felix peeped his head out. "I can see that. Give me the woman. You do what you came to do, and leave. How's that?"

Latif thought. He couldn't give up something he didn't have. "You saw her run inside the building yourself. "

"Right, I did." Felix traced his eyes going towards the back door, right at Ice. "I also see your friend at the back door." Ice stood perfectly still. He had his sights dead on him. "Now, she must be okay if he came out, right."

Latif turned towards Kokomo. "We need to find out where she's at." Kokomo kept his gun Felix's way and looked over at Ice. "Ask him where she is."

Latif cocked his head. Hell, he was right. "Ice! Where is the woman!"

Ice responded. "Maria. We got her in here."

"Bring her to me!" Felix demanded.

"Don't think so."

He snorted, "Then you die and we take her!" He pulled the trigger. Ice rolled out the way and avoided the shots by inches. He shot back at the truck and Felix and his men scattered. He sprayed the gas tank and started shooting. One of his bullets blew a hole in the side and gas started to spruce out on the ground. Latif spotted it. It was their chance. He started to take off towards the back door with Kokomo on his tail. They jumped through it just as Felix fired shots their way. He sniffed, then looked and saw the gas. Oh, hell no! He jumped out of the truck and started running, not again! His men ran towards the pier. Kokomo, Ice and Latif skirted inside the building. Kokomo doubled back and took a shot at the gas. It didn't take long. The truck exploded and a huge flame of smoke bellowed into the air. The sound of the blast reverberated throughout the shipyard. They all looked at each other as they made it through. "We got to get the money, and haul it out of here!" Kokomo said to them.

"Do you know where to go!" Latif asked. Kokomo reached into his pocket and pulled out a paper. Schematics of the warehouse. He pointed to a circled area. "Here."

Ice got up to his feet, dusted himself off, and said, "No need for that, we found it."

"Where?"

"Asia and Rasheed are over there now. Right around the corner over there. "He pointed to the aisle. Kokomo took off running that way. Latif stayed behind and asked, "Where is Maria?"

"Right here."

Latif spun around and looked right
dead in her face.

# CHAPTER SIXTEEN

"**S**tay put!" Giovanni told Cookie as he searched through his bag. He pulled out the walkie-talkie "What the hell is this?"

"What the hell does it look like!" Cookie spit.

Giovanni mugged him, and said in response. "Smart ass. That's why you're in the position you're in now, I bet." He continued to search. He came with some rope, a blue steel, left-handed nine-millimeter pistol and three clips loaded with fifteen rounds, and a uniform of sorts. He pulled it out. A black catsuit filled with slippers and hard soles. "Damn. High tech." He put the bag down and faced him. "You're involved in something deep. Don't know what it is yet."

They both looked towards the window as it shook. The explosion from the truck made the shack they were in quake. Giovanni hit the ground, and rolled away from the window. Cookie covered his head as best he could with the cuffs on. "What the hell was that? "Giovanni shouted.

Cookie looked up. His face turned to worry as he peeped over at the walkie-talkie Giovanni watched him. "Where're they at?"

"I don't know." Cookie shot back defiantly.

Giovanni got up and walked up to him and kneeled in front of his face. "Look, this is the deal. There's something going down. Now, from the sound of that blast, I know it's serious. In a few, the police will be flooded all through here. I don't know you. You don't know me, but you need to let me know what the hell is going on, so no one, including myself, gets killed. Because once it comes. Boy oh boy, it's gonna be hell! You understand?"

Cookie nodded his head, yes. He looked down to the ground, then said, "Okay...It's like this."

Giovanni had listened to him intently. Afterward, he shook his head. The only word that uttered from his lips was, damn. He stood up and walked to the door, thinking, then turned back around, and looked at Cookie, and said, "Come on. Get up." Cookie did what he was told and walked towards him. He reached into his pocket and took out his handcuff key. "It's on you. Let's go." He closed the door halfway, looked at him then pointed his finger in his face. "Now, if you haul ass. When they catch you, they will catch you. I don't know you." Hell, he peeped over at the bathroom. "Right now, you're looking at the chair for all of that, anyway." He turned back towards him saying. "But I know this whole thing is more Cartel related than anything, and in all actuality, you're just a bit of a player in this whole twisted game." Cookie picked up his bag, Giovanni opened the door. "Let's go find your people." They were out the door, and Cookies backed up. "Hold up."

"What now?"

He went back up inside the shack, and flipped the switch to open the gate.

"What'd you do that for?"

Cookie didn't answer, hell, he really didn't know why he did it. Something inside told him to. Perhaps, after everything was done, they'd still need a way out, he thought. For him it wasn't over with. Giovanni's mind was elsewhere. After all these years. Contacts that went nowhere, arrests, murders, senseless killings, he finally thought he had them. The Cartel.

They took off running up the street.

Waseema shook as she heard the blast coming from behind the warehouse. She reached into her bag and pulled out a walkie talkie she had, and she switched it on. "Hello! Hello!" She was panicking. "Oh God, what the hell is going on!" She picked up her bag and ran towards the warehouse with the walkie talkie in hand. Praying that everyone was alright. And still alive.

Shaheeda was listening to the radio snoring behind the wheel of the truck. Half dozing, half awake, then, she heard the crackling come from the walkie-talkie It was incomprehensible. She grabbed for it. She pressed the transmit button and screamed into it. "Hello, hello." and didn't hear anything back. She waited, then got the bright idea to turn the frequency button to another channel, listening. At last, she heard some voices.

She messed around and caught the frequency of the police officers coming from the 84th Precinct. In particular, the ones that were in the black van, in front of the shipyard waiting for backup.

"Hey, how many cars do you need?"

"About ten deep. "

"OK that's a big ten-four, over."

"Loud and clear. What's your ETA? "

"About twenty minutes or so. Gotta roundup some people."

"Damn, can you make it any sooner-goddamn, what the hell was that?"

"Sounded like an explosion."

Shaheeda looked over at the warehouse and saw the smoke come from over the wall. She cranked up the truck, and turned it back to the other frequency, waiting. She knew something wasn't right, because an explosion damn sure wasn't in the plans.

Guillermo and Omar stood underneath the trestle of the Brooklyn Queens Expressway when they heard the explosion. "O-shit! What the hell was that, Guillermo!"

"Hell if I know."

They looked up at the wall and saw the smoke coming from behind it.

"Let's get a closer look." Guillermo said,

"Closer? You kidding me or what!" Omar yelled. Then he said backing up, "This place will be crawling with crops in a few."

"No, it won't," he started walking towards the entrance. "Not yet.
"

Omar started cursing Spanish words underneath his breath. Guillermo smiled at him. Hell, it's not like he hadn't heard them before.

Kokomo caught up to Rasheed and Asia. "Start the party without me, why don't ya!"

Asia looked up and ran towards him, hugging him. Rasheed came over and extended his hand. "Yo man, I'm sorry."

Before he could finish Kokomo had given him a bear hug. "Man. No sweat. I'm just glad to see y'all." He turned toward the door and started rambling. "Man, some big dude out there gave us hell. Said for us to get the money, haul ass. He had a couple of dudes with him, all strapped. I suggest we take the advice."

"What's that noise?" Rasheed asked.

"The truck blew up! We need to get on through." He looked around. "Where is it, the money?"

Rasheed called him over to open one up quickly, and looked in. "Damn!"

Grinning, Asia said, "We finally got it. That must be at least one million in there." She pointed to the one that held the drugs. "That one is full of drugs." Kokomo frowned. "Yeah, I know. We're gonna burn that one. "

"Anymore?"

"I think. But I didn't get a chance to really look. There's other crates up there." He pointed to the back of a rack situated near the far end of the aisle.

"We should get one more and call it a day."

Asia looked at Rasheed. "Well, we better get busy then. Asia stay down here and load the duffel bags. You can do that, right. "

"Hell, they're about half full as it is."

"Let's go, Kokomo."

They jumped up on a beam and climbed up to the second landing where they made their way over to a row that held the crates that they thought belonged to the Cartel. Spotting a big letter C on one they started tearing into it with crowbars once they got off the top and peep in. They ripped the cargo netting from off the bundles. More money. Lots more. Rasheed suggested that they throw down a few more bundles, and let it go at that, Kokomo agreed.

A couple of minutes went by, and at least three bags full with stuff. Thousands of dollars, equaling to millions.

"Let's get Ice and them, and go."

"I don't think so."

Rasheed turned around. "You!"

You act like you're not glad to see me.

He rushed him. "You no good son of a bitch."

Kokomo stopped him. "This was the dude I told you about. You know him?"

"Do I. This bastard murdered my brother, my best friend." He tried wriggling out of Kokomo's grip to get at him. "Let me go!"

"Look man. There's more than him." He pointed and enlightened him to the other men behind him with automatic weapons. "We got to play this one cool...and smart."

Rasheed didn't like it, but he backed off. "What do you want?"

"Oh. Nothing much." He felt the burn marks around his face, "Maybe, you're ass on a platter. "

Rasheed didn't like it; he mean mugged him. "Yeah. I know that feeling." Then he glanced over at the duffel bags.

"No. You can have those. Just give me my woman."

"Woman?"

"Come on now. My wife!"

Rasheed looked over at the bags again. "Hell, if that's all you want."

Asia however was antsy. She started reaching for her gun. Rasheed saw it in time to stop her. "No, Asia! "

It was too late. She caught the bullet just below the chest. Kokomo caught her before she fell. "We gotta get her to a doctor."

Rasheed looked over at Felix. "Let her go. She ain't got no beef with you."

"I have no problem with that. But, the next one that pulls a gun, dies on the spot. "

Rasheed kicked the duffel bags over to Kokomo. "Take what you can carry. I'll stay. "

"No need for that. Go. I'll deal with you another time, you hear me."

"Loud and clear. "

Felix backed off, and Rasheed picked up Asia. "She's right around the corner behind you. Right off the large opening." He told him, then ran towards the front of the building. Kokomo was right behind him, slow moving, after all he was dragging three bags full of money.

In a moment of clarity, Kokomo realized. "Yo man. What about Ice? Your brother, Latif?"

Rasheed stopped. "I know. I know. But, I gotta get her out of here."

Kokomo dropped the bags. "We'll hide them. Come back later."

"No, we can't. Like the man said, the cops will be here any minute. "

"You're right. Then, what do we do?"

Rasheed put Asia down gently and started digging through his bag and found his walkie-talkie He pressed the transmission button "Shaheeda! I need you now! Don't have too much time. Just listen." He took a breath. "Come inside the gate and make a right turn.

About a hundred yards or so you'll come to a warehouse with rolled up gates. I'll be there waiting right now!"

Shaheeda heard him. She gunned it down Washington Avenue, and slammed right into the gate, almost crashing on to its sides. She dared not slow down, sirens in the distance prove that. Sweating bullets, she rubbed the back of her hand across her eyes, it stung like all hell, but right now she needs to keep focus.

She glanced over at the guard shack as she zoomed by, and started to slow down, but the urgency in Rasheed's voice made her stomp on the gas instead. She spotted the stop sign almost too late and pumped the brakes, hard, too hard. She almost lost control rolling the truck on two wheels trying to keep control of the large vehicle finally, she got a hold of it, and felt the steering wheel turning right.

She could see it. The huge cloud of smoke still came up behind it.

Out of nowhere, someone jumped in front of her. Her mother. Like a madman she pressed the brakes hard, and pulled over to the side. "Baby somethings wrong."

Shaheeda screamed. "What the hell were you thinking about! I could have killed you."

Waseema got quiet.

"Get in the damn truck. Rasheed just called me!"

Waseema opened the door, and dived in. "You know where, right?"

"Straight ahead, but i still don't see them. "

"Go around the back."

"No. Hold up. One of the doors is rolling up. Oh my God. It's Rasheed. "

"He's carrying someone. It's Asia!"

Shaheeda stopped the truck in front of them, and jumped out. "What happened!"

"Don't worry about that. Just get her to a hospital, now!"

They opened the door to the truck and put Asia in it. Waseema jumped in with her, and then told Rasheed. "Come on. Let's go!"

"No." He looked back." I got to go get Latif an Ice."

"Okay, then. Waseema jumped back out. "Let's get them."

"No," she said as he held her back. "I got it."

"Hell no. You're not going in there by yourself. No! I already lost one son. "

"Ma." Rasheed cuffed her face lovingly. "I got it. I gotta go get my brother. I've got to." He turned toward the opening and pointed inside. Kokomo is struggling with some duffel bags. "Help him, quick, then go! "

"We got it!" Shaheeda peeped her head out the truck. "Where?"

"We need to get Asia to the hospital! She's bleeding, really bad." Kokomo yelled, as he came through the doors lugging the three duffel bags behind him.

"I'll meet you at the store. "Rasheed said,

A tear came down Waseema's eye as she kissed him. "Go get your brother, and bring him home."

"Ice, too."

"Ice, too, baby." She turned and ran toward Kokomo, and helped him with the bags. He looked at Rasheed as he ran back inside the building and questioned it. "Where's he going? I gotta go..."

"No. We...Asia needs you. Come on."

Rasheed disappeared into the darkness and Kokomo focused back on the truck. He tossed the weighted bags in the back and kneeled down to hold Asia in his arms. He said to Waseema, "We need to stop the bleeding."

Waseema ripped the top part of her catsuit off and threw it to him. "Use this!"

He balled it up and pressed it to her chest and said, "Don't worry, baby everything's gonna be alright."

Shaheeda gunned the truck back up the street and turned on the stop sign slowly this time. She slowed and went through the gate expecting the cops. She spotted them off in the background, and turned the opposite way, and didn't stop until she hit Flushing Avenue. "Where to?"

"Woodhull Hospital."

"Won't they ask questions."

"No, I know some people."

They were unaware of the two people in the cut as they zoomed past. Cookie looked back at the truck and said to Giovanni. "That's them."

"Who? Waseema! Shaheeda!"

"Yeah. Rasheed's mother! I gotta go with him."

Giovanni pressed Cookie's arm to pull over and said, He jumped out. "Look. Get the walkie-talkie Tell Waseema that Giovanni is in here."

"You're not coming with me?"

"I gotta go and see what's going on."

"You gonna tell the police about what I did."

"Look. Just tell Waseema what I said, Now, go!"

Giovanni watched Cookie run off, and then, was distracted by some very distinct and recognizable pops coming from inside the building. Gunfire. He ran as fast as he could towards it.

Cookie ran up the steps to the guard shack and burst through the door. "Where is it! Where is it!" He ruffled the place, scoring the floors, and couldn't find what he was searching for. Frantically, he turned towards the bathroom door. He stared. Pausing, he tried thinking, making sure he was there earlier, slowly, he moved towards it. He pushed the door open slightly then backed off from the stench from the dead guards hit him. He pushed the door open some more looking past the bodies on the other side, he saw what he was seeking, but he had to step across the bodies and all the blood that was now starting to harden to get it.

He held his nose, and stepped on the backs of the men, trying to keep his balance. He grabbed his bag and not turning around gradually eased his way back out. He grabbed hold to the top of the bathroom door, he wriggled, but kept his composure, not falling, then backed out the door. He opened it and reached inside. Clothes, wig, all there. But the radio the walkie talkie was gone. He spun around scanning the place, he had to find it. Suddenly, his ears were pricked by the sound of the sirens going off in the distance. He was over brought with fear. Something else was wrong too, he noticed. The other guard. He was missing. Did he take the radio? he questioned.

Searching underneath the tables, he couldn't find it. Perhaps, he thought, at least he hoped, maybe Giovanni might have kept it. That had to be it. As for the guard, maybe he was the one who notified the police. All he knew for sure was that, he had to go.

He picked up his bag, opened the door, and ran outside to the fence. He peeped out the gate both ways, and didn't see anyone. He stepped it across the street, making his way up Washington Avenue. He figured he'd take a cab. Make his way through the store. That had to be where they were going, that was the plan, but he hoped they stuck to it, because so far, nothing else is going right.

Guillermo held his hand over the guard's mouth, quieting him. Cookie missed them.

The guard broke away from Guillermo and hollered. "Who are you people!" Stepping backwards, he picked up a plunger, and raised it above his head, threatening them. "You won't kill me!"

Omar looked at him, and spit. "You're kidding me, right. What the hell are you going to do! Plunge us to death." He turned away thinking. Bathroom full of blood, two dead bodies, and he picks a freaking plunger.

Guillermo shook his head. "No. We don't want to kill you. We want to help you."

"Help me. Help me do what?"

"Found out who killed your buddies." He stepped over them, and found them." Omar followed behind. "Or...are you going to try and explain this mess to the police when they arrive."

"Or, plunge the freaking toilet."

The guard looked down at his buddies, death. He looked over his shirt and pants. He was bruised around the face with a huge gash in the back of his head. He probably could explain that someone came in, sure. But, the hooker, who really wasn't a hooker. Got the jump on his buddies. How, they'd ask too many questions and not enough answers, and then on top of it all. He was an illegal.

He dropped the plunger and walked out. "Wait one second."

"What? Hold up, wait. The police are..."

He grabbed his folder out of the cabinet with his name and information. He found his identification card, and then looked around. He snatched up the logbook. "Okay, we go."

"Smart." Guillermo said as he opened the door and they eased out. He looked behind him at the piers inside the shipyard, and Omar said, "You want to go inside?"

"No. I'm sure they already have their hands full."

"They...they who?"

"Well, the ATF guy...Maria...and Felix."

"Felix? He's in there?"

"Of course. I called him."

They crossed the street and got into a waiting car. Another car was there also, with three other men inside. They drove up Washington Avenue and spotted Cookie. They shadowed him as he got into a cab. It headed up Myrtle Avenue and they trailed closely behind.

FELIX WALKED OVER TO the cage that Edward and Maria were in, and said, "Hell of a predicament you seem to have gotten yourself into. "

Maria dusted herself off. "You're right, but I can explain. "

Felix turned away, and said, "Edward."

Flabbergasted. The stupid fat look on Maria's face spelt double-cross all day long as she backed off. "You, you, you. Know him?"

Felix snickered and looked over at her. "I, I, I do."

Edward lowered his head. Definitely not the way he wanted things to go down. He glanced at his watch. Where the hell is Giovanni? "Maria...I wanted to tell you."

"Tell me what!" He backed her into a corner. "That all this time you were working with, with," she pointed to Felix. This bastard!"

"Edward." Felix said, "You should have told her that I was in the picture. But you did at least tell her you're ATF, right?"

Latif listened; he dare not make a move. Trying to remain as quiet as possible, seeing that this so-called reunion wasn't going too well. He searched the perimeters looking for a way out. Ice stood opposite and caught his eye movements, and he motioned to one of the aisles, and nodded. Felix turned towards him and asked, "Who is this?"

Maria's eyes arched dastardly. Maybe, she thought he was her way out of this after all. "Oh, you don't know." She walked closer. "That my friend here...is your partner."

"Partner?" Felix laughed." This youngin'. I never did business with him."

"Oh, but you have."

He glanced at her, then with the swiftness of a huge cat grabbed her by the neck, jerking her closer to the gate. "Look. My patience is growing thin. Who is this?" He cut his eyes "And, his friend behind me with his finger on the trigger." Maria looked over his shoulder, and Ice indeed had his hands in his bag. "Let me go, then," she said.

He did, and Maria checked her throat out for a moment, then asked, "You got a cigarette?"

"A cigarette?" He turned, and barked at one of his men. "Manny, give me a smoke. "

The ball headed, Latino ran towards Felix digging into his pocket. He took out one and started to hand it to Felix. "No. Give it to her." He handed Maria the cigarette, then waited to light it. Once he had, he scrambled back to where he was at, behind Ice and Latif, along with six other of his cronies.

Rasheed had eased up on them. He hid undercover next to the scaffolding by Ice. He got up slowly. Ice saw him. Rasheed motioned to him not to make a move, at least until Latif was out the way; he nodded.

"Now, tell me. "

Maria took a drag out of the cigarette, and Latif blurted. "I'm the biological son of Malik Hamid Mohammed. "

Felix shrugged. "Who is that? I don't know who that is "

"Malik!" Maria shouted at him. "From Bushwick."

He turned towards him and studied his features. "Yeah. Yeah."

"He owned half of what you. We own. His father signed the papers you gave him. "

"Oh yeah." He motioned to his men. "Then, you're the one I really need." He looked at Maria. "With him...I really don't need you."

Maria backed away. "I'm your wife!"

Felix laughed. "True." He pointed his gun towards her. "That is very much true. Even though you screwed me over, and tried to sell me out." He snarled at her. "But. You can't live with them, and you can't live without them. "

He pointed the gun at Edward and shot. He dropped. Maria looked over at him. "You killed him."

"He was a snitch. No good...he tried to get me to dime out the Cartel, but they knew it, so they offered me a deal."

"A deal?" Maria questioned.

"Yeah." He motioned to one of his men and he pointed the high-powered shotgun at the lock on the door of the cage. He blasted it open. "A deal to restore things back to order here."

"Here? I don't understand."

Felix reached out his hand." Come, they know you stole from them, and yet you continue to steal. But, they're loyal to your old man, so they won't kill you." He looked over at her. "It's funny. You don't have to steal...they're impressed with all you have done." He beckoned her. "Let's go. We don't have much time. He checked his watch. I've already held back the cops long enough."

Maria walked out the cage and looked at Latif. "What about him?"

"Oh yeah." Felix walked over to Latif and started raising his gun. "I'll kill you like I killed your father. Keep the money out of your hands."

"Hell no!" Rasheed yelled.

Felix spun around. "You! I thought I let you go! Why are you back here?"

"You've killed enough of my people...and enough of...my family."

"Family?" He turned and looked at Latif and finally made the connection, "Fuck!" Latif jumped out the way, giving Rasheed enough time to fire off a round. Felix ducked out the way while Maria ran towards the back. One of her men was waiting, and he fired rounds in Felix's direction to cover her. Felix hollered at her. "You're trying to kill me?"

Maria nodded. "Oh well".

"You dirty bitch!" With a motion of his hand. All hell broke loose. A barrage of bullets flooded the warehouse. Echoes of metal to metal, metal to brick, kicked up years of dust as the gunfire continued.

Giovanni made his way underneath the rollup gate, and had just brought up towards the aisle. He spotted Rasheed, Ice. Latif laid on the ground, and was in a bad position. Any move one way or another, and he'd be sure to catch a bullet. Felix had crawled into the cage ducking, shooting, when and where he could. Giovanni needed a plan. He glanced over at the scuffle. He thought he had one.

Ice dove in the direction of Rasheed. He needed cover, and Felix's men were flanked behind them. Latif hugged the ground tightly as Rasheed called out to him. "Don't move. I got you!"

Felix couldn't keep his eyes off of him, meaning mugging. Malik's kid. If I knew where he was when he was a kid, I'd have killed him, years ago. He had him in his sights now, though. He aimed his gun, and said, "You die now." Then, shots riddled the front of the cage, and he jumped back to the side taking cover.

Latif peed up, and Rasheed was beckoning him over saying. "I got you." Ice sprayed the top of the scaffolding with 40 caliber automatic gunfire where Felix's men were. They backed down, given Latif enough time to fall in line with them. "Now what?" He asked.

Ice looked around, racking his brain trying to figure it out, and he couldn't think of anything. "We need to get out. Somehow"

"The building." Rasheed responded. "The shipyard. Is it one way in, and one way out? "

"No. It's not. There's another exit." Giovanni yelled to him.

"What the hell!" Rasheed exclaimed, glad to see him." He asked, "How did you..."

"Behind this building, there is a way out. But you have to keep close to the pier."

"How would we know which direction to go?" Ice interrupted.

"By looking across the water. You will be going Uptown... Follow the FDR. Trust me. "

"We go way back, Giovanni. That's not a problem. But the deal is, we gotta get out of here first."

Giovanni crawled out front and looked around, then came back. "In a few, this place will be crawling with Feds."

"But, why?"

"A Fed by the name of Edwards Gonzalez."

"Well...Felix...dude just shot him." Latif said.

"Who?"

"The guy, the Fed. The one you just named. What's the deal with him anyway?"

"Damn! ATF, on the tail of the Cartel...and Maria. Been on it for years. This was a way, the shipyard delivery, to find who out was controlling the Cartel. That person...was supposed to be here today."

"Controlling the Cartel? Who? I don't see anyone else except that crumb, Felix."

"Hello, Rasheed, he's it."

"No... Don't think so. Latif added. Felix shot that dude. He grabbed Maria. This had to be about her. She pissed someone off. "

"Yeah, Felix was a sent flunky."

"He's gotta know what's going on."

Giovanni shook his head in agreement, he was right. The whole thing was bigger than he thought. Edward was right. So, what's the deal with y'all?

"We're trying to make things right."

"Get our money back that they stole from us." Rasheed said,

"Steal? Hello, y'all got money. Why stick up, Rasheed? "

"Something to do with the Cartel. Dad left us a letter, explaining everything. "Rasheed said,

"Then, you know about the key."

"Yep. How did you know?"

"Doesn't matter right now. Look. It's not about the money, Rasheed. It's about the property, laundering money. "

"You know what, Giovanni..." Ice ducked a bullet that whizzed by his head." I believe you're right. But, right now, fellas, we need to get the hell out of here."

Giovanni stuck his gun out and shot. He downed one. Ice follows suit. Another one was down. "The path is clear to the back." Ice said, "You coming?"

Giovanni nodded his head no. "I'm staying. The cops and the Feds will be here in a short time. Need to buy y'all some time." He grabbed Rasheed by the arm. "You need to get back in touch with me."

"For what?"

"For what? I got three dead in a shack. A faggot that can finger you all, and you," he glared at Ice. "You put Waseema and Shaheeda into this shit!"

"I'll be in touch." He was right.

They took off running for the door while Giovanni shot at Felix's men.

Latif pulled up the rear shooting at Felix. They were out. Maria had just pulled off and was on her way zooming up the street. Making a mad dash for the pier, underneath the cover of the heavy black smoke that smoldered from the truck, and it was just like Giovanni had told them.

The path took them all the way up to a point off Flushing Avenue called High Street. There, they came upon a small brick, utility building. Rasheed kicked at the door and it burst wide open. No herculean feat, years of rust had decayed its latch. They were finally out of the shipyard. Ice said, "Waseema probably took Asia to the hospital. Let's go!"

"No!" Rasheed stopped him.

"It'll be too hot. We made plans to go to the store to remember. Go there. I'll go to the hospital and find out what's up. I know some people that work there. Once I find out." He dug for the walkie-talkie "I'll call."

"Alright," Ice said, as he checked for him. "You ready, Latif. Meet you at the store, Rasheed."

Ice whistled for a gypsy cab, they jumped in and were gone.

Rasheed ran up a ways then made a right going towards Park Avenue before he ran into a cab. He flagged it down. "Woodhull Hospital."

"Woodhull?"

"By Bushwick Projects. You know where that is, right?"

The cab driver grimaced. He knew all too well. Too many robberies for him to count. He sure hoped that this wasn't one...here!

Rasheed handed him a fifty-dollar bill. "Don't worry. Just step on it!"

# CHAPTER SEVENTEEN

The drizzle played lullabies on top of the roof. The rhythmical, hypnotic sounds of the tires running across the black asphalt on the big city street almost lulled her into a nod, if not for the streaking of the old wiper blades against the windshield. It made her roll down the window, keeping her awake.

The overcast sky made the city appear darker grey. The downpour got heavier and the truck kept its pace making its way towards Woodhull Hospital. They were closer, and that was good.

Waseema sat next to her peering closely out the window, trying to see. She didn't say anything, she was quiet, in deep thought. She had wanted so bad to say something, but there was nothing to talk about. Waseema was scared too. She could see it all on her. Worried about Ice and Rasheed.

They were sitting on three duffel bags filled with money, at least close to a mill a piece, if not more. Which would have been good, but for what it was worth, Asia lay bleeding badly in the back, and if they didn't get help for her soon, she'd die. That damn sure wasn't part of the plan. Kokomo was back there with her. She wanted so bad to stay back there with her, but he insisted that she be up front.

Once they got to the hospital, she'd get out and do her thing. Get hold of her people; a nurse friend of hers. A girl she knew from Bushwick Projects. She was strapped down on welfare back in the day, struggling, Asia gave her a hand up. When she strived to go through nursing school, Asia fed her kids until she got on her feet.

She's out of the projects now. A two-story HUD home in Canarsie. Nice ride. Kids go to good schools now and they make good grades. She more than once told her that whenever she needed her, don't hesitate. Waseema just shook it off as a *yeah, yeah* then, but who knew. She just hoped right now she was either working, or on call.

Kokomo comforted Asia the best he could. He held her in his arms gently, keeping steady pressure on the wound. Bleeding heavy, her breathing shallow, she struggled for air. He hoped to God it wouldn't be an issue to get her into the hospital. He figured they'd have to explain the gunshot wound, and once they dug out the bullet, finding out it came from an automatic weapon at that; they'd called the cops, fast. Lots of questions, too many that couldn't be answered. But they couldn't worry about that, now.

He knew Shaheeda was driving as fast as she could. It was close to morning, and daylight was creeping up on them. They had to move fast. Beat the traffic on the street, the hospital. She wheezed, and coughed, he heard her groan, then her eyes came open, and she spoke. "Kokomo..."

"Don't talk."

"We. Did it. Right?" her voice trailed off; it was weak.

"We did. What?"

"We're...rich..."

Kokomo smiled. "Yes, we are...now, be quiet. "

She struggled reaching her hand up to his face. "Now. We can go. All those places. We imagined."

"Sure can, baby." He laughed. "Now, you can shop in Paris."

"Tired of the knockoffs." She coughed. She was getting weaker. Kokomo looked down at her wound, and the blood continued to flow more severely now. "Come on now. Be still."

"No, baby. It's gonna be alright. You know you're...gonna give me away."

"Give you away?"

"Silly. Me and Rasheed... Wedding." She was getting delirious.

A tear came down his eye and landed on her cheek. "Yeah, silly me. Sure I will. Anything for you."

"Don't be sad." Her voice dimmed, and her eyes teared up. "It's gonna be. Alright."

He shook his head, "Yes. It will. "

Her eyes fluttered, she smiled broadly, and with her last breath said to him. "I love you...too..." It was over.

Tears flooded his eyes, and his cry was the cry of deep sadness, and pain. He'd lost his best friend, and the woman he loved the most in this world. He kissed her lips, and said, "Yeah, Asia. Love you, too."

The truck slowed down, and Shaheeda stared out the window. "Mom... Ain't that."

"It is. Stop the truck, and let him in. He's soaked."

Cookie was walking towards Park Avenue when the truck slowed down. He didn't recognize it, thought maybe it was a trick, and he did need a ride. Pissed off, he got kicked out of the cab he was in about ten blocks away. No more money. He stopped. "What's up?"

Waseema called out to him. "It's me, Waseema. Rasheed's mother. "

"Oh my God! He ran over. Where is Asia? And Kokomo! "

"They're in the back. Asia's been shot. It's pretty bad. We're on our way to the hospital, now."

Shaheeda started up the truck, and drove what seemed to be only a few minutes. They pulled across the street from the hospital and Waseema got out. The rain had subsided some. She knocked on the back door. No one answered. "Kokomo! It's me, Waseema. We're here!"

The door opened and he stared at her.

"Come on. Let's get her moving. Take her through emergency, and I'm going inside to get my friend."

"Don't worry about it."

"Don't worry, boy, are you crazy!" She started to climb inside. Kokomo jumped off the truck, outside. "It's too late."

"Too late!" Cookie hollered. He looked inside the truck where Asia was laying. Still, not moving. "No! No!" He jumped in and picked up her head. "Maybe, she needs CPR. I know CPR. I can help."

Waseema pulled at him. "Cookie. She's dead."

"No!" Cookie held her, "No! She can't be...no!" He wailed.

Waseema walked over to Kokomo and asked, "What do we do?"

He took a deep breath. "We go to your store."

"With the body inside the truck like that"

He looked off. "I can't..."

Kokomo was hurting and Waseema understood his pain. "Don't worry...we got her." Waseema glanced over at Shaheeda. She walked over to him and gave him the keys to the truck. "Look these are the keys...the truck...the store."

"We'll take the body inside. I'll find my friend. You just go to the store, ok." Waseema added. "And change your clothes, too." She kissed him on the cheek. "I'm sorry." He half smiled, then turned towards Cookie. "We gotta go."

Cookie was still numb by what happened. He just stood there, staring at Asia, and Kokomo stepped in front of him and said, "Look...we gotta go."

"Go where?" Kokomo sniffled, wiped his nose with the back of his hand and said, "Finish the job."

"WE SHOULD HAVE PICKED him up when the cab driver kicked his black ass out!"

"Calm down, Omar." Guillermo kept his eyes peeled on the truck. Hold up. "Something's happening."

"He's trying to catch a ride, that's what's happening. Probably a trick."

"No...something else." He squinted his eyes. "He knows them. It's a woman...two."

"Where are they going?"

"Keep up behind them...but not too close..."

GIOVANNI STUCK TO THE side of the aisle like glue. He crept slowly, and silently. Felix's men were climbing down from atop their location hidden in the scaffolding. Felix had run out back with two of his men, escaping, and they were right behind him.

Giovanni was in the lurk waiting by the door in the shadows, when one of the men came by. Grabbing him he drugged him underneath the scaffold down the opposite aisle and squeezed tight around his throat. The man tried crying out for help, but Giovanni held him down, flipped him over, and muffled his cry. Giovanni then heaved up on the back of his neck, snapping it. He dropped him, and pushed the body further underneath, the man was now hidden. There were now just two.

He needed to hold them, until the Feds came, and couldn't figure out for the life of him why they weren't already here yet. He'd heard the sirens at least a good hour ago. He was perplexed, but he had bigger fish to fry right now.

He moved up to the aisle where Rasheed and Ice were earlier. He looked around, and saw the crates they were in. Getting closer he noticed the top was ajar. Empty. Nothing, except a ripped-up cargo sack. He looked in another and there were wrapped bundles of drugs. Kilos. It had to be a Cartel stash. He looked around and there was one other, open. He peeped in that one, and it was halfway filled with money.

Tens and twenties. If he had to guess, they had to be at least one million still left inside. Looking around at the others, there were probably more. He heard footsteps. He turned, and one of Felix's men was right up on him. He cracked Giovanni's jaw and staggered him, putting him down. He fell to the ground on his back, and the man jumped on him. They wrestled. The punch hurt him, slowed him, but there was no time for the pain. He got up to his feet and shook it off, oblivious to the pain to his grill, then he heard the others coming. He couldn't fight them all, especially in the pain he was in. He ran.

They were on his ass. He couldn't make the move for the hole at the bottom of the door at the speed he was going. He'd never make it. He had to make a stand, but where? He bust a quick left towards the shops. There was an opening to the far right when he came in, he saw it. He just hoped the door wasn't locked. One of them opened fire, and he ducked as the bullet ricocheted around the warehouse. He only had one more clip. He loaded up and fired. He got one. Two left.

He crouched down trying to figure out how to make away for the door, when he heard the sirens outside. Felix's men heard them, too. One took off running for the back door while the other stayed. He was left by Felix. He knew he had to shut Giovanni up so when the police came, he could tell his own side of the story. The one that hopefully would keep him out of prison.

He launched towards him shooting wildly. Giovanni stood his ground, and started shooting back. When the smoke cleared, and the dust had somewhat settled, Giovanni had caught one in the shoulder, he grimaced. Luckily, the bullet went straight through, but Felix's man wasn't so fortunate. He was dead. Giovanni wobbled to his feet. He could hear men outside barking orders. He banged on the rollup door and yelled out. "It's Giovanni!"

"Giovanni?"

"Yeah, hold up. I'm gonna open up the roll up door."

"Which one?"

"First one...left." He made it over and pressed the button. It rolled up and there were five squad cars, three Fed, but no van. "Where's the ATF guys?"

"Who?"

"The ATF guys...I was with them earlier."

A tall man in a suit helped him to an ambulance and flashed his badge, and said, "I'm ATF, and I don't know anything about no van."

"Damn. Cartel." Giovanni said under his breath.

"This is some sort of work. Stash spot?"

"Cartel. To the left, on the scaffolding. Crates filled with dope and money. Also, you got a man down back there."

"Who?" The man waved his men inside.

"Gonzalez...Edward Gonzalez."

"Damn... you know we have to brief you later, detective."

"Giovanni's good...I'm retired."

He looked at the cops, and said, "Not what they tell me. You're a good cop. Got to go, see you later."

"Trying to get yourself killed these days?"

"Goddamn, Ravenel."

"Captain Ravenel, now." He reached out his hand. "What gives? Still chasing Cartel?"

"Yeah...stash spot. You wouldn't believe who I saw."

"Who?"

"Felix...he's still around."

"Damn, hmmm...anyone else?"

Giovanni looked at him suspiciously, he seemed to be probing for something. He knew, he trained him. He had a hunch, but it couldn't be, but what the hell. "Oh, what precinct are you over at, Ravenel?"

"The eight-four"

"Oh...okay...just got the call then, huh."

"Yeah." He scanned the area like he was looking for something. "Just came in. Shots fired."

"Wow..." He didn't say anything about the truck or the smoke. He had to be the one who held back the squad cars. Damn, he looked up at him with disgust. He's being paid off by the Cartel. He knew Felix was here then, and probably helped him get away. "Hey, look. I need a car. Got to get back to the station house, and make a report for these guys." He pointed to the Feds. He was on the bullshit too.

"You can go later. Go to the hospital." Ravenel knew.

*Hmmm*, Giovanni thought, *he damn sure didn't want me anywhere near the precinct, and the Feds, at least, not now. The hospital though?* He could make it from there. "Sure, okay. Let's go." He scrambled into the ambulance, but before the door closed, he said, "Did the guard see anything?"

"Naw...we didn't bother to stop there. You?"

"I didn't either. Alright Ravenel, see ya around." The door closed and the ambulance took off. Halfway up the street the siren came on. Strange. He asked the paramedic, "Did something happen by the precinct, let's say about an hour ago?"

"Not really...crazy ass captain had everyone respond to a call by Farragut Projects...over near the piers."

"What happened?"

"That was the thing...nothing, but he had his men wait there. Search. Made us wait, too...with the damn sirens turned on. Now, how crazy was that?"

He couldn't believe it, Ravenel was being paid off by the Cartel. He was the one who held the police back from the Navy Yard. Set up a phony surveillance van. He wondered who else was involved and why him?

GUILLERMO AND OMAR watched as Shaheeda and Waseema directed the orderlies to Asia's body. They did the best they could carrying her to the entrance of the emergency room without a gurney. Waseema eventually found Mona, the person she was looking for. She told her that she'd be back a little later on and not to toe tag it as a Jane Doe, not just yet. She said not to ask any questions, told her she'd explain everything later. Mona Agreed and took the body in and Waseema and Shaheeda hailed a cab to the store.

"Felix's men must have shot the girl...killed her." Guillermo said as he and his men followed closely behind.

"Why do we care?" Omar smirked.

"The only reason we let Felix loose in the first place was so he could prove to us that the broad..."

"Maria?"

"Yeah, Maria was stealing. No problem. We found out that the ATF guy was dirty, but..." he pointed his driver right at the light. They'd lost the cab for a sec. "There they are."

"But, what, Guillermo?"

"Why the others? The homo guy...the woman? What are they doing?"

"Probably stealing."

"Yeah, but who told them about the Cartel stash in the first place? How'd they know to go there? And..."

"You ask a lot of questions."

"And...why'd Felix spend so much time trying to kill them?"

"Look!" Omar pointed to the store. "They are getting out of the cab, and there's the truck."

"Felix's?"

He looked over at Guillermo and said, "Now...hmmm, I see what you mean. I wonder who that store belongs to?"

"Me, too." Guillermo told his men to duck down in their seats. "Oh shit... Felix, and the ATF guy."

"There's more than what he's letting on."

"That bastard. I bet he's been double crossing us all the time." He reached underneath his seat and pulled out his gun, got out of the vehicle and with the rest following suit, said, "He'd better have a damn good story."

"Or, lie."

"Yeah, Omar...or lie."

RASHEED JUMPED OUT of the cab and ran into the entrance of the emergency room, yelling. "Where is she?"

The small petite woman that cautiously approached him said, "Please sir, calm down. You're disturbing..."

"Where is the girl that was just brought in?"

She pulled him to the side, out of ear reach, and asked, "Are you Rasheed?"

"Yes! Do you know where she is? She was brown skinned...about your height..."

Waseema's friend Mona hadn't expected Rasheed to come to the hospital. Waseema probably thought he'd go to the store first. She recognized him from around the projects. Irate, she needed to calm him down before security, who were already watching, and would eventually start asking questions. She had to tell him something.

"Sir...Rasheed, please, sit down. Be cool." She cut her eyes at the guard. Rasheed looked, and followed her line of sight. He sat, but he could tell by the look in her eyes, that what she was about to say wasn't going to be good. He gripped the sides of his chair, and put down his head. "Just...where...is she?"

Ice and Latif were behind him. They'd heard everything and peeped the guard also and immediately knew what it was. Mona recognized Ice and nodded to him, then spoke softly to Rasheed. "Your mother said she was going to see you..."

"At the store... I know..."

"I'm very sorry." She rubbed his arm gently. Rasheed turned toward Ice and his brother and said, "I need to see her for a minute. Say goodbye, that's all."

"Do what you gotta do." Ice answered.

"I won't be long..."

Mona took him by the hand through some double doors marked "Morgue". They took the elevator to the basement. Rasheed hung his head down solemnly as the door opened. She guided him by the hand, then pointed him to her body. "That one." He nodded and she left out, "I'll be back in a few."

"Won't be long." He walked over to the metal table where she lay. She was Already covered, he pulled back the white sheet.

Her skin had just begun to pale. Hair still soft to the touch, he swept his hands through it. She had a pleasant smile on her face, like everything was blissfully peaceful. He bent over and kissed her on the lips. He reached for her hand, and with his other, dug into his pocket and pulled out a ring. A dazzling, five carat diamond. He put it on her finger, and said to her. "Till death..." He started crying. And for the first time, in a very long time. He was hurt.

Mona came back through the doors, and spoke, softly. "Your friends said they need to talk."

"I'll be right there."

By the time he turned, they were there. Latif hugged him. "I'm so sorry, bro," Ice sighed when he looked at her, and walked off. "Damn." Rasheed followed, and said, "You alright?"

"I'm alright...I should have...done something..."

"It's cool. It wasn't your fault... just one of those things. So, what's up?"

"I just got a call"

"A call?"

"Here...at the hospital." He turned towards him. "It ain't good."

"What?"

"Felix...said if you're not there in a half hour."

"There?"

"He's going to kill Shaheeda ...and...your mother."

"My mother! He's got them, where?"

"The store."

Rasheed walked back over to Asia's body, kissed her, then covered her up. He looked over at Latif and said, "You still got everything?"

Uzi. 40 Cal." He turned towards Ice. "What are we waiting for?"

"Rasheed!" He grabbed him. "This could get really ugly." Rasheed exhaled, then gently caressed his friend's arm. "Ugly?" He glanced over at Asia's body then said, "It's not ugly enough? Look, Ice...we can't run...change...this is who we are...what we do."

Ice just shook his head, "you're right." Then looked over at Latif. "Let's go get them...back".

Latif was right behind him, then turned back. Looking at Asia, all he could do was think of Felix. He killed her, his father, his brother, and now he was threatening to kill his mother. His sister. He banged his hand against the wall. It had to end. Today was about redemption... Khalid's.

GIOVANNI ARRIVED AT the hospital surrounded by a bunch of drama. Evidently, someone had called in a police shot, distress call, at 10:13 A.M., and by the time he got there, a bunch of reporters, off duty and on duty cops, and about as much hospital staff one would not expect to see, was there waiting. He was escorted into the emergency room by doctors and nurses, a lot of shouting, orders being barked by security, questions, and cameras being poked in his face.

Eventually, he was finally left with a couple of doctors in an examination room. Once it was determined that his injury was not life-threatening, the crowd slowly disbursed. He was literally left by himself. He pulled back the curtain, and a nurse walked by. "Hey... Is anyone going to see me?"

She shrugged her shoulders and kept on moving.

"Damn, Woodhull. I gotta be dying to get some help huh." He tried to raise himself up and grimaced in pain. "*AHHH!*"

"Hey...aren't you Mic?"

He struggled putting on his shirt. "Yeah, yeah... The cop that got shot. And, no... I'm not dying."

"It's me. Mona." She had seen them bring him in, and when all the pandemonium started, went upstairs doing rounds away from it all. She came back down later when it was finally quiet.

She eased over. She remembered Giovanni from the projects also, but it was during a time when they were both younger. When she was catching hell. She faintly remembered about him and Lisa, but she never forgot that he was a cop though. From Bushwick projects?"

Giovanni looked up at her, he didn't actually remember her but politely said, "Oh yeah...Bushwick." He tried putting out his hand, and couldn't. "I'm sorry, my shoulder hurts like hell."

"Hold up, let me help."

"Is there anyone available?"

She looked at his arm. "Gun shot."

"Bullet went straight through."

"I see." She walked over to a cabinet and pulled out some gauze. "Here let me see." She cleaned up his wound and applied a salve, then bandaged it up. "There, much better."

"Damn thanks." He got up. "I appreciate it." He reached into his pocket and pulled out a few dollars. "Why don't you buy lunch? On me."

She pushed it away. "I'm just doing my job."

"I didn't mean anything by it, but thanks."

She helped him with his shirt and down off the bed. "You, uh, still see, Lisa?" she asked.

Giovanni smiled. He did. There was no need to tell her any more than that. "Yeah. Still do."

"Tell her I said hi."

"Sure will."

"It's the strangest thing. Seeing everybody from Bushwick today, it seems like. Least people my age."

"Excuse me." He gawked.

"I'm sorry. Remember, Waseema. Her son, Rasheed. Ice. "

"Yeah. What about them?"

She peeped out the curtain both ways, and then closed them shut. "Look. You're still a cop, right?"

"Something like that."

"I hate to snitch, but."

"Look. If it's incriminating for you, then you better report it to a precinct."

"No. It's not that," she said, "Waseema brought in a girl. Dead. Bullet wound. Just like yours."

Giovanni's eyes were wide open now. He got up and peeped out the curtain too. "Tell me what you know."

"I'm not going to get in trouble. Lose my job, or anything."

"No, I promise. Between us only."

"Well. They brought this girl in, like I said, Dead. She's downstairs in the morgue now. But Rasheed and Ice came in right after they left."

"They?"

"The daughter. Shaheedah. But anyway, they had some other guy with him. He looked familiar, but."

"Latif?"

"I believe that was his name. Anyway, they were talking about something. I mean, I didn't want to be nosy, but I was just coming back into the morgue. And, I overheard him say something about Waseema and her daughter Shaheeda being kidnapped or something."

"Kidnapped? Did you hear where it was?"

"The store that Waseema opened up on Broadway."

Giovanni buttoned up his shirt and took a look out front. There were still cops outside. "Is there another way out?"

Mona thought for a moment then said, "Follow me".

They crept behind the examining room curtains toward the end of the corridor, then she told him to lie down on a stretcher. "Here. Put this over you." He covered up with a sheet, and she pushed him out towards the back past the elevator to a door reserved for funeral home pickups. She said, "This way is Park Avenue."

He searched his pockets. "Damn, forgot my keys, but my car is parked downtown." He turned towards her. "I need you to call a cab."

She reached in her pocket, and took out her keys. "My car is parked on Park Avenue. Across from the park. Red Toyota. Here." She tossed them to him. "Just go get Waseema and them."

"I'll bring it back, I promise."

"Hell," She smiled, "If you don't, I'll report it stolen...by a cop."

A grin came across his face, and he said to her, "I won't be mad at you." He went outside and after a small search, found her car. He hopped in it, and took off towards Broadway, to the store.

He couldn't help thinking about the last time he made a run like this. About ten years ago. Hopefully, this time things will turn out differently, but he still took the time to say a silent prayer.

FELIX PACED BACK-AND-forth. Every now and then, he would stop and look at the windows where his men were posted as lookouts. Gonzalez was off in the cut by the sneaker section, towering, every now and then, he too, peeped over at the window, thinking to himself that he never should've let Felix talk him into this.

Located in the back, behind the hanging jackets, high dollar sweat suits, and display cases, was a door, an inconspicuous, gray door with a shiny brass knob. Outside on the right was a light switch, and once you flipped the switch, the light came on showing the stairway going down into the basement. On the bottom to the left was a large board with stock, numbered according to style, date, and even a ledger stating how fast merchandise was moving.

Directly behind that was the shipping and receiving area, along with an electric hoist that carried freight up to the sidewalk outside. Opposite that was another door, the office. Usually where Waseema did the books. Inside of this room was the safe.

Neither Felix, nor Gonzalez had bothered to check it. Probably assumed it was a bathroom. Underneath the stairway was a storage room. A small space that held items such as extra bags, wrapping paper, shrink wrap, and the like. It also held enough space to fit small storage inside. Outside of the door to the left, sitting low-key, were three duffel bags.

The door was pushed open slightly. "Stay here, while I see what's going on upstairs." It was Kokomo and he was talking to Cookie.

They were already inside the store when Felix and his men stormed in. Kokomo had disabled the alarm system when he came in, and never reset it, thinking Waseema and Shaheeda were a few minutes behind them. Felix and his man had accosted and overpowered them, then tied them up.

Kokomo crept up the stairs and opened the door ever so slightly. He saw Felix, then looked over to his right, and saw Gonzalez ducking down in a corner, with a gun in his hand. Behind him was Shaheeda and Waseema. He also checked out the three other men that were posted by the windows.

He closed the door back and slowly slid back down the stairs to the room. He bit his lip but didn't see it. There were about five men up there. Waseema and her daughter were tied up in the back. He reached for the small Arsenal they had, specifically the 40. Cal. "The way I figure. I can take at least two-maybe three. The big Mexican dude and the white boy near the back." He opened the barrel and held it to the light. "If I play it right, I can get close to Waseema and then hopefully untie them and let them go." He aimed it. Then got a bead on one by the window.

Cookie gawked at him. "But what about the other two."

He looked at him and sighed, "That's where you come in."

"Me?"

He nodded a little, opened the door and grabbed one of the duffle bags. "Here you go."

"What?"

"Look. Take this. It's yours. You earned it. Don't know exactly how much is in there, but."

"No. I'm not leaving you. He reached for a gun. I can take out those two. I can!"

"I hear you. He reached for the gun. You don't owe no one anything. You did your part." He grabbed his jacket, and said, "Just do one thing for me."

A tear ran down Cookie's eye. "What?"

He reached in the pocket, and pulled out a paper. "Take this address. Go there, and tell her to leave." He leaned outside, and grabbed a duffel bag, and Cookie stopped him. "I can't carry two. You know that."

"You're right." He reached in and pulled out three big handfuls of money and stuffed them in Cookie's bag. "Don't really know how much that is, but it's a lot. Give it to her." He exhaled, then looked off. "Tell her to find a good man, a house. Stuff like that. "

Cookie rubbed his back. "I know what to say. I got you." But he glanced outside the door, and asked, "How do I get out of here?"

"Come on." He helped him with the bag, and they went over by the hoist. "I'm going to have to lift you up through here." He pointed upward to the iron gates.

"Can't we use the hoist..." he pointed to the panel.

"No. Makes too much noise." He climbed up top, and pushed open the gate. He climbed back down and pulled up the heavy, weighed down bag. "Come on, grab my hand." Cookie did, and he helped him up and out. "Now remember."

"I will. I'll be back."

"No! Go! Go somewhere...far."

"Go? Where would I go?"

He grinned. "You know... Try Paris. Asia always wanted to go to Paris."

"Paris?"

"Why not? You got the money now." He grabbed at the handle on the gate inside. "Now, go. Take care of your punk ass." He smirked.

Cookie smiled back at him. "Yeah...love you, too."

"And Cookie..."

"Yeah."

"You did good." Kokomo closed the gate and climbed back down. He loaded up the guns he had, the Uzi, 40 caliber, and a 9 mm, and looked up at the door. "Well, Kokomo. Let's get it over with."

Cookie grabbed the bag and drug it to the curb. He glanced up the street, and then back at the gate then wiped away a tear. Maybe, he should put the bag up somewhere, and go back. He opened the paper that Kokomo had given him and it was a letter written to someone named Shante saying he was sorry for the way he treated her, and to take the money, leave New York for good. That he really cared for her, just didn't know how to show it. He had to deliver it.

Once he got to Kokomo's apartment, the cab driver asked if he should wait. He said, "Yeah," then asked where else he wanted to go. Cookie laughed. LaGuardia airport.

"Going on a trip?"

"Yeah...going to Paris."

# CHAPTER EIGHTEEN

"Hey, Felix...someone's coming to the door." Felix damn near broke his neck turning around, then once he realized who it was, he cursed, "Shit," and stopped in his tracks.

Guillermo and Omar, and the men that were with them, now five deep approached the door. Their hands stuffed into their pockets, bulged. Felix knew what it was, they were strapped. He exhaled heavily, then barked an order. "Open the door!"

"What!" His man said, knowing full well who Guillermo was and the danger that came with him. "Are you sure?"

"I said, open the door." He turned towards them, "Just be on point...if I were you".

Guillermo stepped through the door behind three of his men who immediately positioned themselves in front of the men Felix had posted. Omar, right behind them, surveyed the area. When he saw Waseema and Shaheeda tied up, he got Guillermo's attention and pointed. "There..."

Guillermo pointed his men, the two that were behind him towards them, and said, "Untie them!"

Felix barked another order. "No! Stop!"

Guillermo looked over at him, dismayed by the action, and then calmly walked over to a chair by the counter that held the cash register and crossed his legs. Not taking his eyes off Felix, he asked, "What is this all about, Felix?"

He was fidgeting, but at this point it was a direct standoff against the Cartel. Dead serious. He walked over towards him, had his man pull up a chair directly in front of him, and sat. Omar kept Guillermo in his sights, sized Felix up, never taking his hand out of his pocket.

Felix, then said, "It's about what's right, Guillermo."

"What's right? I don't understand."

"I've been faithful to the Cartel, and I need some respect. "

Guillermo laughed, and looked up at Omar, and said, "Did you hear what he just said, Omar? I've never heard anything so absurd."

Felix put out his hand. "The Cartel owes me."

"We don't owe you shit!" Omar spit. "I ought to..." He started to pull out his gun, and Guillermo stopped him, but not before Felix's men turned towards them, with theirs pointed at them. He looked. "I see."

"They feel the same way." Felix said, the venom evident in his tone.

"So, I see."

Omar stepped back at Guillermo's directive. "Talk to me, Felix. Why do this? Why bring all this attention on us?" He pointed towards the back. "Kidnap these women?" He uncrossed his leg and leaned forward. "We. The Cartel, don't do this."

Felix sighed and leaned back. "Then, let me tell you why."

RASHEED AND ICE INCHED their way outside the building, peering inside, trying to figure out a way in. The sun was up, and already people started to commute, on their way to the J-train station a good half block away. They had to be sneaky, so as not to alarm anyone, keeping their guns hidden in their pockets. Once the people and the traffic subsided some, they huddled up. "They're deep inside." Rasheed said.

Ice asked him, "Did you see how many there were inside?"

"Naw." Latif answered. "When I walked by, there were just two at the window. That's all I saw."

"What about Felix?"

"Couldn't really tell. Had to move fast, ya know."

"Yeah, yeah...it's all good."

Time was racing against them, and they needed a way inside, quick. Once the day began, then they were at their mercy. No telling what Felix would do, then if they started popping caps, the area would be flooded with cops in a matter of minutes. Don't know if they'd kill Waseema, Shaheeda, or if they'd move them. Too much was at stake.

It was going to be risky, but they had to make a move, now. But, what? Ice looked over at the iron grate in the sidewalk and moved towards it. "Rasheed, doesn't this go to the basement?" he asked.

"Yeah."

"Well, if we can get in, then-"

"Naw...won't work." Latif shook his head. It's got a lock on the bottom side. It's bolted. "Hell, I'm the one who had it installed." He walked off to the sidewalk and yelled out. "Damn, I messed up!"

Ice walked behind him and soothed him. "It's not your fault, but," he turned towards the building. "Is there another way in?"

Rasheed said, "Think Latif. Remember, when those young boys tried to rob the place."

"Yeah...yeah,". He looked up, "they came through the roof, but we sealed it, remember?"

"Sure did." Ice agreed. He walked up and down the sidewalk pacing, then Rasheed threw up his hands and went over to the grate and lifted. "It's open, oh shit!"

They turned and looked his way. "What's up!"

"It's open!" They surrounded it, and Ice said, "Hold up. It might be a set-up! This might be where they're keeping Waseema and Shaheeda."

"In the basement...you might be right."

Rasheed peeped around at the traffic coming up and down the street and gathered closer to them. "We gotta make a move."

"Okay, cover me." Ice reached into his pocket, pulled out his gun and hid it behind his thigh. Rasheed pulled it open. "Fast. Then."

"You have to jump."

"What?"

"Look," Latif explained. "If the electric hoist isn't there, or up. It's gonna be a straight drop to the floor."

"How much of a drop?" Ice asked.

"Least eight feet."

"Well, then I hope I land on my feet." He sighed, "Let's do this."

Rasheed grasped the handle, and Latif covered them. Waiting until traffic had subsided some, Rasheed snatched open the gate, and Ice jumped.

He landed on his feet, and his ankle twisted. The pain shot up his leg, and he grimaced, but still he managed to roll, and then with all he could muster, he held up his gun. Something had moved. He pointed, and was just about to pull the trigger. "Don't move. Or you're dead!"

From out the shadows with his hands up, was Kokomo. "It's me, man!"

"Oh shit!"

"Let me help you up."

Ice pointed upstairs. "Never mind me. Get Rasheed and them."

Kokomo ran to the opening and waved his hands. "It's me, Kokomo!"

Rasheed peeped in, and nodded his head. "Be down in a few. Hey! Is the coast clear?"

"Yeah! But you need to get down here, fast? "

Rasheed looked over at Latif and asked for his gun. "C'mon I'll toss it down. Then I'll help you down." Latif did, and he tossed the gun to Kokomo, then Rasheed turned, and looked at him. "Go!"

"What? No...I'm staying."

"Can't have that. It's going to be too dangerous. I got this. Believe me. Momma would want it that way."

"Fuck that! First, y'all toss me to the wind when I was little. Well, I'm grown now. I make my own decisions."

"Damn it, Latif! I need you to get my daughter. He kicked at the side of the building. Look after her. Don't do like us. Me...Mustapha...Derek..."

"That's my mother down there, and my sister."

"I got them!" He implored. "You can do better up here."

"Rasheed...Latif...c'mon!" Ice yelled from the basement. "We ain't got all day!"

"Alright, alright!" He turned towards Latif. "Find a car, then. This way when we get out, we'll have a ride out of here. You understand?"

"Well, that makes more sense, but I'll be back."

"Yeah, yeah. Now just go up the street and there's a car lot there."

"Where." Latif looked up the street. "I've never seen no lot-*uhhhn*!"

Rasheed had knocked him upside the head, then drugged him behind a dumpster that hugged the building. "I love you, bro," he said as he ran toward the grate and started to climb in, but then he looked back. "Make daddy proud of you...of us." He eased his feet down and Kokomo caught him and held him up. Rasheed's long body allowed him to easily close the gate behind him, but before he jumped down, he closed the latch and locked it shut. No one could get in, now. He peeped back up before he jumped down and said, "I love you, bro...one day, you'll understand. I hope."

"BACK IN THE DAY. THE mid 80s, me and Carlos were running things around here."

"Running things? You mean, like in this neighborhood, right?" Guillermo let the sarcasm spit out of his mouth.

"This neighborhood? How 'bout, this whole side of Brooklyn." Felix smirked. We ran it with an iron fist." He turned towards Waseema. "Her man, her husband, he opened the doors for us, and we made lots of money."

"Yeah..." Guillermo looked over at her. "I see."

"I just found out that her son took over his father's inheritance. I knew he wouldn't have a normal meeting with me, but with her, I know he'd come."

"There were better ways."

"I'm sure, but this way is guaranteed." He turned back around facing him, "Besides, if I kill him, then I'm the sole owner."

"Sole owner of what!" Omar spit.

Felix turned his way, and frowned up. "You know...I'm tired of you already." He started to raise his gun, and Guillermo stopped him. "You don't want that type of trouble."

"Why not!"

"He's the one the Cartel sent to make sure that I brought you in."

"Him?" Felix looked him up and down. "This little..."

In a flash, Omar had his gun up, aimed directly at Felix's mouth. "And, I was starting to like you."

"Stop!" Guillermo stood between them. "Cool it!" He turned back around towards Felix. "Right now, you have two hostages, and a federal agent you're protecting. Why? That's all we want to know." He beckoned at Omar to lower his gun. "Right now, you're expecting this guy, Latif to come in...quietly, really. He looked over at Waseema. You're holding his mother."

"And, his sister."

"You're kidding me. His sister, too?" Guillermo looked over at Omar. "Felix, I swear, I'm trying to work with you here."

"I don't care what you think!" He ripped open the front of his shirt and showed deep scarring, burns. "I should kill them both for what her other son did!"

Waseema squirmed fighting at the gag on her mouth.

"What the hell? What happened?" Guillermo asked as he observed the disfigurement on his neck, back, and hands. "I've heard about that." He turned towards Omar. "He was the one who told me. But I thought you were killed. Along with the other one..."

"No! He got away." He pointed to Waseema." Her son!"

"Whoa." Guillermo said, "You mean to tell me that your partner, this Malik, 20 years ago, or so, had a son you didn't even know about. And, on top of that he gave his inheritance to him. Then, his brother tries to kill you. And you want to...uh..."

"Lure."

"Yeah. Thank you, Omar. Lure, this Latif, the one who inherited the money in. Oh yeah, but of course, kidnap his mother, and sister. Then, make him sign paperwork to get out of the partnership. Then kill them all." He started to laugh. "Really."

Felix looked at him, then at his men. They all turned towards him at his nod, and started raising their guns. Omar shook his head, and stared at Guillermo. This was going to be trouble. He raised his gun, and trained it on Felix. The surprised look on Guillermo's face spoke volumes. "Felix, you don't want this."

"I don't know Guillermo. Maybe, I do. Maybe, I don't, but maybe, just maybe, you're the one I really want. I mean You know quite a bit."

"What are you talking about?"

"The name."

"What name?"

"I never told you the boy's father's name...Malik." He started to pull the trigger, and then.

"Back off, Felix!" Guillermo shouted." He started walking towards him with his gun pointed. "Let's be reasonable. You get him to sign the papers over, and we can all split the money between us."

"I don't like the math." Omar shouted. "The Cartel doesn't like the math."

"Forget them!" Guillermo yelled back. "For years, Felix did what they wanted, and looked at what it got him. Hell, you're even trying to kill him now."

Felix nodded his head. "He's right."

Omar started to back away from them. "I see. So, you both want out of the Cartel?"

"No! I am now...The Cartel." Felix hollered out.

"Yeah right!" Omar snarled.

"I am. Here in New York."

Guillermo's mouth curled into a grin. "Okay, then. What do you want?"

"No, Guillermo." Omar turned towards him. "We don't give him anything, except his head on the plate."

"Fuck you." Felix shot him. "I don't like you anyway." Omar's body crumbled in a heap to the ground. A standoff. All around the room was silent except for the cocking of triggers ringing out. Guillermo looked over at Omar's body and said, "Me, neither."

Felix smiled. "So, You with me?"

Guillermo threw his hands up, and his men lowered their weapons. "For now."

"Good enough."

Edward started backing up a little. "What about me, Felix?"

He turned towards him, and said, "What about?" He pointed his gun. "With you, I still have the ATF in my pocket. Right?"

"I thought we'd split the money! Us two. Like we agreed!" He screamed.

"No."

"I can't go back to work. I'm in too deep. I need the money."

"There's your problem." He turned away from him. "I don't need you...If, you're not with the ATF."

Edward couldn't believe his ears. After all he'd done, and sacrificed. But he didn't put it past him. He raised the gun at him. "I ought to kill you!"

The door bust open, and Rasheed stood there with an Uzi in his hands, cocked, locked, and loaded. "Felix... This time you won't get away!"

Immediately, without thinking, perhaps even scared, Felix started to shoot, wildly. Bullets littered the door jamb above Rasheed's head as he dove for cover behind the counter to his right. He picked up his head and sprayed the Uzi in Felix's direction. Enough distraction for Guillermo to break the opposite way diving for cover himself.

"Damn, Rasheed. You should have waited until we put together a plan!" Kokomo screamed.

Ice peeped out the door, then looked back at him and said, "It's too late for that now." He pointed to the area where they saw Felix run to and try to hide, "I'm going after Waseema. You get Shaheeda. We'll cover each other okay."

Kokomo slid a round into the chamber and said, "Got it."

There was a lull in action for a moment, and Ice called out. "Rasheed!"

"Yo!"

"Need cover."

"A'ight!" He got up and sprayed heavy gun fire over at Felix's men. Ice ran out the door and dived in the same spot as Rasheed and rolled behind some counters too. He tried getting a bead on where he was.

Felix crawled over to where Waseema was. She kicked at him as he grabbed for her. Then, using her as a shield, he stood up. "Okay...this is what you want!"

"Let my mother go!" Rasheed said as he slowly stood.

Ice slithered towards him. He peeped his head up and saw one of Felix's men off to his left, who hadn't seen him yet. Twisting the silencer on he took aim and shot. He dropped and Felix crouched. "Keep it up...I'll kill her." He pointed the gun directly to Waseema's head. Rasheed yelled out. "Nobody makes a move." He turned towards Felix and said, "What do you want?"

"I need your brother. Latif is his name, right? I need him to sign some paperwork. That's all. Real simple."

"What paperwork?"

"Come on. You know." He dragged Waseema over to a counter that held a briefcase, and opened it. "In here are the papers that sign over everything to me."

Rasheed sighed, "Damn! What the hell does that have to do with us! You need to be fucking with your people. Your wife knows more than us!" He hollered out to him.

"Oh... I did, and believe me, she told me about just how rich you are. Rich with Cartel money. Money that me and Carlos gave you."

"I don't know about all that. Besides, Latif's not here!"

"I know, but I'm sure he'll be here shortly." He picked up the phone. "Why don't you call him?"

"Look Felix. I don't know where he's at." Rasheed said, "But...Hell. If all you want is that. I can make it happen, but you have to let her go, first."

Kokomo spotted Shaheeda. He gave her the eye. She was being watched over by the last of Felix's men, who was paranoid as all hell. His partner was just killed and he damn sure didn't want to be next.

Kokomo had to use a distraction to get him to look over his way. Ice also peeped the game. He raised up his fingertips, and counted down. *Three, two, one,* blip-blip! He fell.

Kokomo crawled over as quickly as he could, and finally he had Shaheeda in his arms. He needed her to be able to run, stay low. He pulled out a razor from his pocket, and cut the duct tape off her mouth then pulled the gag out, telling her to be quiet. He pointed towards the basement, and she nodded her head like she understood.

Felix fired several rounds in his direction. He only had one more man left, and then there was Edward. He scanned the area, and didn't see him. He spotted his other men over by the door. That was where he needed to be. He backed up slowly towards it, and when he reached it, he told his man. "We go through the door. I'll hold them, while you get into the truck, and crank it up. Be ready to go."

"Okay, boss. But. What about the papers?"

"Have to deal with that another time."

He turned towards the double doors, "I'll go get the truck-" and then he dropped. Rasheed popped him in the head. "Oh, no you don't, Felix." He now stood right in front of him. Face to face. Tightly holding the gun to Waseema's head. Finally, she bit through the gag, and shouted. "Shoot him, baby!"

Rasheed aimed, but he didn't wanna chance firing a round into his mother's head. Not at all. "Look Felix, there's nowhere to go. Let my mother go!" Felix grinned that sickening sneer of his, instead. "You sure." Then looked over Rasheed's shoulder.

Rasheed moved swiftly, but Guillermo had already lined him up in his sights. He shot, and Rasheed felt the bullet rip through his side. He instantly lost his breath as the bullet ripped savagely through his lung. He fell over in pain, wheezing for air. Guillermo rushed over and grabbed the Uzi. Rasheed still struggled to stand, but it was useless. He fell back down.

"Okay, Felix." Guillermo said as he dropped the clip and reached into his pocket for another, then jammed it home into the butt of the 45 auto he brandished. "It's me and you now. We can still make this right." He pointed to Waseema. "Let her go. We'll deal with her another time. We gotta go. The cops will be here in any minute."

"No!"

"No?" he gasped. "What? Are you kidding me?" Looking over his shoulder, he could see that a crowd was starting to form. He backed up, grabbed a skully, and slipped it on over his head. "We gotta go."

Felix shot at the window where the crowd was, causing them to scatter. Waseema struggled biting his hand and she ran towards Rasheed. Felix fell back, losing his balance, squeezed the trigger and shot Waseema in the back.

Guillermo tried catching her. She fell dead in his arms. Felix scrambled over and tried to run. Edward tried to stop him. Ice ran through the door after Edward and caught him. Kokomo pointed to Waseema, and yelled. "They shot her!"

"Who!"

"Waseema!"

Giovanni looked over at her, and gasped, then a little past her he saw that Rasheed was also down. He tried to get up. "Ice... Look, Rasheed. Help him!" Ice was still choking Edward. He stopped and turned. He realized that Rasheed didn't know that his mother was dead. He scrambled for him, but it was too late. Rasheed wailed as he saw the body of his mother dead on the ground. He staggered over, and fell on his face, crying. "Mama... Mama..." Ice came over trying to comfort him. "I'm sorry...I'll get you to a hospital."

"It's too late, Ice." He grabbed him by the collar. "We need to get that bastard, Ice."

"We will."

"Now!" he said as he tried standing.

"Now? We don't even know..."

"A truck rode past, and people jumped out the way as it sped up Broadway. Giovanni hollered out. "That's him!"

Ice put his arm around Rasheed, helping him up. Then he walked into the door. Rasheed looked over at his mother's body and said, "To God we belong and ..."

"To him, do we return," Ice finished, then said, "Do. Or. Die."

Giovanni held his gun on Edward as Ice and Rasheed staggered past. "Take care of things, Giovanni." Rasheed uttered. He looked at his mother's body and said to him, "We. Gotta go."

"Where y'all going?"

"Handle the business." He looked back over at Shaheeda and said to her, "I'll see you, Okay."

She got up and ran over to him. "Let me go, too. I can help!"

"Sis! Sis! You need to be here to handle this And mommy." He looked off. A tear came down his eye, and he struggled getting the right words out. "If I don't see you..."

"You'll be back!" She cried.

"Take care of Khadija."

"No." She pulled at him. "Don't go Ice!"

"I've got too." Ice hugged her. Kokomo yelled out to them, asking. "What do you want me to do?"

"Get her out of here, before the cops come."

He nodded. "Alright, Ice. I got you." He walked over to Shaheeda, and watched as Rasheed and Ice slipped into the throng of people peeping, and gawking at the insides of the store. The bodies. The blood. Then he snapped his fingers and ran back to the basement door. "Be right back," he hollered at Shaheeda. He jumped down the steps two at a time going downstairs, and grabbed the duffel bags. He lugged them back upstairs to the door then suddenly without warning, one of Felix's men who wasn't dead, yet, got up and shot him. Kokomo fell on top of the bags. Giovanni turned and started shooting, catching him with two slugs to the chest. He ran over to Kokomo, and he too, was dead.

Giovanni looked at the bags and sneered. Go Shaheeda! Get a cab. Go now! He had to pry her away from her mother's body, and that gave Edward enough time to escape. He turned and watched as he dipped into the crowd and disappeared. "Damn..." he said.

Latif woke up rubbing the back of his neck. A wicked bruise had risen as he stumbled about before getting his bearings. Once he did, he saw a cluster of people standing in and around the store, and he staggered over to the front. All he saw was Mayhem as he pushed through, once inside he saw Kokomo's body sprawled out, and about six other men, all dead. And then, his mother. He fell to his knees and cried out. "Oh God! What the hell happened!"

Giovanni heard the gut-wrenching scream, and spun around. His heart grieved as he stepped over to him, and kneeling down in front of him said, "I'm not quite sure, Latif, just got here myself."

Shaheeda slumbered over, and he got up and hugged her. "You Okay?" He looked her up and down, then she pulled him off to the side and said, "You've got to be strong now. For us."

He scanned the room, and didn't see his brother, or Ice. "Where is Rasheed?"

She lowered her head, sniffling, and said, "He's gone, Latif. He went after that, that...demon, Felix! He's the one who killed ma!"

"Where'd he go?"

"He's gone."

"Gone? How do you know for sure?" He started to turn and run out the store but Shaheeda grabbed his arm, then looked over at her mother's body and said, "Please stay...don't go. I'm scared."

He dragged his tired body over to a chair, sat down and wailed. "I've lost my whole family over this damn..." He ripped the chain that held the key from around his neck, and started to toss it away, then Shaheeda stopped him. "Don't you dare!" He looked up at her.

"Remember what Mama said, We'll get through this as a family. You hear me! We will."

Latif looked up in his sister's big, brown, teary eyes. They had never before looked like this. But then, never before had anything like this happened. It was a nightmare. His mother was dead. Like his father. He was numb.

Deep down in his soul, he knew what Shaheeda said was true. He looked over at his mother, got up, walked over, and dropped to his knees by her. "Shaheeda, get one of those shirts." He kissed her, then whispered, "I love you, mom." When Shaheeda came back, he took the shirt from her, and gently covered her. Shaheeda knelt down beside him, and after a while, reached over to him, grasping her hand, and said, "We'll get through this." He rubbed the key that hung around his neck. "We will...I promise."

Ice and Rasheed had managed to push past the crowd and made their way towards Halsey Street. Ice said, "We can get a cab."

The hole in Rasheed's lung caused him to wheeze and gasp for air. He was getting weaker by the minute, and could barely walk. "We need to get him..."

Ice held him up, and pleaded. "Let's get him another time. I'm telling you; I need to get you to the hospital."

Rasheed grabbed at his collar. "I might not have time."

"Come on, stop talking like that. I need you. I just lost...Waseema, I don't need you to go nowhere."

Standing in the cut of a building next to a weed house, a man in a dark hoodie hollered at them. Then, he started to approach. Ice reacted, and reached for his gun. The man in the hoodie stopped abruptly and said, "Whoa man it's me."

"Me, who?"

"Cutty, from Bushwick Projects ..."

Ice recognized him and said, "Yeah. What's up man. Yo, we ain't got time to talk..."

He walked over to them, helped Ice with Rasheed and said, "Let me help."

Ice asked, "Do you know anyone with a ride?"

Cutty walked them over to an old Buick, and said, "This is mine. Man, Rasheed don't look too good." He reached into his jacket and pulled out the keys. "I'll get up with you. Can't leave right now. I'm on the hustle." He kept watching up the street, doing the job of a lookout "Gotta go."

"I'll make sure you get your car back."

"I know. I trust you."

Ice helped Rasheed into the car. Still in pain, he struggled to breath. He sounded bad, so Ice made a decision to go to the hospital. He turned left on Broadway, and Rasheed raised up. He grabbed his gun, and poked him in the side. "Is this the way Felix went?"

"What the hell are you doing?"

"If you don't follow him, Ice. I'll shoot you and then kill him, myself. That bastard killed my mother."

Ice looked in his eyes, and he knew he was dead serious. Even though he couldn't possibly pull it off. He'd damn sure die trying. He turned the car around, then sighed, "Put the gun down...you won't need it. We're going after Felix. Okay."

"Do or die, right..."

"Fuck you and your do or die. It's not worth it." Tears formed up in his eyes. He was hurt. The only other time he remembered being this hurt was when his grandmother who raised him died, and now, Waseema. The only woman he'd ever loved since.

Latif and Shaheeda somberly watched the paramedics try to revive their mother. Standard procedure. The paramedic turned towards the medical examiner and nodded her head. Waseema was officially dead; it was just a matter of time, and an autopsy. Latif's expression turned dismal as he could do nothing but watch as the paramedic called for a body bag.

Giovanni walked over, and deliberately stepped in front of them in an attempt to distract them from the sorrowful scene, and asked, "Are y'all gonna be alright?"

Latif just rubbed on Shaheeda's shoulders gently and said, "Yeah...we'll be alright."

"You'll probably have to get the body from the morgue."

"Does it have to go to the morgue?" Shaheeda asked.

"Yes...I'm sorry." Giovanni looked around at the other bodies. The police had finally arrived and were caught up in analyzing the scene. No one asked Shaheeda and Latif any questions, yet. "You think we'll see Rasheed?"

Latif just nodded his head no. "Naw...no telling where he went."

"Yeah, him and Ice took off after Felix."

"Wish I knew where."

A police officer came through and spoke to Giovanni. Witnesses say the perp that you described jumped in a truck and headed up Bushwick Avenue. We got cars going up that way, now.

"Yeah...I guess. I didn't see anything, though."

"We'll talk later..."

"Did anyone else see another vehicle...maybe behind it?" Giovanni asked him.

"Well. Someone did say something about another car."

"Where did that one go?"

"Up Bushwick Avenue as well."

"Towards the cemetery." Shaheeda candidly said to Latif. Remember when mama used to take us to the Burger King up there when it first opened?

Latif smiled and reflected then rubbing his chin, said, "The cemetery...Evergreen?"

"Yeah. A lot of mausoleums there. Had a case there once...drugs..."

"Tombs. He rubbed at his key."

"Yeah, so what." Shaheeda smirked.

He got up walking towards the door, and said, Look...I gotta go. Go up to Harlem Shaheeda. I'll call you there."

"Oh, no you don't!" Shaheeda was right behind him. "You know something."

Giovanni yelled out. "Be careful!" He walked back over to where the officer from earlier was standing and asked, "Uh, who is in charge?"

The officer looked around, then said, "Ravenel. He should be here...or on his way."

"I see." Giovanni said to him, then stepped away. This whole thing had Cartel written all over it. He looked over at the other bodies, and they were being whisked away. No bodies, no evidence...no crime. First Edward, and now Ravenel. Something wasn't right. It stunk like all hell. "Hey, uh, officer. You don't mind if I stick around?"

"Naw...just don't mess with anything. Like I said, Ravenel will probably be here in a short bit."

"Thanks, officer." He pulled up a chair and sat watching over Waseema's body and thought to himself. "I'm gonna find out who did this, Waseema. And I'm gonna make them pay. I promise you."

Latif whistled for a cab when he got outside, and him and Shaheeda climbed in. She asked, "Where're we going, Latif?"

"Evergreen Cemetery...the entrance." He told the cab driver.

Shaheeda didn't quite understand, but she knew something was up. She didn't ask any more questions. Latif leaned back and quietly rubbed on the key, thinking about the account he used to pay every quarter of the year for Maria. The check was for a tomb, inside a mausoleum, located at the Evergreen Cemetery.

# CHAPTER NINETEEN

Rasheed and Ice parked on the corner of Chauncey Street and Evergreen Avenue. Up the street from the entrance to the cemetery. They watched Felix jump out of the truck. They got out right behind him. After about a three-minute walk past hundreds of tombstones, grave markers, and even a few searching moments by Felix; he finally came to where he was going. A white, tomb mausoleum. He peeped around, opened the dirty door, and went in.

"You need to stay here while I figure out what he's up to."

"Hurry up, *cough, cough,* Ice."

Ice crept behind and opened the door slowly. The door creaked some as he walked through. Once inside the dark, damp vault he saw Felix lurking about in the shadows. He peeped around a corner and saw him stop in front of a sepulcher. It had a distinct golden lock that he pulled on, and fought at trying to get it open. Ice reached into his pocket and silently pulled out his gun. "Got you now..."

Felix turned. "Oh shit!" He dived on the ground for cover as Ice fired a shot. Ricocheting around the tight tomb, Felix stayed low, but took out his gun and fired back. Ice tried to get a bead on him, and then suddenly his gun emptied. Felix heard the clicking sound and got up. He pointed his gun at Ice, and snided. "Yeah...you got me, huh." He got closer to him. And pointed it to his head. "I'm going to kill you." Click. His gun was empty also.

Ice threw a right to his head and floored him. Then he tried to stomp him out. Felix rolled out the way and threw dirt in his face. Ice coughed and rubbed at his eyes. Felix got up, punched him square in the jaw. And Ice hit the ground. He jumped over him, and ran to the door. He swung it open, and ran straight into Rasheed.

Rasheed grabbed at him and with all he had, wrestled him to the ground. Felix fell, and struggled with him, but Rasheed was too run-down and couldn't hold him much longer. He'd left his gun, and all he had on him was a knife. He reached for it and opened it. He jumped to his feet, then dived on him with it open to stab him. Felix grabbed his arm and tried to keep him at bay. Ice was up now. He dived at Felix too. Felix managed to push Rasheed to the side, and turned his back trying to avoid the beating that Ice was putting on him. He saw that Rasheed was weak, and that it was difficult for him to stand. Then, Rasheed messed around and dropped the knife. Felix dived on it, picked it up and grabbed Rasheed in a choke hold with the knife to his throat.

Ice stopped in his tracks. Rasheed fought, but he was too weak. Gulping for air, and losing blood, his shirt was wet with it, he gave in. Felix yelled at Ice. "He's dying. I'll make it quicker, if you don't back away, now! "

"Kill him Ice! Don't worry about me. Kill him!"

Ice was torn. Rasheed, his friend. Felix, the one who killed the woman he loved. He had to do what he had to do, but at what cost. He didn't know, so he hesitated. Felix grinned. "Oh. You don't know what to do!" He raised the knife to slice Rasheed's throat. "Felix!"

He turned. "It was Latif. I think I know what you want."

"What? Oh yeah, it's you. Malik's son."

He ripped the key from around his neck. "You want this!" And held it up.

"The key. How did you get it?"

"Don't worry about that. Just let my brother go."

"No." He drug Rasheed over to the tomb where he stood, and said, "Open it."

Latif walked cautiously over, then he inserted the gold key into the dirt laden lock, and it popped open. He tried to remove it, but it broke off inside the rusted keyhole. Felix barked at him. "Pull it open." Latif did. "Open the casket."

"I'm not into this creepy stuff!"

"Open it!" He held the blade tighter to his brother's throat. "Now!"

Latif did as he was told. Inside there was no body, just an old, flattened briefcase, and he handed it to him. "Open it up!" He ordered. Latif did however grudgingly, and it revealed old sheets with pages of deeds. He looked at the signatures on them and it was all the same, his father's. "These are the deeds to the properties in Bushwick. Bed-Stuy. Williamsburg."

"Their mine."

"There in Malik's name... My father."

"But, with my money. I told him to buy them. All, prime property." He moved away from the tomb, and said, "I'm glad you came, anyway. Sign them over to me."

"No."

"Yes. Or I'll kill him. Just like I killed your mother. Your brother! I even killed your father behind this. All he had to do was sign the papers! Now, I've grown tired. Sign them! "

Latif reached for the papers. "Okay, I will. You can have it all."

"No!" Shaheeda came around the corner. "You'll get nothing, but hell." She pointed her mother's gun to his head, and squeezed. Felix's head swung to the side, and blood spurted all over the tomb as he dropped face forward in the dirt. Rasheed fell down, and Ice rushed over. "Hold on. We're gonna get you out of here."

"Wait." He beckoned for Latif to come over. "You did good. It's all you now, bruh, you hear! Ours...keep it in the family." His breathing feigned some.

"Hold on." Ice pleaded.

Rasheed looked up at him and smiled. "Make sure they do the right thing."

Shaheeda cried, and he called her over, too. "Take care of Khadija."

"I will...I will..."

Rasheed looked up at Ice again and said, "Told you...we had one more in us..." then he died.

Latif opened the door of the building. The sun was up high, bright. He glanced away from it and happened to glimpse up at the top of the tomb. There was a name. He squinted, then read it out loud. It said, *Redemption.*

Off in the distance, on top of a ridge inside the vast, sprawling cemetery. Someone stood; Maria, watched as they carried Rasheed's body off. She stood by a dark blue Mercedes Benz. It was hers, and one of her bodyguards was in the driver's seat playing the role of a chauffeur. "He found it," she said.

"I thought you wanted him to."

She looked over at the person who spoke and said, "Felix...yeah, but not Latif."

He got out of the car and walked next to her. "So what. We'll take him out, too."

She smirked. "No...it's not that simple."

"Why? Who's going to stop us, now?"

She stepped over by the car and leaned back on it. "You did say you saw Waseema get killed, right?"

"Yeah..." Edward turned around. "I told you that."

"And, you said that you and Felix had that whole shooting thing at the warehouse faked to fool me huh."

"Yeah..." Edward walked back around to the car. "I told you everything."

"You did, but," The bodyguard stepped out of the car, and pointed a gun equipped with a silencer, at him. "I didn't."

Edward raised his hands, surrendering. "What is this? I thought we had a deal."

"No...you and Felix had a deal. You were going to do me in, kill me, but I got away, right?"

"Not true, Maria. I had to do that to make it look good."

"Not good enough." She turned away from him and walked off looking down at Latif. "Damn...the little girl...I got you, Waseema."

Edward still had his hands raised, yelling. "You said we were going to be partners!" He rushed her. And the bodyguard shot him in the knees. He fell down in pain, hollering. "You said we'd split the money. Go south...Columbia."

"I lied..."

"You bitch..."

Maria stepped over him and got in the car. She told her bodyguard, "Kill him, will ya, then take me to the airport. It's time to go. The Cartel's...waiting."

THE END

...it's not over, yet.

**Dunya 3: Khalid's legacy**

# About the Author

# Dean Hamid Presents

The author Dean Hamid was born and raised in Brooklyn, New York. In his youth he read the works of Donald Goines, Iceberg Slim, as well as Richard Wright, throwing in the poetic banter of James Baldwin over and over.

Growing up in New York City's hardcore Bushwick-Hylan Projects, his writing is not necessarily intended to glamorize the quote-unquote gangsters, or even the street life; but to emphasize the presence of the drama that was involved and surrounded around it.

It's been said that his work swings towards what is described as Urban Fiction Drama, with a strong propensity towards a slick old school literary voice.

Dean Hamid works hard and tirelessly to keep his work as professional, and gritty as it can be, but yet stay literally solid. His work successfully proves and drives home this point.

www.ingramcontent.com/pod-product-compliance
Lightning Source LLC
Chambersburg PA
CBHW051234260626
47162CB00002B/419